This book is dedicated to anyone who has ever felt like they weren't good enough.

I thought about dedicating this book to all the awful people who inspired it, but I decided they don't deserve any credit.

Who does deserve recognition, are the people who have made my life beautiful.

My husband, the most amazing man I've ever known, who's given me a life I never could have imagined. And who stuck by me when I needed it most.

My close friends, who I can't name but I think they know who they are. At least I hope so, because they're the family I chose.

& My therapist for convincing me to finish this book and publish it.

Trigger Warning:
This book contains discussions of suicidal thoughts, self-harm,
depression, and anxiety.

Chapter 1

"Do you always wear black to weddings?" He asked her.

She looked over at him silently, her mind elsewhere, not quite seeing him walking beside her on her right. She tried to refocus, bring his face into view, but she could only stare out at the raging water of Lake Michigan beyond him. On a Saturday afternoon in mid-May, the sky was eerily grey, the wind howling, the lake dark and angry.

Her mind finally caught up with his question. She smirked, "I wear black everywhere, Matt. You know that."

"So, what are you? Goth?" He quipped, his hands shoved in the pants pockets of his blue tailored 3-piece suit.

"No, I'm just… me." She said sadly.

"And who is Ariettea?" He queried, chuckling, his low, gravelly voice slowly rolling over each of the five syllables in her name. His tongue holding onto that last 'ia' sound.

She didn't have an answer for him. She finally was able to bring his face into focus, able to watch his chiseled features, his slight dimples, pop like they did every time he laughed. She was always pretending not to notice them, to not show that she enjoyed seeing his smile, those white perfectly shaped teeth shining out against his dark cocoa complexion.

"You've known me for ten years, why don't you tell me?" She asked him.

After the ceremony had ended, he had slipped over to her side of the aisle, pulled her by the elbow, weaving through the rows of folding wooden chairs, knowingly taking her away from the crowd.

He was always able to pull her out of a crowd.

His sparkling bourbon brown eyes flew up to meet her own, dull chocolate brown and hidden under layers of black eyeliner, before she could rip her gaze off him. He looked at her with that look, that look that made her feel like she was the only girl in the world. The only one that mattered. That look that made her try and fail to control her heart rate. That look that would soften his usual sarcastic air as he asked, as always,

"Are you ok?"

She forced her typical tight, fake smile as she hollowly recited the lie she told everyone every day,

"Yeah. I'm fine."

He nodded, both of them knowing he didn't believe her. She studied him again, not even knowing why she was, as he looked out towards the water himself, the wind pushing his suit coat back away from him, throwing the coral tie that all the groomsmen that day wore over his shoulder. Again, he caught her glance before she could tear it away.

"What?" He asked suddenly, grinning, keeping his hands stuffed in the pockets of his suit pants.

She tried to find an answer, an excuse, quickly, "I'm just surprised you haven't ripped that flower off yet." She said, nodding her head towards his chest, towards the single calla lily boutonniere, white and pristine, on his lapel. Her own arms were tightly crossed around her chest, her fingers clinging to her heels she'd given up trying to wear in the sand. Her arms were trying to reign in the hoodie she was holding closed against the wind, the one she'd thrown over her black high waisted pencil skirt, her tucked in lace blouse.

"I'm comfortable enough in my masculinity to wear a flower, Ariettea!" He said in mock offense, throwing a hand over his heart, feigning sincerity.

She nodded, tried not to laugh, a smile creeping onto her face anyway. "Right."

He laughed himself. "Price of being the favorite cousin and best man. I was threatened with the guillotine if I took it off before the reception."

Her eyes wandered back down the shoreline, the wind was picking up, and the waves were starting to crash along it, the storm threatening to unleash itself at any moment. "Well, it was expensive, I'm sure." She mused absentmindedly, having to push her hair out her eyes as a gust of wind tousled it.

"Just like everything else about this wedding. Ugh, that girl...My poor bro." He rolled his eyes. "God, I hate weddings..." He scoffed.

She started to mutter, "I don't know, I think-"

"Ariettea!" He cut her off, throwing his head back in frustration. His voice bellowed, making her jump. Every muscle in her shoulders contracted as she felt the exasperation dripping off his exclamation. "You always take everything so seriously." He whined.

She hugged her arms around herself even tighter, dropping them to around her waist, letting the wind push her hoodie back and away from her as he ranted on.

"This whole wedding is ridiculous. Most weddings are! People should go out and have more fun before sinking into miserable chains."

"I mean, we're 17," She said thoughtfully, slowly, carefully. Hoping he wouldn't cut her off again. "We're getting older...You don't think about your future? About what you want? You really think that you and I are still just kids? That everyone we know are too? That none of us are capable of making any major life choices? Or will be soon?"

"So many questions, Ari! This is our childhood! Why can't we just enjoy it?" He waved his arms out, gesturing wide, making sure she was picking up on his displeasure.

"Why?" She asked hotly, "Because this next year we are supposed to decide what to do with the rest of our lives. College, jobs, relation-...Real life." She kept her eyes fixed on the ground. "And I haven't been a child for a long time." She muttered bitterly, painfully, but mostly to herself.

The sand underneath her was cold and wet, compact and hard, it had already absorbed the damp foggy air, it knew a storm was coming. But going barefoot was proving more difficult than she thought. She tripped and stumbled, but Matt quickly reached out, grabbed her forearm, then her back, to steady her. She wished his hand, his touch, would linger, but it wouldn't. It never did. They were just friends, of course. But that fact didn't stop the tingling feeling his touch left.

"You always think too much, Ariettea." He said as he let her go, steadying her quickly with both hands, the feel of his hand on her back sending sparks down through her toes. "Just enjoy the now!"

Her face burned, and not just from the cold pockets cutting through the wind. 'What's there to enjoy in the now?' She thought bitterly, coming down off the tingling feeling that his touch had left. What kind of 17 year old had no friends, no boyfriend, no job, muddled through school a good student, but had no college aspirations, no goals? She hated it. She hated all of it.

"I just think it's nice to know where you're going in life." She said softly. "Your cousin found this great happiness, he has this solid life and direction now, I just think that that's beautiful."

"Ugh." Matt blurted quickly, thoughtlessly.

She shot her eyes over to him, trying to hide the hurt, the feeling like she'd been slapped. She scolded herself for oversharing, offering an opinion at all. To even have an opinion. The siren was going off in her head, to conceal, to wall up. That maybe she was as foolish and as wrong as everyone said she was.

He felt the hurt radiating off her and softened, but only slightly. His head leaned towards her, and he dropped his voice an octave, "I hope they're happy, honestly. But I think it's stupid to try and settle down, especially so young."

"So, what," She angrily jumped in, throwing her hands and head up at the sky, her heels threatening to whack him in the head as she motioned. "We're just supposed to party it up until we are considered 'old enough' to settle down?"

"If we ever are!" He laughed, clapping his hands in jest.

For Ariettea, she felt like she lived on a different planet than everyone else her age. She wanted direction, stability, meaning, goals, but everyone around her just wanted to have fun and nothing more. She wanted to see things, places, people, help people, to do something that meant something to someone, but she didn't know how. She needed something solid to hold on to since everyone around her left and slipped away so easily. She was homesick for a place she wasn't even sure existed. She felt a sense of empty that she couldn't quite put into words.

"Come on, Ariettea, what's the look?" He asked her.

An all too familiar question, one that her usual lie of 'Nothing, I'm fine' didn't work for.

Her eyes still on the ground, she stopped abruptly, about to step into a bed on sand lilies growing in clusters in the middle of the sandy beach.

They were in full bloom, early for that time of year, and standing out as gorgeous against the ever-darkening sky. Deciding to ignore his question, she knelt down, tucking her long, thick, raven black hair behind her ear, and plucked one up off the ground, traced the petals with her fingers.

As she stood back up, the wind gusted and threw her hair into Matt's face. "Why's your hair so long?" He asked irritated, batting at it, having to spit some of it out of his mouth. She tucked it behind her ear, adding the lily with it. She fluffed it down her back, the volume on full display, and the length reaching all the way to the small of her back.

"Because I like to annoy you, the center of the universe, obviously."

"Always so serious!" He rolled his eyes, and getting genuinely irritated with her, he took a step away to create more distance between them. "You take a party day like a wedding and turn it into some sort of philosophy session."

"That's your problem, Matt! A wedding is NOT just a party day! It means more. You say I'm too serious, but you never see the serious side of anything. We have two weeks left of being juniors, Matt. This fall, we'll be seniors, and it makes me nervous! I want to know exactly what I'm doing next year; I need to know; I'm desperately trying to find which direction I'm heading."

"Senior year is for fun." He waved a hand.

"Senior year is for decisions." She pointed a finger.

"And you can't have it both ways? Well, wait, look who I'm talking to…" He said derisively, waving a hand at her dismissively. She tried not to let the statement bother her, but it did. She was never good enough for anyone, and never good enough for anything. She didn't belong anywhere. She didn't think she ever would or could.

She sighed. She turned around, letting her arms limply fall to her sides, her shoes flopping into her side and cutting into her leg. She saw her parents waving to her to come back. "Time to leave for the reception, I guess." She conceded quietly. She made sure the lily was still secured behind her ear as she took a step, but Matt grabbed her arm gently before she got far.

"Hey," He said, in that low voice yet again, that breathy, husky voice he had mastered so well. His arm lingered on her elbow, his fingers fighting the urge to stroke it. "I was only kidding." He coaxed.

She mustered up a smile, heart fluttering in her throat. "I know." She swallowed hard, lying to him yet again. She could never quite figure him out. Joking or serious, mean or kidding, liking or disliking.

His fingers trailed down her arm, then he pointed to the lily in her hair. "Looks good." He said simply, bruskly, making her heart jump again. "But this one will look better." He took off the calla lily boutonniere from his lapel, unwrapped it, and handed it to her.

She smiled at it, unable to look at him at all, not wanting him to see her cheeks warm, her pale complexion never hiding much. She added it to the one sitting behind her ear, the two lilies sitting one on top of the other. "I guess lilies are the thing today." She stole one last glance at the lily bed, feeling like it meant more than it should have for some reason.

She looked at him and laughed, her eyes crinkling at the ends. "But what about the guillotine?"

"Ah, they'll get over it." He flashed her a smile. "You need it more than I do. I know how you much hate these things. Why do you think I pulled you out back there?" He kept his gentle gaze on her, knowing her all too well.

For a flash of time, her heart swelled, she felt understood.

"Besides, the flower'll break up the 'all black'. You need some color. You always do."

And just like that, her heart dropped, and hard. There was just no hope for her, she was never good enough, and she never would be. Even though he had pulled her away from a situation he knew she hated, that the next Monday at school, he would be back to telling her to quit being stuck up and shy. As if it was that easy. As if it were a choice, a switch she could just flip. As if it was she hadn't tried that before.

She felt her eyes fix on nothing and glaze over, the hard steel feeling in her stomach starting to taking over as it always did, as she trudged off to yet another social occasion that she didn't belong to, or even wanted to be at.

Chapter 2

Summer barreled into Michigan, wet and heavy as always, and tediously dragged itself out. Most people in the Midwest live for the long summer days, the ones that they believe offset the relentless and bitter winters of the Great Lakes region, but it made no difference to Ariettea. Both extremes left her feeling trapped.

The pockets of cool lake air that hit her in the face as she walked down the concrete lighthouse pier did little to combat the thick, humid pall that hung in the air. She was trying to find somewhere where her own personal pall, ever-present, felt less heavy, somewhere quiet, where she could actually think without someone popping up over her shoulder.

Besides telling her that she was too young to know or decide anything, every single person that she talked to; her parents, her parent's friends, everyone in the congregation, people at the grocery store, took every chance they could to remind her that high school was nearing its end and she had decisions to make. But no one could just state that simple fact, everyone had to tell her what the 'right' thing to do was, what she WOULD be doing after school was over because of course, they knew how her life was going to play out.

Everyone's life played out the same there. She was foolish to think she would be any different. Everyone was destined to stay in their small town, bouncing from job to job, either because they didn't go to college, or they came back with huge student debts, or because what they went to college for was of no real use. So you work a job you hate to squeak by. You get stuck in an unhappy marriage, pregnant before you have a chance to hang your high school diploma up on the wall.

You stay there and darn you if you don't be happy about it.

She was so determined to not have any of that, to be able to stand on her own two feet, to build a life she loved. But she wasn't sure it was possible, after listening to so many people say it wasn't. Anyone who actually bothered to genuinely ask her what she wanted ended up regretting they asked and angry with her.

Because didn't she know how hard real life actually is? Didn't she know she needed to take a step off the pedestal that she had so clearly elevated herself onto?

The only child of her parents, they would tell her to make her own choices, but they really just meant whatever choices they felt were right. Shoot, she didn't even know what her options were anymore.

She sat down at the very edge of the pier, the spot that had ten million signs saying to stay out of the water, that rip currents kill. The hot concrete burned the back of her legs as she swung her calves over the edge. Her feet dangled over the water, her old, worn, black combat boots loosely laced, laces hanging, nearly skimming the top of the calm water. If you looked closely, you could see the ripples of the undertow crisscrossing on top of the lake, even though it was as still as glass.

She sipped the iced coffee that was ever-present in her hand, the one that was her last-ditch effort to stay awake after nights and nights of insomnia. Or nights of oversleeping til early afternoon, not wanting to force herself out of bed and into the cruel world she lived in, the one that more so lived in her head than out of it.

She was supposed to be out buying new school clothes since none of hers fit anymore, she had lost too much weight for her old clothes, but the mall crowded with her classmates was too much. So she did what she always did in those situations- she ran. As far as she could from any other human.

She sighed as she shoved her hands underneath her thighs, black skinny jeans absorbing all the cloudless sky's heat. The little gravel bits of concrete dug into her palms and burned, but she liked it. Her jeans were two sizes too big, acting like a ziplock bag holding in condensation, sweat pouring out of her, but she didn't care.

Even when she wanted to eat, her stomach wouldn't allow her. That pit that was always there, that cold hard feeling, the clamping of a cruel hand around her waist, it got angrier when she tried to eat. Of course, people always compliment weight loss, so no one cared how it happened, how miserable it was.

Ariettea whipped her head around as she heard familiar laughter from behind her. A small group from her school, sophomores, screeching, laughing, threatening to push each other off the pier. A small group of best friends. Something she'd never had. Something she'd convinced herself she never would.

She turned back around, shaking her head. She wasn't sure if she was annoyed at their immaturity, their noise, or if she was jealous of the fact that they all had each other. 'Everyone always leaves, anyway.' She found herself thinking. 'People aren't worth it.' Names and faces flashed through her head like a movie montage, one she was always trying to cut off.

She moved her feet back and forth, daring her laces to sink into the water. Thinking of what it would be like to slip beneath the glass herself. She sighed again, frustrated her quiet had been ruined. It was getting later in the afternoon, more and more people were arriving at the beach, her cue to leave.

She sighed a third time as she stood up, swinging herself back off the edge of the lighthouse, throwing her messenger bag crossbody over her chest, the one full of books that she kept with her to keep her mind occupied on something other than her real life.

She ran a hand through her straight hair, wavy in the humidity, and sweaty and wet at the roots, wishing she had a hair tie to pull it back. But it was so long, a ponytail didn't help much anymore, and her hair was so thick that a bun was too heavy to stay put. She was always being accused of having extensions, but her hair just did its own thing, no matter what she tried. She took a strand and twirled it in her fingers as she walked, wrapping it over and over and over around them, as she weaved silently through the crowds, head down, not wanting to look at anyone. She hated being around people. She couldn't see them give her the up and down look, wondering why she was wearing jeans in the summer, and she couldn't bear having to fake a smile anymore. She just couldn't. She was too tired anymore.

The only thing that she did look at were the lilies that she and Matt had walked past weeks earlier. Still blooming strong, even though half the little clusters scattered all over the sand were trampled by people who didn't care, the ones who left their half-eaten McDonald's just sitting on the beach. But her glance to them was only fleeting, as she had to swerve through another crowd of people not watching where they were going.

She reached into her bag for her car keys and phone and was surprised to find a missed call waiting for her from her Aunt Nadette.

Dr. Nadette Vermeule, the much younger sister of Ariettea's mother, lived far from Michigan, in a coastal college town in South Georgia, practicing obstetrics. Her husband, Trent, was a doctor as well, happily running around as an ER attending. Trent and Nadette were two of the rare people that she actually quite admired, though from afar. She loved talking to them at family reunions, seeing their Instagram posts. Smart, funny, accomplished, full of faith, and incredibly kind. They always spoke to her like she was a real person. Like she was someone worth talking to. Even though she knew she wasn't. She thought they just tried to be cordial.

But still.

They were different. They were everything she had dreamt of being and more, what she based her dream life on. But that's all it was- a dream. They were only something she could envy, wish she could be. Of course, they weren't normal. Of course, no one could find the happiness that they had. It probably wasn't even real.

Ariettea wondered if the call had been a butt dial, but there was a voicemail waiting. "Ari!" Her Aunt's warm, full voice rang out clear, even through the phone. "Sorry to bother you, you're probably out with your friends enjoying your summer vacation!" Ariettea's stomach flipped at the statement. If only.

"I was calling because the hospital that Trent and I both practice at is having this super cool charity event, it's called Hair That Cares. It's a donation event for making wigs for childhood cancer patients. What's really cool about it is that it's a local program, the hair stays local, and you get to meet the child that your hair goes to. I mean, of course, multiple donations go into a wig, but, still, you get to meet them! Anyway, I remembered that the last time I saw you, your hair was still super long, so I was wondering if you'd be interested in donating, give yourself a fresh summer cut. Give me a call back if you are, and I'll give you all the details. Even if you're not, call me! I'd love to hear from you, this is kind of an excuse to just catch up, you've been MIA on social media. Love you. Bye!"

Ariettea kept the phone pressed to her ear even after the message was over. Of course she was absent on social media; she wasn't social.

She could picture her aunt, her long honey blonde hair, dishwater blonde mixed in so perfectly that no one believed her when she said they weren't artificial lowlights. Nadette had a penance for the color navy, the same way Ariettea did black. When she wasn't in navy scrubs, she was usually in some sort of form-fitting navy pencil skirt and girly blouse that hit her slim body in all the right places. The only thing that detracted one's gaze from her deep hazel eyes was her beaming smile, ever-present.

But when Ariettea thought of Nadette, she thought of her achievements; doctor, wife, established, happy.

All before 30.

Ariettea leaned against her car, her parent's old Ford SUV, handed down to her, red and rusty, as she twidled with the ends of her hair. Even as she played with the ends, the curl of her hair still reached her waist.

Would she have to go down to Georgia to do it? The thought did excite her. A chance to get away from home.

But, did she even want to do it? Some random deed? She didn't know what she wanted in life, but she knew she wanted meaning. Meaning besides faith and family.

Maybe this could be her first step, her first chance!

But she immediately got mad at herself. Like some small deed, some short trip could change things. People were the same everywhere.

She'd still be alone.

Still wouldn't have any friends.

Still would be the epic disappointment of.. well, everyone.

Still would have to face senior year.

She'd still have to choose a life and then live it.

But…

Something was gnawing at her nonetheless.

Something in her still felt excited about it.

But she still couldn't answer Nadette.

The next day, the smell of burning, cheap hot dogs, and lighter fluid filled the air. Red solo cups littered every bit of surface space that wasn't already home to a plate of half-eaten potato salad or a bottle of MGD.

Ariettea's own plate of food sat untouched, the smells overwhelming. Her stomach seized up even at the sight of the charcoal when she had picked it up at the store.

At an end of summer picnic on her parent's acre large property, Ariettea scanned the crowd, a mish-mosh mixture of her parent's friends and their families. She had popped up her own lawn chair as far away from the group as was possible without getting yelled at by her parents.

She caught herself looking for Matt, as she always did in a crowd, and once she found him she watched him as he ran alongside a group of boys, only to be tackled by three of the younger ones all at once. She turned her bottle of boring plain black unsweetened tea over and over in her hands. She smiled seeing him interact so well with kids who completely adored him, but then shook her head at the thought that he was rolling around in the dirt when they were starting senior year the next week. They were forever trapped between go play with the kids, and sit down but shut up with the adults.

One of her dad's friends saw her shaking her head, "What do you think you are shaking your head at, missy?" The large tank of a man bellowed, hot dog in hand, sauntering over to her.

She looked up at him from her lawn chair, but without moving her head. She kept her long legs crossed over each other, staying still all over, refusing to move her body towards his. Her eyes simply glared into his judgmental ones silently and coldly.

"You need to learn to loosen up." He laughed at her, rolled his eyes. "Boys will be boys, kids will be kids!" He said, mouth full of hot dog he was suddenly pushing down with a PBR.

Ariettea stood up slowly, keeping her eyes trained on him. She felt the adrenaline. The fight or flight. It had always been fight. But anymore, she didn't care.

Anymore, it was always flight.

She suppressed a pure snarl as she responded, "I'll be sure to keep that in mind when we need jobs in less than a year."

She waited until he broke her gaze, not willing to be the first to look away. Once he did, she shook her head, disgusted, and started to bolt.

Matt's mom, Cirise, caught her arm at the elbow before she went far. Her long fingers dug themselves down into Ariettea's skin as she leaned in far too close, her breath beating down on to Ariettea's neck, Ariettea resisting the urge to rip her arm away forcefully. "Yes, but that's still a year away," Cirise lowly hissed in her ear, "Even then, you still won't be old enough to hold your own. Being 18 and graduated doesn't make you an adult. Show some respect." She finished sharply, each word trying harder and harder to degrade than the last.

Ariettea refused to respond, to give her any semblance of a win. She stared into her eyes hard, unwaveringly, her expression refusing to change as she silently waited for Cirise to release her arm. When she finally did, the spots her fingers had been leaving red marks, Ariettea ran.

She ran through every back door and hallway she could through her house to avoid as many people as possible.

She ran to the closest bathroom and shut the door, her hands trembling as she latched the lock.

She watched her hands shake, not knowing if it was in fear or rage, as they trailed down the white six-paneled bathroom door. Her vision fixed on her already white skin, paler than usual, the blue veins jumping out at her. She turned and sank down to the floor, back to the door, her butt hitting the old linoleum so hard, sharp pain shot up through her spine.

She pulled her knees to her chest. 'Breathe, breathe, breathe.' She commanded herself, futilely. She knew full well there would be no calming down. She drew in air, with the knowledge that she was getting oxygen, but she still somehow felt a struggle to breath.

She wasn't fighting tears, but the urge to run even further. Maybe to a place she could never return from.

The cold, hard, familiar feeling enveloped her stomach and spread to the rest of her body as she sat there, stoic, staring at the dust on top of the baseboard. Her mind was somehow empty and yet full of echoing words. 'And no one understands why I hate to be around people.' She thought as she laid her head on her knees. She closed her eyes until she stopped shaking, absentmindedly playing with the deliberately frayed hem of her baggy black denim shorts. Not baggy by choice, but by circumstance, as with all her clothes.

She sat there, eyes squeezed shut until she was able to shove her emotions back into the black pit from which they came. She was just so sick of being demeaned, being told to grow up, but also told she was nearly an adult and needed to act like it. Then someone would follow it up with telling her even when she would be an adult, even that wouldn't be good enough.

The door suddenly rattled and shoved her body away from it as someone knocked, trying to get in. Another sanctuary, lost. Ariettea sighed and stood up, straightened her faded band tee, ran the water for show, and exited, looking for a new spot to be alone. She knew if she went to her bedroom, her parents would throw a fit about her oh so typical anti-social behavior. Because of course, that's why she didn't have friends. It was always her fault.

She found an empty picnic table at the edge of her parents' property, skirting the forest, dilapidated and damp. She gently sat down, pulled one knee to her chest, letting her other leg dangle. The toes of her beat-up converse trailed the tops of the blades of grass, long missed by the lawnmower.

She tucked her hair behind her ear, interweaving it in between her fingers as it pooled into her lap, once again considering her Aunts' proposal. There was a fire in her, slow-burning, and lately, dimly lit, but it was ever burning. Sometimes she fought to squelch it; other times, people did that for her. She shoved everything down that she could to smother it, to smother all emotion, both negative and positive, it had turned out. But the fire was unwilling to be put out. Something in her kept it fueled. Something in her was still searching for meaning.

Her phone vibrated in her back pocket with a text tone. She jumped at the feeling, it wasn't a very familiar one. Her phone usually remained devoid of contact and silent at all times.

Matt's name lit up the screen. ***"I see you THINKING over there. Told you to lay off that."*** A winking emoji playfully at the end. She felt her face flush as she smiled and looked up, searching for him, as always.

She could envision the look on his face. That look, that serious, caring look. The one where he stopped being an immature boy for just a minute, looked into her eyes, and calmed her soul while making her heart race.

All while they both denied the feelings that fueled it.

"Come stand by me, I'll stay with you." Another text came in, ***"We're having a great time over here."*** She knew he was asking because he'd never seek her out in a crowd, not when people were around to see. She caught sight of him throwing his head back, his sharp jawline protruding towards the sky, laughing at a joke that someone in the group had told. Yet another group she wasn't apart of.

She reasoned, she could always walk over there, of course, join the group, that's what Matt was always telling her to do, to jump into the conversation… But it just…. Never turned out well for her. She was always saying the wrong thing, or even the right thing, but someone would take issue with it just because of her age.

Because she was her.

She wished she could just be fixed. Part of her longed to be like Matt, to feel, to just be, to be young and carefree, but that fire. That fire always overwhelmed that longing.

Phone still in hand, she dialed Nadette: "Hey, Nadette! I'd um, actually really like to hear more about that donation event…"

Chapter 3

The Midwest likes to play a cruel joke of getting even more mercilessly hot its last few days before school starts. So Ariettea was enjoying having short hair for the first time in her life.

Two weeks before she was due back to school, she stood and flipped her head from side to side, examining her reflection in a fitting room mirror. The weight removed, her raven locks bounced with a wave in them now, length barely brushing the tops of her shoulders when she cocked her head to the side. Sixteen inches cut off left a razor cut long bob that she liked to call choppy and punk.

"You are doing SUCH an amazing thing, Ari!" Nadette had exclaimed over the phone. "Really! You yourself- You're going to change a life!"

Ariettea had struggled not to roll her eyes, trying to keep her voice upbeat for Nadette's sake. A lot of, well, most, people took Ariettea's unexcitable nature as plain teenage brooding. But it was something more than brooding, right around apathetic on the scale.

Her baseline was melancholy on a good day.

She didn't know why, but for some reason, she didn't want Nadette to think of her that way.

Part of her wanted to just be normal, like any other 17 year old. To have friends, even only one, to not be relentlessly alone. She felt like she was always surrounded by people; in the congregation, at school, even at home, her parents always had people over, yet, she never felt more alone than when she was in a crowd of people. That feeling came from the belief that relationships did nothing but give you false hope and hurt you in the end. Because all her relationships had done so. All the people who called her cynical could never seem to remember how many times she had been hopeful. That, or they just didn't care.

She sighed as she threw a pair of blue jeans over her arm and left the fitting room. As she walked out, she nearly bumped into a tall bottle blonde heading in with an arm full of push up bras.

Samantha.

"Ariettea!" She exclaimed, shoving her items under her arm, her voice an octave too high, a notch too loud, as if to alert someone nearby to come save her.

"Sam." Ariettea snipped, trying to remain cordial, wearing that fake pursed-lip smile that people use when they're trying to avoid someone.

She winced internally, knowing she was the only one to still call her Sam. Samantha had adopted her full name once she decided she was an adult at 13. The same time she had decided Ariettea wasn't good enough to hang out with anymore.

"Wow, I haven't seen you in so long!" Samantha said, going in for a hug. Ariettea stiffly extended an arm as Samantha gave her a limp, barely there, barely meant, hug. It made Ariettea's skin crawl. She hated being touched.

Samantha looked down at the jeans in Ariettea's hands. "School clothes?" She said, nodding to them.

Ariettea looked down, finding herself trying to hide the size tag, all the years of 'who can weigh the least' flooding back to her. "Yeah, it's that time." She said with a shrug, drawing out her words, desperately wanting to escape.

Samantha shook her head. "I am SO glad to be done with that!" She said, throwing her head back, her hand smacking the side of her painted on denim capris. "It's awful!" She whined, "And ugh, all that reading!"

Ariettea nodded solemnly again, that fake smile still stuck on her lips. She tried to view school as a means to her escape. Being there felt like she was accomplishing something. But for people like Samantha, it was the social game that was all the fun, the only reason they showed up. And it was the reason the two of them never got along, no matter how badly their mutual friend parents wanted them to.

Small towns, small minded people, but big mouths, big opinions.

Samantha looked her up and down. "But I guess you always did your own thing anyway…"

"So how's life outside of high school?" Ariettea asked her suddenly, trying to hide a smirk.

Samantha shifted her weight, suddenly uncomfortable. Which, of course, was why Ariettea had asked her that. "Oh, you know…" She said, looking around her, unable to meet Ariettea's eye. "It's busy!" She said with a large arm flourish.

Ariettea knew full well what that was code for. Boys and parties and clubs and booze and avoiding getting a real job. All because she played the game, the game of lying through life, telling your parents what they wanted to hear so you can keep your free rent and freedom, tag along on all the free family vacations.

Samantha stared at Ariettea awkwardly as a moment of silence lasted a moment too long. A moment Ariettea both cringed and relished in. "Did you cut your hair?" Samantha blurted.

Ariettea blinked hard to avoid rolling her eyes. 'Have I ever in the 15 years we've known each other cut my hair?' She wanted to blurt back. But that same smile still stuck on her face; she answered, "Yeah, yeah I did. Donated it."

"AW! How SPECIAL." Another sickeningly sweet and loud voice rang out from behind Samantha. Her best friend Jayelle came sauntering up.

Ariettea glared at her, cocked her head slightly, and answered, "Why thank you." In the most level voice she could muster. For Ariettea, the more annoyed she got, the more level her voice got. The more robotic she became. The more emotions she tried to shove down and away.

Jayelle smiled at her and shook her head, saying so much with that little motion. Without breaking her gaze on Ariettea, but shifting it up and down her body, examining every perceived flaw, she said to Samantha, eyes on the size of Ariettea's chest, "I'm heading in to try on my stuff." She linked her arm in her friend's and started to pull her along.

"GREAT to see you, Ariettea!" Samantha said, stifling a giggle as Jayelle pulled her away.

Ariettea could hear their whispers as she walked away. "Did you see her-" She rolled her eyes so far back that she closed them. She shook her head as she walked towards the register, memories of years of abuse flooding back into her mind as she desperately tried to throw up dams to keep them in. 'And yet everyone loves them and wants me to be like them. Wonders what I did so wrong that those oh so amazing people cut me out during junior high.' She thought bitterly, remembering all the people that packed into Samantha's graduation party the summer before, the dozens of them giving speeches about how amazing she was and what great things she was going to do. And where was she? Still in that small town, unemployed, still going on mall runs midday, mid-week, no aspirations, but still carrying everyone's admiration. And for what? All because she did exactly what she was told and answered everyone in all the right ways, even if she never meant a single word she said.

Ariettea knew her problem was that she refused to play that game, refused to blindly follow what others told her to do, but she also knew it wasn't a problem at all. Even if it kept her alone, shopping for yet another smaller size of jeans, not sure where she was going to end up by the end of her own senior year, at least she wasn't a liar.

She was getting into her car when her phone rang. Nadette's name popped up on the screen.

"Hello?"

"Ari! Hi! Guess what! We've got a name! THE name! Of the patient who is getting your hair!" Nadette babbled excitedly.

"What, it's just my hair?" Ariettea answered flatly, drained from her encounter with Samantha.

Nadette wasn't even phased. "No, but actually, it is mostly yours! The girl wanted a shorter wig. So less hair. The other donors weren't interested in meeting her. I did mention she's a girl, right? And that she's 13? Well, I did now. Sorry, I am SO excited!"

Ariettea tried to jump in, "Nadette, are you saying she wants to meet me, though?" She said, worry creeping into her voice. She didn't want to barge her way into some poor kid's hospital room, demanding to meet her when she didn't have any interest in meeting her herself.

"Oh my gosh, YES!" Nadette exclaimed. "Remember how I told you that was the best part of the drive being local?"

Ariettea's mind wandered. Nadette had said that… But all Ariettea wanted was to DO something, not meet anyone.

"So she is absolutely begging to meet you! And how cool is it, you get to do this amazing thing, see how you impacted someone, come to visit us, it's just so exciting! You do want to come to visit us, right?"

Ariettea bit her lip. The thought was more appealing than she wanted to admit, a vacation away from home, from everyone there… "Yeah, yeah… I mean… if you wouldn't mind and she… really wants me to… I guess I could-"

"Oh, AWESOME! This is so cool. Right?! Well, I've got to start my rounds here at the hospital but get me some dates before the school year starts! Love you, by-"

"Wait, Nadette, you didn't finish- what's her name?" Ariettea interrupted.

Nadette laughed as she caught herself. "Sorry, I'm overly excited and in a hurry. But it's Lily." She said. "Her name is Lily."

Ariettea looked over to the calla lily, the single one wrapped in an orange ribbon, along with the wild one from the beach, that now both hung from her rearview mirror. "Maybe lilies are my thing now." She muttered to herself as she started the car.

She wanted to take it as some kind of sign… But she had long learned to not look for things that weren't there.

Chapter 4

Ariettea sat on the plane, aisle seat. The middle seat next to her was empty, thankfully. But the window seat was occupied by a woman who clearly didn't believe in silence. Or holding your pee for any length on time, as she had made Ariettea move three times so she could go to the bathroom before the flight had even begun its taxi down the runway. After the taxi began, THEN she tried to get up a fourth time, but the flight attendants made her stay put, much to her chagrin.

And of course, Ariettea was the closest target for her word vomit. She tried so hard to be nice; she smiled, nodded, agreed when prompted. Everyone always acted like Ariettea was a rude and mean person, but she wasn't. She even put in a few agreeable affirmations here and there while the old lady was talking at her.

But once her temples started to throb 20 minutes into the flight, she had had enough. She nodded one last time, and as the lady stopped to take a breath, Ariettea put her headphones on, which produced a heavy and annoyed sigh from her aisle mate that Ariettea could hear even through her full volume music.

She could hear the woman speaking to the lady in the seat in front of her, "Teenagers these days! I tell you WHAT! They are SO RUDE!"

Ariettea slowly turned her head and stared at the lady until she caught her eye. She held her eye contact long enough to make the woman uncomfortable and then turned back forward and closed her eyes.

She could still feel the woman's self-righteous huff back into her seat, her large leopard print encased body shaking the whole row.

Ariettea leaned her head back against the headrest and sighed herself. No matter where she went, she was the target of some adults' 'my word is law' opinion. Everyone judged her by her age, even before speaking with her. Her age alone defined who she was. And it drove her crazy. Even her parents did it.

Two weeks prior, while telling her parents she was going to Georgia, the conversation kept going back to her age, the most irrelevant point there was.

"You think you're going to TELL us where and when you're going?"

"You can't go on a plane alone!"

"No, you can't drive yourself there, either!"

"Maybe when you're 18."

She believed that she was more than just a number. But to everyone else, that's all she ever was.

"I'm smarter and more responsible than you give me credit for!" She had fired back. "You say when I'm 18, but I'll be 18 in a few months, so what would that number change? So then it would turn into an 'our house, our rules' thing. Why can't you just say that you don't want me to go somewhere where you can't monitor me?"

The back and forth continued, but at that point, they knew she was right. So instead of acknowledging it, they had to push harder to show her who was boss, no matter how correct she was.

She opened her eyes once she felt the row moving again, the old woman next to her was getting up, carrying her knock off Louis Vuitton purse to the bathroom with her. She hugged it close as she looked at Ariettea nervously. Apparently, she could no longer be trusted because she didn't do what the woman had wanted- agree with everything she said and did just because she was older.

Ariettea watched her walk away, her orange-red hair, fried from over coloring, bouncing as she shuffled in between the flight attendant and her cart, complaining to her that the plane was too cold.

The flight was less than two hours, but once the plane landed in Atlanta, Ariettea was relieved to be getting off it, away from all the prying eyes wondering why she was flying alone. She thought about announcing to them all that she was going to rehab, just for fun, but decided against it. It would only reinforce their preconceived perceptions of all teenagers.

She immediately saw Nadette as she came through the security doors. Her multifaceted blonde hair, curled so perfectly, bounced as she waved excitedly. "Hi, Ari!" She exclaimed as she pulled Ariettea in for a hug.

Ariettea felt her body stiffen rapidly. She tried so hard not to, but it was just a thing her body did on its own. She loosely tried to place her arms somewhere not awkward, she was so bad at hugging. It felt so foreign to her. So unnecessary.

Nadette's thin frame produced a much tighter grip than one would expect, Ariettea mused as she felt her face bury into the cedarwood and floral smelling ivy green sweater that had the perfect amount of slouch and style to make Nadette look even more perfect than she usually did.

"We are SO excited you could come!" Nadette said pulling away, shoving her hand casually in the back pocket of her dark wash straight cut jeans, keeping the other hand tightly on Ariettea's shoulder. "Trent is working, but today is my day off, so I thought we'd go to lunch, catch up?"

Ariettea nodded stiffly, trying to force a smile, feeling even more uncomfortable and awkward than she already did every single day. Once Nadette started to head out of the airport, Ariettea started feeling maybe her being there was a stupid idea. She was feeling foolish for trying to force connections that weren't even there. Or connections that would just shatter like all do eventually. She slightly shook her head, trying to rid the dark thoughts that were ever-present.

Nadette led Ariettea to the car, an arm around her the whole way. Ariettea scolded herself for feeling so uncomfortable, being so cold when Nadette was literally welcoming her with open arms. She just had a hard time believing it was sincere, well, that anyone in life was sincere.

They stepped out into the sweltering heat, humid and sticky, almost slimy. Nadette noticed Ariettea wince and laughed. "You're used to being on Lake Michigan! Much cooler breeze up north. There's a cool breeze once we get back to Ducreis, though. We have a bit of a drive to the coast, but trust me, it's worth it! Not only is the air cooler, but it's absolutely gorgeous."

"I'm sorry you had to drive so far." Ariettea muttered, hopping up into the passenger side of her Aunt's old Jeep Wrangler, the laces of her combat boots lapping around her ankles.

"Oh, it's no problem, really! Lily is so excited to meet you! She is the sweetest little girl. Let alone how excited Trent and I are to have you." Nadette smiled warmly at Ariettea as she started the car.

Ariettea kept her eyes down to her feet, nodding.

Nadette leaned back into her seat before starting to car and turned towards Ariettea. "Are you ok?" She asked gently, her eyes soft and warm.

Ariettea forced a smile, taken aback. Not many people bothered to ask her that anymore. No one except Matt, but only on a good day, when his friends' backs were turned.

"Yeah." She said, trying to smile, nod. Her one-word clipped, short, with false excitement put into it.

Nadette nodded softly, but knowingly, and then turned back to the wheel. She pulled out of the parking garage, asking Ariettea how her flight was.

"Fine." Ariettea said quickly, wincing at her unintentional shortness. "It was ok." She corrected, trying to seem more congenial. "There was a lady next to me that got up so many times I nearly lost count."

Nadette laughed heartily, her hazel eyes shining in the Atlanta sun. "That's rough!"

Ariettea smiled, tightly, almost sarcastically. Her usual smile.

Nadette's own smile stayed genuine. "So, we have a long drive to talk, we have a lot to catch up on! I haven't seen you in what, three years?"

Ariettea nodded stiffly, remembering their last family get together, the one where she had hid in the barn the whole time, playing candy crush, desperately trying to avoid any human contact. "Yeah, I guess that was the last time."

"And now you're about to be a senior! Tell me about school, do you like it? You have lots of friends there?"

Ariettea felt her chest tighten, her heartache. "School is school. I'm there to do the work and not much else." She said, hoping that answer would explain itself. She couldn't, wouldn't admit the truth. That she was a loner that didn't belong anywhere in any situation.

"That's not necessarily a bad thing, though," Nadette said thoughtfully. "I would have stayed out of a lot of trouble if I hadn't been running around with my friends instead of concentrating on the more important building blocks. But I guess that's part of being young."

Ariettea leaned her head against the headrest, eyes out the passenger window, watching the city grow smaller and smaller as they drove east. "Yeah I guess it is." She muttered, not even sure what she was agreeing to. She appreciated her Aunt's sincere effort to connect, most people gave up on her after 2 of her one-word answers.

As Nadette looked over at her again, Ariettea could feel the concern radiating off her. Before she could ask again if she was ok, Ariettea turned back to her and quickly asked,

"So, tell me about Lily. Can you explain to me what it is exactly that she has?"

Nadette swallowed as she chewed on her words. "Miss Lily Abonet. Gorgeous girl. These eyes that pierce…." She cleared her throat. "I actually sat down and pulled up some articles that my colleagues have written, and I talked to Lily's doctor who is a friend of mine, not that he could discuss her in particular, but just so I could try to explain it in a way that makes the most sense." She took another breath,

"Lily has Hodgkin's Lymphoma. It's a cancer that starts and spreads in the lymph nodes. To treat it, for Lily being so young, the first choice is chemotherapy. Lily just loves beating the odds, because Hodgkin's Lymphoma isn't usually found in someone her age, and it usually doesn't recur."

"Recur? This is her second time with it?"

"Yes, she's 13, and her first go-round with this was at age 9. That's what I mean by being younger than most patients."

"Why did it come back?"

Nadette shook her head. "There's no way to say. But because it has, that has made her treatment more intense this time around. They start with so many 'cycles' of chemo, then check to see if or how much more chemo is needed, and then it might be a different chemo."

"There's more than one type?"

Nadette laughed. "Ohhh yes, sadly. People tend to think chemo just means this one poisonous drug but saying chemo is just like saying painkiller, there's a lot of different types."

"So how long does she have to be in the hospital? I mean, if she's been here all summer already…"

Nadette silently changed lanes. "That's another thing that just depends on the person and disease. Lily has been admitted for about two months. For Lily and her parent's, they're native to a small town in South Carolina. Most people go to the hospital Monday-Friday for their treatments and then go home. But coming here to Ducreis is a five-hour jaunt, well worth it since it's a university hospital, but because of the drive, Lily stays full time. Her current chemo plan is a six-cycle treatment, and each cycle lasts for four weeks."

Ariettea did the math in her head. "So basically, six months just for the chemo?!"

Nadette nodded sadly. "And with her maintenance therapy, they probably don't want to constantly be driving for, she probably won't leave, or at least go home, until after the first of the year."

"Her parents live there or like, where do they all go when they're there but not admitted?"

"There's programs for things like that, and they have a friend in town, I think."

"So, you know them?"

Nadette nodded, waved her hand up and down. "Somewhat. I've gotten to talk to them a lot through the drive, actually, so I have you to thank for our new friends!" She laughed, and Ariettea got that pain in her stomach like she always did whenever she heard about how easy it was for other people to make friends. "Even before, when you work in the same building for years and years, and the same people are always coming through, you're bound to cross paths. Even when she's not your patient, most everyone in the hospital are familiar with Lily. She's just that special."

Ariettea stared at her for a minute. "Special...How?" She asked incredulously, thinking Nadette was just gushing over some sick kid for no good reason.

"Kids in her position are forced to grow up pretty quick. So, she's this combination of old soul and spunky. She is hilarious to talk to, but insightful. You could see a kid like that being bratty, but she is the sweetest person, the whole family is. Positivity is important, Ducreis hospital is big on mental health and therapy in general, so I'm sure they've all been through their fair shares of therapy sessions."

Ariettea shifted in her seat, uncomfortable. Why was Nadette talking about THAT? Her head couldn't comprehend it.

Nadette turned her signal on to get off on an exit to a two-lane roadway, winding through seas of greens and blues, and they neared the coast. "But you'll have all the time in the world to see just how special she is!" Nadette said, looking over at Ariettea reassuringly.

Ariettea tried to muster up a smile for her, even a fake one, just to make her happy. She could tell Nadette was trying so hard. And she knew that she wasn't the easiest person to talk to. Which is why most of the time, she just didn't talk to anyone. Ever.

"Are you good with Italian food? There's this great little place Trent and I love; it's on the way back to town." Nadette asked.

Ariettea nodded silently, feeling the weight of being a burden starting to crush her. "I'm sorry again, that you had to drive all this way to get me."

Nadette waved her hand at her. "Are you kidding? Look at this view!" She said, motioning in front of her.

Ariettea looked around her, rivers running into each other, bluffs of sand dancing on the edges, sprinkled with thousands of little white beach lilies, and a million hues of green spread out over all the massive old trees, tangling together, as the highway faded out into an old natural road the further they got.

"It's gorgeous out here. It's like our own little world. When we get to Ducreis it's a bit more built up, but it still has that fun coastal charm. I think that's one of the big draws for the college, personally. At least that's why I loved it."

"You and Trent met there, right?"

"We did!" Nadette answered quickly, coming close to blushing. "I was a sucker for the floppy blonde hair on that beach bum, his tan skin, and soft, kind green eyes. Lucky for me we had all the same classes. Although looking back I have this theory that Trent rearranged his class schedule to match mine. And then of course one thing leads to another and here we are. It took me forever to convince him to cut his hair...And medical school convinced him to stop spending all his time at the beach, so it's not as blonde anymore, but sometimes I still see that same surfer boy."

Ariettea stared down at her hands, wondering how it could be so easy. Wondering if it would ever happen for her.

"So, is it a small town?" She asked Nadette, feeling a sudden but familiar claustrophobia clamp down on her throat.

Nadette shook her head. "I wouldn't call it that. Quaint, yes, charming, yes, but small, no. The college and hospital put together make a huge campus and there's so many people in and out that 'small' isn't really a word that gets used much around here."

Ariettea tried to let her chest relax, her heart stop pounding. The small-town fear was all encasing, she wanted out so badly, even when she wasn't there.

Nadette droned on and on the rest of the way back to Ducreis, desperately trying to make small talk and 'catch up' with Ariettea, who tried her honest best to comply. Nadette seemed so sincere, she felt terrible that she didn't realize, at least not yet, the kind of person she was. The type of person people left. Over and over... She scolded herself for going there. She silently shook her head to jar her from that place.

Nadette saw the slight jerk of her head but pretended not to notice. "Here we are!" She said cheerily, smiling over at Ariettea encouragingly.

They rounded a corner, and Nadette braked on top of a hill, looking over yet another vast expanse of green and blue.

The ocean jumped out at her more than she thought it would. Living in a lake town, she was used to the blue-hued brown lake, but the blue there was a totally different tone; crisp and deep bright blue. The way the sun's rays hit it made it look like millions of diamonds sprinkled the surface, with soft white caps lapping all their way to the shore. And unlike the lake at home, you couldn't see where the ocean ended.

White sandy beaches trailed the edges, leading into seas of green, with trees lining every street.

Small quaint little condos and houses trickled their way into larger apartment buildings the closer you got to what in the distance were massive brick buildings, literally covered in ivy, stained glass windows trailing their way up the sides- Ducreis University. And a glimmering blue wall of windows going up 20 stories high set behind that. Ducreis Hospital.

The way the hospital was situated left it locked in by the sea, with both the back and one side of it literally on the beach. In front, it shared a courtyard with the college.

Leading away from both was a two-lane street with, in perfect succession, perfectly shaped little trees with twinkle lights you see even in the daytime.

The further away from campus, the more little stores and restaurants crowded in. Ariettea could see so many little bistro sets she lost count.

Off to each side of the town, the houses got bigger but not massive. Sweet little suburban cottages lining the beach on the right and off into land on the left.

Nadette sighed happily. "Every time I come back into town; I love seeing this view."

Ariettea could nearly see the hearts in her eyes. She said hollowly, "I hope someday I can look at wherever I live with as much love as you."

Nadette turned to her and laughed at herself, her hazel eyes dancing. "What can I say, I've lived the best years of my life in this place."

Ariettea felt that familiar pit in her stomach burn once more, the pain that made her wonder if she would ever feel that same sense of peace and belonging. Again, she shook her head, trying, as Matt always was telling her, to live in the now.

Nadette couldn't ignore the head jerk a second time. "Are you sure you're ok, dear?" She asked, not in the condescending way Ariettea was used to when someone called her dear, but in the way a friend would ask.

Ariettea mustered up a smile. "Yeah, of course!" She said shaking her head, shrugging her shoulders. "I just must be tired from the flight."

Ah, her age-old, ever used excuse, 'I'm tired.'. When her first go-to lie of 'I'm fine' didn't work, those two little words hid the war being fought in her head.

Nadette smiled, knowingly, but tried to hide that fact, let Ariettea think her secret was well hidden. "Alrighty. Let's just get you home, we'll order in for dinner instead of going out for lunch." She said still smiling, patting her gently on the leg.

Not even five minutes later, Nadette pulled up in front of the two-story walk-up condo she and Trent called home- a sleek, narrow brick building with trendy black trim.

Nadette led Ariettea inside to a shotgun-style layout. Entryway faced the stairs leading to the second level bedrooms, but to the left of that were the living, dining, and kitchen, all in a row.

Ariettea repositioned her old duffel bag on her shoulder, uncomfortable and unsure of what to do next. She couldn't remember the last time she'd slept over at someone's house.

"Well your bedroom is upstairs, turn right, and you'll be facing it; it's the first door. Trent and I are down the hall, and there's a bathroom in between. I'm going to set dinner up for when Trent gets home. Make yourself at home and call me if you need anything." Nadette smiled.

She was always smiling. Ariettea found it a little off-putting.

She made her way upstairs and to her room. She sat her bag down on the queen bed, covered with a yellow quilt she recognized as her grandma's. She sat on the bed, quietly musing. Georgia seemed...Nice. Charming, but sleek. Busy, but calm. Ivy league, but beach bumming.

For a split second, her mind wandered as it always did, and she imagined herself living there, in Georgia. Maybe going to college, living with Trent and Nadette, making amazing friends-

But it stopped there.

Friends, they would hurt her. Trent and Nadette would quickly tire of her, as everyone did. And college was a dream that when reality hit, would be a nightmare.

She sighed. That wash over of hardness that went through her chest always stung a little.

She was always telling herself not to live in the past, Matt was always telling her not to live in the future, and everyone around her made her feel like there was no point or joy living in the present.

She had no idea where she belonged.

If anywhere.

Ariettea stayed in her room. She didn't want to bother Nadette. No, more like she didn't think Nadette would want to be bothered with her. She pondered why Nadette and Trent had offered to have her come down. What was the real reason? Purely to be nice? Was there some underlying scheme to get her to do something? She looked around the room, paranoid. Softwood furniture scattered about, too big for the room itself. It should have felt claustrophobic, but it landed more on cozy.

She flopped back from her sitting position to lay staring at the ceiling. She reminded herself of the real reason she was there, for Lily. The girl that wanted to meet her. She wasn't sure what she was expecting. A thank you? A nice to meet you, have a good life? She shook her head, mad at herself for ever thinking this trip was a good idea.

She heard Trent come in. Voices downstairs...Probably talking about her, she thought. There was a soft knock at her door.

Ariettea sat up quickly. "Yeah?"

Nadette opened the door gently and stood there, her body language cautious, as if she were afraid of what she would find. "Hey, dinner's ready, if you're hungry." She said with a smile.

'I'm not. I never am.' Ariettea thought. But she forced a nod, a smile, a thank you, and put one foot in front of the other to follow Nadette downstairs.

Trent was waiting, still in blue scrubs from work. Nadette was right, his blonde hair had darkened with age, but it was still a little floppy on the sides. His green eyes crinkled at the sides ever so slightly when he looked at her, soft and welcoming as he opened his arms to embrace her quickly, warmly. "Ari!"

What was with these people and their hugging? She wondered as she waited for him to release her.

He did quickly, laughing, explaining, "These are clean scrubs, don't worry!"

She could smell the deep warm aftershave on him as she pulled away. She always forgot he wasn't very tall, 5'10 at the most, but a muscular build made him solid. His was a hug you could easily feel safe in.

"How are you?" He boomed excitedly.

She wasn't quite sure if boomed was the right description for it though. Trent's voice was strong and authoritative, but somehow soft and compassionate all at once. It was the perfect doctor's voice.

Ariettea tried to force the same smile she had been forcing all day. "I'm good, and you?" She shoved her hands in the back pockets of her jeans.

Trent kept a hand on her shoulder as he smiled enthusiastically down at her. "Good! Starving!" He laughed again. "These 12-hour shifts kill." He said, pulling out a chair at the dining table and motioning for Ariettea to sit. She did, awkwardly as Trent and Nadette took seats at each head of the table.

The usual pleasantries were made, how was the flight, how is school, how are your parents? Ariettea tried her best to give more than one-word answers, to elaborate and converse. It wasn't easy for her. Partly because it wasn't what she was used to. She was used to being talked over, and when people asked her a question, they didn't really listen to her answer, they just listened for what they wanted the answer to be.

She braced herself for the more invasive questions, college, boyfriend, future goals?

But to her surprise, well, to her utter shock, those questions didn't come.

She realized all Nadette's questions on the car ride home had been non-invasive as well. It was such a breath of fresh air, that she hadn't even realized. She wondered why they weren't asking. She wondered what it was that was holding them back.

Appreciative of their treating her like a real person, she tried to start asking them questions. "What happens in a typical shift for you, Trent?" She twirled spaghetti round and round on her plate, trying to make herself eat it. Nadette had gone on and on about how this was her favorite restaurant, and she didn't want to hurt her feelings.

Trent swallowed hard on a big mouthful of salad, and excitedly answered, "Chaos!" He laughed as he reached for his glass of water. "I work 12-hour shifts, and in that time, I see everything from the flu, UTI's, self-harm, and bumps on the head, all the way up to heart attacks, car accidents, dismembered limbs-"

"Trent!" Nadette interjected, "Ariettea is eating!"

Ariettea held her hand up, shook her head, as if to say no, really it's ok, as Trent pointed to her with his glass of water and laughed, "See Nade! Ari is cool! And it's not like you don't come home and tell me about the placentas the won't detach and the blood and-"

"Ok, ok, truce!"

Trent and Nadette laughed at each other playfully. Ariettea could see the love in their eyes as they gazed at each other across the table, each gleefully shaking their head at the other.

"But no, honestly, I love my job," Trent said, tearing his gaze from Nadette back to Ariettea. "I'm seriously lucky I get to say that. It's not like I'm saying it fulfills my life on its own or that I don't have days I hate it, because lord knows some days I don't think I can chart one more thing, but I love that I get to spend my days helping people."

Ariettea stuck on that term, helping people. And how many times she had thought about that, how she wanted to do something that meant something. But she hadn't believed that to be a reachable goal for a long time.

"That sounds really cool." She said quietly, not able to keep Trent's gaze for longer than a second.

She waited for him to ask her about college, what she wanted to do for work. She tensed as she braced for the question, but instead came, "It is. But of course, what I come home to is what matters most to me."

Nadette waved a hand at him, but Ariettea could see her cheeks flush ever so slightly. After all their years together, he could still make her blush.

She found herself remembering all the times she'd caught Matt's gaze from across a room- him already staring at her, the feeling it gave her. She tried never to let herself wonder about that feeling. But it was times like that when she did let the thought linger. The way Trent and Nadette looked at each other, and the more they told Ariettea about their life there, how happy they were, she started to wonder if maybe there was a hope for her future.

Even if she didn't believe there was.

Chapter 5

"The hospital started out as the center for a tiny town. Back then, no one thought anything of a hospital on a beach. It was their main hub, after all. Now, zoning laws would freak out about preserving the shore, I'm sure, but lucky for us, Ducreis is such an institution, we get to keep this view, and add on to it too! They're always growing and building and adding…"

Nadette was going on and on as she drove into the hospital the next morning. Ariettea tried not to tune her out but couldn't help it sometimes. She was always bubbling something…bubbly out of her mouth. It gave her a headache if she concentrated too much on the jumping from subject to subject. So, she just watched the view go by.

Massive oak trees, hundreds of years old, lined the street into campus. They drove past the university first, literal cobblestone on the road and sidewalks. It was massive and daunting. The dozens of high buildings made of solid stone, stained glass windows, ivy crawling everywhere, was right out of a novel about some far-away boarding school.

Once they faced the hospital, it was hard not to notice the beach on the right and back sides of the building. The white sand stood stark to the bluest blue Ariettea had ever seen. Whitecaps crashed into the shores, where only a few hundred feet away stood the massive building that was Ducreis Hospital.

Once parked, the heat slapped Ariettea in the face as she hopped out of the jeep. She ran a hand through her hair as she always did to pull out the tangles, but it stilled jarred her to find it not sticking to the back of her neck, most of it gone.

She trailed Nadette into the building, going in the back way, but still catching a glimpse of the massive round lobby a couple stories below. A glass dome circled above the first few open-air levels before branching off to all the different wings.

She had to jump to keep up with Nadette, surprised how briskly she could move in heels that perfectly matched her high waisted navy-blue skirt, with gold buttons on the front, and a tucked-in white collared shirt. Ariettea looked down at her own black jeans and standard t-shirt, thought of the ever-present black eyeliner smoking out her eyes, and wondered if she should have dressed up for this… meeting.

She followed Nadette through the marble-tiled hallway, up an elevator, and rounded a corner into another long hallway. But then the view changed from marble and glimmer to linoleum and floor to ceiling windows.

"I should have mentioned this, but don't be taken aback by Lily's appearance. The chemo has her looking pretty battle wounded, but hey, that's why she's got your hair on her head, right?" Nadette laughed, but Ariettea was suddenly slightly worried about what state she would find Lily in. Because no matter how high tech Ducreis was, it was still a hospital. There were still sick people there. There was still the overwhelming smell of disinfectant, the faint scent of a used bedpan. The feeling of hope sadistically extracted from the air.

They walked down a long hallway where the right side of it was 100% glass, windows overlooking the shaded campus and beach. The other side of the corridor was lined with a row of sliding glass doors into patient rooms, something a bit more high-tech than the standard heavy wooden door with the funny handle.

Nadette stopped outside the corner room at the end of the hall, the glass windows from floor to ceiling shielded with long blinds. She knocked on a halfway open sliding glass door and waited for the call to come in. When it came, she slid open the door and stepped in, smiling. Ariettea followed a few steps behind.

Her eyes were immediately drawn to a little girl sitting straight up in her bed. Pale as anything, little blue and green veins visible all over her thin skin, her tiny frame. An earlobe length black bob framed the most effervescent teal colored eyes Ariettea had ever seen. They sparkled, but were sunken into her frail face, her eyebrows nothing but a shadowed memory.

The loud, clear voice that came out of her didn't seem to match her body as she exclaimed, "You must be Ariettea!" Lily leaped out of the bed sitting on the left wall and gave Ariettea a ferocious hug, arms wrapping tightly around her waist. In addition to being thin, Lily was short, years of chemo stunting her growth.

Ariettea once again stood stiffly in yet another hug, her arms pinned to her sides. She waved her hands limply, awkwardly trying to hug Lily back. A man and a woman, looking all too comfortable for being in a hospital room, immediately tried to corral their daughter.

"Lily! Calm, remember? Healing!"

Lily dramatically rolled her eyes and flopped herself onto the edge of her bed.

"She doesn't like to admit how bad she feels, even to herself," The man said, laughing. He towered over Ariettea, a muscular build showing through his navy-blue polo pullover sweater.

"I'm Alex." He extended a hand. "And this is my wife, Elaina." Ariettea shook his hand, his grip strong and confident. His dishwater blonde hair swooped up and was brushed back, and his square jaw showed a couple days worth of stubble. He gave her a glowing smile as his wife stepped around him to gently hug Ariettea.

Elaina was much shorter than her husband, a contrast in every way, soft features, soft kinky curled dark hair brushing her shoulders. "So nice to meet you!" She exclaimed softly, pulling up both of Ariettea's hands in her own and holding tightly. "Truly. We are so grateful you agreed to come all this way. What you did for Lily was just…amazing." Elaina's deep brown eyes filled with tears.

Ariettea tried not to shift from foot to foot to stay grounded while this stranger held on to her, crying. It wasn't as if she'd picked Lily out or anything…She tried to uncurl her lips from where she had sucked them inside her mouth. "It was uhm… No big deal." She managed to murmur. "I mean, there were others that donated…"

She couldn't look anyone in the eye; instead, her gaze raced around the room. Every hospital looks like sparkles and chrome when you first walk in, and no matter how high tech and fancy it is, somehow all hospital rooms share certain items. The TV mounted on the ceiling, a sink in a corner with a shiny paper towel dispenser, some sad green plastic chairs. The walls behind hospital beds always hold ten thousand different ports and plugs, and a BP monitor was hanging out somewhere.

Ariettea's eyes landed on the breathtaking view outside the window. Lily's corner room had a full view of the beach on one side, and the college on the other. But the view of the beach, the pure white sand against the glimmering deep blue Atlantic, was amazing.

"Lily wanted her wig to be exactly how she's always kept her real hair-short. So, in all honesty, your donation made up the largest portion of the piece!" Ariettea snapped her attention back to Elaina. "And no other donors wanted to meet with us!" Elaina beamed at her, thanking her with her eyes way more than she felt she deserved.

Ariettea fought the urge to jump in and tell them all she didn't necessarily want to meet them either, she never wanted to meet anyone, but for some reason felt compelled to for Lily, even if it was just a means to escape small-town misery for a week.

As she tried to avert her gaze from mindlessly staring out the window, or catching Elaina's tearful stare, she glanced around the room and jumped when she caught sight of a man sitting in the corner behind Elaina.

He stood up slowly and laughed. "Sorry," He said, pulling up a heaping messenger bag of textbooks and loose papers onto his shoulder. "I'm not supposed to be here, didn't want to impose. I'm Peter, the tutor."

"You are MUCH more than that!" Lily's voice boomed across the room, still surprising Ariettea at how strong it was for someone so ill.

Ariettea looked over to see her shaking her head in disapproval, a sly smile dancing on her lips. Keeping her eyes on Peter, she said to Ariettea, "Peter is going to be a teacher in one more year, and most important, Peter is family."

Ariettea could see him out of the corner of her eye smile and stare at the ground, avert his green eyes from everyone's gaze, scuff his loafers against the floor, and run his hand through his messy cut of dark honey hair. "I think they've adopted me." He said with a sheepish laugh, his eyes flashing over to Ariettea briefly. "But I do have to get to a pre-semester study group now. I'll see you tomorrow, Lils."

He took a step to shake Ariettea's hand but then stopped himself, kept both hands on the shoulder strap of his bag. "Nice to meet you."

Ariettea watched him leave and thought to herself how she appreciated getting out of at least one awkward hug.

"Peter is a student at Ducreis," Elaina explained in her still soft, fragile voice. "He is studying to be a teacher, we know him from our congregation, so it just fit perfectly when Lily couldn't…" She stopped herself and forced a smile, "When Lily needed a tutor for her homeschooling."

Another awkward silence followed.

"Well… Ok then guys, bye!" Lily piped up, trying to woosh her parents out of the room with sweeping arm motions.

Alex laughed as he grabbed his wife's hand, interlocking fingers. "I have to get to work anyway. Wonderful to meet you, dear." He said to Ariettea, patting her shoulder with his free hand on their way out, pulling Elaina along to prevent another hug.

"You two as well." Ariettea replied with as much enthusiasm as she could muster.

Nadette smiled at the girls and turned to talk to Elaina as they walked down the hallway, leaving Ariettea suddenly alone with Lily.

Lily looked her up and down, her bright eyes peering and inquisitive, and blurted, "My hair used to be just like yours, you know."

Ariettea took a breath, as if to respond, but instead looked side to side, unsure of what to say.

Lily made it easy for her and just kept talking. "Mine was about as long as yours is now, the same color, but super curly. No matter what my mom did to it, it was always full of ringlets."

Ariettea laughed softly, "Yeah, no matter what I do to my hair, how often I get it thinned, it always does what it wants to, which is to be thick and in my way."

"Well, it served me well. So, thank you." Lily grinned hard.

"You're welcome." Ariettea said, her eyes locking onto Lily's, her voice finally free from mumble.

She wondered if that was the end of it, if she would now be free to go. She faced the thought of was that what she really wanted? To just leave? Did she really not want to converse with this kid at all?

But Lily laid all her questions to rest, "Sit down! Hang out, let me bombard you with overly personal questions!"

Ariettea looked at her, feeling unsure of how to take her. As Lily's eyes sparkled and just purely danced, Ariettea knew she was kidding. For the most part.

She blew out a breath of a chuckle and sat down. "Well, you guys all already can pronounce my name right, so you know more about me than most people."

Lily laughed, turned to face her head-on, crossed her legs Indian style, her pink flannel pajama pants sticking out against the dull blue and white hospital gown that allowed for cords to come out of every pocket. "How do most people pronounce it?" She asked.

Ariettea shrugged. "Arietty, Arietta, Aritea…" She laughed. "I guess it should have been spelled 'Ariettia', because everyone misses the 'ia' sound, but no matter what, I'll never be able to find my name on a souvenir key chain, so…" She shrugged.

Lily clasped her hands in her lap. "So." She repeated, "Let's get me out of the way first, even though my name is far less interesting… I'm sure your Aunt has filled you in on the diagnosis, prognosis, and treatments. Hopefully, if things keep improving and I'll be back home soon enough."

Lily took a breath as if she was suddenly short of it. Ariettea glanced at her pulse ox, seeing it had dipped since she arrived. She stopped to wonder why she was on the machine at all, if she was just sitting in her room. Just how sick was she?

"So, where is home for you then?" She asked, giving Lily the chance to take in some air.

Lily smiled, a different smile from the one she had had on her face since Ariettea had arrived. This smile was a soft, reminiscent one.

"Baringvale, South Carolina. This tiny town on the ocean. Literally, super small, like 400 people, quaint small. Our house is literally on the beach." She continued, "It was my grandmother's and got passed on to my dad. We have this amazing massive deck in the back that could hold 50 people or more, and it has a walkway that goes all the way down to our private portion of beach. The front and sides of the house are completely overwhelmed with bright orange and purple lilies, hence where I got my name."

Ariettea fought a laugh at Lily's use of 'hence'. She talked as if she were way older than she was, but in a believable way, not like some child trying to play adult.

"Hey, you said your name was less interesting than mine; I don't think so; I think that's a cool backstory." Ariettea said.

Lily grinned wide. "Yeah, and so I love the beach, even beside the lilies part. It's where I grew up, where I live. It's why I don't mind staying here for so long, because of the beach beside the hospital. You can see it from the window here," Lily pointed out the window on Ariettea's right, the one that stretched both exterior walls.

"So they always make this my room," She laughed again, "I go down there as often as they let me. It feels like home."

Ariettea tried to smile for her, but panic welled inside her and the silence loomed. She felt compelled to say something, anything. "Yeah I come from a small town too," She said, looking at the floor. "Well," She shrugged, "Not so small. Big enough to have two Starbucks, but small enough that you go anywhere and meet someone who knows someone who knows your teacher's ex-boyfriend."

Lily laughed heartily. To her it was funny, to Ariettea, it was torture. Her fake smile faded. "I can tell you love your little town, though." Ariettea said softly. She pulled a knee up to her chest and hugged it. She resisted the urge to lay her head on her knee, close her eyes. Escape from anywhere and everywhere, like she always did.

"I take it you don't like yours." Lily said pointedly, matter of factly.

Ariettea hesitated. She spent so much of her time telling everyone how eager she was to leave, and everyone always took it as the biggest personal insult, told her she would change her mind, that she didn't know what the rest of the world was really like, that she needed to enjoy being a kid while she could. She thought of what she had told Matthew. 'I haven't been a kid for a long time.'

She met Lily's gaze. "I really don't." She admitted slowly, drawing out the vowels in each word, waiting for the bomb of disapproval to drop. Instead, Lily laughed. "What do you hate about it most?"

Ariettea felt taken aback at the question. That was one question that, if anyone ever asked it, was asked in a such a disapproving tone that it made her feel like she had just kicked a dog. But Lily's tone was different, sincere. Ariettea had spent so much time defending her point of view, her feelings, her thoughts, trying to justify it by generalizing it all, that she didn't even know what the true flat out plain answer to that question was anymore.

She stared at the floor. "I... I guess that it just feels like a black hole. Everything around you looks the same, and the harder you fight to leave, the harder it tries to suck you back into it." She paused, trying, and failing, to bring her gaze back up to Lily. She shook her head, eyes tracing the lines of linoleum tiles. "Everyone has the exact same ideas, goals, and thought process. And if you think any different, want anything different, there must be something wrong with you. And the harder you fight against it, the harder you struggle to keep your drive to leave alive, the more everyone tries to rip you back down to what they call 'reality'."

"Why does their reality have to become yours?" Lily asked suddenly.

Ariettea felt the corners of her mouth turn up by themselves, naturally. Almost smug. "That's what I'm saying." She said, finally meeting Lily's gaze again.

Lily's teal eyes danced and sparkled as she smiled back. "So, what about your friends?" She asked, leaning back into her hands. "From what I can tell, you wouldn't keep company with anyone who sucks you down. You must have a pack of great people around you!"

Ariettea felt that lump in her stomach. She felt the blood drain from her face, ever so slightly. Surely, she was supposed to have friends, everyone did.

"I, uh… I guess I haven't found that group yet." She admitted. "I've tried," She said with a shrug. "I've gone the older girls route, and even the older older girls route, where both groups always treat you like they are babysitting you until they need something, and every so often they let you go somewhere cool with them. I've gone the younger than me route, with girls that I feel like I'm babysitting after I get home and need a nap. I've done the single best friend thing, multiple times, the guy friend thing, and that's just…" She shuddered, thinking of Matthew and all the feelings surrounding him. "Guys my age are jerks. And I've seriously tried the big group of peers route, but…" She trailed off, many names and faces rushing to her head. "That might be the worst group of all. As far as like-minded people, that is."

Lily nodded, she understood. "I think being different is hard, because then in any group, you're the odd one out, whether you were "supposed" to fit in with them or 'not'." Lily said, air quoting with her hands. "Me, I know what it's like to be in a group of adults who humor me, but also wait until I leave the room to truly talk about anything. Or, until they leave MY room, rather, or around a group of people who are all my age, but who have lived totally different lives from me, and/or they are going a totally different direction BECAUSE they've lived a totally different life from me, or a lot of times, they just were never on the same wavelength as me, sick or not. I've been detached from home far too long and too often to be very close with anyone there, and here I'm stuck in bed, anyway."

Lily threw her hands up in the air. "Trust me, I'm with you!" She said with a laugh.

Ariettea pulled up a smile. "So then how do you deal with it?" She asked flatly, but more sincerely than she wanted to admit.

Lily shrugged. "I just take what I can get and try not to look too much into it aside from the fact that, at that moment, I'm with someone who's company I enjoy. So, if it's just for that moment, I'm happy, and if it turns into friendship, I'm ecstatic. Not that I ever go into something pessimistically, quite the opposite, actually. I guess I just kind of wait on the other person, because I tend to like everyone."

Lily smirked. "But I guess that's why I love to meet people, why I wanted to meet you, and even more so than anyone else I meet, I really hope we can be friends."

Ariettea dropped her eyes to the floor, unsure of what to say to that. She was very much Lily's opposite; her view of everyone and everything was clouded with a quite opaque veil of cynicism - she never expected much good to come from anyone. She hated meeting people, she hadn't even wanted to meet Lily, yet there she was.

"I guess we are all just waiting on that rare connection." Ariettea mused aloud, trying to not answer, to agree or disagree with Lily's proclaimed hope.

Chapter 6

The conversation continued between Ariettea and Lily, branching off into all sorts of topics, serious and funny, light-hearted and dark. Faith and goals, favorite movies and books, where they saw themselves in 20 years, Target vs. Walmart.

Ariettea tried to throw her usual walls up, but somehow Lily found a way around them. "So then don't take offense to this, I'm not asking with any opinion on what you should do, but what do you want to do after you graduate? You're going to be senior, right?"

Ariettea nodded. "Yes, this is my last year... And as often as EVERYONE asks me that," she lamented, throwing her head back, "I never have a good answer. I've wanted to do a few different things. I've always wanted to... Help people?" She winced, used to an eye roll to that response. She tried to quickly recover. "Honestly, I think I'd just like a gap year. Time off to maybe travel, or... I guess whatever I want."

"Party?" Lily asked, playfully.

Ariettea scoffed. "Not that type of a girl."

"So, what type of girl are you? Wanting to help people and all?"

"Roundabout way of asking how I spend my time?"

"Much nicer, I think."

Ariettea conceded and laughed. "It is..." She giggled. "Uhmmm... I... I read, I go to school, I tell my mom I'm going to get an iced coffee then drive down by the beach." She paused. "Then I get interrogated when I get home, but then again, I always do."

"Strict parents?"

"An understatement."

"What do they think you should do, or want you to do, after high school?"

"What everyone else wants me to do... Find a job I hate to pay the bills to get by in a world that sucks and whatever else THEY decide I need to do."

Lily shook her head. "I can see why you feel suffocated."

Ariettea looked at her, realizing she had just pinpointed precisely how she felt, without judging her for it, or trying to change her mind. But then again, she was only 13.

Lily could see the dubious look on her face. "Ariettea, I've spent a ridiculous amount of my life in the hospital. I read books, I watch people, and the only people I get to talk to are adults. I grew up fast." She shrugged, as if to say, it is what it is.

'But you're still a kid...' Ariettea couldn't help but think.

Thoughts raced through her mind, it doesn't matter what she thinks, it doesn't matter what she says, there's no way she can know anything about anything. And then she realized she was just repeating what she had been told about herself her entire life.

"So then what plans do you have in life?" She asked, the question coming out sounding completely different than she meant it. "I mean, like, what do you-"

"Stop backpedaling!" Lily laughed. "I know what you meant and, more importantly, what you didn't mean, and honestly, I just try to spend as much time in the here and now as I can. Eventually, one day, I want what everyone else does; to travel, live, fall in love, but for now, I just want to go to the gala in the spring, and get home to see the lilies."

"What gala do you mean?"

Lily rocked side to side and smiled wide. "Ooh it's this gorgeous, glamorous event they have here every year," She mused, staring off into space. "It's white tie formal, fantastic food, a big band, and it's all for charity. Usually, that's not something I'd be considered 'old enough' to go to," She said, her hands in air quotes. "But if I was here, and not bedbound and weak, I could get away with going!" She giggled but then pulled her attention back to Ariettea. "But every year, I'm either way too sick, or at home, and can't go."

Ariettea smiled at her, consolingly, knowing exactly how it felt to be told you're too young for an amazingly beautiful thing that you want so badly. "Well I hope you get to go."

"If I do, you can come back for it!" Lily looked at her with such gleeful enthusiasm, Ariettea almost felt guilty about brushing her off as she said, "Well this being senior year, I may not have much time to get away."

Lily pursed her lips into a smile. "This is awkward, right?"

Ariettea let out a breath and dropped her leg back to the floor. "Kind of." She said with a genuine, albeit nervous, laugh.

Lily giggled with her. "Ok, let's make it more awkward, tell me, what made you join the hair drive?"

Ariettea shifted uncomfortably. She didn't have a clear answer for that. There was no way to explain the flickering spark in her, how she wanted to do something with meaning.

"I guess it just sounded like something nice to do. It was something to do for someone, something that mattered." She tried to find the words to make up an excuse, how long her hair was and she needed a reason to cut it anyway, but the words couldn't form before Lily asked, "So, then what was the reason you wanted to meet me?"

Ariettea felt a chill run down her arms as heat raced up her back and into her face. She had no idea how to answer that either, as, truth be told, she didn't want to meet her.

"Well," She began, desperately trying not to stutter, "I mean, you guys asked for me, right? You wanted to meet me?"

Lily nodded. "Yeah, of course, I wanted to thank you and see just where this gift came from, I guess like any organ transplantee wants to meet their transplanter's family. But what made you want to meet me?"

Ariettea dug around her brain for words, for any explanation, other than the truth. She looked all around the room, searching for an answer. Her eyes darted from object to object, out the window, along the wall, until her gaze finally was forced back to Lily. Her expression reading as if she already knew the answer.

"I guess I don't really have an answer for that either." She admitted to the floor. "I… I didn't really want to." She was used to being blunt, cold. But for some reason, she was struggling against her normal tendencies with Lily. Lily wasn't trying to correct her thinking every other sentence.

"But you came," Lily responded without hesitation. "So something in you must have wanted to." She said, smiling.

Ariettea tried to smile back but couldn't quite make it happen.

"So," Lily piped up, clapping her hands. "Tell me where you'd like to travel during your gap year."

Ariettea shrugged. "To be honest, I usually tell people that to get them off my back, and I mean it's true, I do want to travel, but I have no idea where. I think more so than anything I just want the freedom to go where I want, see what I want, meet who I want. I honestly was thinking of coming down here to see Trent and Nadette along the way. I've always wanted to see the east coast."

"Oh my gosh!" Lily exclaimed. "You should totally come to visit us when I get to go home! You can come compare my small town to yours!" She said with a big laugh. "But no, seriously, I would LOVE that!"

Ariettea smiled at her, then found herself staring at the floor again. She looked back up at Lily and kind of squinted her eyes, shook her head. "Lily," She said hesitantly, "You BARELY know me, how can you invite me to your house?"

Lily smiled at her as if she knew something Ariettea didn't. "I think we're off to a good start." She said softly. "Are you ok, Ariettea?" She asked, her voice still soft.

Ariettea didn't know how to answer that. She didn't quite understand the question, or at least, that's what she told herself. "Am I ok?" Ariettea repeated, as if the term was foreign. "I'm sorry; I don't understand your question."

Lily smiled some sort of consoling, kind, almost, but not quite, patronizing, smile. "I mean, you seem sad and dejected; disconnected. Like, you were once a happy vibrant spirit, but now are a lonely, sad soul. I don't know why, and I can't pretend that I do, but I just have a knack for reading people and…I guess you read as…hurt. In a word."

That one word did sum up much. Not that Ariettea would admit it.

She thought a million thoughts in one second. 'I'm not hurt. Well, in a way. How would she know? She can't. No one has ever described me as hurt. No one has ever paid attention. No one has ever cared enough to pay attention. I'm not…I…am. I am hurt. DENY DENY DENY!' It was like an alarm going off in her brain. 'No, you're fine. Quit whining.' Then came the cold, rock hard front. "Sad? Me? What do I have to be sad about?" She asked.

"You haven't spoken of much to be happy about." Lily said plainly.

Ariettea searched inside for an answer but came up with none; because she knew Lily was right. "I guess…I guess I'm searching." Ariettea said vaguely.

Anyone else would have pushed: 'Searching? For what? What does that mean?' But Lily didn't. Somehow she understood. She knew what Ariettea meant, even if Ariettea herself didn't.

"What keeps you so happy?" Ariettea found herself saying, coming close to spitting the words at Lily, who wasn't fazed. "We keep talking about me, but who are you? What is Lily?"

"Hopeful," Lily said, expression changing, becoming somber. "I mean, I do look at and accept and experience everything here and now, but what keeps me going is hope. Contentment. Other than cancer, nothing bad has happened to me. I have faith in God and all His promises. And hope keeps me going. Hope that one day I will get better. Hope that I will get out of here and get to go home to South Carolina. I look forward to all the things I want to do in life. I have hope that one day things will get better."

'Hope that one day things will get better.' It repeated in Ariettea's head. It sounded like something she had once said to herself a long time ago. Something she had stopped saying to herself. Something she had wished she hadn't lost, but still not anything she wished to get back.

She didn't have hope anymore. She hated to admit it to herself, but she didn't see a light at the end of her dark tunnel anymore.

"I think that's what we're all trying to find..." She mused.

"And who am I besides all that?" Lily continued. "You could say not much, you've seen what my day looks like, I've told you what keeps me going, and who are we besides the things we live for?"

Ariettea kept her gaze on Lily, thoughtfully. Contentment. She mulled over the word, for the first time really considering what that meant or could mean.

"I've come to realize contentment is more about where you head it at, as opposed to your body." Lily said quietly. Ariettea realized just how many meanings she could take from that. "Or sometimes it's with someONE?" Lily suddenly asked, trying to lighten the mood, smiling playfully.

Ariettea scoffed and rolled her eyes.

Swiftly, she apologized, "Geez, sorry, that wasn't an eye roll at you. More of an eye roll at a lot of people."

"You get that question a lot?" Lily asked, laughing.

"Yes. Mostly about one particular person." She found herself admitting, finding comfort in the fact that Lily had no idea who she was talking about.

"And so what's the real answer?!" Lily asked excitedly, throwing her hands in the air, her hoodie too long for his slim frame, sleeves covering her fingers.

Ariettea laughed, feeling like she was at some sort of sleepover, like all the dozens of ones she had never been invited to. The ones she had to hear about in detail the days after… She jolted herself out of the memory and looked back to Lily.

"No, we aren't a couple. Not at all."

"So, where does the speculation come from?"

"He's basically my only friend back home. But he's also a royal pain and child who happens to be the same age as me so…"

"So, you're just friends?"

"…Yes." Ariettea said, pausing slightly.

"Well, there's where the speculation comes from!" Lily exclaimed. "Why the pause?"

Ariettea mused on that one for a second. "Because…" She sighed, trying to will herself into admitting the truth for the first time out loud. Lily didn't know him. Why not?

"Because I find myself always looking for him in a crowd." She admitted, eyes fixed at the ceiling. "I love the way he says my name. And I love the way he knows what I'm thinking."

"But?" Lily's 'but' came out before Ariettea even finished talking.

"But." Ariettea sighed again, bringing her gaze back down. "But he is an immature, selfish, egotistical, immature, child who has no direction and panders to what everyone wants him to do, but is too suave for anyone but other teens to realize how full of crap he is."

"So what I'm hearing…" Lily said slowly. "Is that like you, he doesn't know what he wants, but unlike you, he does the pandering you refuse to? And he's majorly immature?"

Ariettea nodded. "Yeah, that's it." She said, suddenly bursting out into a huge belly laugh.

"Well… Give it time. We're all growing, all our lives. But it sure sounds like he has a lot of it to do."

Ariettea nodded. "It's the growth that's the hard part to wait on." She paused, shoved her hands under her legs. "So for now… I'm just watching. That's pretty much all I ever do. Watch the world around me move and wonder where I'm supposed to be moving in it."

"Same!" Lily's way of balancing lightheartedness with serious conversation was unmatched.

Ariettea pulled her hands out from underneath her and stood up abruptly. Suddenly feeling her version of normal -- uncomfortable, raw, and on edge again. Suddenly feeling like they had talked way too much about her. She scolded herself for being so selfish and self-centered.

"I really don't want to take up all your time, tire you out, or anything." She said sheepishly, shoving one hand into her back pocket.

Lily shook her head. "You're really not doing either, but I'm sure my parents will be back soon anyway."

"Do your parents work?" Ariettea queried.

"My mom, no, my dad goes back and forth between his office back in South Carolina and working online while being here with me."

"Where do they stay?"

"With me or at Ronald McDonald here or even sometimes with Peter." Lily shrugged. "Soon enough, we'll all go home, though." She smiled at Ariettea, her teal eyes sparkling and dancing again, "And YOU can come to visit."

Ariettea smiled. "I… will look forward to it."

Lily beamed back and nodded. "It's a date. Can we keep in contact in the meantime, though?"

Ariettea nodded. "Of course! Here, let me put my number in your phone."

As they exchanged info, part of Ariettea truly and honestly believed that then, right there, would be the end of their relationship. Yet another part of her felt something tying her back there.

Lily jumped up and gave Ariettea another hug, and Ariettea still felt awkwardly stiff.

"I'll see you soon, Ariettea." She said, stepping back.

Ariettea herself took a step back towards the door. "See you soon, Lily."

Chapter 7

With all the talk about the fantastic Ducreis beach, Ariettea found herself wandering down there, wanting to avoid meeting with Nadette for as long as possible.

It was much larger than she had expected; a good football field's distance of sand separated the sidewalk around the hospital and the edge of the tide. All white sand, immaculate, surely kept up by a large staff of gardeners each morning to pick up seaweed and cigarette butts.

And then there were the lilies. Beach lilies that sprouted and pushed their way up through the sand. Lilies skirted the edge of the sidewalk, they grew through the sand at random spots, and they encircled the massive grey rock boulders on the water's edge.

But for some reason, the gorgeous beach was totally empty. For that time of day, the sun was high in the sky, and the hospital was beginning to overshadow the area.

She scanned the horizon; nothing even graced the water for as far out as the eye could see. Pure ocean, crisscrossing waves where the current ran underneath, sun glistening off the top.

The sun radiated off the side of the hospital as well, blindingly, and she suddenly wondered if Lily was watching her from her room. She couldn't see inside, but Ariettea counted up the floors to that corner room, the one that had overlooked the view that was now before her and wondered. Would she ever actually see Lily again?

She walked across the beach, having to knead her feet through the sand step after step until she finally plopped down. She dug the heels of her combat boots down into the hot sand and set her arms over her knees. She had expected it to be the same sweltering hot it had been since she stepped off the plane, but by the ocean it was cooler. The wind suddenly and loudly whipped around her, deafening her, throwing her hair up in her face. She batted it away, figuring the tall hospital building somehow made for a makeshift wind tunnel up against the sea.

Then she thought of Matt, throwing her hair out of his own face. When she told him she was going down to Georgia, she expected him to be as excited as she was trying to hide she was. Instead, he shrugged, and told her to make some friends while there. The same thing he told her before every school year, every party, every time they went anywhere. As if it were that easy. She rolled her eyes, at least she had made a friend for once.

But was Lily her friend? Even if she was, or were to be, it still wasn't the typical friend everyone around her was always telling her to make. It wasn't anyone near her age. It wasn't anyone close by. And it wasn't anyone that everyone would approve of and fawn over. The glory of everyone knowing everyone where you live -- you either make the 'right' connections, the 'in' connections, or you don't. And she never did. Sometimes she was amazed that Matt even bothered to talk to her. But then again, he only ever did when no one important was around. She was forever fighting the inner conversation of why she even liked him, but that was on the rare occasion she actually admitted to herself that she did.

She shook her head, trying to push all that away. She was always pushing every feeling as far away as possible, until she could lie to herself and say that they didn't exist.

She took in a deep breath of the salty air and felt an odd sense of calm wash over her. She was alone, in a quiet place, in a new town, where the only people who knew her actually liked her. Or so they said. She wasn't sure if she just felt relieved to be away from home for a bit, or if there was something drawing her to Ducreis. She turned her head and looked towards the campus. She was always telling people that she didn't know what she was going to do after she graduated high school, and everyone always took that to mean that she didn't think about it at all. Which couldn't have been farther from the truth. She thought about it constantly. And fought with the voices inside her head and out, each telling her to do something different. So as she looked at the sprawling cobblestone buildings, she could hear the inner voice critiquing her, telling her she knew nothing about the place, so how could she ever feel 'drawn' to it?

She shook her head and tried to push the thoughts away; surely, she was just being an idiot. Even more so, she didn't know the people. She had just met Lily, and this was the first time she had ever spent any real time with Trent and Nadette. But… She really liked them all. She tried to fight it, telling herself, 'They'll probably just hurt you like everyone else has.'.

She shifted to pull her phone from her back pocket. A lone message, one from Nadette, and still one more than she usually found, sat on her screen, "*I've finished up my work here, I need to run to my office now, so I'm ready whenever you are :)*"

Ariettea sighed, looking out at the ocean one more time. The calm was suddenly gone, and she was immediately the bad kind of all alone again. As much as she found comfort in solitude, she didn't enjoy it nearly as much as she put on.

She pushed herself up to return to a world she just couldn't understand, one that didn't understand her. She texted Nadette that she would meet her back at the car. She trudged through the sand, feeling it seep deep into her boots. The boots she had fought tooth and nail with her parents over, the ones that looked 'rebellious', the ones they pretended not to see until they wanted to pick a fight. Ariettea shoved her phone back into her rear pocket and crossed her arms over her chest, another so-called stance of rebellion. She walked wondering what would happen now, before she went back home. She wasn't sure what to expect going through another evening with Trent and Nadette. They'd had their one nice night, and now she braced herself for the badgering of questions and 'suggestions'.

Nadette was standing outside her Jeep, still gorgeous and put together, with an armful of patient charts. She looked up from one she was making a notation in and flashed Ariettea a huge smile. "Hey!"

Ariettea mustered a small smile back. "Hey."

"So, how was it? How was she?" Nadette gleefully asked as they got in the car.

Ariettea pulled her seatbelt over her chest and shrugged. "Lily is very special. That's the best way to describe her."

She waited for Nadette to ask for details, to push, but she didn't. "Are you hungry?" She asked, not waiting for an answer before she said, "I am STARVING. There is this adorable little cafe in the heart of town I'd love to take you to!"

Ariettea nodded. "Sounds great." She lied. Eating with other people was agonizing, and they were all starting to notice. It was already hard enough for her to eat, no matter how hungry she was because everything inside just physically hurt when she did eat. She had laid in bed so many nights after dinner, in a fetal position, shaking with pain. It didn't help that she could never sleep as it was, so being up until 3 am while in pain was just not something she liked to do every day.

Nadette chatted and blabbered on about her patients from the morning while trying not to violate HIPAA while Ariettea tried to nod in all the right places.

Nadette parked in a flat open lot, still in view of the ocean, and announced they would be walking from there.

They walked side by side down the sidewalk of a narrow two-lane street; the one Nadette had pointed out on the drive in. As awkward as she felt, it being just the two of them, her feeling overly exposed, Ariettea relished in the adorable little shops they walked past. A florist, a formal dress shop, a bakery, souvenir shops, cafes, and of course, the lovely little trees with the string lights she had seen from afar. She found herself drawn in and wonderstruck.

Nadette looked over at her and smiled, linked her arm through Ariettea's. "Enjoying the view?"

Ariettea felt her smile, the one she hadn't realized was on her face, fall immediately, and her cheeks flush with embarrassment. "I, um," She stammered, looking for words.

Nadette purposely ignored what she had clearly seen happen on her face. "I know. I get the same feeling every time I walk down here. That's why I prefer to park and walk."

Ariettea smiled at the ground, thankful not to have suddenly been lectured for being silly. "I just think it's funny how much I seem to like this place, even though I've barely seen it." She found herself saying, self-deprecating.

Nadette shook her head. "Why would you feel silly about that?" She said with a laugh. "I told you from the second I drive over the hill and see the town I feel like I'm home. Some places are just like that."

"You really think so?" Ariettea blurted out, surprised.

"Of course! Don't you?"

Ariettea tried to find words that wouldn't get her in trouble, as they usually did. "I don't know. I've always wished there were places like that. But most of the time, everyone tells me that's a child's dream." She said, sheepishly, blushing once more. She was used to blushing, blushing from embarrassment, anger, shame. Shame seemed to be everyone's favorite tool against her. She was always 'too' something. And it stung.

Nadette pulled her into a small cafe and to a small wrought iron table for two on the outside terrace before answering swiftly. "Well, personally, I fully believe that there is that place for everyone. And if you don't believe it, you haven't found it. Honestly, I think it's silly that people would pretend that a place has to mean the same thing to everyone, or that there's not a place each person can find to fit in. I think once you find that place, it can be magical."

Nadette's eyes twinkled at Ariettea from across the table. "But what do I know." She said playfully, grabbing a tiny menu of the stand on the table.

Ariettea smiled to herself. She liked the idea. Not that she'd admit it. She was afraid of someone jumping out and making fun of her. Thinking a PLACE could be happy? Ha.

She grabbed the other menu. "So, what's good here?" She asked, scanning a list of coffees and pastries, her stomach suddenly seizing up. She agreed to let Nadette buy her Nadette's favorite coffee.

As Nadette ran off to order, Ariettea pulled her phone out of her pocket. Any time she pulled it out, she'd wish there'd be a message from some old friend, suddenly interested in her again, or Matt, suddenly checking on her. She either had a glimmer of hope that there'd be a message from someone, anyone, or she had a bone-chilling fear that there would be some other person from her past, showing back up to tell her off once more, to twist whatever knife they'd left.

A paper coffee cup plopped down in front of Ariettea, and Nadette with it. Ariettea set her phone down on the table and picked up her coffee.

"So," Nadette said in between bites of her panini, "Are you excited for your senior year, or is it just something you're not into talking about?"

Ariettea wasn't sure how to respond to that, no one ever asked her permission before asking her anything. "Uhm, it's not that I'm against talking about it, I think I'm just against being TOLD about it."

She smiled down at the shiny lid. "But thank you, for asking before asking, I mean." She said, looking up to meet Nadette's soft eyes. She could see in them why she made such a great doctor. She was gentle and kind and happy, confident, and Ariettea could feel the firmness that dwelt within her when she talked about something she loved.

"Of course..." Nadette mused softly. "Ari, I vividly remember being your age, in your position, and what's more, I see tons of college girls as patients of mine; I know how hard it is to be where you are." She stopped, looked off into the distance. "I just wish I had had someone to tell me when I was your age that you have to fight for your truth. Of course, set all the right priorities, but you're told that so much you don't need to hear it over and over. So just make choices that will lead you to the best happiness you can imagine, set those dreams in place and don't be afraid to hold on to them, but don't pressure yourself into fitting into any type of mold or expectation, even if it's one you set yourself."

She set her cup down and sighed. "I hate the notion that senior year is do or die, make all your choices now! At any point in our lives, we are making choices that affect our future. I don't think it's fair to put all that on someone who isn't even legal yet! But, then again, if you know what you want, go for it." She laughed at herself. "What I'm trying to say is that I've been there, I work there, and I'm here for you. Trent and I both, of course. I know we don't see each other or talk much, and I'd love to change that, because I know all too well what it's like to be where you are, and I want to give you as much support as you want."

"As much as I want? As in, I get to decide?" Ariettea blurted out before she could stop herself.

Nadette nodded emphatically. "Of course! What I've been trying to get at is that you are in control of your life, embrace it, and don't forget it or give it up." Nadette swirled her coffee around in her cup. "I really want you to know that you will always have the option of coming here and going to school if you ever choose to. Or just coming here whenever you want. But I won't push you for answers on what path you want to take within the next couple of years."

Ariettea spoke slowly, "I appreciate that." She paused. "It's just that right now; I have no idea what I want to do. Especially because any time I get an idea of what I want, I get ten more people telling me that it's the wrong idea. Everyone says it's my choice, but I never feel that way."

"Well, it is. And I will back you up with whatever you choose."

"Well, what if you don't agree with what I choose?"

"Ari, unless you're doing something harmful, I don't see why I would disagree."

"What if I do something harmful?"

"I have more faith in you than to think that. And you should have that faith in yourself."

Ariettea shook her head and silently ran her right thumb over her left wrist underneath the table.

Nadette took a final swig of coffee and picked up her bag. "Alrighty you, I've got some appointments this afternoon, so if you're all good, I'll drop you off at home?"

Ariettea nodded, picking her phone up off the table. She looked at the screen, as was her custom. But instead of it being blank, there was a message. ***"Thanks again for coming today! Can't wait to see you again.***" It was from Lily. Ariettea smiled down at the screen.

As she slung her bag up onto her shoulder, she caught sight of a little florist shop across the street. The windows were choked full of lilies.

Lilies on beaches, lilies in a florist's window, a lily hanging from her rearview, and now a Lily on her phone screen. Ariettea was beginning to like the sight of them. All of them.

And all of them against what she thought was her better judgment.

Chapter 8

After Nadette dropped her back at their townhouse, Ariettea sat on the couch in their living room, in darkness. She couldn't turn on the light, let alone the tv, and her phone sat on the ottoman in front of her, silent.

The message from Lily still unread on her lock screen.

She felt an overwhelming sense of empty, more so than usual. She was alone, and soon she'd be going back home, where she'd somehow be even more alone. At least there she had Trent and Nadette, and for some odd reason, she had Lily. There were people that were nice, and invested in her.

She shook her head. 'You're being absolutely ridiculous.' She yelled internally. 'These people are new to you; they don't know you well enough to see you for who you are yet.'

She flopped back onto the overstuffed cushions behind her. She tried to relax into them, but could only feel stiff, rigid. She traced her hand along the green, soft fabric.

Her self hatred welled up inside her like a geyser, hot, ready to erupt. Her eyes started to burn as she fought tears. She never cried. She wouldn't let herself, not anymore. She had spent night after night lying in bed until 3, 4 in the morning, tears silently streaming down her face for years. She finally got to a place where she refused to let them come anymore.

And her pain showed elsewhere on the outside of her body.

She ran her hand under the sleeve of her left forearm. It was smooth, for once. She was afraid it wasn't going to stay that way. And what was more, she didn't want it to.

She got up and started to pace, she walked around the house, exploring whatever was out in the open. Wedding pictures of Trent and Nadette, framed college degrees, Pottery Barn and Williams Sonoma decor perfectly placed around the house. Their life was what she had spent so long yearning for, but what she had given up hoping for.

Everyone around her told her that she melodramatic; she was only 17, how could she possibly feel so lost? But she did. She felt no hope that her future held anything happy, or even could.

She leaned against the wall and pushed her forehead into the rough paint job. She scolded herself for being so stupid as she leaned away and wiped the makeup off the wall with her sleeve. But the roughness had felt good, on her forehead, the pain. She couldn't shake what Nadette had said. 'As long as you're not harming yourself.'

If only she knew.

Ariettea shook her head, fighting a headache, and rubbed the inner corner of her eye, her finger coming away black from the eyeliner.

The emptiness was too much.

She couldn't fight it.

She gave in.

She found herself laying on the bed in her guest room, awhile later.

Most teens would have been found scrolling through Instagram, Snapchat, anything, but she just laid there. There was no point. She followed no one she cared about except Matthew, and all his pictures were that weeks new friend. He made them so easily. Everyone did. Everyone but her.

Lily's message still lingered on her lock screen. She wanted to reply but was stuck between why bother, and maybe. If she replied, it would only be a matter of time. Lily was just a kid, anyway. What kind of pair would they be?

Her stomach ached, rejecting her coffee from hours earlier, whilst yearning for food, that would only end up making her sicker.

She had started listening for a car, footsteps, anything to signal that it was time for her to bolt up and pretend she hadn't been fighting sleep for the last three hours. Staring at the wall like she would all night. And that her arm wasn't stinging under her sleeve.

She rolled over onto her stomach and buried her head into the pillow. She held her breath for as long as she could, until her lungs started to burn, before pulling herself back up to the world.

She had already packed her duffel bag for the return flight home. She pulled down the sleeves of her shirt self consciously, dreading having to wear it in the heat the next day.

Back home, back to reality.

The reality of senior year, of everyone she had grown up in front of watching her every move and choice, even if they barely knew her.

Then there was Lily. Lily, who barely knew her but offered not a single judgment the whole time they talked. She kept trying to convince herself that that would change once she knew her better; it always did. But she couldn't shake the feeling that there was more to Lily than everyone else.

She picked up her phone and finally opened the message. Her fingers stood erect but motionless as she realized she had no idea what to respond. She still had no idea how she fully felt about Lily.

She heard the front door lock start to jiggle. Her ever perfected acting began as she flew from the bed and fluffed her hair up from the flatness that resulted from lying down for hours. She switched the light on and straightened her clothes before the front door opened, and Trent came in. She poked her head out the doorway and glanced down the stairs that led straight to the front door.

She waved a hand and forced a closed smile. The one you give when you pass someone on the street that you don't want to talk to.

Trent, in contrast, smiled big. "Ari! Hey! How was your meetup with Lily?" He asked, enthusiastically.

"It was good," She started, shoving her hands into her back pocket. "She's a sweet girl."

"That's so awesome! Hey, I'm going to get out of these scrubs and start on dinner. Any requests?"

Ariettea's stomach turned. "No, thanks."

Trent bounded up the stairs. "Well, let me know if you need anything. And make yourself at home, Ari! Turn on the TV, some lights," He flipped a switch as he passed her, "Our home is yours!"

She smiled as he walked away, that time not as forced, but still found herself pulling as far away from him as she could as he walked by.

She wandered downstairs and back on to the overstuffed chair. She curled her feet under her, trying to make herself as small and inconspicuous as she could as she tried to find something to do on her phone. Staring at the wall always made everyone around her feel uncomfortable, like they could sense just how unhinged she really was.

Trent came back downstairs in sweatpants and a Ducreis t-shirt. He took one look at her and stopped. "Are you feeling ok?" He asked, an eyebrow raised.

She forced another smile. "Yeah, just fighting a headache."

'As usual.' She added silently.

"We've got some Advil around here somewhere, do you want anything?"

"I took something already, thanks."

"Well, let me know if you need anything else."

She nodded wordlessly. She hoped her presence would be enough to keep Trent happy, but he started chatting with her from the kitchen. "So, what are your plans before school starts?" He yelled.

Ariettea sighed, too tired to yell back, and walked through the dining room to the kitchen. "I'm not sure." She said quietly, leaning against the doorway. "I don't really have much to do when I'm not at school."

"Oh, come on," Trent said, pulling out a mixing bowl. "I bet you've got a lot to do with your friends."

Her heart hurt, stabbing and burning in her chest as her stomach seized. "I'm a bit of a loner." She admitted sheepishly, playing with her hands. "I read a lot."

"Oh yeah? What do you like to read?"

"Pretty much anything that takes me far away."

"Ah! So, any places you specifically want to visit?"

"This was one of them, actually."

"You're always welcome here!"

"I appreciate that."

"Well there's always time before you settle in anywhere, if you even want to." Trent completely ignored the option most people tried to give her - settle down where she was and accept monotony.

She grinned, and genuinely.

Nadette came in just then, more like breezed in, still looking fabulous somehow after a day's work. She rubbed Ariettea's shoulder as she walked by to kiss Trent.

Ariettea silently backed out of the kitchen, feeling like a nuisance as they started discussing their days.

Dinner was ready soon after that, a nice simple meal Ariettea thought maybe she could get down as they gathered around the large rectangular cherry wood table.

Trent and Nadette both futilely tried to get Ariettea to open up. "So what did you and Lily talk about? Did you find much in common?"

Ariettea chewed her chicken thoughtfully. "More than you'd think. She's very observant and easy to talk to."

"Most kids in her position are," Nadette said. "They adapt to be."

"She said she'd like me to come visit again." Ariettea said softly.

"That's great!" Nadette exclaimed. "Seriously, though, come back soon! We love having you, and apparently Lily does too!" She said, smiling.

Trent nodded in agreement as he asked, "Can you pass me that plate of green beans?"

Her fork in her right hand, Ariettea absentmindedly picked it up with her left, and her sleeve lifted. She flushed hot all over as she knew from where Trent sat; he could see what was underneath.

She quickly passed him the bowl, trying to ignore the look of worry that immediately crossed his face.

Her mind raced to find words to distract him. "Yeah, she has a lot of good advice, outlook."

She let Trent and Nadette do the talking through the rest of the dinner.

Once everyone was done eating, Ariettea quickly picked up her plate and the empty serving ones and ducked into the kitchen.

Trent quietly and swiftly followed. "I've got it all, Nade. Go ahead and change."

Nadette left to go upstairs as Trent came and stood in front of Ariettea before she could get the dishes into the sink. His not so tall but solid frame in front of her, she couldn't look up to meet his eyes.

He gently took the plates from her and set them on the counter. "Ari," He said clemently, "What you have up your arm, please keep it clean. Do you need help? In any way?" He asked, placing his hands on her shoulders, his strong, warm touch, somehow making her feel even more guilty than she already did.

She hung her head; no one had ever seen her cuts before. It had been a few months since her last run with them.

"You're not going to yell at me, commit me?" She said to the ground.

"Of course not," he said quietly.

"Or ask me if I want to kill myself?"

"Well, do you?"

"No." She whispered.

"People who self-harm don't do it as a means to kill themselves, or to say that they want to. People are still ignorant of that fact. But me, that's nothing new to me. I'm an ER doctor. Even though it concerns me, makes me sad, both from a doctor's and an uncle's perspective."

He gently lifted her chin up to face him. "Just please talk to someone, or at least think about it, ok? Even us, Nadette and I, we're here for you."

She began to shake as she nodded silently, looking back at her feet. She couldn't look him in the eye.

"Can I bandage you up?"

Ariettea began to shake harder. She immediately wanted to say no, to push him away from her, but she found herself weak in the knees and starting to get dizzy. They both cared so much. And for real. And non judgmentally.

But she was so ashamed.

She knew had her parents ever seen what she was hiding, she'd never hear the end of it. It would be an ordeal for months, overdramatized and stigmatized, never-ending threats and embarrassment.

But Trent, she could hear it in his voice that that wasn't going to happen.

She nodded, still too guilt-stricken to look up at him. She let him help her without saying a word. Once the bandage wrappers were safely tucked away in the garbage, she finally looked up at him. His blue eyes were full of concern.

"Please don't tell my parents." She whispered. "I could never handle that."

He nodded. "It's between us."

She nodded as he pulled her in for a strong hug. She let herself bury her head in the smell of cologne coming through his sweatshirt.

"Please get yourself some help, Ari. If you can't right now, talk to us. Please."

She nodded, still unable to speak.

Nadette appeared, in her perfectly matched VSPink sweats and top, and leaned up against the doorway. "See? I meant it when I said we are both going to miss you!"

Ariettea found herself scoffing as she pulled away from Trent. "Are you sure about that?"

Nadette shook her head in reassurance as she stepped towards her. "Of course! We've loved having you." She threw her arm around Ariettea's shoulders and pulled her in, her other hand reaching for Trent's. "You're special, Ariettea. Don't let anyone tell you any different."

Feeling somewhere between awkward and comforted, she wasn't sure what to say to that. She didn't believe it, even if for some odd reason, they did.

Nadette pulled her arm back to grab Ariettea by the elbow. "Come on, let's let Trent start the dishes while we go pick up a Redbox movie."

Ariettea pulled her phone out of her pocket as she waited for Nadette to grab her purse.

She opened Lily's message back up and began to type. ***"Let's keep in touch."***

Chapter 9

Ariettea felt entirely conflicted on her flight home. There was the ever-present self-deprecating voice telling her that everyone in Georgia was happy she was leaving, and then the same voice telling her that no one at home wanted her, either.

As much as she was certain that everyone down south wanted her gone, she hated the thought of having to go home and being expected to report on every move she had made while away.

As soon as she slid into the backseat of her parent's car, the questions started, rapid-fire: "How was the trip?"

"Fine."

"Well, what did you do down there?"

Ariettea rolled her eyes, staring out her window, annoyed at the ever-present tone of accusation in her mother's voice. "Not much, went to the hospital, watched movies."

"Oh, well, with anyone new?"

She cringed at the poorly veiled attempt at digging. "Just Lily."

"And what's she like?"

Ariettea softened internally, but simultaneously threw up walls to try and keep her parents out of that soft, sweet world. "She's sweet, considerate, mature-"

"Mature? Isn't she 12?" Her father butted in, scoffing.

"No, she's 13." Ariettea said, her answer sharp and final.

"Don't take that tone with me." Her father warned, in that voice that made her skin crawl. "She can hardly be 'mature' at 12, Ariettea. Don't be silly."

There was that phrase.

The one that always ran through her head.

'Don't be silly.'

Ariettea's stomach turned. As usual. She had no desire to defend herself or her answers. Not anymore. There was no use.

She sat silently, waiting for the barrage of questions to continue.

"Well, if you're not going to tell us what happened, fine." Her mother snapped. "I'll just ask Nadette."

Ariettea's jaw clenched. "And she'll tell you exactly what I just did." She all but hissed, disgusted at the insinuation she was hiding something.

Part of the reason she was such an introvert was to avoid conversations like this. Not going anywhere saved her from the assumption that she was out doing something 'wrong'.

"I'm not sure that visit was such a good thing for you." Her mother huffed, hunkering down in her seat, putting on a grand show of offense.

Ariettea shook her head. She could give them every logical explanation available, and it would never be good enough. It wasn't worth the fight. She didn't have the strength anymore.

She threw some headphones on and stared at the dreary forests, all the same color of poop brown, the rest of the way home.

There was one last weekend before school was set to start. Ariettea wanted to stay home and mentally prepare for Monday, but instead, she was dragged to a beach party.

A big group of people, the usual suspects, gathered in the dunes. A circle of beach chairs, lawn chairs, and blankets sat around a pile of wood, being prepped for a bonfire. Each seat was filled by someone laughing, smiling, joking. But at something Ariettea couldn't relate to. Or at least would be told she couldn't relate to it. Matt was there, of course, but tossing a football with the kids.

She stayed as far away from them all as she could. The past week she had grown sick of being asked the same questions over and over again about her two-day trip. And what was more, even as silly as she felt about loving it there, and even as lonely as she had felt there, she was becoming more and more hesitant to share that little private part of her life.

She stood knee-deep in the waters of Lake Michigan, watching the sun go down, firing shades of orange and pinks all through the sky.

She crossed her arms over her chest and sighed. Matt had ignored her all evening. They hadn't spoken a single word since she had come home a week before. She was never too sure where the two of them stood. No matter how much she tried to lie to herself about her feelings for him, they were always there. She could hear the giggles of a girl and the smooth undertones of his tenor behind her. She turned around to see who she was, only to see Mandy.

She cringed internally. Why did she always have to show up? The girl who was constantly being arrested and suspended from school, but somehow was revered by everyone that she gave the 'right' answers to, the answers Ariettea refused to lie and give.

From behind them all, she watched Mandy cock her head to the side, and get everyone in her immediate vicinity to laugh with her at whatever smart-alecky thing she had just said, including Matt. Ariettea could never do that. People only ever looked at her confused, disappointed, when she tried to fit in, be funny, contribute to a conversation.

It's funny how when people accept you, you can get away with anything. And how easy it could be for her to be accepted. The simple lies she could tell. Or how easy it would be to just do what they wanted, to free-fall into monotony, to settling.

But she couldn't.

It wasn't in her.

It never could be.

She watched Matt slowly saunter, turn himself from beside Mandy to directly in front of her, obtaining her full view and attention. He handed her a can of Coke, and as she took it, she leaned back, thrusting her hips forward towards him, in a pair of cut-offs that were at least a size too small, laughing coyly. He smirked, pleased with what he was receiving from her. He kept his eyes immersed into hers, bending over laughing every few seconds, as she held the can up to her neck, throwing her hip out as she laughed with him.

Ariettea shook her head, knowing full well she was being unfairly jealous, and turned back around.

The sun was beaming out its last rays as it sank down into the waterline. The water lapped at her knees and she stared down into in, murky and brown. She reminisced on the blue, sparkling Atlantic, and tried to make herself believe she was just idealizing the place. Surely, the water there was murky, too.

She wrapped her long-sleeved jacket tighter and around her, trying to feel calm, safe. But that feeling never came.

Darkness falling fast, she trudged back to the group. As much as he drove her insane, she always gravitated towards Matt. But more and more often, that also meant being close to Mandy. She crossed her arms as she silently slid up beside Matt and watched as one of her parent's friends poured lighter fluid onto the pile of wood.

"Hey Ariettea!" Mandy suddenly screeched from the other side of Matt.

Ariettea winced, jumped a little, every muscle in her shoulders now tense. She forced the smallest smile. "Hey, Mandy."

Mandy jumped over to her, high kneed, Baywatch style, her white t-shirt, suddenly not hiding much. At least not hiding anything leopard print. "How ARE you, girl?" She yelled, throwing an arm over Ariettea.

Ariettea left her arms crossed, her body rigid, and waited for Mandy to let go. Matt saw her stance and rolled his eyes, shook his head in disgust at Ariettea, scoffing.

Her eyes on him, she forced out, "I'm good, Mandy. How are you?"

"SO great!" She exclaimed, looking up towards the sky. "Can't WAIT for our senior year!" She beamed, linking her arm into Matt's while keeping her other around Ariettea.

Ariettea couldn't help but let her eyes linger there on Mandy and Matt's linked arms too long, and then she accidentally met Matt's eyes. He stared at her, annoyed at whatever look he saw on her face. "What's the look, Ariettea?" He said, calling her out, purposely loud enough for everyone there to hear.

Her arms still crossed, she shook her head. "No idea what you mean." She said pushing her lips out, trying to appear indifferent.

Mandy's arm finally dropped, as Matt shook his head again, the look of disgust ever more prominent. Her heart ached at the look on her face. How could he be so kind, then turn whenever people were around? She tensed, her stomach rolled and hardened, trying to block out the feeling.

"Well tell us how your trip was, Ariettea." He said, still loud, mockingly, already knowing the answer.

"It was great." She said simply, feeling the eyes of dozens on her.

She wanted to disappear, but there were no bathrooms to hide in at the beach. Unless you stole away in a darkened putrid port a potty.

She swiftly strode away and pulled her own Coke out of the cooler, settled down into a beach chair, as far from everyone as she could.

Suddenly Matt was beside her, flopping down into the lawn chair on her left. "So really, tell me about the trip." He said, suddenly sounding vaguely sincere. "We missed you."

Her heart fluttered. She shrugged, sipping her pop. "It was... Amazing. I really loved the place." She admitted. She beamed at the ground before meeting his eyes once more. "Lily is a sweet kid. She's happy and kind and way more interested in you than you could ever be in yourself."

He nodded. Ariettea's heart calmed, swelling with happiness that he understood what she was saying for once. Swelling with the thought they maybe he'd be proud of her for finally making a friend.

"So is she bald?" He asked suddenly.

Ariettea jerked away from him, to the other side of her chair, not having realized she had been leaning towards him. "What?" She asked flatly.

"Is she bald?"

Ariettea blubbered. "Sh-She just got a wig. I cut off my hair, and she got part of it in her wig." She said carefully emphasizing each word.

"So, she's bald?" She looked at him, confused.

The look on his face was somewhere between mocking and quizzical, she couldn't tell which was more prominent.

"Yes, but, but what does that matter?" She asked, trying to smile at him.

"I just wondered...Does she look funny?"

"How OLD are you, Matthew?" She snapped, jumping to her feet.

He laughed, a scoffing degrading laugh, the kind that sends fire up your spine. He looked up at her. "Same age as you. Which you seem to always be forgetting."

"And what exactly does that mean?"

He stayed eerily calm, as if this was the conversation he wanted. "You aren't older or better than me or anyone else Ariettea. So don't act like it."

"Then don't act like a jerk when you're talking about a kid who's sick." She shot back, her own voice becoming hard and all too even.

He leaned back in his chair, crossed a leg, chuckled. His voice sounded smooth, flirty as he said, "Sor-RY! Didn't know you'd get so riled up about your new BFF."

She felt her cheeks get hot. He was touching on the one thing he knew was her sore spot. And he was mocking it. "That's jerkish."

"It's the truth."

"WHAT is? You don't make any sense."

"All of it is the truth." He looked deep into her eyes, brushed his thumb on his nose, bobbed his head, and smiled sinisterly. "All I'm saying is that I was wondering if she looked weird, and your golden girl is perfect, apparently, and you get all defensive." He said, motioning up and down her body.

"She's a sweet little girl, and you're being disgusting."

"I'm not going to talk about it."

"Why, because you're wrong?"

"Ariettea!" Her mother suddenly warned out of nowhere.

Anger boiled up in her. She could now see from the corner of her eyes that they had an audience. And of course, it was all her fault. She was too serious, too cold, too arrogant. She turned and glared at her mother, then turned away before she could draw out a backhand.

Rage churned inside her; it was as if she were a child who's conversations needed censoring. Where was Matt's censorship? He didn't get any, of course. He played the game. He was the poster child for everything she rebelled against.

She scoffed down at him, rolled her eyes, and started to walk away.

"Yeah, stalk away," Matt muttered.

She flinched, wanting to stop dead in her tracks, wanting to whirl around and slap him across the face.

This was why.

This was why she fought so hard to feel nothing, avoided opening up to anyone, and why she felt like she had no choice but to take it all out on herself, internally and externally.

She trudged herself up a sand dune and plopped down. She watched the night sky light up as the bonfire below her lit. Everyone clapped and cheered, grabbed another beer from the cooler as the kids grabbed marshmallows.

She sighed as she rubbed her palm across her forehead and closed her eyes. She felt so lost, so alone. All the time.

Her ever silent phone buzzed in her back pocket. She rolled her eyes, heisted to pull it out, awaiting an angry text from her mother saying to just be nice to people.

The phone buzzed again and again. 'Oh good,' she thought. 'Either a rant from my mother or now multiple people are mad at me for telling Matt he was being rude.' She grabbed her phone and saw the awaited texts.

But they weren't from her mother.

They were all from Lily.

"Missing you, Ariettea! I really want to keep in touch! Please keep me posted on your school year! When you came to visit that day, Peter was here working out my homeschooling plan for the year. I've been trying to convince him to take most of my lessons to the beach that you can see from my window, especially since it's just a short walk from his classes at Ducreis. I'll keep you posted on that request lol. I can tell you don't like to share much, like you think you're selling your soul every time you open up. But I want to be there for you! I can tell we can be close friends."

Ariettea smiled. But COULD she be trusted? At least, she thought, Lily was far enough away that if she did turn out to be like all the others before her, she'd be easier to avoid.

She looked around her. No one had followed her up the dune to check on her. Everyone was down at the bonfire, laughing and dancing and having a great time.

She was alone. Except for Lily.

She didn't leave the message on read like she had the last one, she replied right away. *"Funny to hear from you just now. I'm at the beach and was just thinking of you. The lake water here is grey and murky compared to that gorgeous Atlantic blue by you. Yes, please keep me posted on those beachside lessons so I can be jealous lol."* She paused. *"And I'll keep you posted on my final year here, too."*

Send.

Ariettea watched the message send, be read immediately, and then saw Lily's little bubbles of a typing reply pop up.

She waited.

"I hope I'm not taking your attention away from anyone there! Have a great time! We can talk more tomorrow."

Ariettea scoffed at herself. SHE had already taken HERSELF away from everyone. *"No, I'm kind of a loner in this crowd."*

Again, she paused.

She felt the inner struggle to hold back.

But something else inside her was fighting too.

"I have time to talk now."

Chapter 10

Ariettea walked down the school hallway, bright blue lockers lining each side of it, trying to scream PEP! At the girl in the black eyeliner. A long black duster sweater covering all the way down to her knuckles and a messenger bag slung over her shoulder, she kept her head down as she wove in between the crowds of teens hustling to their next class.

Someone bumped into her, running towards the stairs trying to scale the five flights the school had so kindly placed in between their classes before the bell rang. She heaved her bag back up onto her shoulder, having to readjust her slightly too big shirt as it slid down her collarbone. She realized then that she should have focused more on tops that day at the mall before running into Samantha. Too late, she supposed, as it was now the middle of the first semester.

She sighed. She just wanted to get to her next class. She was tired. So tired. Despite having slept 12 hours the night before. Which no one found abnormal. Just another tired, busy, angsty teen.

She pulled her phone out of her back pocket as she checked the time. She had made herself late by stopping to talk to Matt. Or at least, trying to talk to him. "I feel like this class schedule has us on opposite planets." She called out, approaching him at his locker.

He glanced over at her and shrugged. They had never discussed what happened at the beach the weekend before school started. It just kind of went away, but nothing went back to normal. Or what was their own version of it.

"You doing ok?" She asked him, hugging her books to her chest, nervous. "I feel like we haven't talked in ages. I can never seem to catch you on Sunday's, or here, either."

He shook his head. "Just busy, I guess. I've got a lot of friends to keep up with." He said, looking her up and down, as if she didn't qualify to be one of them.

She felt the sting in her throat. "I've texted you a few times, but I guess if you're busy…" She mumbled. She felt so disgusted with herself. The girl who took no crap from anyone, avoided anyone who gave her a hard time, pining after someone who was doing just that.

He nodded again and slammed his locker shut. "Well, I'm sure I'll see you Sunday." He brushed past her without looking her in the eye.

She felt humiliated. Even before she left, he had been getting more and more distant. She was terrified she was losing the last person she had.

She made it to her class with a few minutes to spare. Her head down as she went in, she all but dropped her bag over her chair and fell down to pull her book out.

When she stood back up, she caught a glimpse of Matt in the back of the classroom, over Mandy's shoulder, laughing at something she was showing him on her phone. His cheek was just a little too close to hers, and Ariettea could see Mandy soaking it in from the corner of her own eye. His cheekbones popped like they always did when he found something genuinely funny, which made the feeling in her chest cut a little harder as she found herself wishing he still smiled at her that way.

She shook her head and scolded herself, looking away. What did it even matter? She got angry at herself for even caring. For feeling anything regarding it. Who was she to have any opinion on who he talked to?

She sighed again as she whipped her book open to the correct page. She turned to grab a notebook from her bag when her phone buzzed in her back pocket. She furrowed her brow, confused, then remembered that she had actually been receiving texts the last couple of weeks.

All from Lily.

It first started out just small, weather, memes, but somehow it went from Lily describing the college campus to Ariettea's thoughts on college. From Ariettea's feeling stuck to Lily's same feeling.

She shifted so she could pull the phone out from her moto jeans. She looked around to make sure no one was watching. Her parents already were so confused, after being surprised too that her ever silent phone was showing life, that her texts were coming from 'that little kid'. She wished they would understand, that they were even capable of understanding. But she just hid the messages the best she could; she didn't have the energy to explain that talking to someone, even a kid, with a positive light was somehow calming to her charred and black world. And not in the annoying, fake, imitate me, way all the adults around her tried to be positive. It was real. And genuine. A genuineness the people around her couldn't seem to grasp or apply to their own lives.

"*Actually, they're saying I'm improving,*" Lily had text, continuing their conversation from the day before. "*I probably won't go home as soon as I'd like to, but it's good news! How is school today?*"

Ariettea glanced back at Matthew and Mandy once more before replying, "*I'm glad to hear it. School is the same as usual. I'm currently watching Matt shove his face up against Mandy's. Earlier, he had some other girl up against her locked laughing. Sometimes I wish I had that charisma.*"

Send.

She always felt an immediate sense of regret every time she hit send. Like she had made some terrible mistake, that she was oversharing, that Lily couldn't possibly care. Or if she did, she'd end up using it against her later.

She quickly typed, "*Sorry to be unloading on you. You've got enough to care about already.*"

Lily text back immediately. "*Oh please, when I ask about school you know I'm also asking about Matt. You're not exposing yourself by telling your friend what you're thinking. And you have more charisma than you know.*"

Ariettea smiled, loving the feeling of having a friend to confide in, but still fighting the sense of shame that it had to be a kid. But wasn't that what people always made her out to be when she tried to talk to them?

Lily continued, "*I just don't understand why he doesn't actually ask all these girls out? He probably can't commit to one.*"

"*That, and his parents won't pay for his car, gas, or college if he does. They want him focused on school. But I'm sure his texts and DM's show a different story.*"

"Hahahaaa. Alright. So spill it then. Why do you put up with it? Him? Being in your life at all? I mean, aside from your parents being friends, no excuses you." Lily already knew her and her excuses, her self deprecations, all too well.

Ariettea stared down at the text. She knew the answer. But she couldn't bring herself to type it out. Not at that moment, at least.

"Phones down, books out!" Her science teacher suddenly bellowed.

Ariettea threw her phone back in her bag as Matt walked by. He looked at her quizzically, raising an eyebrow, knowing all too well she never had anyone to talk to. He looked at her almost approvingly. Like she was finally trying to be normal. Ariettea couldn't look at him in the eye, or even at all. She ignored him all through class, even though she could see him glancing over at her periodically, the first time since the previous school year.

When the class was over, she jumped up, not even slinging her bag onto her shoulder before bolting out of class.

It was lunchtime, and the last thing she wanted to do was stay inside. The school, of course, didn't care about any student individually and did everything they could to keep them all inside, no matter what anxiety-inducing situation could make them need some air.

Nevertheless, Ariettea knew which door to go out of so that she could eat in her car in peace. And think about how to answer Lily's question.

She slammed the driver's seat all the way back and curled her legs up in front of her, resting one across the steering wheel.

She flopped her head back against the headrest and took a deep breath in.

She stared at the two lilies hanging from her rearview. They were always there. Always a reminder of two different people.

She pulled her phone out and opened Lily's message thread. As much as her heart ached looking at the question, she knew exactly how to answer it. *"You know, everyone, including my parents, are always asking me why I don't have friends. Why don't I invite anyone from school to do anything? Someone from our congregation? A friend of a friend? What they can't and won't understand is that I've tried all that."*

She sighed. Unsure if she should keep going. She figured at least she could type it out and delete it if need be. *"Matt always tells me to just walk up to groups of people and strike up conversations, but I do that, and everyone looks at me like I'm from another planet.*

"I was always too old, too young, too quiet, too opinionated, too cocky, too brainless, too much of a rule follower, while too much of a convention breaker. The ones that did stick around, always moved or lied or betrayed or were barely there from the start. Were never my friends to begin with.

"But of course, according to everyone, that was always my fault as well, I just didn't try hard enough.

"No one knows about the texts I had sent, outings I tried to join or score an invite to. The times I've been cancelled on, stood up, for better offers.

"What Matt is constantly telling me to do, just walk up to a group of girls and try to make friends, he doesn't know that I've done that so, so many times, and everyone just stares at me like I have a disease. I can never find the right things to say, I can never just fit in.

"But then that is all my fault again, because it must be me that's the problem. Most often I'm told that I'm too picky, stuck up. But mostly I just want to find someone who I can talk to, who isn't doing drugs or something shady, and who won't end up lying to me or about me.

"Which, to answer your question, is why I put up with Matthew. As much as I hate him some days, as much as I disagree with things he does, I've seen the good in him. I see the good heart he tries to hide. He ignores me, he's rude to me, but he still shows back up.

"He's the only one who hasn't completely left me yet."

She read it back. It hurt. It hurt to relive those moments.

She shook her head, trying to shake the feeling, to bring back the numb. The comforting numb she was so used to.

She thought about Lily, what would she think when she read all that. Would she even care? Would she turn around and agree with what everyone else said? Ariettea figured, if she did, might as well get rid of her now.

Send.

Her phone buzzed immediately after. She looked down, expecting a 'wow' or some other scolding phrase.

But she saw a message from Trent. "***Just checking in on you. Hope your first weeks at school are going well! I hope you're doing ok, too.***"

Her heart jumped. Partly scared her parents had received some similar message, and partly because he was the first one to ever even know what he was hinting at asking about.

"***I've been ok. Thanks for checking.***" Was all she could bear to reply.

She placed a shaking hand over her mouth and leaned it against the door.

She was embarrassed.

She felt so stupid and weak.

She suddenly had multiple people in her life asking if she was ok. It made her defensive and suddenly humiliated over what she had just sent Lily. She was a kid. Why did she even think she'd understand?

She dropped the hand and banged her head against the window. "What am I even doing here?" She whispered to herself. She wanted to crawl in a hole.

She closed her eyes, tempted to sleep the rest of the day, blow off her classes. But that was a yelling at that she did not want from her parents. She was too tired for it.

She tore off pieces of her peanut butter sandwich, tried shoving them in her mouth, just to have eaten something.

She tried to ignore that fact that it was taking Lily longer than usual to respond. She tried to calm herself, maybe Lily was doing her own schoolwork, or maybe she was getting a blood test done.

But she also knew Peter didn't see Lily until after 2 O'clock and she had blood drawn yesterday.

The curse of being anxiety-driven observant.

As Ariettea pulled her feet off the dash and got ready to get out of the car, Lily's answer came.

"***I'm sorry, Ari. If it's any help, I know where you're coming from. It's not like any of my friends stuck around when I got sick. When you're as young as I was, I guess you can't expect them to. At least you and I know how to treat people ourselves. But*** *sometimes even the ones who don't leave, you have to stop and make sure you're not allowing them to treat you badly just because they've stayed around, however little interaction that may be. Or because of what we wish they could be."*

Part of her felt angry. Who did she think she was? Telling her to write Matt off like that? She barely knew her, let alone him.

But then another message came through. *"But unlike everyone around you seems to do, I won't tell you what to do. I'm ONLY here as your friend, I'm on your side. 100%."*

The sting of irritation was still biting as she got out of her car. How could she say she was her friend when they still barely knew each other? She'd end up just like everyone else, eventually.

She typed as she walked. *"That's nice. But still. You don't know me very well. Most people end up telling me I'm wrong."* She was throwing walls up, fast and hard. Which made her feel like even more of an idiot because she was the one who opened up in the first place.

She ran to her locker to grab a book she'd forgotten when Lily's next text came in, *"You keep saying that- that you must be 'wrong' and the odd one out and that I'm wrong about you, too, because I'm not there to see it.*

"People are always telling me that I'm too young to understand anything.

"Like people tell you.

"But once you've been absent of anyone your own age for years, you adapt to what's around you. You observe. A lot.

"So I know people. And because we talk constantly, I DO know you.

"You're a way better human than you think you are. You're trying to push me away to prove that you're as awful as you think you are.

"We are so different you and I- you didn't even want to meet me, even now you could ignore me, but you don't. So, you are not a picky jerk, and you're not an undesirable person. I chose you because you're awesome, and I'll keep telling you that until you know me well enough to believe it."

Ariettea wanted to believe it. So badly. But names and faces ran through her head like a freight train. Loud and shaking and unforgiving.

She didn't want to make the same mistakes again. Open up to the wrong person. She always fought so hard to stay numb, to stay walled off, because that's the only place she was safe. From everyone but herself, the harshest critic of all.

Trent's reply then rang in. *"Please reach out if you need to."*

She slammed her forehead into her locker shelf and closed her eyes.

She had people, multiple people, begging her to have faith again.

She heard a commotion, opened her eyes slowly.

Out of the corner of her vision she saw a group of girls that she had once spent a few weekends with, before they started ignoring her texts, walk by, not even glancing at her.

And then Matthew's group of guys ran down the hallway, laughing, someone throwing a shoe at the guy furthest ahead. She saw Matt with his arm slung around his best friend as they brought up the rear.

She closed her eyes. She felt the grit of her eyeliner crunch as she squeezed them shut. She took in a deep breath, then let it out heavily, opening her eyes.

All the people around her were constantly a reminder that she just couldn't give her trust out that easily anymore.

An algebra book sitting open in front of her, Ariettea couldn't keep her mind on homework that evening. She still hadn't responded to Lily. She stared at her phone for a minute before finally picking it up.

"Thank you, Lily. I appreciate all that. It's all too kind for me." She paused, chewing on her bottom lip. *"I feel so conceited, you hear all about my crap, but I never asked about your friends. I guess I never quite know how to. But that's no excuse."*

Lily's typing bubbles always popped up right away. **"It's ok. It IS a weird question to word the right way. I don't have friends either. Kids I grew up with were too young to understand what was wrong with me when I got diagnosed, and by the time they did, it felt like I had aged ten years past them, and we just didn't click anymore.**

"I talk to kids here, but we usually all end up in our own rooms, trying not to spread germs amongst our little immunocompromised group.

"And see, it's words like that that get me in trouble. No one my age understands it, and anyone who does thinks I'm too young to say it.

"I love talking to people; I talk to anyone that comes in my room. Nurses, aides. If I can sneak down to the beach, I'll talk to whoever is down there. But it's so secluded it's usually no one lol. I talk to Peter a lot, ask about his friends. But as far as my own, I really appreciate you being there for that."

Ariettea's heartstrings pulled, feeling special while guilty. Some friend she was, with loads of baggage for a sick kid, always trying to kill the friendship that Lily so desperately wanted for herself. *"Talking with you is my utmost pleasure. You're always being something for me more than I am for you. Sorry."*

"It's called friendship, Ariettea! We take turns being there for each other."

"Ok. So let me be here for you tonight. Tell me about your day today."

"Typical. Someone woke me up for vitals way too early. I ended up watching some terrible reality tv for a while, then my mom got me started on school before Peter came. He always shoos my mom or dad out when he comes so they can get a break, then we do homework together more than he teaches most times lol. He keeps telling my parents they pay him too much and that I don't need him here as often as he comes. But they like paying him and getting a break they don't feel guilty about."

"How do they seem to cope with it all?"

"They lock it up. I can tell. My mom sees a therapist; my dad still works but can do a lot remotely. So, I see him but not as much as my mom, who hardly ever leaves me. I feel like such a burden on them. Especially because I know they wanted a big family. Then got stuck with me."

"Meeting them, I'm positive that's not how they feel."

"It's not. I know that. It's just guilt is all. Which I also know isn't my fault, but oh well. Good days and bad. Speaking of, they loved meeting you! They see me texting you all the time and keep asking when you're coming back."

"Trent and Nadette are the same way, said I could come to visit anytime. I can't help but think they don't really mean it, though. But I did love Ducreis."

"Nadette likes to stop by between her rounds. I'll hint how much I miss you! ;) Maybe winter break?!"

"I'll think about it."

"So, what was it you loved about Ducreis so much? I'm curious, everyone here loves it for all the same reasons and completely different reasons at the same time."

"I wish I had a better answer to that. I think part of it was just feeling free."

"You know one thing I've learned is that happiness can be found anywhere. But my heart is always happiest at home for sure."

"That's the thing. Sometimes I don't know where my home is. Or will be."

"You've got time."

"Do I really, though? We're already heading into winter, college advisors are at school every week, kids I grew up with are already leaving town because they turned 18, and I still have no idea what I'm doing. Or what I even want. Although everyone keeps TELLING me what I want..."

"Ariettea, I think your faith may be the problem here." Her mother announced to her one day.

Ariettea looked up at her silently from her spot on the floor.

"You have faith, don't you?"

Ariettea rolled her eyes. "Of course I do."

"So you have faith in God and all His promises, you have purpose! Why are you searching so hard for it somewhere else?"

Ariettea stayed silent.

"So maybe we need to work on strengthening your faith, then you'll be happier." Her mother crossed her arms in triumph as if she'd won a war.

Ariettea sighed. "Mom, I've never said that I'm looking for purpose somewhere else. That's you putting words in my mouth. That's everyone twisting my words to fit their narrative: that all I need is more faith! Just because I know what my deeper purpose in life is doesn't mean that everything I do has meaning. I can have faith and also look for happiness in the day to day."

"But faith gives you that!"

"Ugh, mom, you're not hearing me." She moaned.

Her mother raged on, "I just don't understand, why don't you want to spend time volunteering or go to vocational school or even liberal arts! Why do you think you need a set path?"

Ariettea folded one last towel and threw it on the pile of clean laundry. "I've waited my whole life to be able to make that choice for myself. MYSELF." She said evenly, slowly standing up from her spot on the floor and picking up her laundry basket. "I'm not going to let others make it for me."

"No one wants to make the choice for you, Ariettea!" Her mother whined earnestly, following her down the hall.

"No, but everyone wants me to choose what they think I should." She said over her shoulder, not breaking pace.

"And what's wrong with that?"

Ariettea threw her laundry on the floor inside her bedroom door and stopped. She whirled to face her mother. "MOM. I CANNOT have this conversation again. I'm not going to do what I'm 'supposed to'," She said, her hands in air quotes. "Just because it's what everyone wants."

"Everyone just wants what's best for you!"

"What they THINK is best." She crossed her arms and leaned her hip against the door frame. "All these people, from our congregation, from my school, all your friends, they think they know me, know what's best for me, and they don't. On either account. Just because I'm the only one who's ever said no, doesn't make me wrong."

Her mother sighed. "There's no need for you to set a flight plan and not deviate from it. You're being too rigid. Stay here, volunteer, get a part-time job, most people your age BEG to hear that from their parents! We just want you to be happy!"

"And mom, I get that." Ariettea said, bouncing up off of the door frame. She recentered her jeans on her waist, clasped her hands together, and looked at the floor. "But what makes me happy isn't going to be what makes everyone else happy. That's the only thing I ask people to understand about me. But it's the one thing no one can grasp."

"Because maybe we all know what's best for you, Ariettea. Maybe we all want you to have an easier life than we did!"

"Mom, I keep hearing what 'we want', even what 'I want', none of you seem to care that whatever it is that I actually want, even if I don't know what it is yet, could make me happier and be the 'right' and 'easier' path for me. And that's all that I want. You should know by now I'm never going to be happy if I don't make the choice myself."

"So then make the choice yourself to be reasonable!"

Ariettea rolled her eyes and dropped her arms to her sides. "Ok, I can't talk about this anymore. I can't." She waved her hands and went the other way. "I'm going to go get a latte. I'll be back soon." She said, grabbing her keys and coat in one swoop, desperately needing to get out of that house, get some air that wasn't thick with judgment.

But her mother ran up behind her before she could open the front door, "Why is it that you think you deserve all these people's respect, anyway?" She suddenly asked.

Ariettea whirled back around, felt her face scrunch up in disgust. "What do you mean?"

"I MEAN, what have you done to earn anyone's respect?"

She stared at her blankly. "I...Was born...? Shouldn't everyone respect everyone?"

"Oh, don't give me that crap, Ariettea!"

How she hated hearing her name spat at her.

How she hated everything about her life.

How it wasn't even worth living.

A thought she tried so hard to bury but was coming up into her mind more and more frequently.

As her mother turned around and started to walk away, she crossed her arms and widened her stance, planting herself firmly on the ground. "You know mom, the way everybody treats me, a lot of times I think I would just be better off dead. That I should just kill myself."

The words left her mouth in a flurry, but as soon as they did, she knew she'd made a mistake. Her mother turned to her slowly, disgust enveloping her face. She dramatically took in a deep breath and theatrically let it back out, slowly tipping her head forward in fury.

"I… Am going to make you an appointment with a psychiatrist," She said obstreperously.

Ariettea rolled her eyes and dropped her arms to her sides. "You do this out of nowhere- I am not going to see a SHRINK, mother." She spat.

Her mother grabbed her arm and yanked it so she'd face her. "YOU say this out of nowhere! So, you say that just to hurt me then?"

"No, I-"

"Oh, so it is true? Then you do need to see one?"

Ariettea stayed silent, not willing to feed into her mother's fantasy.

But she also couldn't admit the truth- that it WAS true. She DID want to give up more often than not.

"You're just saying that to hurt me, and try to make me feel guilty, and that's low.

"It's disgusting.

"You need to sit with yourself and think about how terrible you make people feel." Her mother marched away, and she let her.

She wasn't willing to fight the fight.

She already knew how miserable she made everyone else's lives.

She really did just want to go to sleep.

She found herself driving in circles, which, in a small town, didn't take her very far. She ended up where she always did, at the beach.

She got out and started to pace the concrete walkway. The sand on the sides of the path was hard and packed, the waves dark and white-capped as the grey sky started to rain down soft flurries that you had to squint to see. She looked for the lilies, their spot in the sand empty.

She sighed, leaning up against a lamp post. Her fingers trailed down the side, the paint on half of it missing from being sandblasted over and over.

She looked down the beach and thought about Matt. She thought about Lily's question. Why did she put up with him?

She set her coffee down and plopped herself at the edge of the concrete, where it started the slant upwards from the sand, let her legs dangle over the good three feet of air below her feet.

She fluffed her scarf around her ears and pulled out her phone. "*You know Lily; I don't think I've ever told you about Matt's good side. Like, at the beginning of Freshmen year, one of the girls I had been 'friends' with came up to me at school randomly. She started going off about how she just HAD to come over and tell me that my hair was way too dark for me and that I needed to color it to look more 'normal'. Matt sees my face even though he was all the way at the other end of the hall and came running up behind her to cut in and say, "You're being a brat, cut it out." The girl batted her eyes at him and said, "I'm only kidding." He took one look at my face and said, "No, you're not. Drop it. She looks great." And she just...walked away. The bell rang, and it got loud, and I could only mouth 'thank you' to him. He just shrugged and nodded, mouthed 'you're beautiful', and backed away into the crowd.*

"We used to talk, him and I, about everything. He would laugh and ask about my future kids' names, and I'd ask about his. It was like all the things you learn from dating someone, were already knew.

"He'd come find me every day at school to make sure I was ok.

"He was the only one who knew that I wanted to be a nurse, and I was the only one who knew he wanted to be an architect.

"Sometimes we can still look at each other from down the hall or across the room and know what the other is thinking. Even though we haven't had a conversation in weeks.

"You ask, even I ask, what changed? And I still don't know. But I know that he doesn't talk about being an architect anymore. He just agrees to whatever it is his family says he should do. And sometimes I worry that that's exactly what's changed. He started letting everyone else tell him what to do. And maybe that's why I can't listen when anyone tries to tell ME what to do. I don't want to lose myself. Even though I laughably have no idea what losing myself would look like."

"Ari, have you ever stopped to think that you're so busy shutting others out you've shut yourself out too? You dig your heels in

against what they all want, but then you're stuck in the sand and can't get to what you want either. This is first time I've ever heard you put a label on something you'd like to be. Just don't lose yourself in the fight like Matt did."

"You think he lost himself?"

"Sounds to me like he just wants to have fun. So he does whatever he's told so that he can do whatever he wants and have a good time. But what I know for sure, is that you're nothing like that. So don't think it."

Ariettea sighed, took a swig of her coffee, and stared at the water. Ice caps would start to form soon, despite it only being the end of October. She let her mind drift back to Georgia. That blue Atlantic. She tried not to let herself idealize it. Surely it was cold there too.

But she missed it. She missed Ducreis and the people in it. She wondered if Lily was on to something, if maybe Trent and Nadette would have her for another visit?

But then her stomach flip-flopped. She had to set down her coffee to steady herself, place both hands on the cold ground, let the air burn and nip her fingers as the concrete dug into her palms.

She was simultaneously trying to ground herself but also dive headfirst into the panic wrapping around her chest.

She was damaged.

In more ways than anyone knew, except now Trent. There was no way they'd want that mess back in their house.

She hung her head, defeated, knowing she needed to get back to her own house before her mother flipped a lid. Another lid.

She stood up to leave but heard her name being called from down the beach. She recognized a couple of people from her congregation waving at her. She held her coffee cup up in a half-hearted wave and tried to hustle back to her car before they could catch her. But no such luck.

"Ariettea!" Her mom's friend Heather came up breathlessly.

"We were trying to get you to stop!" Laura said from behind her.

Two non descript people, people she'd seen a million times, knew a lot about, but not people she could describe past average builds and brunette hair.

Ariettea tried to force a smile. "How are you both?" She blurted.

"Oh good,"

"Yeah, great."

Ariettea stood, crossed her arms, nodded. "Yeah…" She said expectantly. She didn't want to be there, she didn't want to talk to anyone, not in the mood she was in. 'Curse you small town.' She silently whined.

"We just wanted to say hi!"

"Did you bring your homework down here?"

Ariettea tried not to roll her eyes and the poorly veiled, nosy, underlying question of what she was doing down there, all alone. Because some secret must be had if she would do something as ridiculous as take her homework down to do out in the snow.

"No, no… Just… taking a walk." She said slowly, casually, her eyes shifting up and down the coast.

"So, how IS school going?"

"So far so good. School has never been an issue for me. Just trying to finish now." Ariettea put out, trying to force some singsong into her voice.

"That's great! And after?"

Still avoiding eye contact, her eyes still scanning the coast, still subconsciously looking for the lilies, that time Ariettea did sigh. Shrug. Even when there were no lilies to see, there was always at least one in her thoughts. Lily's words were always running through her head, warring against the cruel ones Ariettea hurled at herself. She knew what she wanted to say, and she also knew Lily would tell her there was nothing wrong in saying it. So, for the first time in a long time, not feeling guilty, she kept her eyes trained on the lighthouse as she finally began to answer the question.

"You know…" She smirked, "I just really want to find something I enjoy; I'd like to help people."

"Oh, so like, ministry or travel or a nice job here?"

Ariettea finally met their eyes, flicking back and forth between them. "No." She said confidently. "There's actually a few things I'm considering. Nursing, psychology, social work, I've got all these options right in front of me."

She watched their faces fall ever so slightly. "Oh, well… Good for you! So, you must know of places hiring here in town for those… jobs?"

Ariettea bristled under the anything but subtle scolding undertone. "No, no, actually, I don't." She smiled, shook her head. "But there are lots of places to be besides here."

She took a slow swallow of coffee as she watched the two exchanged a glance.

She smiled sweetly at them both. "Nice seeing you, ladies! I've really got to head home now." She waved over her shoulder as she made it to her car.

She looked up at the lilies hanging from the rearview and smiled. as she picked up her phone and texted Nadette. ***Hey! I was wondering if your offer to come back for another visit still stood?***

Ten minutes later, Ariettea stepped in her front door feeling a little lighter, like there was slightly less pressure in her chest. She closed the door and placed her keys on the dish beside it, and then suddenly, her father appeared.

Angry.

"Ariettea!" He boomed, making her fight the urge to flinch. She wouldn't let herself. She wouldn't give him the pleasure. She knew he was trying to goad her into a fight.

One he wouldn't let her win.

"What do you think you're doing, storming out of the house after fighting with your mother? Making THREATS? Who do you think you are to make a threat in MY house?" His eyes wild, face scrunched in disgust, he waited for an answer.

And Ariettea made sure he was waiting, because she didn't want to be accused of talking back. After he shook his head at her in anticipation, she spoke. "We weren't fighting," She began before he cut her off right away, as usual, not giving her a single chance to speak.

"No no no, don't change your story." He raged, shaking his finger at her.

Ariettea shook her head. "What story?" She asked, squinting her eyes, confused.

Her father turned around, hands on his hips. "Is this that little kid?" He asked, his back to her.

"Is WHAT, WHO?" She asked.

He whirled back around, got in her face. "YOUR ATTITUDE." He yelled into her eyes, his yells so close that she could feel the spit on her face, the hot air of his breath burning.

She fought the urge to take a step back, to relent, to fear him the way he wanted.

"This attitude here! The look on your face now! Wipe it off!"

Ariettea looked to the ground, then down the hall where she saw her mother watching from the shadows. Rage boiled inside her, but even being emotionless was enough to make her father enraged. He wanted her crying, scared, begging.

And she wouldn't.

"This pathetic dreaming!"

Ariettea's eyes snapped back to him, flashing with anger and hurt. "What dreaming? What fight? I told mom I wanted to choose my own path, and I didn't want to fight about it." She said, emotionless, tired, exhaustion creeping in her shoulders already.

"You don't know ANYTHING, Ariettea. Is this all that little cancer kid? Filling your head full of pipe dreams and once in a lifetimes and dramatic quotes?"

"My head is not one to be filled with anyone else's ideas." She said, each word even.

He took a step towards her, then stopped himself. Clenched his fist beside him. "I have a feeling that's it. Well, get over it, Ariettea. Pull your head out of your butt and grow up. I'm not sure I want you talking to that kid anymore."

Ariettea felt the rage build up inside her. He was finally getting what he wanted, a rise out of her, even if she refused to show it.

Her one friend, the only person who cared about her, and talked to her, kept her from spiraling further down the rabbit hole she lived in.

And he was threatening to take her away, as if he could, just to prove a point.

Just to punish her for thinking for herself.

She wanted to scream. She wanted to be a normal teenager and scream at him how much she hated him. How much she hated her life. But she had already gone down that route with her mother and look where it had landed her.

She knew what role she had to play to survive, to avoid getting backhanded. She knew things would be far worse for herself if she ever tried to fight back against her parents.

Her father shook his head, and her again and waved a hand.

She took it as her cue to leave for her room, that she'd been degraded to his liking.

She wanted to bolt again, in her car, on foot, six feet underground, anything. But she knew that would end up even worse than what she had just experienced.

It was times like those, when she couldn't escape, that she wanted to find a way to let the pain out of her soul and on to her body.

Was he right? Was Lily just shoving a fantasy of happiness down her throat? Surely that'd make more sense than her actually getting to be happy for once.

She silenced her phone and then whipped it into the back of her closet, telling herself she was stupid to respond to any more messages from Lily, and for thinking that Nadette would never answer her.

She locked her bedroom door and threw herself into a corner. She hugged her knees up to her face and deep into the sockets of her eyes, held her breath as long as she could.

She was alone and trapped.

Literally.

Chapter 11

It was December, and the snow had definitely settled into the region. The sharp wind bit Ariettea's legs through her lace tights, whooshing up through her thin pencil skirt as the usual dune party group gathered at some local, non-chain, Mexican restaurant after a Sunday morning meeting.

As the large group of people scattered around the table an empty seat was left next to Matthew. The one that had always been reserved as hers but had so often been quickly filled by Matt's mother or Mandy or anyone else but her for months. But, it stayed empty as the table filled, so Ariettea reluctantly slid in next to him. His eyes didn't divert from whatever sports show was on the TV above them all on the wall.

She pulled her phone from her pocket as she took off her coat and looked down at her last exchange with Lily.

"I'd talk to him next chance you get, any chance you get. It's gone on long enough. Just ask him what's going on and why he's been wonky? It got worse after your visit here in the summer, right?"

"We had been off before then, but yeah, it was like over the summer I just lost him. But you're right. At least I'll know if he hates me or he's just... grown out of me."

"That's not a fair statement, and you know it. Everyone deserves friends that actually treat you right. Because you deserve more than past tense and asking why he stopped talking to you. At least you can stop torturing yourself. And maybe know what feelings he has for you?"

"Or doesn't."

She put her phone face down on the table and took a breath. She knew it was a rare chance, to have him alone. They were at the end of the long table, so at least the conversation would be semi-private.

She turned to Matt on her left. "So, how's it going?" She asked him, her voice an octave too high.

His eyes didn't move from the TV. "Fine."

She fought the urge to sigh and roll her eyes. "How are your finals going?"

"Good."

She dropped the fake smile she had forced on to her face. "Alright dude. What happened to us?" She asked, turning her head towards him, her voice dropping low so no one but him could hear.

He shook his head, eyes still on the tv. "I don't know what you're talking about." He mumbled.

She slapped her hand down on the table in front of him, enough to make him break his gaze on the tv, but quiet enough no one else noticed. "Matthew. You haven't even looked at me in weeks. We used to talk about everything. Even when we didn't, or disagreed on something, we were still friends. What's really going on?"

He met her eyes, but only for a fleeting second. "Nothing's awkward on my end."

"So something is on mine?"

"You tell me. You haven't been talking to me either." He muttered, eyes drifting around the room.

She felt her shoulders droop, suddenly ashamed of herself. "You're right." She whispered. "I guess I've been sensing something...weird between us for a while. I just wanted to give you space to... figure things out." She said, trying to imply but not imply what she actually meant.

"What do I need to figure out?" He said, his eyebrows furrowing together, lip slightly curled as if in disgust.

She felt her cheeks flush in embarrassment. He clearly had never felt what she did towards him.

She pulled her hands off the table and started to wring them in her lap. Her eyes fell there. "I just meant that I wanted to give you space because I thought I had offended you somehow."

"Have you done anything offensive?" He asked, tone scolding, his gaze now fixed on her bowed head.

She lifted her eyes, keeping her head low, to meet his. Indignation burned in her heart, but somehow shame with it.

Of course she had done something wrong. She always did. Some advice Lily have her, to be open.

She didn't know how to answer him. "I think we all take offense differently." She finally said evenly, again, meaning something she wasn't saying.

She turned away from him and picked up her menu, stomach-churning at the thought of eating anything.

"Well. Nothing taken on my end." He said, cordially, mockingly.

She nodded silently to her menu.

"Ariettea?" Matt's mom Cirise called from down the table.

Ariettea whipped her head around. "I'm sorry?" She asked.

"That's alright, dear; I was just asking about your plans for Georgia? What are you going to do?"

Ariettea shrugged, pushed her menu away, knowing no matter what answer she gave, it wouldn't be right. "Oh, I'm not sure." She started hesitantly. "The main thing is to visit Lily-"

"Still with that weird little girl with cancer?" Matt piped up.

Ariettea turned to face him. She felt every muscle in her face harden, her jaw clench. "What is that supposed to mean?" She asked him, her words short and clipped.

He shrugged. Eyes glazed over and locked on something in the distance. He stayed silent.

"Excuse me?" She pushed, and sharply.

"Matt." Cirise prodded. "Quit ignoring Ariettea."

He shrugged. "Look," He said, shaking his head at the ground. "I just don't get why you wanna hang out with..." He trailed off, seeing her face. "I don't know." He finished lamely.

Ariettea finished for him. "You think I'm weird for hanging around with a kid with cancer? Why is that weird? Don't you hang out with kids all the time?"

He shrugged again. "I-I..." He shook his head, waved a hand at her.

Ariettea wasn't going to let him worm out of answering. "'I-I' what?" She asked, her own tone starting to mimic his mocking one. "Maybe I like her; maybe she's my friend. Maybe I'm going to visit my Aunt and Uncle in a place I love. Maybe you don't know what you're talking about!" Ariettea felt the electricity running through her explode, as everyone grew quiet.

She saw her parents give her nasty looks out of the corner of her eye, disgusted that she was embarrassing them. As always.

Finally, she saw Matt's jaw tighten as he turned to look at her. "Why is it that you will hang out with no one here, but run down there to be with those people? Why is it that you talk about Georgia being this magical place? What makes those people, that place, better than everyone here?"

She had never seen his eyes show such contempt, and her own eyes burned. "I never said that they are, or that it was." She said, her own jaw tightening, words clipped.

He scoffed. "You didn't have to."

She stared at him. Making the silence awkward on purpose, until he continued.

When he did, his eyes showed rage, disgust. "You think you're better than everyone else, Ariettea. You think this town is beneath you. And now you think you've found people and a place worthy of your time and attention. But you know what?" He hissed, leaning in towards her, "If these people are as stuck up as you, then soon enough, you won't be good enough for them either, and they'll be as tired of you as you are of this place, if they aren't already."

Everything inside her hurt. Everything burned and ached, her chest, her throat, her stomach, her eyes, everything. He hit her most sensitive nerve, and he did it on purpose. She already knew she wasn't good enough for anyone, let alone people as wonderful as Trent, Nadette, and Lily. She already knew they were tired of her, or were going to be soon.

And he was confirming it.

She wanted to rebuttal, to tell him she had tried so hard to fit in there, that she didn't hate her life before it hated her. But maybe he was right.

She turned away from him, silently, careful not to let her face fall, not to let him know he had gotten to her.

But he knew he did.

He kept his gaze on her, smiled, sinisterly, satisfied, and sat back in his seat. He turned his head to tune back into ESPN, tuning her out of his world, having made it clear that she had been tuned out for a long time.

She bit on her lip, purposely hard enough to taste blood, feeling like walls were collapsing on her from all sides.

Every negative thought she had about herself seemed to be confirmed in that moment. She was desperately trying to block out the emotions, the feeling, like she always did. 'Deny, deny, deny!' Her mind was screaming at her like a siren.

She gripped her phone tightly in her lap, waiting for someone, anyone, to tell Matt that he was out of line, to defend her in some way. But no one did. The helpful defense never came.

"Well, we all hope you have a good trip." Cirise said softly, almost sarcastically.

Ariettea nodded, full of anger and hurt, not even able to lift her head to look in her direction.

"But I mean, Matt is right, dear. You don't need that ridiculous big school. You should really find your place here."

Her eyes flashed over to her for just a moment, full of rage, but she knew it wasn't worth the fight. There, or at home later.

She didn't want to be there. She wanted to run. She wanted to run from that place, away from her seat next to Matt, but more so from everyone and everything there. That town, those people, these people with her then.

But now Matt had clearly let her know that she was a fool for thinking she could run, no one anywhere wanted her.

And if you can't run, what is there left to do but give up?

To just… sink?

She went from wringing her hands to rubbing the insides of her arms, feeling the raised scars and wishing she could make more right then.

She was worthless.

She instinctively unlocked her phone to look at the screen. She saw she had missed Lily's last text. "*Whatever he says, at least you'll know. If he likes you, that's great. If you're still friends, awesome. But if he's a jerk, it doesn't matter, because you have other people that love you way more than he ever could. Like me.*"

Ariettea let her fingers dance above the screen before she began to type back. She wanted to recoil, but she also wanted to lean into the love. "*Sounds like you already knew what his answer would be. Because*

that's all he is, all he will ever be. A jerk. I'll tell you more later."
"Love you, Ari. Chin up princess, or the crown falls ;)"

Matt insisted she was haughty, but Lily wanted to see her in a crown.

She smiled down at her phone, enjoying someone finally sticking up for her.

But for some reason, when she got back out to her car, she couldn't bring herself to rip Matt's calla lily from her rearview.

Trent and Nadette both stood waiting for her as she came to the edge of security.

Nadette had her in a tight hug before the, "Hi!" Even left her lips. Trent laid an arm around both of them, squeezed her in even tighter.

Since she had at least expected all the hugging this time around, she was slightly less tense about it.

Trent took her duffel bag out of her hand and slung it over his shoulder. He brushed his hair out of his eyes, "It's so great to have you back, Ari," He began, striding through streams of people. "The three of us really have to go out and have some fun this visit."

Nadette's perfect soft curls bounced as she nodded in agreement. "We really want to take you around town some more, spend some time after Lily gets hers in." She grabbed Ariettea's hand and squeezed, as she threw the other arm around her shoulder.

Ariettea smiled softly at the ground, enveloped with warmness, but the sting of Matt's words still ringing in her ears. "I can't wait." She said, looking up to meet Nadette's smiling eyes.

She hoped they meant it, because she really did. There was a gnawing feeling inside her stomach, the one that always warned her that there was a shoe waiting to drop.

'They'll be as tired of you as you are of this place, if they aren't already.'

She was sick of that happening; every thought she had was countered by the voice of some old friend

'You can't do that in this town.'

'You'll get it when you're older.'

'What's wrong with living here?'

'If you live thinking that you're above things, you're going to have a very hard life.'

'Quit being so dramatic.'

'You need to make more friends!'

IGNORE IT! She finally screamed at herself.

"You ok?" Trent asked.

Ariettea looked up at him, raised an eyebrow.

"You're shaking your head." He elaborated, his eyes soft around the corners, brow furrowing ever so slightly in what she could tell was deep concern that he wasn't masking well.

"Lost in thought, I guess."

He nodded, trying to seem like he accepted that answer, even though they both knew he didn't.

'If they aren't already.'

Trent and Nadette took her to a wing restaurant once they got back to Ducreis. A local college bar and grill type place, packed with students cramming over fries and beers.

Ariettea felt flustered that she was always having to eat with Trent and Nadette, it was getting harder and harder for her to make excuses why she wasn't hungry.

"So," Nadette began, flipping through her menu. "You're halfway through your senior year! You must be excited!"

Ariettea gave a half-smile and flipped her head from side to side. "It will be nice to get out of that place, that's for sure." She said slowly, not sure if she had meant the school or the town.

"So, do you have any ideas about what's next for you?" Trent asked.

Ariettea tried to hide a wince. She should be grateful, she thought, that she had managed to avoid that question on her last trip.

"What's the look?" She heard Trent ask with a laugh, bringing her attention back to him.

She looked at him, knowing his laugh was sincere and answered truthfully. "I just never have a good answer to that question," She said with another half-smile, shoving her hands underneath her thighs, a subconscious effort to make herself as small and inconspicuous as possible.

"Well you don't have to have one right now, or even anytime soon," Trent said to her.

Nadette jumped in, shaking her head in agreement, "Really, take your time, change your mind as many times as you want, even as adults, we aren't locked into anything in life."

Ariettea looked down at her menu, laying open to some random page that she had only pretended to read. "I guess I get so caught up in the-becoming an adult, turning 18, leaving school, make your choice now, mindset. Especially being in a small town, it's not like you have many options to choose from, anyway."

Nadette nodded, her eyes soft, understanding. "So, what if you had all the choices in the world available to you, which you do," She pointed a finger at her smiling. "What would you choose?"

Ariettea mulled. "I ask myself that a lot, actually. And I never quite know." She paused. "What was it that made you guys choose to do what you do?"

They shared a knowing look.

Trent answered first, "Personally, I wouldn't endorse my path," He laughed, "It was way too much school, especially after we started dating, I found myself wishing that I had more time to give to Nade."

Nadette answered, "We are both SO glad we have jobs that we love, and we will tell anyone all day long that you absolutely have to do something that you enjoy in this life. That doesn't always have to be a job, though. But if you want it to be, that's your choice, no one can make it for you. So don't let anyone."

Ariettea found a laugh escaping her mouth. "Can you tell that to everyone back home? All I ever hear is what I 'should' do and choose." She shook her head, waiting for either of them to jump in with some platitude. When it didn't, she found herself continuing, "I guess I just get overwhelmed by how many choices there ARE open to me, and also overwhelmed by how many people there are trying to take those choices away from me."

Nadette nodded. "You forget that I grew up near that area too," She said with a sad smile. "I know the feeling. It comes down to you knowing what it is that you want, knowing what's right, and tuning out people who have no basis for telling you that it's wrong."

"What about the people who do have a basis?" Ariettea fired back right away.

Nadette squinted. "Do they really, though?" She asked, cocking her head to one side. "No one else lives your exact life, feels what you do, has gone through what you have. Everyone can give you a unique perspective on their life and choices and cause and effects, but that doesn't really give them law to tell you what to do.

"I'm not saying to discount people's own truths, but just consider the source, and compare it to you. No one's circumstances are ever the same, even people living in the same house! You have to do what's best for YOU, and only you and God know what that is."

Trent put down the beer he had been nursing to add, "If you feel like your options are that limited, we can always grab you a course catalogue from Ducreis," He winked. "Or you can come down here and hang out while you look for what you want other than school. But I'm not saying you can't do that at home, either."

Ariettea smiled at him, then at Nadette. She could still hear Matt's words in her head, and her smile fell ever so slightly. "Well, a course catalog could never hurt. It might even give me some ideas for things to look at back home." She said, trying to strongly imply that she didn't want to impose on them by going to school there.

Trent nodded, "I'll grab you one tomorrow, maybe meet me over on campus after you're through seeing Lily?"

Ariettea nodded. "I'd like that."

Chapter 12

Ariettea and Lily had agreed to meet at noon.

Trent took Nadette to work so Ariettea could use her car. She slid into the driver's seat, somewhat surprised they had just left her with their car, no lectures, no sideways glances, only the keys, and a smile. She kept telling herself that it was just what Matt had said, that they didn't know her well enough yet.

His words had left her in a perpetually bad mood.

Ariettea's combat boots seemed to hollowly thud with each step across the massive hospital, until she finally stood outside Lily's open sliding glass door, not exactly sure how she even got there, she was so tuned out.

She knocked lightly and stepped in.

Lily sat on the bed; atop the covers, lap wholly covered with books. Her skin with a bit more color than the previous visit and her eyes still glowing with the same effervescent sparkle. Her head still held a wigged collaboration of hair, most of which had belonged to Ariettea.

Lily's head turned and lit up, "Ariettea!" She exclaimed, trying to push all the books off her lap.

"Woah Lils, woah," She heard, suddenly realizing that Peter was in the room too. He jumped up and caught a book hurtling towards the floor and smiled scoldingly at Lily as he handed it back to her.

Ariettea jumped over and placed a hand on a shifting pile of books on the bed and smiled down at Lily. "Hey." She said grinning.

"Hey!" Lily replied, climbing up her arm for a hug.

Ariettea placed her free hand around Lily and hugged her back.

Lily suddenly released and looked apologetically at Peter. "Ohmygosh, Peter, I'm sorry I forgot to tell you we'd have to finish early. I was so excited I forgot to tell you Ariettea was coming."

Peter shook his head, his dark hair slightly bouncing, a curl dropping down to his forehead. "It's ok, Lils. I mean, I kind of wonder if this is an attempt to get out of doing your schoolwork, but I'll allow it." He winked down at her with a smile.

"Love you, Peter!" She said sweetly, half sarcastically, as he started packing up his messenger bag.

Ariettea couldn't help but notice he was a bit more buff than he was on her previous visit, his bicep shyly coming through the sleeve of his pullover. He looked over at her, stopped on his way out the door. He hesitated, unsure of what to do. He just placed both hands on the shoulder strap of his bag, his standard stance, she noted, and gave her an awkward smile. "Nice to see you again."

Ariettea nodded to him. "You too."

Peter left and Lily started to squeal, grabbing onto Ariettea again. "Ahhhh I can't believe you're here!"

Ariettea smiled and sat on her bed, pushing textbooks out of her way, letting Lily keep hold of her arm. "I'm happy to be here." She said with a sigh.

Lily leaned back and raised an eyebrow. "Are you really?" She asked, knowingly.

Ariettea shook her head back at her. "What do you mean?"

"Are you ok?" Lily asked softly.

Ariettea sighed. "I... Yeah. yeah, I'm fine."

"No, no, you're not." Lily patted her arm before she sat back against the raised head of her bed and pulled her knees to her chest.

Ariettea stared at the sheets, her fingers trailing the thread pattern in the cheap, thin hospital bedding. Her chest ached, suddenly worrying about the day when Lily was tired of her, as Matt had warned. When she'd turn on her, spill any secrets Ariettea had shared, dump her off like everyone else had.

She sighed, not able to look up and meet Lily's eyes. "Why did you ask me to come, Lily? Why do you want me here?"

Lily answered without stopping to think, "Because I like you, because we're friends."

"What about me makes you want to be my friend?" Ariettea asked, chest burning, waiting for an answer she was afraid to hear.

Lily responded, "Let me ask you a question, why are you so afraid of friendship?"

Ariettea felt her jaw clench, her eyes narrow, as she jerked them to look out the window, fighting waves of emotion. Emotions she didn't want. Emotions she had long blocked out. Things flooded back to her mind. Names, places, events, events she wasn't invited to. She tried to push the block back into the wall, to keep the pain, the hurt, and the anger back shoved down where she kept them.

"It sounds like you think you already know the answer to that question." Ariettea answered, finally meeting Lily's eyes. She found them soft, yearning for understanding.

"I know the answer; you think that you can't trust me, because you can't trust anyone."

Ariettea sighed, crossed her arms. "You wanna know why?"

She stood up and started to pace across the scuffed linoleum.

She took a slow, shaky breath and began to speak, slowly, like each word had to be formed inside her before it could leave her body. "I have dealt with nearly every single kind of…" She let out her breath, then lifting her chest upward, her arms still tightly holding it, she took another. "Jerk. The… Immature friends. The popular girls. The crazies. The partiers. The loners. The crazy loners that everyone warns you about, but you give a chance to, anyway. The mentally unstable girl, and her friend,"

She turned around, laughed slightly, walked back and forth from Lily's bed to the window as she spoke. "The multiple: 'I think I'm grown and can act like your superior' girls, the actual adults who claim to take you under their wing but turn out to be like the rest. The boys who spread rumors about me, probably led up by the boy who used to like me," She let out another breath, "But who now hates me."

She placed her forehead in the palm of her hand and shook her head. She felt like her brain was being ripped apart. "I just keep thinking that Matt is right, I am just stuck up, that it's all my fault that I can't make or keep friends, and that it's just a matter of time before you all get sick of me, too."

"Wait, he actually said that to you?" Lily gasped.

Ariettea let her hands drop from her face. "It doesn't matter."

"Yes, it does!" Lily said in outrage. "That's so incredibly ignorant, blatantly mean!" She shook her head in fury. "And then everyone gets mad at you for wanting to get away from that."

Ariettea walked towards Lily's bed and stood at the foot of it. She placed her hands on the footboard, shaking her head. "Look I'm sorry," She said quickly, trying to backpedal, eyes on her hands. "This isn't something that I should have dumped on you. That's not right. I'm here to visit you, trust you, not revisit my past or let it affect our visit together. Besides, I don't even care anymore."

"Now you and I both know that's not true."

Ariettea's head snapped up and met Lily's eyes. "What?"

"You care. You care a lot. You care too much, actually. So, you tell yourself that you don't, you try to believe that you don't, but if you really didn't care, well then, you wouldn't care. All that stuff wouldn't bother you." Lily's eyes never left Ariettea's.

"Well if I care that much, then I really must have been the problem after all." Ariettea walked her way to the chair by Lily's bedside.

"What could you have done that was so wrong to warrant all that hate and hurt?"

Ariettea shook her head. "I'm sure I was rude and immature and wrong and-"

"AND why do any of those things warrant whatever it was that you went through? Can you give me a specific thing you did wrong?"

Ariettea hesitated. "I'm sure I could think of something…"

"Then the answer is no! You did nothing evil or mean, and you yourself aren't evil or mean or unworthy. So stop trying to push everyone new away."

"Usually everyone just leaves." Ariettea muttered, crossing her legs.

"Sometimes, Ari, we will only accept the love we think we deserve. And if we hate ourselves, then what good does that do for who we let into our lives?"

"So that's why I just don't let anyone in. Problem solved."

"Yeah, but does that make you happy?"

"It keeps me safe."

"That's not what I asked. And I'd hardly call lonely and sad 'safe'."
"Lonely and sad are emotions," Ariettea jumped in, "I try to avoid them all."

"All emotions?"

"For the most part, yes. It's easier."

"What if I told you that being cold and overly rational, emotionless, is DRIVEN by an emotion. Fear."

Ariettea bowed her head and sighed, heavily. She knew Lily was right. She just didn't want to admit it. "And what other terribly insightful words do you have to share?" She asked, bitterly, annoyed, keeping her head low.

"Just the ones I've learned from spending my entire childhood around adults and in my own hours of therapy."

Ariettea pulled her head up, surprised. Threw her leg onto the ground and leaned forward in her chair. "They make you go to therapy for cancer?" She asked, disgusted.

Lily shook her head, "No," she answered with a small smile. "That's something I chose. Something that should be more common. Something people should see as the same thing as drinking enough water each day. A simple task to better benefit yourself."

Ariettea tried to process the thought. She spent so much time running away from emotion, from her school guidance counselor, from anything that would make her confront things she didn't want to. She said as much. "I just spend my emotional energy running away from emotions."

"And how well has that worked out for you?" Lily asked gently.

Ariettea blew the air out of her lungs, flopped back into her chair.

"Look," Lily began, shifting into an Indian style sit, facing Ariettea head-on. "There are pros and cons to letting people into your life. You always have the chance to be hurt. But you gain the chance to have amazing fun. To have people in your life who love you, who are in your corner, and stay there. To have this great happiness."

"Well I haven't found them yet."

"Well, then let me be the first."

Ariettea looked into Lily's sparkling teal eyes again.

"Let's be that person for each other."

Her heart calmed, because she knew Lily was making sense, that her logic was sound. She nodded slowly, at first not realizing it. But she continued once she did. "Ok then." She said softly. "I'm here to see you, so let's stop talking about me."

"From my understanding, friends share things about themselves." Lily quipped, suddenly jumping out of bed, pulling her hoodie up into her shoulders.

"Woah, wait, where are you going?" Ariettea asked, jumping up as well.

"You and I are going to go hang out by the beach." Lily said matter of factly.

Ariettea fumbled for words as Lily put her shoes on. "But all your IV's…"

"Can come with." Lily reached up and took the bags from their poles, handed them to Ariettea, who looked at her flabbergasted and confused.

Lily smiled and started to walk away. She stopped at the door and turned around. "Well don't just stand there!" She commanded, "The tubes only reach so far. Come on!"

Ariettea hesitated. "Your parents-"

"Know full well that I force Peter to do this all the time. C'mon." She motioned for Ariettea to follow her, which she found herself doing.

Lily led her to a side door that revealed flights of stairs. "Staff stairs," She explained. "Leads straight outside to the beach directly." She said, starting down them.

"But your energy, your breath,"

"Ari I'm going home soon! The chemo is done, I just have to be strong enough to go! This helps. Keep moving!" She said, doing so herself.

For some reason, Ariettea found herself wordlessly following her.

When Lily flung open the door at the bottom landing, the sunlight slapped them both in the face as the wind gusted inside, nearly pushing them back in.

The blue ocean spread out in front of them, the little beach was quiet and empty as always.

"I'll never understand why there are never more people here," Lily called over her shoulder, the wind trying to carry her voice away. "Once we move away from the building, the wind will die down."

Lily finally plopped down into the sand once they were close to the shore. Ariettea sat beside her pensively, on her knees.

"I love coming down here," Lily sighed, eyes locked somewhere in the distant horizon. "It reminds me of home."

Ariettea shifted to sit in the sand comfortably, crisscrossing her legs under her as Lily had. "Tell me more about home for you." She asked, squinting over at Lily through the sun.

"It's a lot like this," Lily said, eyes staying on the sea. "When I said our house is on the beach, I wasn't kidding. It's strange; it's literally the only house on the beach for miles each way. I think they passed some sort of building restriction, but since the house was already there from when my Grandpa built it, they let it stay. The house is small, like, big enough we have three bedrooms, but small enough that everyone is always close by. But when I think of home, I really just think of the beach."

Ariettea stared at the IV bags sitting in her lap. "I wish that's what I thought of when I think of home."

"Well, what do you think about?" Lily asked, bringing her gaze to Ariettea.

"I think of…" She paused, hesitant, chewing on her bottom lip. "I think of cramped hallways at school where I'm always dodging out of people's way. I think of bonfires where the other girls always forgot to hand me the bag of marshmallows. I think of a beach that I wish felt open and free, but just ends up feeling like another room closing in on me when I'm trying to run away from a group of people."

She shook her head, taking her own eyes out towards the horizon. "I spend so much time wanting to get out of that place. But maybe I just fit right in." She mumbled.

"It just sounds like you're always running from something when you talk about home," Lily said slowly. "But that doesn't mean you think you're better than everyone, Ari. Matthew was NOT right."

Ariettea shook her head, not wanting to talk about him. "Then why am I always running from everyone?"

"What are you actually running from, though?"

Ariettea took in a deep breath and shrugged silently.

"It doesn't sound to me like you're running away because you think you're better, it sounds like you're running away because you think you're not good enough to be where you're at."

"Then why aren't I running now?"

Lily laughed, "Excuse me, but just how many times have you tried to get me to stop texting you? Just because you push, or run, doesn't mean you do it out of arrogance. Sounds like self-preservation to me."

"If that were true, why can't anyone else see that so clearly? Why can't Matthew?" Her voice cracked rolling over his name.

"I think you'd be better off asking yourself why you care instead."

Ariettea sat on that thought.

"And if you really need to know, people can only see what's clear to them. They can only see what they understand. Just because someone can't see something, doesn't mean it's not there. And it's not your job to make them see it." Lily paused.

"We as humans are not all-powerful, Ari. You can't control what people think of you. But you try to stay alone and obsess over what people think. Or if you can't control what they're thinking and doing and saying, you run, to try and remove yourself from their brains. That's why you hate being around them all so much. People do what they want with our words and actions.

"If someone dislikes you, you can't change that. You just can't. No matter what you do, it can't change the outcome. You just have to accept it and learn not to care. And I'm not saying that not caring will make things less awkward, but it WILL make it more comfortable for you."

Ariettea twiddled with the fringe of plastic on the end of the IV bag. "I guess if anything, at least I know how NOT to treat people. I know how I hate being treated." She paused. "But Matt makes it sound like I treat everyone as beneath me."

"Why do you put so much stock into this one person's opinion? Do you agree with all his life choices, the way he does things?"

Ariettea scoffed. "Not a bit."

"Then why do you care?! Why do you care when clearly the way he controls his life is different than the way you control yours? When he puts into your head that the way you do things is wrong, when you disagree with everything he's doing? If you do, then I'd think you should be happy that he disapproves."

"I guess it comes down to that even though we are opposites, this is someone that I like, this is a friend, and everyone seems to hold the same views he does, and what if I'm wrong?"

"Explain to me how he's a friend to you?"

Ariettea hesitated to answer, knowing Lily was right in what she was about to say. "I guess I can't answer that anymore. I don't know how to." She said softly.

"Was what he said to you right?"

"I don't know."

"Ok, well, was the way he said it ok?"

"Maybe I deserve it."

"Ariettea, come on," Lily said gently, but loudly. "If you have this person be a total jerk to you, that you've been nothing but kind to, come at you like that, how does that give any credence to what he says? Especially when he's saying YOU'RE the jerk?"

Ariettea shook her head silently. "Maybe I haven't been as good of a friend as I thought. I don't go up to him either; I don't text him first, I always tell him I don't want his advice. Maybe I'm the bad friend."

"Do you actively avoid him? Do you give him terrible advice?"

"No," Ariettea said, all above a whisper.

"What if I agree with you? Does that make me wrong too? Are you going to tell ME that I'M wrong? Girl, we've had this conversation already!"

Ariettea bit her lip, chewed on it.

"Right and wrong are not these two black and white things that people try to convince you there are. There are more than two choices in life."

Ariettea stayed silent, and Lily continued, "What if there's a grey area? A middle ground?"

"Altering their mold still means I don't fit in it."

"I don't know why you think you have to fit anything. If people are seriously so closed-minded that their way is the only right one, I think that's more of a 'them' problem than a 'you' problem."

"But 'them' is a whole town. And the next town over. And the one after that. How can I survive in a place that hates me?"

"Maybe you need to work more on thriving than surviving. Happiness comes from you, not anyone else's approval."

Ariettea suddenly tried to change the subject. "This feels like an extremely one-sided conversation." She said, brushing sand off her hands. "You know all about how I want to get away from my beach," Ariettea laughed at herself, and Lily scoffed. "But what about you? What do you want to do?"

Lily paused; her own gaze averted to the water. "It's taken me a long time to even think about it. I was afraid for a long time to make a goal I wasn't sure I could reach. So, I've always just done the best I can to do what I can for myself and others while I'm here. That's really what I try to get everyone else to do, too. Find the happiness in what's here and now."

She squinted at the sun, "It's funny, the only thing I've ever wanted was to go to the gala here, but now I'll be home again." She laughed at herself, trailing her hands through the sand. "But I think it's really important now to set that goal. All I know is that I want to help people, like I've always tried to do. Like I hope I've helped you, as a friend."

Ariettea smiled at her lap. "That's what I always say, too. But everyone tells me it's silly."

"Well, then we'll be silly together." Lily smiled, throwing her head onto Ariettea's arm.

Ariettea looked down at the moppet of black curls on her shoulder and smiled.

She didn't stiffen or move away.

"I can't believe there's never anyone down here," She mused, scanning the beach.

Lily popped back up and looked around. "Yeah, I mean, it's not a cool spot for tanning or anything,"

An ambulance siren blared, and she laughed. "It's not a quiet space always either. I just think the students find better places to hang out, the hospital and college staff already have nice break rooms, and everyone else just doesn't know it's here. It's nice that the sun comes up on this side, but by the afternoon, it gets shadowed."

She paused, "I like looking out my window after a thunderstorm, or just before dawn. There are no lights on, it's pitch black, and the wind hits the building so hard that it makes a wind tunnel against the cool ocean air and everything is flapping, and the waves are black and raging, but in an hour it all dies down and the sun is out and it goes back to calm."

Ariettea nodded and tried to stifle a laugh. "You make it sound so easy for everything to just come back down to calm."

Lily looked over and met her eyes. "In the right place, at the right time, everything calms." She leaned over and bumped Ariettea with her shoulder.

Ariettea bumped back and giggled.

"Hey," Lily exclaimed, "If you love the beach so much, come spend the summer with us!"

Ariettea felt her stomach flip, suddenly uncomfortable, trapped. She could feel that all the blood had drained from her face.

"Woah, Ari, what's the look?" Lily blurted.

Ariettea caught herself, and laughed, shaking her head. "You know everyone always asks me that?" She said, still giggling to herself.

She bubbled up more giggles that turned to belly laughs, and she couldn't stop. She laughed and laughed and finally flopped back onto her back, squeezing her eyes closed at the sun. She panted trying to get her breath back.

She stirred the sand with her hands and kept her eyes closed as she spoke. "Everyone always asks what the 'look' means. And I honestly don't even know myself. But everyone tries to tell me anyway. Either it's disrespect or annoyance or arrogance or indifference... But none of those feel quite right to me, because it's a face that I don't even know I'm making. It's an emotion that I can't even identify." A

long pause ensued as Lily waited to make sure Ariettea had nothing else to add. "From my end, it looks like someone who's trapped and can't find a way out."

Ariettea kept her eyes closed as she dug her hands deeper into the sand. "That's how I always feel." She said softly. "I'm always looking for a door in every room I enter. I'm always looking for a way out of a conversation. I'm always trying to dodge the cage everyone tries to put me in. Everyone wants me to be complacent, but I just struggle against the chains and do nothing but hurt myself in the process."

Lily laughed in response, playing with handfuls of sand, pouring one handful into the other.

Ariettea shook her head, feeling sand crunch through her hair, stick the back of her sweaty neck and scalp.

Then she sat up, tilted her head to the side, tried the shake the sand out of her hair with one hand. "It sucks being somewhere that doesn't want you." She said, sadness creeping into her voice, overshadowing the usually annoyed tone.

"Then I guess you have to decide if you want them."

Ariettea turned to look at her.

Lily shrugged. "Hey, you're in control here. You can kick them to the curb if you want."

Ariettea laughed. "I struggle between wanting to stay and just wanting to run."

"So, why do you hesitate to run?"

Ariettea paused.

She scanned the horizon. You'd think there would be sailboats, windsurfers, but not that day. It was just empty Atlantic stretching out for thousands of miles.

"Because I'm afraid there's nowhere better. There's nowhere I belong. There's nowhere that I'll be happy."

"And that, my friend, is why happiness isn't a place. You've got to find it in yourself first."

Ariettea smiled sadly. "But I don't even know how to do that."

Lily laid her head on Ariettea's arm again. "Maybe try chasing that first before chasing a life."

Ariettea found herself laying her head on top of Lily's, as they sat in silence for the rest of the morning.

Chapter 13

Ariettea had agreed to meet Trent in front of the Ducreis administrative building, where the admissions and dean's offices were.

She was unsure of what they were going to do together; if he wanted to take her on a tour of the university or just show her the course catalog that he had to grab from the office.

Walking from the hospital, she wove her way through crowds of college students. She expected most of them would have left for home for the holidays, but somehow the campus was still thriving. Fairy lights were wrapped around each of the bare little trees she passed, and the rich red velvet Christmas ribbons waved in the wind.

She was terrified of being alone with Trent; she hadn't been since that last night of her previous visit. Her cheeks warmed at the memory as she rubbed her left arm, smooth and healed. She was hoping he wouldn't bring it up.

She finally caught sight of him chatting with a scholarly looking man on the bottom half of a tall line of concrete steps leading up to an imposing mahogany faced building.

Trent wasn't in his usual baby blue scrubs but stood with one hand shoved casually into flat-front khakis, a navy sweater covering a plaid button-down. Ariettea drew closer to see the older man wasn't all grey, but salt and peppered grey and black, with a soft beard to match. He wore a maroon sweater vest with the Ducreis logo proudly and loudly sewn onto the chest, over his barrel of a belly.

"Ari!" Trent yelled out warmly when he saw her.

She sheepishly smiled, ducked her head down as she approached. She stood on the step below the two men, the older now towering over her even more than he already was Trent.

"Ariettea, this is an old friend,"

The older man started to laugh as Trent placed a hand on his shoulder. "Old friend as in former professor who busted his chops-" His deep voice rumbled.

"-And who I now very much respect for that!" Trent spoke over him with a smile, patting the hand on his shoulder.

"Well, he brings me coffee and gory ER stories, so I let him call me what he wants." The older man bellowed. He extended a hand to Ariettea. "Dr. Quillian Abbott."

She gently shook his hand. "Ariettea."

"I've heard." He said, smiling down before letting her hand go. "I've heard many things about the smart girl with the lyrical name."

Ariettea's cheeks burned. "Well, then whoever's had my name in their mouth has been much too kind." She said shyly.

Dr. Abbott shook his head, waved a hand. "Nonsense! When an accomplished old study of mine comes along with a new young mind he believes in, young lady, you listen."

Ariettea smiled up at him and then at Trent.

"Dr. Abbott has gone from my professor to head of admissions here at the college," Trent explained.

Ariettea felt her eyes widen.

"He would be very interested in talking to you after I get a chance to show you around the school."

Ariettea nodded towards the Doctor. "I'd be very privileged." She said as clearly as she could muster.

He nodded towards her. "Then, I'll have tea waiting for you in my office." He nodded towards Trent. "Doctor."

"Doctor."

They smiled at each other as Quillian started up the long line of stairs.

Trent shoved both hands back into his pants pockets and hopped down the step and next Ariettea. "Shall we?" He asked, waving a hand. She turned to face out towards the campus.

"Let's."

They walked down the steps together.

"I have to take you to the library here first," Trent said, hands wildly motioning, eyes dancing over each building in the courtyard. "It's the best description of how many subjects you can choose from here."

Ariettea kept her head to the ground as she kept pace with him. She could still feel sand crunching in her boots. She felt his eyes on her.

"How was Lily?"

She nodded, eyes still down. "She's great. I'm going to stop back by tomorrow for a bit, hang out some more before I fly back." She hesitated. "She asked me to come to spend the summer with them in South Carolina." She said, looking up at him finally.

He smiled wide. "That sounds like fun! Hey- you could even split some time with us!"

"So, you think it's a good idea?"

Trent shrugged. "I don't see why not. Unless you're uncomfortable, but from what I hear, the two of you are quite close, so I'd say go for it."

Ariettea paused. "From what you hear?"

"Yeah, since you and Lily met, Nadette and Elaina clicked, then Alex and I, it's been fun. They're great."

Ariettea stared at the ground, suddenly uncomfortable with people sharing her little Lily world. It was the one place that had stayed untainted. But then again, Trent and Nadette were mostly untainted as well.

Aside from his knowing…

"So, how have you been?" He asked her, looking at her sincerely.

She could feel the load of the question, and he wasn't trying to hide it.

She sighed.

She stopped walking and looked up at him. He wasn't much taller than her. But his comforting air made him seem so.

He stopped a couple of steps ahead of her and turned around. He didn't say anything, and she didn't either.

She rolled her eyes hard and threw her hands up. "If you want to ask me something, Trent, just ask it." She said, tired.

He broke the gaze they shared and motioned towards a bench off to the side of the brick path that was still full of students.

She threw one leg on the wrought iron bench and sat on it, pulling the other up to her chest, trying to close herself off from what she knew was coming.

Trent sat and leaned towards her, one hand on his knee, one hand on the bench. "It's a genuine question, Ariettea. How are you?"

She rolled her eyes again. "It's a genuine question with a genuinely loaded meaning."

He smiled, tried not to chuckle. "God, I can see the stubbornness that Nadette has is in you, too." He shook his head, but stayed silent, looking at her expectantly for an answer.

Another eye roll. More of a casting upwards of the eyes, anything to avoid looking at him.

"I'm fine." She finally said, eyes locking onto his.

"All that drama, for fine?"

"You're the one who keeps asking."

"You're the one who doesn't want to answer. And why is that?"

"You know why."

"Then you're not fine, are you?"

She laid her head on her knee and watched ants scurry in and out of the bricks. "I'm as fine as I ever am." She said, muffled, her face in her sleeve.

"So again, you're not fine."

"I'm surviving." She said, hoping it would end it. It always did. Hanging in, surviving, still breathing. It was always good enough for whoever was pretending to care.

"Surviving is not thriving, Ari."

She fought the urge to roll her eyes again, but then realized he was repeating what Lily had just told her. "Does anyone ever actually describe themselves as thriving?" She spat.

"Yes."

She jerked her eyes over to his.

"Yes." He repeated, nodding towards her.

He hesitated, then reached out to place his hand on her left arm. "You can only tread water so long before you drown. You can only survive for so long before you can't anymore. There has to be more."

She scoffed, expecting him to pull away as she jumped, but he didn't.

"Nadette and I see you. We see YOU. We see who you could be, who you WANT to be. Who YOU want to be. I wish you could see it too."

"Is that why you brought me here? To help me… find meaning?" She asked, trying to hide disgust. "What's the real reason you brought me to campus? What's the real reason you guys keep asking me to come to visit, keep offering me to come to stay long term? It's not just you; I asked Lily the exact same thing an hour ago. What message am I missing?"

She threw her foot onto the ground, knocking his hand off as her arm fell off her leg. "What am I supposed to do?" She finished, crossing her arms tight over her chest.

She waited for the eye roll, the sigh, the walk away. But he stayed. He stayed, and he smiled at her.

"You're supposed to do whatever you want, with the support of those who love you and respect you enough to let you do what you want."

"But?"

"But what?"

"Where's the 'but'? The but- you have to do XYZ. But- you have to be reasonable. But- you have to put god first. But-"

"But you know all those things. You know what to put first, you know what's reasonable, all that's left is to support you in that. And that's all we want. We aren't going to have kids, Nadette and I. So, we just want to be who we would want to be as parents to whoever needs us. You're the only niece, so you get the lucky draw."

"So, your message is to find meaning in school or work?"

"My message is to find it yourself, and here's a giant vending machine of choices I know you don't have back home. Heck, maybe you don't like anything in the vending machine and decide to go get something out of a drive-through. Maybe there's some drive-in back home."

He shook his head, laughing at himself. "I think you know that's why you're here, too. You've found something in Lily, that's how friends work. How people work."

He repositioned himself on the bench. "Look, it's clear that you want something that you don't currently have. Even if you don't know what that is. Nadette and I want to be available to help you find it. That's it. That's why we're here. And that's why I keep asking if you're ok; because I want to see you find it. Whatever it is."

The wind came through the courtyard and stung her cheeks, the sun hidden by the buildings, the air in the shade nipped.

"All I want is happiness." She murmured, kicking her foot against a raised brick. "That's the only thing I find myself chasing. It's the thing I can't find."

She scolded herself immediately for saying that. 'Stupid, pathetic, ignorant, immature-'

Trent looked at her sadly, eyes lingering on that left arm of hers. "Ari," he began hesitantly, "If you really are feeling that way, you know there are... medications that can help-"

She shook her head fiercely, squeezing her eyes shut. "And explain one more completely un-understandable thing to my parents? No. Absolutely not."

"It's not un-understandable if you have an illness-"

"Trent, self-harm, and lack of happiness doesn't make me crazy."

"I would never say that. But what I am saying is that you don't have to be this sad. It's not normal to be this sad. To just try to survive."

"Have you met any teenager ever?"

"Yes, constantly, you know this." He said, not in the annoyed way one would expect, but gently, encouraging her to keep talking.

"So, you know we're all this way?" Ariettea raged on.

"No, you're not."

"It's just another thing that keeps me grouped in with the immature kids of my generation." She ranted, hand gestures flying. "Depressed teens, utterly incapable of choosing their own life path-"

Trent grabbed her waving hands and held them both tightly in his. "You're not like everyone else, Ariettea. In more ways than one."

She let her hands drop into her lap as he let them go.

"You want a direct question, I'll ask. As long as you promise not to lie to me, I won't bother you anymore, at least today."

She nodded.

"How ARE you?"

"I'm... Surviving. Treading water through senior year. I'm fine. I've also been... 'fine' since I saw you last."

"Ok. Well. If ever there's a time you're not going to stay fine, you can talk to us. We can help you."

She shook her head, trailed her fingers along the bench. "I'll let you know." She looked up at him. "I promise."

He nodded softly with a smile and stood. "Are you ready to go?"

Just like that, he was letting her out. No lecture, no dramatic disgust, just a smile.

She sighed. She looked up and out through all the buildings to catch a glimpse of the beach where she and Lily had just been.

She hung her head and stared at the brick again, not even seeing it, dissociating.

She thought of all the reasons she was wrong in wanting to be there, dreaming of being in Georgia, away from her hometown. All the reasons it wouldn't work, the tuition, the burden that she was on everyone, the chances she would even succeed.

But then she looked over at the beach again.

She thought of Lily.

She took a deep breath and stood herself. "Well." She breathed out, "Show me the vending machine. And if I don't see anything I like, maybe I'll check out the drive-through in South Carolina over the summer."

Chapter 14

When Ariettea rolled onto her stomach to turn her alarm off the next morning, she saw a text on her screen. She rubbed her eyes, expecting it to be from either her mother or Lily, but it wasn't from either of them.

It was from Matthew. "*I'm sorry for what I said to you. I was out of line. I just wish you would give people here a chance. I'm having a party next weekend; I'd really like for you to come. You can meet some cool people.*"

Her stomach turned as she did to flop onto her back.

She didn't know what to say to that.

He was more than out of line. He was cruel.

But… He had never apologized like that to her. Ever. Through all the snide remarks, that was the first full-on apology she'd ever gotten from him. She knew he meant well, underneath it all. At least, she thought he did.

She inwardly moaned at the thought of a party. She always ended up hiding in the bathroom. And here he was inviting her solely for her to make friends. She had always wanted them — more than anything.

Past voices started echoing through her head, and she couldn't stop them.

"You're eating that?"

"You wear WHAT size?"

"How dare you ask me about that! You can't possibly care; you're just nosy."

"You know, you're the one with the problem if you're alone all the time."

"I can't believe you watched that show. What's wrong with you?"

"You were condescending this whole friendship, Ariettea. You have a frequent, stubbornly prideful attitude and think your opinion trumps all."

"I guess you're too young to hang out with us after all."

"Why would you wear that here?"

"Did you seriously think you're on the same level as those girls? You're not old enough to ask them to respect you."

"You'll understand when you're our age."

"You have no idea what it's like to do anything or go through anything difficult."

"You just have a bad attitude and need to cheer up."

"WOW, I can tell you were an only child."

And finally, "If they're as stuck up as you, they'll get tired of you, too."

Every single criticism and personal attack rang through her head and socked her in the chest. Which was why she fought so hard to stifle them all.

She shook her head, told herself that none of those things were harsh or wrong. That she deserved it all and was too sensitive. She told herself she was the problem. Like everyone else did. She told herself yes, she was arrogant; she was nosy and not caring. Yes, she was fat and ugly. Yes, she did choose the wrong movies and clothes and music. Yes, it was wrong of her to think she'd be invited to the sleepover she helped plan, the movie they had talked about seeing, the concert they looked at tickets together for. Yes, she was too young to be friends with anyone more than a year older than her because she was ignorant of anything outside herself and immature. Yes, nothing she went through was ever that bad. So yes, she did have a bad attitude and just needed to cheer up.

She hated herself. She wasn't good enough for anyone, anywhere, ever, and she would never be. She wanted to hurt. Her eyes burned, part of herself wishing to talk to Trent and ask for help, the help he had offered, just to talk herself out of hurting herself, but the other part telling her she didn't need help. She was so stupid for thinking that. Even if she did ask for help, she didn't deserve any.

She shook her head, suddenly feeling hot and deeply ashamed, ashamed of being there, thinking she was worthy enough to be a friend to Lily, for thinking Trent and Nadette actually wanted her to stay with them, and of everything she had said to Matthew before she left. She remembered as if frozen in time, the looks of shame and fury on her parent's faces that day in the restaurant. He must be right. She was the problem.

She texted him back, *"**Apology accepted. Send me the details. Will talk soon.**"*

Elaina was with Lily when Ariettea arrived that morning. She rushed over to hug her as soon as she walked into the room. Ariettea put one arm around her, trying as hard as she could not to go stiff.

"It's so good to see you again!" She said, pulling away, pulling one of Ariettea's hands into hers.

"It's nice to see you too." She smiled softly.

Elaina beamed. "I wanted to make sure I caught you today; Lily mentioned she asked you to come stay with us during the summer,"

Ariettea's stomach flipped, her heart smacked into her chest, her face hurt, and she couldn't tell if it had flushed or drained, but it was hot and cold all over. 'Here it comes,' She thought to herself. 'The rejection. And I didn't even invite myself this time. I learned to stop doing that a long time ago… Ten sleepovers ago…'

"And we really hope you will!"

Ariettea felt her heart slow. "Really?" She found herself asking incredulously.

Lily laughed from her bed. "Of course!" She hollered, trying to see Ariettea from around Elaina.

Elaina softly laughed, squeezed her hand. "Yes, absolutely. Whether it be a weekend, a few weeks, the whole summer, you're more than welcome."

Ariettea shifted from one foot to the other, fighting to urge to take her hand away from Elaina's hold. She stammered, trying to find words that weren't insulting, but would convey how much she didn't want to impose. "I mean, I just…"

She looked into Elaina's soft brown eyes, so bright she could see her reflection in them. She took a shaky breath. "You guys don't know me." She finally let out. "I know Lily, I love Lily," she abruptly stopped, realizing just how much Lily meant to her. Even though she felt like she was foolish to think she had any right to say it, she said, "She's my best friend." She saw Lily radiate with a smile out of the corner of her eye. "But I would hate to impose on you guys."

Elaina squeezed her hand once more and let it go. "Trust me; it wouldn't be an imposition. Peter usually comes and stays the summer with us, but he's graduating this summer and is going to be looking for jobs, going on interviews, then setting up a classroom…" She waved a hand. "We'll feel lost without a guest!" She said with a laugh.

Ariettea smiled cordially.

Elaina crossed her arms gently. "But we wouldn't want you to feel uncomfortable either. We know your aunt and uncle well now, they know us, you know Lily, but you're right, we don't know you, and you don't know us. But all the other things combined, I think it would make up for it."

Ariettea felt herself smile, naturally, this time. "I will definitely think about it. Thank you."

Elaina rubbed Ariettea's arms up and down. "No need to thank." She smiled. "We're family." Elaina looked back at Lily. "I'll see you in a bit, Lils."

Lily nodded as Elaina looked back to Ariettea as she left the room. "Hopefully, I'll see you soon."

Ariettea waved goodbye, her heart aching at the thought of how she didn't deserve these kind people, then sat down next to the bed.

"Sooo…" Lily smirked, dangling her feet off the edge of the bed. "How'd the tour go yesterday?" She asked, nearly bursting with excitement.

Ariettea chuckled, Lily's laugh calming her wounded heart. "You sound more excited about my life choices than I am."

"I'm excited FOR you! Now really! Tell me!"

Ariettea smiled and shrugged. "There's not much to tell. It's a beautiful campus. They have so many programs that… I, at least at one time, considered."

"At one time?" Lily cut in.

"Well, you know," Ariettea sighed. "I'm trying to reconsider considering. Trent knows the admissions director; he had me sit down and talk with him."

"How was that?"

"Terrifying!" Ariettea sat back in her chair. "The man is over six feet tall and has that huge booming scholarly voice and a huge echoing office to match with books and degrees all over... But he had me pull up my grades online and basically told me that if I keep them up, with a written recommendation from Trent, an alumnus, I'd have a good chance of getting in."

"And you said?!" Lily squealed.

"I said that I wouldn't be able to afford it! But then he gave me a list of scholarships to apply for, helped me fill out the paperwork for some of them."

"Seriously?" Lily yelped.

Ariettea looked at her, taken aback. "Yeah, why?"

"Ariettea! That's a major deal! Like omg, you're basically in if you want to be!"

Ariettea shrugged. "IF I got a scholarship, IF I keep my grades up, IF Trent and Nadette ACTUALLY mean it that I could stay with them, and IF I can choose a program." She sighed. "IF I want to go at all." She finished quietly.

Lily shook her head with a smirk. "'If's' aren't 'no's', Ari."

"Yeah, but they're not 'yes's' either." She said, pushing herself up from her seat.

She stood and looked down at the beach from the floor to ceiling window. Her eyes trailed all the lilies. "I don't know what I'm supposed to do." She said quietly.

Lily hopped up and walked up next to her. "How about what you WANT to do?"

Ariettea smiled sadly and scoffed. "I wish it were that easy."

"It's not because?"

"Because... I just... it's me. That's why."

"So, you don't have a reason!" Lily said pointing a finger, smiling, backing away. She turned and jumped back on to her bed. "Just think about what you want, Ari. It's ok to do."

Ariettea turned around and smiled at her, let her hands fall from their position of tightly crossed around her chest. "So, what are you going to do when you get home?" She asked Lily.

"Well, I'll still have to finish out my school year. Peter will video chat with me to help out, so that'll take most of my time, like any kid I guess. And then I don't know. I guess I'll have to relearn what life is like outside of doctors and treatments."

Ariettea sat on the bed across from her. "You get to join all us losers out in the world."

Lily shook her head. "And I can't wait!" She grinned so big; her smile seemed to take up her whole face.

"What do you like to do in town at home?" Ariettea asked.

Lily smirked. "Trying to get a feel for what you'd be in for, eh?" She giggled. "It's a resort town, you know? So it's like, quiet in the offseason, but then AirBnB guests take over in the summer. When it's summer everything really comes to life. There's this restaurant on the beach called 'The Shack' that everyone flocks to, they have karaoke nights in the summer and you can hear it from anywhere in town. It seems like it's been so long since I've been home, one of my favorite things to do was get ice cream and just walk around town, go into all the seasonal shops by the shore. It's similar to here, really. Except here stays busy with the school. You know what I like! Movies and music and books that are too old for me."

They both chuckled.

"But honestly, I just love our house. I love the back deck, our strip of beach. Most days I just sit out there and do nothing. I love opening the patio doors and smelling the ocean. I love having people come over, our congregation, our family, being around people is my favorite thing!"

Ariettea smiled at her. "Sometimes I wish it was mine."

"You don't have to love being around people."

"But I should."

"Says who?"

"Says, everyone! Says god!"

"God says to love people, but that doesn't mean you have to plan your life around hanging out with people. He did give us all free will, after all. 'Should' is a thing that YOU make up."

"Not really. It's what my parents make up. What my congregation, my school, my town makes up."

"Ok so it's what they make up. Doesn't make it right."

Ariettea sighed. She played with the fuzz on her jeans.

"What do you do when you're at home?" Lily lobbed to her.

"I…" Ariettea laughed at herself. She didn't do much. "I go to school, in the ministry, I do homework, I go wherever my parents take me when they have dinner out with friends. So usually, that means I play on my phone, scroll through Instagram, pretending I actually have friends to follow when I'm really just looking up memes and quotes and places to travel. In the summer, I do all the same things, just without school. It's sad."

"Why?"

"I just wish there were more. There was more to anything."

"I'm sorry." Lily's teal eyes fell. "I'm so sorry you feel that way, Ari. I really am. You know I'm here for you. To help you have that 'more'. You do the same for me."

Ariettea shrugged. "I guess that's why I focus on school so much. It's the one thing I've got to do, that I've got no choice in doing, but if I do it well, maybe one day I can do something more. But I have no idea what."

"What did you ever picture?"

Ariettea scanned the ceiling. "Honestly, I pictured being a mom, a wife, but also having something I enjoy doing outside of the house, a job I like."

"Like what?"

"C'mon Lily, you know what."

"You just took a tour of your options. So you c'mon, say it out loud."

Ariettea rolled her eyes. "A nurse or a social worker or a therapist or anything where I feel like I can make a difference. Especially for people, for teens, like me." She paused. "I've never wanted that to be my whole life, though. I don't want to be in school for a long time. I just want to enjoy whatever it is I do in my life. At work, at home, working for God's glory. But outside of all that, too."

She started to shake slightly, as she finished: "Not that I deserve any of that."

Her mind felt like it was stuck in a game of ping pong. Ping to happiness and a future, all the things she and Lily had spent months talking about, and then pong to undeservedness and shame from all the years of torture that she took as meaning that she was damaged.

Lily took her face in, suddenly very concerned. "Ari, where is all this coming from? I'm starting to worry about you."

Ariettea felt even more guilty as she waved a hand. "I got a text from Matt this morning, apologizing, saying he just wants me to give people a chance, inviting me to a party next weekend to make new friends."

She shook as she took in a breath, trying not to cry, the shame burning in her stomach. "I mean, he's right, everyone is right. I'm too picky and rude. I feel terrible taking up all your time, too. You've got so many better people than me to spend time with."

Lily shook her head, grabbed Ariettea's arm, and held on. Ariettea tried to take her arm back slowly, but Lily pulled harder, warmth radiating on to Ariettea's pallored skin.

She couldn't answer. It hurt too much. She tried to shove it down.

"I'm glad Matt apologized to you. Even as half bootied as it sounds to me."

Ariettea couldn't help but giggle but was still shaking.

"But don't you dare take the apology as him being right in ANY way. Don't you dare take it as evidence that every awful thing ever said to you somehow has credence. That you're picky and mean and wrong and deserved anything less than kind. Don't give that boy that power."

She wagged a finger on her free hand. "I know how you think by now, after all these months. Don't give any belief to any of the awful things those awful people say."

She scooted closer to Ariettea and hugged her around the waist. "You deserve SO much more than you think you do, Ariettea. You said I'm your best friend. Well, you're mine. LET ME love you. Let my parents love you. Let Trent and Nadette love you. Maybe someday you can learn to love yourself as much as we all love you."

Ariettea laid her chin on the top of Lily's head, suddenly finding a tear on her face. She brushed it off but Lily still caught it as she pulled away.

"Great," she laughed again, "You made me cry! Thanks a lot!" She laughed through another tear.

Then another.

Lily paused, unsure if she should say what she was about to. "Do you think that's why you've held on to Matt for so long? Why you're so willing to forgive him and think he's right? Because you want a family that you're afraid you won't have? You think he's the one and only option for a family?"

Ariettea closed her eyes. She knew what the answer was. She always knew. "Probably." She said rolling her eyes as they opened.

"There are more men in the world than him."

"He's the only one to ever look my way."

"Yeah, but he's also looked past you, he's also told you that when he looks at you, he doesn't like what he sees. And don't say he's right because he's not."

Ariettea wiped her eyes, black mascara and eyeliner coating her fingers.

Lily shook her head. "I just hate to see you tear yourself down over someone, someone's, who don't seem to have very good qualities themselves."

Ariettea smiled down at Lily. "Well, as the kindest person I've met, I guess I can't tell you that you don't have good qualities."

Lily bounced on the bed and grinned. "Yes, so me and my good qualities," she said sarcastically, "want you to be happy and say that you deserve it. So, you must accept my love until you believe it yourself. Even if you think it's too nice."

Ariettea sniffled and then flopped onto her back. "So, what would we be doing if I came to visit then?"

Lily beamed, her teal eyes sparkled and danced, black curls framing them as she answered, and they planned together.

Chapter 15

Nadette slammed the brakes and listened to them grind in her old Jeep Wrangler. She looked over at Ariettea apologetically. "Sorry," she laughed, wincing, self-deprecatingly.

They were on their way to the airport.

Ariettea shook her head and laughed hard. "Nadette, you have your own OB/GYN practice, Trent is the ER attending, WHY do you drive this hunk of metal?"

Nadette looked over at her, exaggerating an aghast look. "Ari!" She said with a dramatic flair, "THIS, is STELLA! She's been with me since pre-med! She transported every single one of Trent's surfboards since we've been together. You don't just INSULT Stella!"

Ariettea doubled over laughing, and Nadette joined in.

A car honked behind them, and Nadette floored it through the stop sign.

Nadette looked over at Ariettea and smiled softly. "It's good to see you laugh like that." She said gently.

Ariettea smiled at her lap. Her heart ached as she knew that smile, that laugh, would leave as soon as she got on the plane back to Michigan.

"So, tell me really, what did you think of Ducreis?"

Ariettea shrugged, stared out the window, watching the blue and green hues of land and rivers slowly disappear the closer they got to Atlanta. "It's gorgeous." She said, shaking her head. "Amazing." She paused. "Intimidating." She finished.

Nadette chuckled softly. "You think you might consider going there?"

Ariettea stayed silent. "I don't know, to be honest. I don't even know for sure what I want to study. I wouldn't know what program to apply for." She added softly, "Let alone the tuition and housing. Given I even got in."

"Ariettea!" Nadette exclaimed, shaking her head. "You know we said you can stay with us! And you WILL get in. You're special."

Ariettea suddenly turned to her. "You and Trent keep telling me that. That I'm special. Why? Why do you guys think that? I can't figure it out."

Nadette shook her head again. "You are smart, so smart, and so mature. It's like you sit back and watch the world go by just waiting to see what you can learn. You have this spectacular mind. You are so sweet and polite. It's like you-"

"Like I don't belong in this world?" Ariettea finished.

Nadette looked over at her, slightly worried. "That's not how I would put it."

"How would you put it?"

"That you're special. Unique. You're different than everyone else but in a good way."

"That's just another way of saying I don't belong."

"No, it's saying that you stand out."

"Trust me, Nadette, I don't know a single person who would call me kind and polite. I've got a mouth that gets me in trouble far too often."

"I hardly think anything you say would be malicious."

"Yeah, well talk to some other people, I'm sure they'll change your mind."

"I don't want to talk to anyone else. I don't need anyone to tell ME my opinion of you."

Ariettea stayed silent.

"Ari, don't let anyone tell you what or who you are. We all have a different version of ourselves that lives in everyone else's mind. None of them matter."

"But doesn't what people think of you matter?"

"That's not yours to worry about."

"But if you have to build the right appearance-"

"That's on that person. You just have to focus on yourself."

"That doesn't work in a small town." Ariettea leaned her head against the window.

Nadette sighed in solidarity. "That's why you have to not care what anyone thinks but you. You literally cannot change what anyone thinks of you."

"That's why my parents say you have to make the right impression, and that you have to be perfect all the time so no one thinks bad of you, so that way you won't have to try and change what people think."

Nadette groaned. "Ugh, Ari, honestly, why would you need to care?"

"Because I want to be treated well. With respect."

"If you have to fight to win someone's approval, it doesn't sound like a person whose respect is worth anything."

Ariettea couldn't find anything else to refute. Nadette was saying the exact same things as Lily, word for word. She sat back in her seat and sighed.

She looked over at Nadette. Her multifaceted perfectly loose blonde curls gently cradling her face, her green eyes focused on the road but still holding so much care in them. "Thank you, Nadette." She said softly. "For believing in me."

Nadette reached out and patted her arm. "Just time for you to start believing in yourself."

Ariettea had convinced her parents to let her drive herself to the airport, so once she jumped up into her car after she landed in Michigan, she relished in the silence. She laid her forehead on the steering wheel and took a deep breath.

She didn't want to do it.

She didn't want to start the car and go home. To her parents, to Matt, to everyone's expectations. To everyone's scorn when she talked about how much she loved Georgia. And how she was considering moving there.

Moving there.

It repeated in her head. She'd live there for school, of course. But what if she stayed after? There was just so much to consider. There was an entire world at her fingertips.

There she was, 18 and legal, just waiting on a diploma.

Trent, Nadette, Lily, they were all telling her things that she had spent her life believing herself, that she had wished other people believed. But the vast majority of people she knew sang a whole different tune.

She sighed as she started the car up, shivered as she turned up the heat. Winters up north are never a joke. She rubbed her hands together and then picked up her phone. She opened her photos and scrolled through all the ones she had taken of the campus. She finally got to one that Trent had insisted on, a selfie of the two of them in front of the library. The building towered behind them in all its glory, their smiles prompted by some lame joke Trent had told. Ariettea thumbed past it and then went back. She smiled down at it, then set it as her lock screen background.

She paused, and then opened her Instagram and posted it. Her first post in months. She tagged the location, and captioned: ***"Had the best visit with family this week."*** She wondered if Matt would take issue with it. But then she decided that she didn't care.

She pulled out of the parking garage and began the drive home, a sly smile creeping onto her face without her knowing.

By the time she got home and settled, she curled up next to the fireplace in the living room. She pulled up the Ducreis website on her phone and began scrolling through different programs.

She was smiling down at her phone when her parents both entered the room and stood, looking down at her. "Ariettea, we need to talk." Her mother said sternly.

Ariettea uncurled and crossed one leg over the other, now sitting on the ledge of stone. She raised an eyebrow.

"You seriously don't know what this is about?" Her father asked, sitting down in the leather recliner across from her.

Ariettea shook her head. "No…"

"Drop the attitude. Now."

"I seriously don't know what's wrong. I haven't even been home for more than a few hours."

"That's exactly it," Her mother said, crossing her arms, widening her stance. "It's not anything that happened at home. It's what you did. It's what you posted."

Ariettea looked around the room. "On Instagram?" She asked slowly.

Her father nodded. "Yeah… You don't see a problem with it?" He asked sarcastically.

Ariettea shook her head. "I really don't."

"We won't tell you again to drop the attitude." Her mother nearly exploded.

Her father waved a hand at her to calm down as she sighed and rolled her eyes. "You posting that picture," he began, with an air of fake calm, "You don't see how that could be embarrassing to us? To you?"

Ariettea stayed silent.

"To everyone who saw it!" His voice began to rise to the level she had been expecting.

'Ah, there it is…' She thought to herself.

"It screams rebellion, that you are going against everyone else, that you aren't doing what's normal. What's right."

"By posting a picture with Trent?" She asked, still trying to grasp what the issue was.

"At a college!" Her mother said, enunciating every syllable. "A university! A big, expensive school on the other end of the country!"

Ariettea shook her head. "Trent really, really wanted me to tour it with him. He wanted to show me all the options I have."

"How is that an option for you? Where would you live? How would you pay for it?" Her father asked, shaking his head, his tone degrading, incredulous, sarcastic.

Ariettea sighed, brought her hands up to gesture. "Look, I got there, and the night I flew in, they asked about senior year, how was it going, what was I going to do after. I said I don't know, like I always do," she said, annoyed, trying to say something they couldn't argue with, "and Trent and Nadette asked me to tour the campus the next day after I saw Lily. So, we did. Trent made me take a picture with him after he showed me his favorite spot. I never post anything, and I thought it was a fun picture, showing that I had a great time."

"That's just it," Her mother said, walking towards her. "You are acting like you're going to go to this massive school. And again, tuition, housing?"

Ariettea didn't want to answer. She knew what the response would be. "They asked me to tour Ducreis because they said if I went there, I could stay with them."

Her father rolled his eyes. "For 2, 4, 6 years?" He spat.

"They offered. I never asked."

"And tuition?"

"The admissions office helped me fill out some scholarship forms that Trent could help with and-"

"You filled out paperwork there?" Her father asked, angrily, suddenly leaping up from his chair.

"And Trent was in on this?" Her mother jumped in. She shook her head. "I'm going to have to call Nadette and squelch this whole thing."

"But why?" Ariettea asked, standing.

"You think any degree you earn at that fancy school will do you any good here? That they actually want you to live with them for free?"

Ariettea felt her cheeks flush. Embarrassment churning. "I never said I wanted a huge career or degree. Honestly, I don't even want one. I just want a job, a life, I'd actually like. And I never said I wanted to get a job here."

Her father rolled his eyes as he turned in a circle. "Not this again…"

"What?" Ariettea asked, her voice wavering in confusion, but also knowing what was coming.

"You think you can just waltz out into the world and be fine. You can just pick up, and land god knows where. It's not that simple, Ariettea. You don't get a job for anything other than to pay bills. That's how it works. That's what everyone on the planet does. And you know full well people are the same everywhere. It's not like you can run from everyone, find some magical town where everyone thinks like you. People all feel the same way about things."

"I don't believe that anymore," Ariettea found herself saying.

Her parents looked at her silently.

"I just want to be something, someone, that matters. Plus, I've had a great time each time I've gone down there. Everyone is kind and laid back and-"

"Ariettea, you've been there two times. Please."

"And I've talked to them all continuously."

"Oh, what, three people?"

Ariettea stopped. She knew it was a battle she wouldn't win. She thought about what Nadette had said. "It's time I stopped caring what everyone else thinks of me." She said firmly, but gently. "And just go after what I want."

"That's a pipe dream, Ariettea." Her mother said, getting up to leave the room. "And that won't fly in a small town like this. It matters here what people think of you. And don't kid yourself, it matters everywhere else, too."

Ariettea stood there as her father followed her out of the room, too. Humiliation stung her cheeks, her shoulders shaking in shame. They had to be right, weren't they? Her parents were only echoing what she had heard her whole life. Why did she think they and everyone else she knew were wrong?

'You know the answer to that.' She could hear Lily saying in her mind.

She opened her phone to delete the post but saw two comments had been left. One from Nadette and one from Lily.

"***Can't wait for the next visit!***" From Nadette.

"***Look at that gorgeous smile!***" From Lily.

She paused her finger and then set it down on the side of her screen. She decided against deleting it. Instead, she responded to the comments with a single one: "***I can't come back to you guys soon enough.***"

Chapter 16

Ariettea left early for school her first day back. She left early so she could go to the beach, try to clear her head, try to think of a happy place with Lily.

She parked her car so that it faced the water. It was too cold and windy to get out. Ice caps had taken over the lakeshore. Everything was dark and utterly desolate. All the Christmas lights had been taken down. The lifeguard's stations had either been taken down entirely or boarded up for the winter. The trash cans were bolted shut and the pier was closed off.

She stared out at the water. She could see herself and Lily, sitting on the Georgia shore just the week before. Laughing, sunbathing, talking. Making jokes, finding things in common, sharing dreams of finding their places in life. She had felt such pure happiness, such a freeness. She had felt the elephant that always sat on her chest be lifted off. But it came crashing down as soon as she landed back home.

It was funny, she figured, that on the beach with Lily she had felt so happy and free. But the beach at home, all she could see was the dunes where she hid at parties. The ones with her parents, and then the parties she saw by accident, the ones she was told she was going to be invited to, but then wasn't. The parties that she wasn't supposed to know about, the ones were everyone scattered so she wouldn't see all her 'friends' together without her. She could see herself sitting reading a book, her beach chair just a few feet away from the circle of everyone else, while they all laughed and talked. When she tried to join in, offer up an opinion or joke, everyone would roll their eyes, wave a hand dismissively.

She saw herself with Matt, that day last spring. Their last normal day.

The first day she saw lilies.

She still had the two hanging from her rearview. She looked to where she had plucked hers and of course there weren't any there. But there were in Georgia. Literally. Lilies on the beach, and Lily on the beach.

She hadn't even mentioned spending the summer with Lily. It was a fight she didn't have the energy for. She felt her energy slipping each day she'd been home. She felt her mood slipping, diving past sad, past indifferent, down back into the numbness that she tried so hard to stay in. The numbness that feigned off the hurt. At least that's what she told herself. It was the numbness that somehow faded when she would go down south. But maybe her parents were right. It was three people that made her happy, not the actual place.

Her phone chimed in her bag, Lily's own personal ringtone chirping. *"Missing you, bestie! Don't go forgetting all our summer plans in that Michigan snow! Let me know what happens with Matt this week. Talk soon!"*

Ariettea responded. *"Trust me; I can't forget. Because I don't want to."*

For the first time in months, Matt came and found her at her locker in between classes.

He leaned his back up against the one next to hers and turned his head to look at her, with the look that he used to give her. The look she knew meant he was apologizing.

She smiled at him slyly. "Matthew."

"Ariettea." He taunted back.

She laughed. "What's up?" Her cheeks flushed.

He shook his head sheepishly and stared at the floor for a moment, scuffing his Nike across it. "Not much. Have a good trip?"

Her stomach flipped as she tried to decide what tone he was using. She tried to play it cool. But she also knew she was over trying to hide things. "I had an amazing time." She said nonchalantly.

He nodded; his face expressionless. "So the party Saturday," he said, abruptly, suddenly, turning his body towards her, leaning his shoulder against the locker, crossing one leg over the other. "You still in?"

Ariettea took a breath and tried not to let him notice. "Of course." She said, turning to face him finally.

He nodded. "Cool, cool," he muttered. "So, everyone'll be by around 7."

Ariettea felt her heart hit her ribs. The total ambiguity of a party she really didn't want to go to was killing her inside. "Who's all coming?" She asked, struggling to keep her voice still and loud enough for him to hear.

"Yeah you know, just the usual crew, my buddies, their sisters, their friends, there'll be lots of girls you can hang out with."

Her eyes dropped as she tried to find words but then instead, turned back to dig in her locker, pretending to look for something. She was talking to him for the first time in months, she didn't want to ruin it right then.

He caught onto her hesitation. "C'mon, Ariettea," He said, turning his back to the locker again, and angling his body away from hers, leaning his head back, "you know you need friends. I'm trying to get you some!"

Ariettea shook her head. "Who says I do? And who says I don't already?"

He rolled his eyes. "Seriously, dude. We've had this conversation a million times over the years."

"Yeah, but I never had the people I do now." She pushed, waiting for the outburst, not caring what he thought of her exclusive little world of people.

"Yeah, but they're not here. How often are you really going to see them anyway? You'll get to meet people you can see every day at the party."

Her eyes fell to the ground. "Matt…" She muttered, voice wavering. "You have always told me, as long as we've known each other, how easy it is to make friends. But Matt… I don't think you know how many times I've taken your advice."

He gave her that look. He stepped forward to face her again, his presence closer to her than he'd been in months. He looked softly into her eyes, silently, at a loss for words, but she knew he was trying to find some way to tell her he was still right.

"I just… don't fit in, Matt." She found her eyes roaming the hallway. Her eyes landed on someone in particular, someone throwing her head back laughing with a group of ogling guys. "Mandy coming too?" She asked, trying to make it seem casual.

"Yes…" he answered, drawing it out, as if to ask a question he already knew the answer to. "You know you should really give her more of a chance. She's super chill."

She shrugged. "And YOU know I've went there. Many, many times."

"A few hangouts hardly count. Besides, that's when she had crap going on. Which shouldn't matter to a friend, but whatever."

She tried not to show the sting on her face.

"She's in a great place now. She's met some good influences."

Ariettea caught sight of her down the hallway, now with a group of girls. The more she looked, the more faces she recognized. All the ones, even the older girls, that had kicked her out, uninvited her, mocked everything about her. Everything she believed in. Her face stung even more.

Mandy caught sight of Ariettea and Matt and came running over alone. As soon as she was within 20 feet, Ariettea saw Matt's whole demeanor change. He went back to leaning against the lockers, crossed his arms over his chest, and somehow managed to make his biceps sort of puff out. She watched his jaw set and become more prominent as well. His eyelids dropped to make himself look more indifferent yet alluring.

"Hey, guys!" She ran up, screeching.

"Sup?" Matt said, lowly.

Ariettea looked at him and tried not to laugh and roll her eyes.

"I'm gooood," Mandy said drawing out her vowels flirtatiously, hands behind her back, pushing her ample chest forward, through a thin white T-shirt, sucking her stomach in as far as she could, rocking side to side. She giggled lowly, at nothing, as Matt nodded at her.

"How'd That algebra test go for you?" He asked, a cool smirk across his lips.

"I did good!"

Ariettea winced.

"Hey, I told you that you could do it." That half-smile on his face. The blush on hers. "You've got it all handled." The growl in his voice.

Ariettea felt the back of her neck tingle and cringe. She was shuffling books as fast as she could, she had grabbed the wrong ones while trying to avoid Matt's glances. She still wanted to check her messages to see what Lily had said that morning before the next bell.

She tried to drown them both out, but all she could see was the smile on Matt's face, the twinkle in his eyes, the genuine expression that would flash across his face every now and again, the same way he used to look at her.

Mandy finally remembered that Ariettea existed. "Ariettea! How ARE you?"

Ariettea felt like fainting from the noxious air coming out of her butt.

"Will we see you at the party?"

She couldn't help but latch on to the 'we' in that sentence. Her stomach turned, and her shoulders burned at the sheer thought of going and having to watch her all night, and all the others like her.

She glanced over at Matt. "Yeah." She said, eyes locked on his. She looked back at Mandy. "I'll be there."

The look of bewilderment on Mandy's face was indescribable as she blinked a few times and stuttered. "Oh, well, yeah!" She exclaimed, just a little too loud. "Can't wait to see you!"

She looked over at Matt, placed her hand on his upper arm. "I'll text your mom about the food."

Ariettea couldn't help but roll her eyes. Of course, she'd be in on every detail. Matt's mom loved her. Had Mandy planned the party herself? She and Matt together? Together...

Mandy tried to tear her face away from Matt as she fumbled for a new topic. Not wanting to leave him, but not wanting to talk to Ariettea, too. "How was your trip?" She asked exhaling. "I saw that pic of you on Instagram, wow, what a crazy school..."

Ariettea turned back to her locker, cocked her head as she exchanged books slowly. "What do you mean by that?" She asked without turning around.

"By what?"

"Crazy?"

Ariettea saw Matt roll his eyes out of her side view as Mandy tried to cover up with a laugh. "Oh, just that it's... like, so fancy and big!"

"Expensive?" Matt murmured slowly.

Mandy's eyes lit up as if he had hit the nail on the head, but she didn't know what to say. "Just different than around here! From what everyone else does!" She said, pulling up her jeans in the back, restuffing her shirt, still trying to desperately suck her gut in so that her jeans that were two sizes too small didn't show the muffin top.

Ariettea finally turned back around as she responded, "I've decided to like different." She said smirking.

Mandy looked at her like a deer in headlights and turned back to Matthew. "Uhm… Okay…" Her eyes scanned Matt's face as if to look for a sign of agreement about how crazy Ariettea was.

She stepped back, "I'll see you," she said, looking at Matt, then her gaze flickered over to Ariettea as if on accident, "GUYS," she hurriedly added. "See you, GUYS, later."

"Later." Matt put out as Ariettea gave a halfhearted wave that looked more like a salute.

The whole thing felt laughable to Ariettea. She turned and looked and him, up and down, knowingly.

"What?" He asked, immediately knowing what her look meant.

"Nothing." She said, the word clipped but the vowel drawn out.

"What?" He asked, insistently.

"Just watching someone flirt." She smirked.

His entire being immediately got defensive. "Not me!" He said vehemently, scoffing, stepping back.

"No, not you. Mandy." She closed her eyes and shook her head, annoyed.

"Mandy?" He spat, trying, and failing, to sound confused.

"Oh, please, Matt. Everyone KNOWS she likes you. And the feeling doesn't seem to be one-sided."

"That's none of your concern." He snapped. He rolled his eyes, trying to soften his jaw. And again, trying yet failing. "Yeah, well, I can't help who likes me. And why is it every time I talk to a girl, suddenly I like her? And you know what, it's a fact- you for sure need to try harder with her. She's nothing but nice to you, and you roll your eyes at her!"

"Hey, Woah!" Ariettea finally snapped. She slammed her locker shut. "You asked me what I was thinking, so I answered what."

She stepped towards him, "Maybe instead of snapping at me, ask yourself why the thought bugs you so much more than when it's any other girl that usually fawns over you." She flicked her head to the side as she spoke, narrowing her eyes.

He sighed, shook his head. "Okay, okay." He paused. "I apologize."

She nodded at him, firmly and wordlessly, accepting an apology she rarely got from him. The second one in a week.

They were both about the step away when Matt's best friend ran in. "Heyyyy!" He sang tauntingly.

Ariettea looked him up and down, his baggy jeans, some Eko or Nike T-shirt, she couldn't tell, but the same snakelike smile slithering across his lips, his neck just a little too long for his body, and his head just a bit too small, his presence just could never be ignored.

He threw one arm across Matt's shoulders. "So," He said, smirking, his beady eyes looking back and forth between Matt and Ariettea. "Is this thing back onnn orrr what?"

Ariettea felt her eyes widen. "What THING?" She asked harshly.

Matt threw his arm off him. "Man, Lennox, would you just shut your mouth?"

Lennox laughed, stood on one foot, teetering backward. "Oooops!" He pointed at Matt. "Don't let mommy and daddy find out about this again, bro!"

Matt tried to scream at him, but his words got lost in the crowd as Len was already halfway down the hallway, still screeching.

Ariettea turned back to Matt. "Was he HIGH?" She asked aghast.

He shook his head, waved a hand. "He's on some sort of idiot juice."

She knew full well her first question was valid, that her assumption was correct.

Matt furrowed his brow and pinched it. Then he shook his head and tried to look normal again, stepping away. "Alright, anyway,"

"No, no-no-no-no. Nuh-uh." She said, wagging a finger, walking towards him. "You're not getting out of this. What was he talking about?"

"I don't know what you mean." He mumbled to the ground.

"Then why don't you look me in the eye and say that, Matthew?"

His head jerked up and met her gaze, still silent.

She chirped, "Is WHAT thing on? Or BACK on?"

"Don't ask questions you don't want answers to, Ariettea."

"Well, I WANT the answers."

He rolled his eyes, stepped closer to the wall of lockers, looking around like he wanted to disappear. He lowered his voice, almost embarrassed. "C'mon, Ariettea. You've heard the rumors too. They've been going around for years."

She stared at him wordlessly.

"About you and me." He continued.

Still, silence from her.

"Seriously! You know what I mean."

"YES, I know what you mean! I got the texts too, Matt! Sophomore year, from my friends, and then my 'friends', but it's always been a rumor! One that I thought died once everyone finished going through puberty!"

"Yeah, well, once you're out of puberty is when the rumors start to make you look bad- when they start to seem like they're more than rumors." He said, barely above a whisper.

"So, I would make you look bad?" She spat at him.

"No!" He said, holding his hands up. "Look, Lennox is an idiot. He never left middle school. Pay no attention to anything he says."

Matt started to walk away, and Ariettea reached out to stop him. "But what did he mean about your parents?" She asked insistently.

Her hand on his arm, she realized it was a feeling that she had nearly forgotten about. The feeling of strength that you couldn't quite tell was there until you felt it. The warmth that always radiated from him. The closeness to where you could smell his soap. She held her hand there a second too long and then yanked it off.

He shook his head, refusing to answer.

"Is that why-" And she stopped herself.

He looked at her as if he could see right through her- as if she weren't even there. His eyes fixed on something in the distance, and he muttered, "I've gotta go."

She silently watched him walk away.

She let both her arms drop to her sides, not caring if her bookbag slipped off one shoulder and slapped the dirty floor, and not caring that the other hand was being yanked down by too many books.

She watched him until she couldn't see him anymore.

Was that why he had dumped her, why he has stopped talking to her? His parents made him? She and Matt were too close, spurring too many rumors? She shook her head in disgust. Of course. Of course, in their town, rumors would make or break all your relationships.

She hauled her bag back up and her shoulder and threw her books in it, not caring what got dog eared or torn.

She pulled her phone out of her back pocket. Opened her conversation with Lily. ***"You'll never guess what just happened."***

But she couldn't help but notice the smell of men's body spray on her hand as she typed.

She had barely gotten three steps out of her last class before the school guidance counselor jumped in front of her.

She jumped herself and gasped.

She looked up at him, annoyed. "Mr. Hyacinth," She said, trying not to growl.

He towered over her, his somewhat lanky frame well over six feet.

"Excuse me." She hissed, stepping aside him.

He stepped back in front of her, his out of season scarf brushing her in the face. "Actually, Ariettea, I've been waiting for you, could we talk a moment in my office?"

He waved a hand down the hall, and she rolled her eyes behind his back and followed his long strides to the other end of the building.

"You must really have something to say if you came all the way to meet me at my last class." She said, sitting down on an all too comfortable navy loveseat, throwing her bag next to her feet.

He sat to her left in his own armchair, as opposed to behind his desk. He brushed his hand down the dark stubble on his chin. So many girls in the school thought he was adorable, his tousled brown hair, always at least two weeks' growth of stubble to match. Khakis, maroon V neck sweater, some sort of scarf that did not go with anything else he wore. And his brown eyes, always trying to show concern. Everyone else fawned, but in reality, he just always tried to seem 'cooler' than he actually was.

"I just know how much you love to see me, Ariettea." He smiled and laughed.

She had spent nearly four years trying to stay out of his office, and here she was in the home stretch and yet....

"I actually just wanted to touch base with you over your possible college choices, or should I say, choice." He grinned wide at her, pushing his fingertips together, proud of something, but she had no idea what. It's not like he did anything for her, ever.

She looked at him, her heart pounding, already knowing she was about to be infuriated at whoever blabbed about Ducreis. She kept her social media's private for a reason, and yet in a small town, stuff like that always gets out, no matter how hard you try to keep a lid on it.

Ariettea chuckled lowly, tongue in cheek, trying to hide her anger. "Mr. Hyacinth,"

"Brooks is fine, Ariettea, I've told you for four years, we're friends in here."

She sucked on her tongue, bit it, and continued. "I'm not exactly sure where you're coming from?" She chirped.

He blinked a few times, confused. "I... was told, I mean I heard... that you are basically a lock-in at Ducreis University?"

She stared at him.

"In Georgia?" He said, unsure.

She rolled her eyes. "I know where it is, Brooks." She shook her head, pulling her phone out of the front pocket of her messenger bag, checked the time.

"Well, I would hope so if you're going there! And I mean why hide this momentous-"

"I'm not in, Brooks." She said plainly, throwing her phone in her lap.

He blinked. "Come again?"

She crossed her arms. "Where exactly did you 'hear" air quotes, "that I got in?"

He clapped his hands together, then pulled them apart. "It's just one of those things you pick up in the hallways... I mean senior year come on..." He laughed, trying to play it off.

She shook her head at him. "Seriously, whose mouth did that straight up rumor come out of?"

His shoulders dropped, defeated, knowing he wouldn't win a battle against her. He shook his head again as his voice dropped the fake cheery timber. "I honestly couldn't tell you," He sat back in his chair, "I was getting something out of the cafeteria when I heard the university's name, and then your's, how you got in and won't admit it..." He trailed off, waiting for a response from her that wouldn't come. "So, I mean, there's no truth to that?"

She shrugged, crossed her legs, and leaned further back into the couch, furious but indifferent. "All I did was tour it with my uncle. I posted a picture, and suddenly I'm off living the high life. I haven't applied to anything, anywhere, so no, it's not possible I was accepted to any university."

Suddenly, Brooks Hyacinth was grinning like the Cheshire cat.

"Well, hey!" He said, jumping up, literally. "That's where I come in!"

In two steps, he was digging around his desk, shoving a bamboo plant out of the way, pulling succulents and candy wrappers simultaneously out of drawers.

"Let me grab some books… catalogs…."

"My. Hyacinth," Ariettea called from her spot on the couch.

"And I'll pull up their website,"

"Mr. Hyacinth,"

"and grab your student file…"

"BROOKS!" She finally yelled.

He looked over at her, unfazed by the yelling, but his attention finally grabbed.

"I NEVER said I wanted to go there!"

He looked at her, like a wet puppy dog, completely befuddled. "Well… Why not?" He asked, flopping himself down behind his desk, arms dramatically falling down with his hands full of brochures.

He held her student file in one hand and waved it at her. "Ariettea, we've talked about what's in here! These grades, your interests, you can have any pick, of any program, anywhere! Not all kids are that lucky. I don't understand why you just don't want to go to college! Or just pick a liberal arts program somewhere to get your feet wet!"

She sighed and leaned forward, ready to run. She thought about explaining it all again, arguing all over again, but she decidedly stood up, picked up her bag, and stood in front of him at his desk.

He stopped her before she could start. "Ariettea, you don't understand, you're too young, you can set up your entire future! Or you can spoil it! You can go anywhere, become anything! Think of all the money you can make. That you NEED to make."

Ariettea shook her head. "Mr. Hyacinth, I really appreciate your concern. But I don't ever want to choose a job just based on money. I don't want to be stuck in school for something I end up hating or wasting time in some meaningless liberal arts program."

He started to interject, rebuttal, but she held up a hand. "There are things that are more important to me. If I choose to go to college, which I'm not even decided on, it'll be so I can work a job I like. Not for a career, not for money, but for me. For my life. My real life."

He shook his head. "Ariettea, you don't understand. You HAVE to choose a job based on money. How will you live? How would you pay off student loans!?"

"I never said I wouldn't choose a job, just that I'm not going to waste my life, my money, on one."

"But we both know how bad you want to get out of this town! You're going to need a career to do that."

It was always 'that can't happen in this town' with everyone, but then they'd turn around and get mad she wanted to leave. Even the school guidance counselor was now talking out both sides of his mouth.

She was stuck between annoyed, and broiling, livid, at him, at whoever blabbed to whoever else about a simple picture she posted, and whoever it was that decided to turn her life into a group discussion. She was mad at her parents for being right about the picture, and at her town for being what it was.

She looked down at the background on her phone, she and Trent on the library footsteps.

She looked straight into Brooks' face as she firmly said, "Respectfully, Brooks, I disagree."

Chapter 17

By the night of Matt's party, she was still trying to make sense of what he said, what he meant earlier that week. He hadn't talked to her since.

She was standing in front of the mirror by her front door, responding to a message from Lily, who had been trying to help her wade through it all. She shoved her phone in her leg pocket and looked at her reflection. Pale, as always. This was first party she'd been invited to since Sophomore year, since that party she'd be dropped off at home from as the rest of the girls continued the night without her, without telling her. But of course she knew. She always knew.

She pulled the waist of her leggings up, a change from her usual denim. A long sweater reached far below her bottom, over some old t-shirt, covering most of her thin frame.

She sighed. She didn't want to go. She never wanted to go, but this time she REALLY didn't want to go. But her parents were making her. It's funny, she thought to herself, how most teens' parents forced them to stay in, yet hers were forcing her to go out.

Her mother came up behind her. "You should really get going."

Ariettea turned to face her. "I should REALLY stay home and not go be around people I don't like."

Her mother crossed her arms. "You know, maybe that's why Matthew has been so distant?" She said, patronizing, knowing all too well how he had been treating her, as did everyone with eyes and ears.

"It makes him uncomfortable, YOU make him uncomfortable, because maybe you're being too picky with people? Or maybe there are people you are looking over because you want someone perfect? You'll never find a perfect friend, Ariettea, ever."

"I've found someone pretty close, actually." She set her jaw, crossed her own arms.

"Lily is a kid who is a thousand miles away. She's not here. There are other people HERE. You spend all this time with your head somewhere else, when you need to consider the possibility, the probability, that you're going to STAY here. And what people think in this town MATTERS. So, you need to start being nicer, less picky, and make those friends now."

Ariettea boiled inside. She hadn't told them about going to stay with Lily for the summer, but she had a feeling it was about to pop out.

"For you to blame HIS actions on me is not fair! Why does everyone think it's so horrible for me to want something better for myself?!"

"They don't! But when you say stuff like that, it makes everyone else feel like they're not good enough for you!"

Ariettea paused, let out a breath. She was trying to form her thoughts. "Every friend I have ever had has turned out to be a or a loser or a freak, or a sadistic lowlife. I'm sorry if I am trying to avoid that."

She turned to walk away. She wanted her point to be made. She wanted to hear a: 'I'm sorry, I understand.' But she didn't get it.

"Maybe you should just be more careful about what you say to him." Her mom said.

"You know actually," Ariettea said, turning back around, "I've been waiting to bring this up, but I'm not going to be here this summer, anyway."

Her mom turned to face her.

"Lily's family wants me to come stay the summer with them."

Her mother raised an eyebrow. "Oh, really?" She crossed her arms. "So, you're just going to TELL ME, what you're doing? Where you're going? You know that's not how things work in this house. You don't even KNOW those people."

Ariettea took a breath, in no mood for a rager. "I do know them. More importantly, they know me." She looked at her plainly. "I'm 18." She said simply. "I'm deciding where I'm going this summer. If you disapprove, you can consider it a move out."

Her mother's face waltzed a line of shock, hurt, and disgust. "Where would you go after the summer is over then?" She spat, her eyes welling with tears.

Ariettea rolled her eyes. "Don't go and try to guilt-trip me now, mom. Don't cry and make this about you."

"It IS about me when you want nothing to do with me!" She wailed.

"How did I EVER say that?"

Her mother waved a hand and walked away. "You think it's so easy!" She said, wiping her eyes.

"Because they're MAKING it easy for me, mom!" She earnestly tried to reason. "Everyone there is asking this of ME, not the other way around. At the end of the summer, I'll have all kinds of choices. And it'll be up to you if one of them is me being able to come back here."

Her mom turned away from her and cried more.

Ariettea picked up her bag and keys slowly. "I've never once said that no one here isn't good enough for me," she said softly. "That includes you and dad. But you also have to understand that what I want isn't what you want, but that's not a personal affront."

She picked up her coat. "I won't stay late."

She hadn't been sure what time to arrive. Early, to avoid walking into a room of people? But then being stuck with the awkwardness of having to talk to everyone that comes in because you're all that's there? At least until someone better than you shows up.

She also didn't want to get there late and walk into a crowd of all eyes on her, and then have it be obvious who she was actively avoiding.

And most of all, she didn't want to see it, she didn't want to see Mandy cozying up to Matt's mom, making herself comfortable in his kitchen, acting like she was apart of his family. Of him.

She tried to find the middle ground. When she pulled up outside his house, she tried to recognize the cars, to figure out just what she was walking into, but there was no such luck, his white Subaru was all she could recognize. The all too souped-up machine that he constantly lied about street racing in. His parent's car was there, of course. Still, she cringed, literally, knowing Cirise would be trying to force her to talk to people just as much as Matt would, that is, if he spoke to her at all that night, which she seriously doubted would happen. Not with his boys, his bros, around.

'Ugh. 'Why did I agree to this?' She asked herself, laying her head on the wheel, trying to take deep breaths. She texted Lily, "***Do I really have to go in?***"

She didn't wait for a response as she sighed and got out, wove her way through at least a dozen beat up teenage cars before getting to the door of the unassuming midwestern split level.

She hadn't been to a party is so many years. She didn't know if she was supposed to knock or ring the bell or go in. She finally settled on knocking and Lennox answered. He was always either acting high or disgusted with everyone who wasn't worshipping him. He looked her up and down, rolled his eyes and moved aside so she could walk in. She rolled her eyes back as she threw off her coat.

She walked around the corner and saw Mandy first thing. "Hey Ariettea!" She said loud enough to announce Ariettea to everyone there, bashing her hopes to just slip in.

Ariettea gave a half-wave to the room. She recognized more people than she wanted to. Too many ex friends, half friends, ex half friends and their friends. The rest were all people she knew their names, but their reputations made it so she didn't care to know anything more.

Mandy came over and grabbed her arm. "Come over here and meet the girls!"

Ariettea's jaw tightened, and she tensed at Mandy's touch. She KNEW Matt or Cirise or someone had instructed Mandy to do that, to take her around and force her to talk to people.

She led her to a group of girls all either in painted-on jeans or thin leggings. Most with caked-on faces, the others eyeliners smudged down to their noses. Ariettea knew she was generalizing, but she didn't even care. She knew most of them already.

"This is Tinley, Sutton, Raven, Saylor," Mandy droned on and on as Ariettea barely met any of their eyes. "and you know Hadlee and Kennedy and Madison and McKinley."

Ariettea nodded to all of them. One of them, her name already forgotten to Ariettea, smiled. "Nice to meet you. Do you go to school with Mandy and Matt?"

Ariettea nodded sharply. "Yep." Was all she could manage, or even cared to say. She slid her hands in the pockets of her sweater and bounced on her toes.

The girl, maybe Kennedy? Nodded, as if expecting more. When she didn't get it, she continued. "Well my brother Barrett and Matt are pretty close friends. Most of us go to Greyridge." She waved wide at the group of girls.

Ariettea again nodded. Kennedy seemed nice enough. Ariettea tried to smile, tried not to appear as miserable as she was. "Oh, I know some people that go there." She commented, then instantly regretted.

"Oh, really? Who?" Sutton inquired.

Ariettea fumbled with her words. There were names she never said aloud, at least not anymore. "Uhm, I know Luna Saunders and her cousin Brielle..."

"Oh, we know them!" Came a comment from one of the president named girls. "Yeah we have movie nights and stuff, Brielle and I are actually planning a party now."

Ariettea nodded bitterly. 'Yeah, we did those things too.' She thought. She fought the urge to roll her eyes.

What was even the point of friends?

An awkward silence followed.

She just wanted to leave.

"Have we met?" Tinley asked, seeming to forget she had already met Ariettea, that they took chem lab together. That they had worked on a project together. That she had made fun of her clothes to her face and her boobs behind her back.

Ariettea nodded tightly, her eyes starting to wander as well as her mind. The girl giggled, exchanging looks with another.

Mandy tried to pull Ariettea's attention back. "So, do you know anyone else from their school?"

Ariettea chewed on her tongue a moment. "Yeah," she paused, staring at her socks. "I knew Iris." She said, suddenly nauseous.

That was the name she hated repeating most of all.

Of course, Mandy immediately came to life at that name. "Oh yeah!" She exclaimed. "I remember Iris! She and I hit it off real good."

Ariettea cringed internally at the bad vocabulary.

"But they moved away right after we moved here." Mandy finished, after some long rant about how amazing Iris was.

"Isn't it funny how we all know everyone around our age group even if we've never met them?" Someone asked, laughing.

Ariettea nodded. 'I wonder what they say about me then.' She thought. She scoffed lightly. 'I already know.'

"I love your hair!" Mandy suddenly screeched to someone who had just come in.

With the blast of cold December air coming through the front door, Ariettea stepped away and tuned them out. She looked around the living room. She saw Matt and Lennox and all their boys in a huddle laughing over a video on someone's phone.

She glanced over at the opening to the kitchen and saw Cirise messing with some frozen chicken. She waved. Ariettea waved back and went into the kitchen.

She wasn't sure she wanted to be in there either if Lennox was right. If Matt's parents had warned him away from her.

"Hey there," Cirise said to her, smiling, the midwestern accent strong. "Havin' fun?"

Ariettea shrugged, smiled fakely, and not hiding that it was fake. "You know me." She said softly.

Cirise laughed. "Oh, honey. Get back out there and have some fun! You know the Taft girls are really sweet."

Ariettea looked at her, confused. "Which girls are those?"

Cirise looked at her, knowingly, tried to force a laugh. "Oh you." She shook her head.

Ariettea knew what she was thinking, what everyone thought of her, what she thought of herself.

But she already made her decision.

Any good friends of Luna or Iris or any of the other names weren't people she wanted to talk to.

"Mandy was really excited you were coming tonight," Cirise commented, bending over the oven.

Ariettea stayed silent.

Cirise turned around and saw the look on her face. "Come on now, Ari, put the look away. You know she needs our support."

Silence.

"It's not her fault, the house she was raised in."

"But it is her fault when she punches people's faces in the school hallway."

Cirise set her face in dissatisfaction and turned away. "She needs friends." She sniped, accusingly.

"Yeah," Ariettea drew a long breath in, "and I took her to the mall. The movies. The beach." Ariettea repeated for what felt like the millionth time.

Cirise pulled ice out of the freezer and dumped it into the cooler on the floor. "Well we all have to be kind to her situation." She repeated.

"Kind to her situation doesn't mean letting her tell me I was the most boring person she'd ever been around after I spent all that time driving her places that I didn't even want to go to."

Cirise rolled her eyes. "I'm sure she was kidding."

"She wasn't kidding when I told her I wouldn't take her to her secret boyfriend's house, and she threatened to slash my tires."

"Just because that happened to someone else doesn't mean she would have done it to you. She's got goals now, and that boy wasn't a secret boyfriend, just a close friend."

Ariettea took in a pained breath, tried not to rub her face. She was already exhausted. How did that girl have everyone so fooled? How could she wallop on a girls face in the school hallway and still have more people like her than Ariettea did?

"OH, CIRISE!" Mandy burst in. "I forgot to tell you!" Her high pitched tenor screamed. "I put in my application for that ministry program!" She said, loud enough for the entire party to still hear her.

'Oh, that's why.' Ariettea thought, bitterly.

Cirise threw down her tray of taquitos. "Really?! Oh that's such great news! We're all so proud of you!"

Mandy tried to fake a humble smile and failed. Conceit was smeared all over her packed on nose highlighter, her over plucked brows.

Cirise rushed to completely envelope her in a hug. Mandy was soaking in all the praise.

"Well you know, it's just like, what else could I spend my time on?" Her eyes flashed over to Ariettea, a look of superiority dancing through her gaze. "It's the only right choice."

Ariettea's chest burned. She could have it so easy. She could tell the same lie. Because, of course, it was a lie. Mandy had been cutting gym to do drugs in some kid's car the whole semester. Going into full-time ministry was not something she'd ever do. But telling the truth wouldn't get her the attention she wanted.

Ariettea couldn't help but feel Cirise's eyes scan her as she answered Mandy. "That's exactly the right attitude, doll!"

Ariettea rolled her eyes and turned around, letting her hand trail the old green linoleum countertop. The one she and Matt had sat at doing homework together during junior high.

The living room wasn't safe; the kitchen wasn't safe; she had nowhere to hide.

She looked over at all the girls laughing. One of them was pointing at the kitchen. Then, Ariettea realized, was actually pointing at her. She turned her head away but strained to listen.

"Why doesn't she talk to anyone?"

Her stomach burned.

"I don't know; we were nice enough. Asked her to sit with us, and she ignored it."

She heard Mandy's voice, suddenly back in with the group. "She's always like that."

Ariettea could see her in her peripheral vision, obstructed by her chunky black eyeliner, reapplied three times that day. She could see Mandy's massively overlined and glossy lips, big hairdo, her black hair curled for the night, like she was out for a date, the bouffant bobbing from side to side as she turned towards the kitchen.

"Ariettea! Come back out here!"

Ariettea pretended like she hadn't heard, just to listen to what conversation came next.

"You see? She's so stuck up. She thinks she's too good for us."

One girl scoffed, "She needs to take a look in the mirror before thinking she can stack up to any of us."

"Maybe she's shy."

Ariettea wished she could look and see who said that before hearing someone snicker.

"Shy? Please. Being shy isn't a thing. Being snooty is."

Mandy suddenly appeared and grabbed her by the elbow, "Come back over here, girl!"

Ariettea saw she and Cirise exchange smiles, poorly veiled winks. 'How long before the party started was Mandy here?' She wondered bitterly. 'Cutting up the friggin cheese cubes? Joking with Matt? Flirting?'

Mandy pulled her arm led her back to the group of girls that had somehow gotten much bigger than it had been. The tiny living room was becoming packed with people. All the 90's era couches were full, the shag carpet now being invaded with everyone else sitting on it, either in little groups or just skirting the edge of a larger one.

Her heart sped up as she examined everyone. They were all talking, laughing, exchanging Snapchat handles, taking selfies, the boys pulling out and plugging into the tv video game consoles that she had no clue about.

She turned back to the group of girls, looked to see who else she recognized. Her head pounded, she saw stars, no, please no. Ava was standing there. Crap-crap-crap! She caught her looking and flashed her a smile. "Hey, Ariettea!"

She was never so tired of her own name. She saw one of the girls lean over and whisper to the other, 'That's the girl Matt was-" She couldn't hear the end, Ava was talking to her. "How ARE you?" She grinned, showing way too many teeth, casually hanging onto a red solo cup.

"I'm great," Ariettea said, trying to stop herself from narrowing her eyes, hiss.

Ava smirked at her, her eyes dashing to one of the other girls that had joined the circle before mockingly asking, "Hey Ariettea, are you and Sofia still not speaking?"

Again, she fought to not narrow her eyes. "What you're not speaking to her either?" Ariettea shot back.

Ava giggled. "No! I realized she was a freak!" She looked her up and down as if to say she was too.

'And you aren't? You weren't?' She thought bitterly.

She still hadn't answered the question.

"Well?"

"Well, what do you think?" Ariettea snapped, crossing her arms, trying to cut herself off from the group.

All the girls busted up laughing as if Ariettea was trying to be funny. One of the girls looked over her shoulder at the 'cute' guy in the room.

She pointed at him to her friends, throwing her hand on her hip, arching her back to try and make herself look enticing.

"Oh, the crazy people we used to hang out with! The ones we don't want to admit to." Again, another up and down critical look.

As Ava lamented, Ariettea was losing her ability to care what that statement actually meant. She didn't feel like caring about anything the more the evening went on.

Ariettea had ignored her but couldn't ignore Mandy suddenly smiling smugly. "Oh yeah, Ariettea has more secret relationships than you think!"

Ariettea's head whipped around to look at her, and suddenly Mandy, sitting on the couch arm, had her full attention.

She raised an eyebrow. "Excuse me?" She asked flatly.

Mandy giggled, elbowed the girl next to her in the arm. "See, I told you she wouldn't fess up to it!"

Ariettea felt her blood pressure rising. "I'm lost." Her words again came out flat.

Mandy took her feet out from under her on the couch and placed them on the floor in determination. "Come on!" She smirked at Ariettea, the look on her face conniving, showing that she was enjoying this all too well. Enjoying the crowd whose attention she had, could always have. She shook her head. "What's really going on between you and Matt?"

A few of the girls started to laugh.

"What do you mean?" Ariettea snapped.

Mandy rolled her eyes. "Ok, should I be asking what WAS going on between you and Matt?" A satisfied smirk slithered across Mandy's face, all too pleased with herself for embarrassing Ariettea, for making herself look better.

Ariettea rolled her own eyes. "I genuinely have no idea what you mean. There was never anything openly or secretly 'going on'. At least not like half the relationships in this room."

She felt the comment hang, hitting too close to home for a few of the girls.

Mandy rolled her eyes and sighed. "Fine, don't tell us!"

More giggles.

Ariettea turned from them, trying not to shake her head. She was watching others file in. More girls walked in. One was standing out more than the others.

Iris.

Ariettea felt her heart and stomach drop to her feet. No. No-no-no-no-no-no. NO! How could SHE be there? She had MOVED! Moved states!

She watched her bounce in, hug everyone in sight, laughing and squealing loudly. She was dressed in a hot pink mini skirt that was completely stupid for the three feet of snow outside.

She was talking loudly like she always did, like she had told Ariettea she did- so everyone could hear her. Back when they spent every waking moment texting. Hanging out. Until… It was all over.

Ariettea knew she'd be coming over, hugging her and simultaneously making snide remarks about her and Matt, as she did at the end of their 'friendship'.

Her phone buzzed, and she pulled it out, thankful for something to steady her now shaking hands. Lily to the rescue, as always. ***"I say leave and go get some better food than dumb veggies or whatever they serve at teen parties. Like I would even know. Lol."***

"Ariettea!" One of the guys suddenly called. She looked over at him, not exactly sure if it was August or Flint or Branson, they all looked alike, and none of them ever talked to her. "Ducreis, huh? Think you're going to fit in there better than here?"

Matt suddenly elbowed him, his eyes suddenly showing the fact that HE was the one that had been telling everyone about her and Ducreis.

Her eyes met Matt's, and they stung, feeling betrayed by him.

Yet again.

His eyes somehow showed a combination of remorse and disgust. Both aimed at her.

Panic started rising through her.

She was suddenly all too aware of her own body, her hands suddenly too big, her height too tall, her sweater too long.

She felt the walls closing in.

She suddenly ran, not caring what everyone else thought of her, not even having the strength to fire back every cutting and vile thing she could think of.

She locked herself in the upstairs bathroom, the one that only someone who had been to the house knew about because it wasn't the guest one.

She had been in that house so many times, before Mandy, before Matt refused to look at her.

Before she stopped nodded nicely at what everyone told her they expected of her and started telling everyone she wasn't going to stay in that rotten little town.

Before everyone rolled their eyes when she walked into their congregation.

She stood at the vanity and looked at herself in the mirror.

Her knuckles were white, clutching the sink.

Her face was pale, paper than usual, making her eyeliner seem even thicker than it was.

Her brown eyes looked muddy, and her the whites of her eyes red.

Why?

Why did it eat at Matthew so much that she wanted to go to college? That college? That she was scared of people? Why did it bother everyone?

'Because you're too picky.' She heard her mother in her head.

That feeling was coming over her.

The one that made her trace her arm, yearning for something sharp.

It was over;

she couldn't-

it wasn't-

there was no reason-.

Ariettea gave up.

She slipped down onto the floor and pulled her knees to her chest.

There she was, at another social event, hiding shaking on the bathroom floor.

She stared at the pink fuzzy cover on the toilet seat lid.

Why?

Why was this all happening? And why did it never end? She was ready to go home but not ready to explain why. Not to Cirise or Mandy or Matt or her parents.

She could say she was sick. Her stomach did really hurt. But that was always her excuse. Every single time. It didn't matter that it was always true.

Her heart was pounding so hard that her entire chest hurt, and her hands felt like ice as she held them to her face.

She envisioned in her mind the perfect outcome, Matt coming to knock on the door, holding her in his arms, apologizing, and telling her it was ok for her to leave the party, that he wouldn't mind.

That he loved her, and he understood.

But she knew that would never happen. Not when his boys were around. And not ever.

She knew someone would be knocking on the door sooner or later. She ran the water just for show in case someone was listening. She was able to slip out of the bathroom, down the back stairs, and out the back door without a single person noticing.

She didn't even grab her coat; suddenly happy her anxiety always made her keep her keys in her pants or sweater pocket. Bra if need be.

She hopped in her SUV and drove around, the two lilies on the rearview seeming to mock her. Matt didn't care about her, and maybe Lily didn't either. Who did?

Ariettea found herself waiting for a text from someone, asking where she went. She wasn't sure she even wanted it to come. Even though she knew it never would.

No one would miss her.

No one ever did, no one on the entire planet.

And no one ever would.

She was worthless.

But what she was worried about was what Matt would say the next time he saw her. He was no master of subtly. If he was upset, everyone would know, and why.

She was driving in circles.

She gasped in air as she slammed her hand up against the dash, the radio, shaking the entire front end. The volume knob dug into her skin, and she liked it.

She came up to a stoplight and slammed her fists into it again.

She wanted to scream.

What was REALLY bothering her? That nearly every single person she had a bad history with had all shown up? Was it she couldn't take all of them at once? That she was afraid of being put down or hurt? That she was upset that Matt didn't even care?

She wanted to cry.

No. No, she didn't.

She didn't want to act like a child.

Suck it up.

She got mad. What was Matt's problem? Why did he even want her there? Why did he even care? All he cared about was Mandy now. He didn't even like her anymore! She remembered when he did. She remembered how he'd never let a school day pass without talking to her. How he could always tell when one day was more sucky than usual, and he'd ask her if she was alright with that look and those big brown eyes…How he'd playfully tease her, and she'd tease him back.

It wasn't there anymore. She wondered how long it'd be until he finally asked Mandy out, officially, and with his parent's blessing. Ariettea was to be stayed away from, but Mandy was welcome in their home at all times.

Sure, high school didn't last forever, but where was she going after it anyway? She didn't have a career picked out, and any relationship was off the table, she knew she wouldn't be getting asked out anytime soon. It was no secret to her what people thought of her.

She had spent so much time as a teen sobbing and begging God so many times for SOMEONE to JUST text her, for her not to be alone, so she could survive. But the text never came. But she was there, wasn't she? Didn't that count for something? She wasn't sure.

She thought of Trent, what he had said about surviving vs. thriving. She wasn't sure she was even surviving anymore.

More things were racing, flooding back to her mind. All the reasons she was glad no one ever texted. All the reasons she had to STAY alone. All the reasons she had to fight to stay numb. Because if she wasn't numb … then she was feeling what she was feeling in that moment.

A deep, dark emotion that was too much.

She ended up parked at the beach. The sun long set, she sat in pitch-black darkness and cracked the window just to hear the waves. But they were all enveloped in ice caps and snow that absorbed the sound.

She leaned her head against the frosted window.

Her breath was coming in gasps.

She was shaking. Not from the cold, but from all the feelings, the emotions. The memories.

It was overwhelming her, and she wanted a way out.

She wanted something sharp in her hand, on her arm.

But then she could see Trent in her mind, looking at her not with shame or disappointment, like everyone else did over tiny issues, but with concern, even when she was doing something wrong. The look on his face when he pulled her aside and talked to her soul.

She wanted out.

She was trapped in her car, trapped in that town.

She was starting to feel like the only way out of there was to die.

It wasn't a threat she made just to upset anyone like her mother thought. It was a true feeling of terror and despair. It wasn't like she had any hope for a way out. Everyone was right, Ducreis was a dream. And everyone there hated her no matter what she did.

She just wasn't sure if she could bear it any longer.

Trying to calm the shaking, the gasping for air, she picked up her phone and thought of Lily. Thought of calling her, just having someone to talk to. But the idea of friends was too far fetched for her at the moment.

The lock screen flashed the photo of her and Trent.

She paused.

She stayed paused, thinking.

She unlocked her phone and hit his name in her contacts. The phone rang in her ear and she pulled it away to end the call after the first ring, she was being foolish.

But he answered.

She couldn't say anything.

"Hello? Ariettea? Are you there?" He was somewhere loud, with lots of voices. It was a Friday night, surely, he had a life. He and Nadette had THE life.

She closed her burning eyes. She couldn't cry. She wouldn't cry. She never cried.

"Hey, yeah, I'm here. Sorry to bother you, I was about to hang up, it's nothing-"

"Ariettea what's wrong?"
She could hear the concern in her uncle's voice as he cut her off.
She fought the waves of feelings slamming her one by one.
Fear, anger, hurt, guilt, worthlessness, betrayal.
Fear again.
Her voice shook. "I'm just…" She took a breath in that shook her whole chest. "I'm just not having the best night and I…, and I want to… do something to stop the hurt… to cause hurt... but every time I want to, all I can see is your face." Her voice wavered as she fought off tears.

She could hear him open a door and step outside of wherever he was, from a loud room into a quiet space.

"You're busy, I'm so sorry to call, I was just alone and was about to hang-"

"No, Ariettea, stop. I'm glad you called. I'm glad you trust me. Tell me what's going on?"

She could picture him, his blue eyes growing deep and vast with concern, hand shoved into one pocket, his brow furrowed on his tan skin, his blonde hair flopping into his eyes.

"Trent," Her voice cracked as she choked on a sob that she'd been suppressing for far too long, "I don't think I can be here anymore."

Chapter 18

"So now, as we accept our diplomas, let's not think of it as an end, but as a beginning."

Ariettea sat, listening to her high school's valedictorian yell out Pinterest found motivational quotes. She hadn't even wanted to come to commencement. But she did want to definitively mark the end of something.

She uncrossed and recrossed her legs, shifting in the folding wooden white chair. A tight black lace dress hugged her body underneath a yellow gown, a dress she had gone out to buy by her own choice, again a size smaller than the last time she had gone shopping. But for once, she was wearing something that actually fit, and she looked amazing. She had on pumps to match, not caring how much they dug into the grass on the football field, and her makeup was actually blowing out her eyeliner into smoke rather than grit underneath her cap.

She looked around, nervous, pushing a soft spiral curled lock out of her face. It had been almost a year since she'd cut her hair, and it was nearly the length it had been. She was going to have to walk the stage, in front of so many people... So many people who had made her life miserable for so long. Her chest ached as her heart rate increased.

"Ok, Ariettea, I'm going to need you to breathe with me," Trent's voice rang through her head, the conversation now six months old. At least the first conversation. The first time she called him, sobbing. She took deep breaths in and out.

She opened her eyes that she hadn't realized she'd closed and watched the principal take the podium and begin to call out names. She tuned out the first few letters of the alphabet, thinking of her conversation with Lily over the phone the week before.

"It's going to be the best summer ever. We've got your room all ready. I can't wait to see you!"

She smiled, her heart calming. She had bought a one-way plane ticket, and her bags were nearly packed. Her flight was to take off that night. She was missing Matt's open house and party that next Saturday, but she was actually happy about that. At least the way his last party had gone. She was ready to be away from all of it, at least for a little while.

"Mandy Forman."

Ariettea watched Mandy walk across the stage like a baby giraffe in her high heels and hair extensions. She knew she was just jealous, but she didn't much care anymore.

She saw Mandy turn and search the crowd. Ariettea followed her gaze. Her eyes landed on Matt's family, sitting with Mandy's, and Ariettea's old friend, Aspen, with them. Mandy waved, somewhat smugly, and they waved back.

Ariettea turned back around. Of course, Aspen wouldn't even text Ariettea back once she'd moved away but would drive two hours for Mandy's four-hour commencement.

She rolled her eyes but tried to focus on the fact that she wouldn't have to see anything like that for at least the next eight weeks.

"Even if you don't want to go to school, you're always welcome here once the summer ends. Indefinitely." Nadette had said to her over the phone when arranging her pick up at the airport.

Ariettea's attention shot back to the present as she heard Matt hoot and holler loudly as Mandy took her diploma.

"She really struggled to make it through and finish," Cirise had said to her, "She really deserves a great party. Would you mind bringing those cookies you make so well?"

Her skin had crawled, knowing the real reasons Mandy almost didn't graduate. As Matt's friends joined in screaming for Mandy, that thought was ever reinforced.

She thought of her response to Cirise, "I'm actually leaving for the summer after commencement." She had said sharply, proudly. "It may end up being permanent."

She had brought her shoulders up to her ears in a dramatic shrug. "Hopefully, Mandy finds something to do since all those other plans of hers fell through." Each of her ministry applications had been denied after her arrest during spring break.

Ariettea hadn't minded watching Cirise's face change after her snarky comment. In fact, she enjoyed it.

"Quit trying to fit the mold. Quit trying to change the mold. Just throw it out and make your cake." Lily had told her one of the many nights she had answered Ariettea's 2 am texts.

Ariettea watched so many people she had once been close to walk across the stage. All the ones that fit the mold and the ones that pretended to fit the mold. She had always been envious that at least they had each other. But she also knew that she had something better waiting for her.

When her name was called, she found herself confidently accepting her diploma, making eye contact with a still disappointed Brooks as she walked by.

"You're going to regret not going to a good school." He had told her during finals.

She had smiled, finally unfazed by his comments. "Well, at least I'll be able to regret it knowing I wasn't a sell-out."

She heard no screaming for her as she left the stage. A few people later, she watched Matt accept his diploma with poise. She was impressed, until he jumped off the stage, completely avoiding the flight of stairs, flailing into the arms of his waiting friends. He had never mentioned her leaving his party. He really didn't talk to her at all after that. He wasn't cold or angry like he had been. Just indifferent. Like he cared nothing about her anymore. She was trying to feel the same way about him.

Suddenly the last name had been called, cheers erupted, and caps flew up everywhere.

She took hers off and chucked it up as far as she could. She watched it float down it what seemed to be slow motion.

It was over; it was finally over.

People started filing out. Matt and Mandy were talking and laughing arm in arm on their way back to their families. Mandy squealed and ran over to hug Aspen and Cirise. Ariettea tried not to stare, tried not to think of Aspen telling her out of nowhere that she wasn't on the same level as her, that she needed to know her place. She supposed Mandy knew her place, that she had found it in everyone's favor.

Her own parents standing with Matt's, Ariettea felt she had no escape.

"Where are we all going for lunch?" Ariettea heard Mandy ask. Someone shushed her loudly and then very obviously glanced at Ariettea.

'Yeah, I wasn't supposed to hear that was I?'

She could hear her mother's voice in her head. 'Now Ariettea, you can't be expected to be invited everywhere.'

'Just somewhere would be nice.' She thought to herself. 'And you can't blame me for wondering why Aspen won't even talk to me anymore but loves Mandy. And you can't tell me that we go out 'all the time' when really we only go with your friends and not mine.'

She was having a conversation with her mother in her head.

'They're your friends too!'

'Yeah, that's why they belittle me. Hm. Funny how Trent and Nadette don't.'

She'd had that conversation with her parents way too many times that final semester. "No one there pushes me to be anything!" She had yelled.

"Well, how is that going to benefit you?"

"By letting me actually think for myself for once in my life."

"You work to make money, Ariettea. That's how it works."

"How's that work for your happiness?"

"That's ridiculous. There's more to life's contributions to happiness other than work."

"Yeah, and how can you enjoy it if you're miserable all day?"

"Be realistic!"

"I am! I'm not looking for a dream job or some perfect life! I'm just looking for happy ones."

There were so many times she didn't think she could make it. But Lily never let a day go by without talking to her, Trent never let a week go by without checking in, and Nadette never let a month go by without sending her flowers or chocolates or edible arrangements.

"I really think you should try some therapy, Ari." Trent has said to her gently months before, during finals.

"Trust me; I can't. My parents would be so ashamed of me. Even more than they already are." She had snipped.

Not that she'd have gone.

She threw her new dress into her suitcase and zipped it tight. She had packed nearly half her clothes to take with her, somewhat thrilled at the idea of being away for so long that she'd need to take that much with her.

She tucked her feet underneath her on the plane, her first flight not being an unaccompanied minor, an empty, quiet, late-night flight, leaned back, and sighed.

She smiled.

She was finally getting what she had always wanted.

She was finally getting away.

But there was always still that gnawing feeling something would go wrong.

She fell into Nadette's arms once she cleared security before she could stop herself, remember how much she hated physical contact. She kept her face buried in Nadette's thick cable knit sweater as she held on tight.

Trent popped up behind her, and Ariettea jumped into his open arms, laid her head against his chest, his warm cologne calming her nerves.

For once, she felt like she was doing something she was meant to.

She looked down at her phone; it had just booted up from the off position it had stayed in for the last three hours. She mindlessly scrolled through her social media's as they waited for her baggage. She paused at a photo that Cirise had posted. All of Mandy's family with all of Matt's family, and Aspen, out celebrating at a local restaurant. She zeroed in on Matt, pulling Mandy in close at the center forefront. His arm tightly around her upper body.

She rolled her eyes and closed the app, opened her messages to let Lily know she had landed. Lily had been home for months by that point, and Ariettea was eager to see it.

Trent heaved Ariettea's bag off the circulating belt. "Holy cow," he set the bag down, "it's like you packed for the whole summer or something." He smiled. "I like it!"

Nadette laughed at him as she took Ariettea's arm in hers. "So, graduate," she grinned, pulling Ariettea close like a couple of girlfriends, "the night is yours! We only have you until tomorrow. Where can we take you?"

Ariettea smiled. "Can we go to the beach?"

A couple of hours later, they all sat, corn dogs and fries in their laps, staring out at the moonlit ocean.

"You know you have a lake at home," Trent laughed, seeing Ariettea captivated by the moonlight.

She watched it bounce and sparkle against the waves and ripples the current was making.

She shook her head. "It's a different smell," She and Nadette said in unison. They both laughed, Nadette leaning towards her.

Ariettea shook her head again, "When I'm at that beach, I'm usually hiding from people, or I'm stuck with them. Every time I've been to a beach down here, it's ended in the best way possible. With people I love."

Nadette smiled as she threw her arm around her and pulled her close. Ariettea laid her head on Nadette's shoulder. "So, you made it through commencement unscathed?" She asked.

"And without falling asleep?" Trent added.

Ariettea laughed. "There were too many people around to relax that much."

She noticed Trent's eyes flash over to her and then back. She knew what he was thinking.

She could hear the conversation from the night of Matt's party play back in her head. "Ari, breathe, okay? Breathe with me,"

Her chest ached, remembering how those shaky breaths rattled her bones. "I. Can't. Do it." She had said, sobbing in between syllables.

She hadn't cried since. She never let herself cry, that night had been her breaking point.

"Did you guys do anything fun after?" Nadette's voice brought her back to the present.

Ariettea felt herself jerk, and she had to unlock her eyes from the sea. "No," she said, feeling far away.

She set her half-eaten corndog to the side and pulled her knees to her chest, her stomach suddenly sick. "I uhm, I wanted to get everything packed."

She tried to force a smile, but she knew it landed flatly.

She could still see the picture of Matt and Mandy clearly in her mind. 'It should be me.' Flashed through her head before she could stop it.

She squeezed her eyes shut and then snapped them back open, trying to block it all out, trying to make it all go numb.

"Well, I'm sorry this isn't much of a graduation celebration then," Nadette said, fighting a guilty pout.

"No, no, trust me," Ariettea waved a hand, pulled her hoodie right around her. "I don't want to be anywhere else right now."

And as much as she meant it with her whole heart, as much as she knew she was getting what she always wanted, something was still pressing against her chest. And those physical feelings made her emotional feelings even worse.

"You really think moving to some big city when you're 18 will solve your problems? Honey, you're going to a hard lesson to learn." The voice of some old friend rang through her head.

Chapter 19

Ariettea examined the scenery as she and Nadette drove north up the coast in Nadette's rickety old Wrangler, taking the long coastal route.

Everything was lush and green.

Georgia wasn't anything like she'd pictured growing up. Most of it was total city living. But then there were those small coastal towns that each had their own stories to tell.

The farther north they went, the scenery changed little by little. There were more palm trees, more soft sands, and more spots you could clearly see the ocean from the road. They passed more beaches than Ariettea could count.

She was taking it all in, wide-eyed, but was still fighting the pit in her stomach that was saying she was being an idiot. For running away, for thinking people were different, for treating everyone back home like they were wrong. Because maybe they were right.

She rubbed her temples, her whole world suddenly shifting and in doubt.

Nadette noticed and tried to pull her out of it. "So, what do you and Lily have planned?"

Ariettea fiddled with the laces on her converse that she had pulled up into her lap. "We don't really know," She laughed at herself. "It's one of those things where you get together and hang out, see what happens. It's not something I'm familiar with, but I'm going with it."

Nadette chuckled. Her blonde hair seemed even more multifaceted in the summer sunlight, sparking and gleaming all different colors. Her big, loose, perfect curls bounced as she shook her head. "Well, I'm sure with your friends growing up, you guys did that all the time! It'll be like one big long sleepover."

Ariettea felt her face fall as she kept her eyes on her fingers. She pulled her hands together and started to wring them. "Yeah, I think my last sleepover was junior high."

She looked out the window, spoke to the glass. "I was so freaked out being around older girls that I couldn't sleep all night. I sat up watching The Goonies until I finally got to go home at seven before anyone else woke up. After that, I only got to hear about the ones I had helped plan but never got invited to."

She shook her head. "So, sleepovers have never really been my thing." She finished roughly.

Nadette stayed silent a moment. "Well," She finally said assuredly, "At least this is your best friend, and you've been this close for this long, I think that says a lot."

Ariettea smiled at her, her cheeks warmed with happiness at the thought. She leaned her head back against the headrest and looked over at Nadette. "I hope you're right."

She looked down at her phone, at Lily's most recent message. *"**Can't wait until you're here! I'm finally going to have someone to hang out with for a summer!**"*

Ariettea sometimes wondered if Lily needed her just as much as she needed Lily. *"**I brought all my tacky shark movies. Lol.**"* She typed back. They were alike in more ways than most people knew.

*"**And I made sure we have the good popcorn! We can open the windows and wonder if the waves are really a whirling tornado forming, full of ravenous sharks.**"*

They went back and forth, making fun of terrible b rated movies, quoting way too many than they'd care to admit to having seen.

Ariettea looked back at Nadette. "Thanks again for the drive. You really didn't have to do any of this."

Nadette shook her head like she always seemed to do when Ariettea talked to her. "We WANTED to!" She looked over at her. "I feel like we haven't talked in ages!"

Ariettea desperately wanted to keep the conversation off of herself. "How has work been?"

"It's good, busy. I have a patient that I'm reallyyy hoping doesn't go into labor today." She stopped, laughed, and then continued, "But I love it."

She glanced over at Ariettea. "Why? Is there anything you need to talk about?"

Ariettea rolled her eyes. "No, Nadette, thank you," she started to laugh, "If there was, I really don't think you'd be the one I'd ask, no offense."

Nadette threw her hand to her heart and laughed despite trying not to. Ariettea joined in, and they giggled together.

"Oh, stop it." Nadette said once she had caught her breath. "You know I'm here for anything you need."

Ariettea smiled. "I'll keep it in mind." She threw her head back against the headrest, looked out the window. "You and Trent, good lord, always asking if I need to talk."

"We just care." Nadette said, genuinely.

Ariettea rolled her head over and smiled at her. "I want to be you when I grow up."

Nadette smiled back. "You can be anything you want, my dear. Pray tell, any closer to deciding what that might be?"

Ariettea shook her head. "I spent senior year just trying to make it out alive." She rolled her head to the other side and stared out the window again. "I think maybe I'd like to just be me for a while."

She paused before adding, mostly to herself, "Whoever that is."

Before long, they had moved off the highway and onto local roads. They twisted and turned, getting closer and closer to the coast.

They passed little local shops, fudge, surfboards, ice cream. There were tons of tourists filing in and out, but not as many as one might imagine.

They were soon in a residential part of the area, where you could tell it was mostly rentals as they all sat directly on or across from the beach. They drove further down along the beach, until there weren't a lot of houses anymore, and then none at all.

They came upon a small house, the only house in the whole town on the seaside of the road, sitting in the sand, lilies blooming all around it. It was a soft cream with turquoise shutters that somehow matched Lily's eyes perfectly.

The front door faced the road, and the house was covered with windows, sprayed with salt from the ocean. Even from the front, you could see a big back porch with a million-dollar view.

Ariettea got out of the car and pulled in a deep breath. It was warm, humid, but the sea air was unmistakable. The sun shone on her head and face, and she squeezed her eyes shut as she threw her head back and soaked it in.

But panic started to well in her as she stared at the door. She was suddenly nervous, scared the other shoe would drop while she was there like it always did, then she'd be trapped in a house with people who hated her, stuck waiting for a ride back to the airport, back to Michigan, back to what would be her ultimate fate and reality. She adjusted her denim cut-offs and pulled her duffel bag up on her shoulder.

Nadette got out of the car and came around. They both just sort of stared for a minute.

"They could be renting this out for a FORTUNE right now in peak season!" She whispered, pulling Ariettea's suitcase from the hatchback.

The front door suddenly flung open, "Ariettea!" Lily called, squealing. "I'm so glad you're here!" She exclaimed, running out of the house, barefoot.

She was so small for her age. But she was up and running, her eyes shining and sparking. She didn't have her wig on. She had a short moppet of curls growing.

"I'm glad to be here." Ariettea said, as Lily ran full force into her, wrapping her arms tightly around Ariettea's waist. "Your hair is beautiful."

Lily smoothed it. "I'm happy it's growing in how it used to be."

She pulled Ariettea inside by the hand as she pulled back to hug Nadette. Ariettea turned and realized that Nadette had seen Lily dozens and dozens of more times than she had. That her little world was a complete circle.

Elaina and Alex came around a corner out from the kitchen. "For goodness sakes, let them IN Lils!" Elaina laughed.

Ariettea sheepishly stepped further inside.

The house was wall to wall bleached wood floors.

The tiny living room was made up of a comfy looking navy-blue loveseat and seersucker chair and ottoman to match. A table that looked like it was made from driftwood sat in the middle.

The kitchen was open to the front of the house and living room and was airy, a country kitchen with a modern-beachy twist. White cabinets, blue backsplash, and cream marble counters were just accents when compared to the view the kitchen windows, wall to wall gave.

The soft sand and sea scene outside looked completely and utterly artificial.

"Wow." Ariettea breathed. "You have a beautiful home."

"Thank you!" Elaina said softly.

"It's all right." Alex laughed. He waved a hand, "No, really, I spent a lot of time here growing up. Of course, we've done some remodeling since then." He smiled, threw his arm around his wife's shoulders. She grabbed his hand happily.

"We're so happy you're here, Ariettea. Lily has been looking forward to this since… Oh my goodness, since she met you!" Elaina laughed, moving forward to hug both her and Nadette.

The two of them were quickly talking like old friends as Lily grabbed Ariettea's hand.

"Let me take your bag to your room!" She said excitedly. "Come on!"

Ariettea followed obediently to what was presumably the guest bedroom. She was surprised to see it had an ocean view as well. The walls were a simple yellow, and the bedspread was a pale blue quilt. A dresser made of softwood sat across from the bed.

Again, a massive window, covered with white wooden blinds beheld an awe-inspiring ocean view.

Lily set Ariettea's bag on the bed. "So, this will be your room…" She ran down the hall and opened a door. "This is my room." She called out.

Ariettea walked down the hallway and took in the sea of pink. Lily's room was girly. A little TOO girly for Lily.

"It needs to be redone." Lily laughed. "I picked out that color when I was 7."

Ariettea looked to see Lily's room faced the street. "Why didn't you take the bedroom that faces the ocean?" She asked.

Lily laughed, "Lilies!"

Ariettea looked out of Lily's window to realize the sea of orange and white that came up halfway covering her window.

Lily led her back out to the great room. "Let me take you outside!"

Alex smiled at them silently as he sat at the dining table in front of the patio doors on his laptop.

Lily threw open the patio and led Ariettea out onto the deck. It was circular, benches in the place of a railing, with stairs leading down to a sand-buried white walkway leading down to the water. The top of the stairs showed just how high the deck was off the sand, lending itself to an impressive view. It had to have been 100 degrees out in the sun, but with the sea breeze, it was somehow comfortable.

Ariettea looked over to see the wind blowing through Lily's hair. Seeing her so well made her so happy. "This is gorgeous." She said sighing.

Lily smiled. "And, of course…" She said, walking down to the sand, around the house. She pointed. "Lilies!" She laughed, her white tunic blouse blowing in the wind.

Ariettea paused, looked around her, dissociating, feeling as if the moment in time was stopped. Lily looked so healthy. She was torn between feeling hopeful, excited, and cynical. What could she possibly have to complain about when Lily was just coming into a good stretch of remission?

"Ari?" She heard Lily's voice break through the wall. "What's the look, Ari? What's wrong?"

Ariettea shook her head and dug her eyes away from the spot in the sky they had glazed over looking at. "Nothing. I don't have anything I could possibly complain about." She smiled at Lily.

But Lily shook her head. "You're not getting off that easy. You can't fool me with those lies." She smiled. "Are you thinking this is a bad idea?"

Ariettea shook her head. "No, just seeing you so happy, healthy, I'm just wondering how I could possibly have anything to complain about compared to you."

"Oh, bull-CRAP, Ariettea," Lily exclaimed loud enough to make her jump.

She looked at her, genuinely confused.

Lily continued, "There is such a thing as an emotional threshold, you know. What one person goes through can NEVER be compared to another. For ANY reason."

Ariettea started to object, but Lily held up a finger and shook her head. "Nope. Nu-uh. Not here, missy. This summer is about you. It's about you and me and having fun and not thinking about if or when it's going to end or how."

She smiled up at her. "It's time for you to find yourself in that head of yours. Separate from what everyone is telling you to be or who they think you are."

She looked away, out at the ocean. "It's my summer to actually have fun and relax and be healthy. I can't remember the last time that actually happened."

The wind blew through her short, black curls. "Let's do it together. Let's have the summer we've both always deserved."

Palm trees lined both sides of the two-lane street leading into town.

Lily, Alex, and Elaina were all excitedly pointing out the local businesses to Ariettea.

"There's fudge there, ice cream there, oh and over there is the funnest little nautical souvenir shop," Lily was blabbering.

Elaina would jump in, "Now we're passing the surf shop, it's newer, but the owner has lived here forever, he also owns that little sandwich shop next door to it. Oh Alex, honey, turn down here let's show her the whole town."

Alex looked back at Ariettea in the rearview mirror. He shook his head and laughed. "I'd apologize for them, but I'm just as bad, I'm partial because I grew up here." He pointed out the window. "My grandparents owned that beach store for the longest time. It's still the only place I'll buy beach towels and sunscreen at." He laughed again. "You must think this place is more on the creepy side than quaint."

Ariettea shook her head. "No, I actually think it's adorable." She paused, bit her lip. "But, it's probably not an easy town to keep a secret in."

Elaina laughed. "Yes, this beauty shop over here is where the old ladies hang out with their sweet tea and gossip. But more so about the tourists than us residents. For the most part, it's so tight not that it ends up feeling like love rather than judgment."

Ariettea felt her eyes widen, tried not to shake her head.

Lily noticed and giggled. "I don't think Ariettea can grasp the concept of a small town not being judgmental."

They looked at each other.

Ariettea found herself laughing, too. "I guess I'm just waiting for you to tell me that this coffee shop up here is run by someone that Alex went to high school with and that they disapprove of the color you painted your house shutters or something stupid."

Alex and Elaina joined in the laughter, much to Ariettea's surprise. She expected defensive, offended looks. "Picture even smaller than that," Alex said to her through the rearview. "There's not even a daycare here, let alone a high school. It's truly a vacation town. That's what keeps it lighthearted."

Ariettea's eyes danced all over the little shoppes as they went by. Yet another ice cream parlor, a boutique clothing store, a mom and pop pharmacy, a tiny coffee house.

They finally reached the end of the street and turned back around. "Now to The Shack!" Alex said, clapping his hands.

Ariettea turned to look at Lily, her eyes wide.

Lily and Alex laughed together.

"You look just like Peter did the first time we told him that." Alex said.

Lily patted Ariettea's hand. "It's this restaurant on the beach. Don't worry; it's actually really nice. The tables are all literally in the sand. You'll love it."

She was right.

Once they pulled in and parked in the crowded gravel parking lot, Ariettea could already see the massive patio facing the ocean.

They sat at a table in the sand that bordered the sizeable wooden patio.

A large, circular stage sat right in the middle of it. "Karaoke stage," Lily explained over the noise of the restaurant.

It was jam-packed with tourists. Everyone around her was sitting behind a burger and sweet potato fries, or a margarita and chips.

The waitress came running up, excitedly. "Ahh!" She squealed, popping up at the edge of the four-person driftwood table. "Your guys' first Shack visit of the season!"

She looked over at Ariettea, slightly disappointed. "But no cute tutor?"

Elaina laughed. "Easy, he'll show up sometime this summer."

Ariettea looked over at her, and then Lily. "Like I said, he comes every year," Lily explained to her, quietly. "He's setting up his first classroom, he just graduated too, from Ducreis. Got his dream job. The girls down here fawn over him all summer."

Ariettea looked at her, worried. "I didn't like, take his place, did I?"

Lily waved a hand. "No, seriously, he's setting up for his first class. But he still wants to come down sometime before school starts."

Ariettea shook her head. "I just don't want to be in his way. I mean, he's known you forever, and I'm just-"

"You're just my best friend!" Lily said, smiling. "Calm down, girl! You're wanted here."

Ariettea smile matched Lily's.

Suddenly the waitress's eyes were back on Ariettea. "So, what'll it be?"

Ariettea's eyes scanned over the menu, her stomach in its usual knot.

She looked over at Lily, and then her brain stopped spinning.

"I'll just have whatever she's having." She said smiling, her heart calming.

Once they were back home, as Lily got ready for bed, Ariettea wandered outside and on to the edge of the large deck.

The composite wood underneath her bare feet, she crossed her arms and watched the moonlight dance across the rippling black water as a soft wind blew through her hair.

She had enjoyed the constant reminder of Lily every time she moved her head after she'd chopped her hair off, but now it was heavy again, the wind swirling it up around her.

The sliding door opened behind her, and Elaina stepped out. "It's beautiful, isn't it?" She asked rhetorically, in her ever-soft voice.

Ariettea nodded. "It is…" She found herself muttering.

Elaina came up and stood beside her, Ariettea feeling ever aware of her small frame compared to her own tall and lanky one.

Her eyes on the water, Elaina kept speaking, "Anytime we've been away long, in Ducreis, I miss this view. There is nothing else that compares."

She stayed silent for a few minutes after. She finally turned to Ariettea, placed a hand on her crossed arm. "I know Lily has said it a million times herself, but just from Alex and I, we really, really, are excited to have you here. You are an answer to our prayers for Lily."

Ariettea turned to her suddenly, found herself blurting, "What?"

Elaina laughed softly. "I think we all feel like Lily adds this special magic to our lives. But the reality for her is that she doesn't have that same magic coming from anyone else. There's us, Peter, but before you, that was it."

Ariettea scoffed softly, her eyes darting back to the black and nearly invisible horizon. "Trust me; I add no magic to anyone's life."

Elaina shook her head. "That's where you and Lily mirror each other, you both don't realize how special you are."

Ariettea turned back to her. "Elaina, you, Lily, Trent, and Nadette, are always saying that to me. And I never have the slightest idea why."

Elaina kept the soft smile on her face, pulled her thin white sweater down over her knuckles as she crossed her own arms. "I think you can agree that you're different, Ariettea. It's just time you start seeing those differences as strengths, rather than weaknesses or flaws."

"But what differences? What do you all see?" "Well, what do you see?"

"I see myself as the antisocial, too quiet, overthinking, rude, cocky kid who has no meaning to her life."

"Well," Elaina said slowly, "What if we all see a thoughtful, gentle, logical, clear-headed, girl who wants to think for herself and isn't afraid to say so?"

Ariettea looked away, looked at everything but Elaina- her feet, and the deck, at the lilies around the house, the water, she just couldn't find a place to rest her eyes, so she closed them. "I just feel like none of you know me well enough to say anything nice," She laughed, self-deprecatingly. "Just give it some time, you'll see it how I do."

"Or maybe," Eliana said, stepping back, "You'll start to see it as we all do." She shrugged and smiled warmly as she stepped back inside the house.

Ariettea turned back to the sea, closed her eyes, and rubbed the bridge of her nose, fighting a headache.

"Breathe." Trent's voice whispered inside her.

She took a deep breath and kept her eyes closed. The air was warm and humid, yet cool and breezy. It smelled like salt and seaweed and lilies and laundry soap all mixed together.

She held the breath inside her for a moment, let the pressure in her chest press against her nervously beating heart.

As nervous as she still was, for some reason she tossed and turned just a little bit less that night.

Chapter 20

On a day that was overly hot for June, even for the South, Ariettea was helping Alex, Elaina, and Lily with their garden of lilies. Weeding and planting and fertilizing, they were laughing the whole time. Alex had lame dad jokes mastered, and Elaina's soft-spoken nature hid a biting sense of humor.

"So, do you see why they named me Lily?" Lily asked, sarcastically dubious, looking up at Ariettea from under her white wide-brimmed hat.

Ariettea laughed. "Still no idea..." She smiled.

Alex came out with a tray of bottled waters and his phone. "We need a picture of you two!" He called out.

Ariettea groaned softly, but still louder than she had meant to. Lily latched onto her tightly and smiled as hard as she could. Ariettea was laughing at Lily's cheesing face when Alex took the picture.

"Perfect!" He called. He stepped over to show them his screen; he had caught Ariettea in mid-laugh, and Lily smiling wide. The sun shone down bright, the camera picking up its rays, the orange lilies blazed all around them, and you could clearly see the ocean in the background.

"Take a break, you two. Let us handle the rest. Go hang out," Alex smiled at Lily, then Ariettea. "This is supposed to be your guys' fun summer."

The two of them settled onto the benches on the deck and sat in silence as they watched Alex and Elaina finish up that side of the house until they moved to the other, where they couldn't watch them anymore.

Ariettea tried to keep her mind on what was literally in front of her, but she couldn't, and Lily noticed. "What's the look, Ari?"

Ariettea closed her eyes.

Ugh that question.

Always that question.

She considered lying, not talking about it, but she knew Lily would goad it out of her eventually.

"Today is Matt's graduation party." She said, eyes still closed. She sighed and opened them. "I'm just… conflicted. Part of me says I want to be there, but part of me says only if it were the old him there, part of me doesn't want to be there whatsoever and still feels guilty, but part of me says forget it and him."

Lily giggled. "I think I like that last part."

Ariettea scoffed out a laugh. "It's just, like, I'm here, and this is the only place I want to be, but I'm still conflicted. I still feel like I should want to be back… there."

She couldn't bring herself to say 'home'.

"Why?" Lily asked, bluntly.

Ariettea looked over at her; at the sweat matting down her curls, her teal eyes squinting in the sun. "Why… what?" She asked slowly.

"Why do you feel like you should want to be there?"

Ariettea stammered over words that weren't really words. "Uh, I, welp, I, just…" She paused, chewed her lip. She looked down to meet Lily's eyes. "I guess it's just since everyone else wants to be there; I should too."

"But why?"

Ariettea stood up, exasperated. "I don't know; I don't know what you want me to say!"

"I just want you to give me a reason why you think everyone else has it right."

"Well if it's me against thousands and thousands of people, I'd think I'm wrong." She started to pace, keeping in line with the boards on the deck.

"Wrong about what?" Lily pressed, sitting stilly, calmly.

Ariettea rolled her neck around and stared at the sky. "Wrong about how I hate it there. About how I rebel against everything they say is right."

"Yeah ok, but how does what they believe make them right? Why is it wrong for YOU to hate it there? For YOU to go against the grain?"

"Because I'm the minority." She said softly.

She sat back down next to Lily, sadly, feeling defeated.

"But you're not saying THEY'RE wrong." Lily shook her head. "Look, Ari, you're not the one making hard and fast rules on what the right and wrong things to do are. You're not going around trying to force anyone to think anything. How could it be so bad to want something different? To want to live somewhere else? Do something else?"

"But aren't I, though? Aren't I telling everyone they're wrong by not wanting to be like them?"

"Not in any way like they tell you you're wrong."

"So I must be then! If everyone else says it-"

"I don't care if everyone else there thinks…" Lily stammered, "That like, mint chocolate chip ice cream is the best thing on the planet, and you hate it."

"I actually like it."

"Not the point, Ari, shush. What I mean is that your hating something doesn't mean you think it's bad or wrong. And EVEN IF you do, you're not going around clearing out everyone's freezer, and then going to Walmart and unplugging their freezer!"

"But I am vocal on how I hate it. Everyone says 'too' vocal."

"Yeah well, I personally hate mint chocolate chip. It tastes like frozen toothpaste with cheap fake chocolate thrown in that doesn't melt, and you just crunch on it and-"

She shook her head viciously. "UGH I just hate it so much, and can't understand how anyone likes it, and think everyone who does is crazy, but I don't tell them they can't have it, or shouldn't! I might say hey, have you thought about strawberry? But I can't set rules on what people eat!"

She threw her hands up. "I don't get to look at them sideways and whisper about how nasty their food choices are,"

Ariettea started to laugh.

"I can think they're totally wrong, and they for sure think I'm crazy and totally wrong, but at the end of the day- I'm going to eat what makes me happy. I'm not going to eat something gross just to make someone else feel better about their choice."

Ariettea stared at her a moment, trying to let that sink in as she panted in the summer heat.

"Trust me," Lily began, standing herself, looking out towards the water. "I know what it's like to live a different life than everyone else. And I didn't even choose to."

She rolled her eyes. "And Lord knows everyone has an opinion on that too."

She stepped back and stood next to Ariettea. "All I know is that I'm here for a finite amount of time until God's kingdom comes. I'm not going to waste my time trying to make anyone else happy."

Elaina popped up from the other side of the house. "Lily," she called, her soft-spoken voice ringing out as singsong from a distance. "Did I hear something about ice cream? You should take Ari into town to try Delicia's!"

Ariettea turned to Lily. "Delicia's?"

Lily rolled her eyes. "It doesn't even mean delicious; it's Latin for 'charming'." She laughed softly. "It actually is pretty charming. Do you want to go get ice cream?"

Ariettea smiled as she stood. "Only if I can have mint chocolate chip."

Lily laughed and shoved her playfully as she stood.

She latched onto her waist in a hug as they walked towards Elaina. "Own that choice, Ari."

Weeks went by.

Anyone who saw Ariettea and Lily immediately thought they were sisters- the raven black hair, the smiles, and the fact that they were completely inseparable.

They fell into routine, the four of them.

Ariettea and Lily spent their days laughing and talking, some days in the ministry, other days in town, but most days at the beach.

But that ever-looming thought of the summer ending was weighing heavily on Ariettea's mind.

On a breezy midweek day, the two of them took bikes into downtown to pick up some snacks for a beach bonfire they were having that night. On their way home, they pedaled slowly, talking.

Lily looked around seriously, taking everything in as they passed all the little shops. "I'm so happy to be home, Ariettea." She said wistfully.

Ariettea looked over at her as she took in a deep breath.

"The smell or the air, the scenery…" She shook her head. "You know sometimes I was worried I'd never make it back here." She commented, looking over at Ariettea.

"I can't imagine how hard things were for you." Ariettea said, trying to put the right amount of feeling into each word.

"Yeah, I just…" Lily's teal eyes scanned the cloudless sky. "Sometimes, when you're lying in bed all alone, and you see the pain on everyone's faces around you, and it's almost worse than the pain you're actually feeling, you start to wonder why you're putting them through that. If there's even a point, if you're really going to get better."

"But you did!"

"For now." Lily shook her head. "I get so afraid that I'm going to get sick again."

She rolled her eyes at the sky. "That I'm going to have to go back to the hospital and put my parents through it all again."

She looked out towards the water. "I know how often you question yourself, where you think you're 'supposed' to be and what you're 'supposed' to do, but I question my own existence just as much sometimes."

Her eyes locked onto something in the distance and she zoned out. "I know my life is never going to be 'normal'. Me, I'm ok with it. I just hate seeing my parents suffer and the thought that it could happen again…" She trailed off.

Ariettea's stomach dropped. "Lily, you don't think… You're …sick, do you?"

"No, no, not at all, just… talking out loud."

Ariettea looked down at the passing pavement underneath her feet. She felt her lashes brush the tops of her cheeks as she blinked slowly as Lily spoke again,

"I guess I'm just understanding where you're coming from when you say you don't know who you are or what you want. Not beating the cancer was never an option for me, and I've always had these big ideas in my mind about what my life would be like after, but now…"

She swallowed. "Now it's a whole new world to me. I keep feeling like I don't belong here more and more as I get back into life here."

She looked over at Ariettea. "If I were to get sick again, I'd feel even worse. I guess I just mean it's scary. It's scary to try and grow up and make choices on who we want to be, especially when you haven't been able to even choose who you want to be for a very long time, and you feel like you've disappointed enough people already."

Ariettea looked over at her suddenly. "Don't you ever say you're a disappointment!" She implored.

Lily looked over at her. "Only if you don't get to say it about yourself, either."

Ariettea smiled sadly at the ground.

"I just hate feeling like I took my parents' lives away." Lily continued. "My mom and dad love kids; they've always wanted a bunch. I feel guilty because they've been too busy with me and too scared to have another one. Like I took away their biggest dream. To have a family. I hate seeing them have to live in a college apartment; I hate that my mom can't go see her family on the west coast, I hate that my dad has to work so much to pay the medical bills, and I hate that my mom just has to watch him work because she doesn't want to leave me at the hospital alone all day."

She paused again; eyes now unable to meet Ariettea's. "I just hope you know that you're not alone in feeling like you're not what anyone wanted. But I have to accept that my being sick isn't, and wasn't, my fault. I have accepted it. I know I'm wanted. And I hope you know that, too. That you're wanted and special, and the world needs you."

Lily's eyes twinkled as she broke out into a grin. "I guess we're both just odd ducks, Ari. But who even gets to decide what 'normal' means, anyway?"

Lily smirked, eager to change the subject, lighten the mood. "Hey, I bet I can beat you home!" She yelled, suddenly ahead of Ariettea.

"Oh, no way!" Ariettea laughed, speeding to catch up with her.

Lily beat her back, threw her bike down out front, ran through the house and onto the patio.

Ariettea tossed the groceries on the counter and chased her out back.

Elaina watched them fly by, approvingly laughing.

Lily was laughing on the deck, bent over. "I win!" She panted, throwing her arms up in the air, triumphant.

Ariettea laughed, she wiped her brow, suddenly realizing she hadn't worn makeup that day. "Hey, I'll race you to the water!" She took off running.

"Oh, you're on!" Lily said from somewhere behind her. But she was laughing too.

Ariettea ran into the water, splashing all the way up to her knees, the cold Atlantic flying into the air.

Lily was close behind; she threw some water onto Ariettea's back. Ariettea yelped and splashed Lily back.

A full-on splashing war broke out until Ariettea fell back on her butt into the water. "Truce!" she yelled, holding her hands up, still laughing.

Lily giggled. "Truce." She agreed. She plopped down in the water across from Ariettea.

Ariettea looked around at the landscape. The lilies still standing out blooming against the quaint little house, the white sand shore being overwhelmed with lapping waves.

"I'm so glad to be here, Lily." She said, leaning back on to her hands, the ends of her hair resting in the water. "I mean, you say you're happy to be back and me, I'm so happy to get a break. A break from thinking about all those people at home."

She hung her head. "I honestly don't even like calling it 'home'." She admitted.

Lily shrugged. "So, don't!" She said simply, waving her hands through the water.

Ariettea smiled, somewhat sadly, leaned forward and skimmed her hand over the surface of the water. "But I still don't know what I want. Even away from it all. And it's really frustrating because I start to think that I have no idea where I'll be happy."

Lily looked thoughtfully at her. "I mean, yeah, we all have to find happiness within ourselves first." She said. "But sometimes, we have to chase it to find it."

Ariettea stayed silent. She looked down at her soaking wet top, her shorts waving underwater. "I feel ridiculous."

She looked at Lily and grinned. "But I love it so ridiculously much."

Lily smiled back, all teeth and dimples. "THIS, is my favorite way to swim, you know."

"Oh, is it?" Ariettea mocked.

"Absolutely."

"Very versatile, I guess."

"Well, I guess it depends where you're coming from. I wouldn't want to do this in a ball gown."

"Why not?"

"...Good question!"

Laughter kept floating through the seaside air for weeks.

Wednesday's were the days that Elaina went to the farmer's market to get fresh fish for dinner. It was Ariettea and Lily's job to tidy up the house and get the kitchen ready for their fish fry.

As soon as Elaina left, Lily would turn the stereo on as loud as it would go, and she and Ariettea would sing their hearts out, dancing around the house like fools.

And it was every Wednesday, in that moment with Lily, that Ariettea always felt the safest.

The moment when she pulled away, trying to save it in her memory.

The two of them were folding laundry.

"I'm walkin' on sunshine! WOAH!" Lily yelled out.

Ariettea threw her head back and laughed, sang the next line. "And don't it feel good!"

"Hey!"

"Alright now!"

Lily jumped up and put the towels in the linen closet, started spinning in circles, her hair flying around and smacking her in the face. Ariettea laughed as she put away the dish clothes and joined her.

They grabbed each other's hands and danced together, spinning in circles and twirling around. Ariettea mentally pulled back from the situation. Describing it to anyone, it would have sounded utterly ridiculous. But in that moment in time, Ariettea felt the happiest she had ever been.

The song ended, and Lily flopped onto the couch.

Ariettea thoughtfully placed the potholders in their drawer and stared out the window.

She fiddled with the ends of her hair that had started to lighten in the sun. Her hands tanned by it; her long fingers were no longer blue and pale.

Lily turned off the radio and came into the kitchen, hopped up onto one of the barstools at the island. She pulled an orange out of the always full fruit bowl and started to peel it. "Is there anything on your mind?"

Ariettea turned, played with the hem of her shirt. She had noticed the hem was a little harder to pull up, her shirt wasn't as loose as she had grown accustomed to. Her stomach wasn't rejecting every bite she took in.

"I'm just trying to figure out what a happy me feels like and thinks."

Lily smirked; hands full of sticky peel. "Personally, I'm happiest when I'm getting my friends a water out of the fridge." She shrugged.

Ariettea pretended to be offended as she laughed and turned around to the refrigerator. "That simple, huh?"

She smacked a bottle in front of Lily.

"Yep. Sometimes it's just the present moment that makes me a happy me."

"I'll have to learn that skill."

Chapter 21

Trent and Nadette still checked on her, albeit less and less, as they could tell she was becoming more and more stable. Her parents checked in too, but no one else, of course. At all. Not a single word from any of the people her parents claimed were her friends. She still scrolled through social media, seeing pictures from graduation parties, summer flings, beach bonfires, all the stuff she'd never have been invited to, anyway. Or would have wanted to go to for that matter.

Her little world was in its own bubble.

But then someone new entered into it.

"Peter is coming!" Lily announced to her one morning.

Ariettea suddenly felt nervous as she pulled her hair into a high ponytail, standing in the kitchen.

A new person coming into things? What if they liked him better? What if everything fell apart? If maybe all her happiness was just tied up in some summer fantasy in that little town? And when someone from the real world came along, it would show her that there was no hope of things going how she wanted when she left?

She took deep breaths to calm herself. She smiled at Lily, looked at Alex and Elaina making breakfast behind her.

"How fun!" She commented, trying to seem happy for them.

"Just for an afternoon," Elaina added, tucking her curls behind her ear as she dolled out pancakes onto a plate and handed them to Ariettea. "We'll just spend a quiet day like we usually do with him; relax at the beach, maybe walk through town. Let him decide as we do you." She smiled.

"Then, get dinner at The Shack." Alex added, smiling, handing her a plate of bacon and eggs.

Both hands full, she sat down next to Lily at the kitchen island and pulled the pitcher of orange juice close.

"So, when will he be coming?" She asked, pouring both herself and Lily a glass.

"Today!" Lily exclaimed.

Ariettea jumped and spilled the juice. Lily noticed the look on her face right away and whispered, "Are you okay with that?"

Ariettea leaned in and whispered back, "Of course, why wouldn't I be?"

Lily gave her a funny look and turned back to her food.

Ariettea mopped up the spill with paper towels and stared down at her food.

She hated new people. What if he came and told them that she was crazy? They'd known him longer; they'd trust him, right? He was established in life, building a career, and she was…her.

She started to panic. She jumped up and excused herself, ran to the bathroom.

She steadied herself with the countertop. Stared down at the faded tan laminate, her eyes tracing the scratches from many years of use.

She looked at herself in the mirror, tan, for once in her life. Her swimsuit lines showing through her tank top. The one that had been too loose a few weeks prior, but now clung to her a little tighter, showing off her curves that had been hidden for so long. She pulled it up the hide the boobs that had suddenly reappeared.

She stared at her face, devoid of makeup, as it had been staying, devoid of black eyeliner.

She wondered if she looked like a fool. An idiot, a glutton for punishment. Who did she think she was, spending the summer with them?

She was spiraling down and fast.

She hadn't been locked in a bathroom since Matt's party, nearly eight months before. The party where she had just wanted him to come and tell her it would all be ok.

A knock that never came, then, or had ever.

But suddenly, a knock at the door. "Ari?" Lily called out softly. She knocked lightly again, "Can I come in?"

Ariettea took in a deep breath, let it out, and opened the door.

Lily rushed in; concern painted on her face. "Hey, what's going on? What happened?" She softly closed the door behind her as Ariettea shook her head.

"I just… I don't know. It's nothing." She squeezed her eyes shut as hard as she could.

"No, no, don't do this, Ariettea. Don't shut down. Don't block out negative emotions, because you'll end up blocking out all the positive ones from the past weeks, and for the future. Don't disappear on me."

Ariettea shook her head again, as if to shake out the thoughts she didn't want in her head.

"Let me in!" Lily implored.

Ariettea plopped down on the floor, on the pale blue braided rug in front of the sink. "I just got afraid. Afraid that Peter would come and then you would all realize what you've been missing, what a good person looks like, compared to me."

Lily knelt down across from her and shook her head. "Give yourself more credit than that. Give us some more credit. Do I need to say it again? Let. Us. Love. You."

Ariettea finally met her eyes.

Saw those teal eyes, the ones cradled by thick black lashes that had been growing back in. She saw the sincerity in them. She wanted to believe them.

After all, Lily was the first person to ever knock on the bathroom door.

She pulled at the hem of her shorts. "Okay." She muttered softly.

Lily smiled, stood back up, extended her hand to Ariettea. "Come on," she said, taking in a glance of Ariettea's ever-tightening clothes. "Let's you, me, and my mom go shopping before he gets here. I saw this adorable swimsuit you just HAVE to try on."

They were in one of the many fancy boutiques in the town square. Lily was throwing clothes over Ariettea's arm like mad.

She shook her head, staring at the rainbow of colors. "Are you trying to tell me something about my taste in clothes, Lil?"

Lily laughed. "I just think your tan skin deserves more than black." She threw a white chiffon dress on top of the pile. "Plus, you've been wearing the same blue dress for weeks now."

She smirked at her, patting the white dress. "There! Go try on!" Lily waved her away.

Ariettea stepped into the small fitting room, drew the long red velvet curtain, fastened it as best she could. "Well, what are you trying on?" She called out to Lily, in the next room over, as she pulled the dress over her head.

"I'm trying on clothes that most girls my age actually fit in to, for once!" Lily called back. "With no chemo, I'm actually starting to grow!" She laughed.

Ariettea pulled the tag out from under the armpit of her dress and examined the size. A full size up from what she had been. She smoothed the dress down the front of her body, examined the cut. A flowy skirt, a white ribbon tied at the waist, and a tight-fitting chiffon bodice. Hitting above her knees, sleeveless, she wasn't sure; it just didn't feel like HER.

"Come on! Show us!" Lily called out.

Ariettea unfastened the curtain and stepped out.

"Wow!" Elaina called, walking over. "That's gorgeous on you!"

Lily, in a green sun dress, nodded vigorously in agreement. "You HAVE to get it! Look how it makes your tan stand out!"

Ariettea turned around and looked at herself in the mirror again, standing on her barefoot tippy toes. She noticed the scars down her arm, the ones she tried so hard to hide. They had somehow become blended in with her new tan, and she was grateful.

Lily smiled at her and clapped quickly, "Well, put that thing in the yes pile! And here, throw on these jeans after I try this swimsuit on." Lily threw a pair of bootcut jeans at her as she stepped back into her changing room.

Elaina came up behind Ariettea, "You look great, honey." She said gently.

Ariettea smiled over her shoulder at her. "Thanks."

Elaina nodded, came around to face her. "So, how are you feeling?"

Ariettea nodded, tried to stay cool. "Everything has been amazing. I can't thank you guys enough for this summer."

Elaina nodded, "It's our pleasure. But that doesn't answer my question," She smiled, scoldingly. "How are you FEELING?"

Ariettea took in a deep breath, started to talk before Elaina cut in, crossing her arms around herself. "And don't just say fine!"

Ariettea let out her breath and laughed. She smiled back at her. "How much has Lily told you about me?" She asked, still laughing.

Elaina waved a hand. "Not much, to be honest. But I see myself in you. And I know how I used to think."

"Used to think?" Ariettea asked, subconsciously passing the jeans to her arm to cover it up.

Elaina nodded. "That quiet, shy, battered by the world look, coupled with the hard fear and defiance you fight to keep buried. I felt that way for a long time."

Ariettea paused, taken aback. "You?"

"Me!"

"So how did you… change? Why did you?"

Elaina looked around her, dropped her arms to her sides, and sighed, smiling. "Why? Because it's all I ever truly wanted, to find happiness. How? I had to find it myself."

"I know, I know." Ariettea sighed, sitting down in a plush navy chair, veneered wooden arms sitting too high for her own. She fiddled with the price tag on it. "You have to find happiness in yourself, or else nowhere you go will be good enough."

"Well, I'm not sure that's exactly it," Elaina said, sitting in the chair beside her.

Ariettea raised an eyebrow.

"It's like…" Elaina paused. "It's like you have to find out WHERE that happiness is for YOU."

Elaina smiled at her, that big, yet gentle smile. The one that was framed by her soft auburn curls. "You have all the time in the world, honey. Make the most of it, of every day. Spend your time doing everything you love. And when you make a decision, have the courage to stand up for it. But to do that, you first have to have the courage to make the decision."

Ariettea nodded, somewhat absentmindedly, trying to take that in. "Thank you, Elaina." She said softly.

She smiled, patted Ariettea's hand. "Hang in there, darling. The world needs you."

Then Lily popped out of the fitting room, dressed in a retro one-piece red polka-dotted swimsuit. She posed dramatically, threw her head back, one arm reaching up in the air and the other on her hip.

"What do you think?" She asked grinning.

Elaina smiled as Ariettea giggled.

"I think," Elaina said, pulling Ariettea up by the hand. "We have two outfits we are DEFINITELY buying."

There was babbling traveling through the house by the time the ladies got back to it. They found Peter and Alex in the kitchen, Alex casually standing with both hands on the counter behind him and Peter sitting at the island.

Squeals from both Lily and Elaina brought a big smile to his face as they rushed over to hug him.

Ariettea stayed back, hands crossed in front of her, feeling extremely awkward. Lily looked back at her, smiled, shook her head, and walked back to grab her by the hand.

"Peter, you remember Ariettea, right?"

She felt her cheeks flush as she struggled to smile and meet his eye.

He smiled warmly, nodded. His green eyes stood out against tan skin, a blue Ducreis hoodie. "Even if I didn't, I feel like I know her well enough already."

He laughed at Lily. Looked back to Ariettea, "I've heard a lot about you since we first met. These guys can't speak more highly of you."

Ariettea felt even more embarrassed, had absolutely no idea what to say. "They're forever too kind." She said sheepishly.

She was thankful he didn't try to force anything, but just smiled warmly at her before turning to Elaina and started asking about her family.

As she rattled off news, Ariettea started to step back, but Lily grabbed her from behind with one hand, her head not even reaching Ariettea's chest she could only hang on to her waist, to keep her from leaving.

She started to feel resentment bubble inside her.

All she could see was the dirty looks Matthew would shoot her from across a room, whenever there was a group of girls he felt she should be talking to.

All she could hear was the whispered threats in her ear that everyone would think she's even more strange than they already did if she didn't straighten up and start making small talk.

But Lily looked up at her with a different look on her face. Pride. She was proud of her, and she couldn't remember the last time someone had looked at her that way.

"Oh! Ariettea!" Alex suddenly said, his eyes widening. "This just came for you in the mail."

He handed her an envelope with the Ducreis logo on the upper left-hand corner.

"Why would this get sent here?" She mumbled out loud, turning it over in her hands.

"What IS it?" Lily queried.

Ariettea shook her head. "I have no idea. I didn't apply for anything…"

She stepped aside into the living room and tore it open, Lily by her side.

She ran down the letter quickly,

Dear Ms. Ariettea…. pleasant greetings…. then,

"We are delighted to inform you that you have been selected as a recipient of one of our Alumni Legacy Scholarships. This comes as a result of one or more family members having attended Ducreis University and sponsoring your admission.

The sponsors we have listed for you are:
<u>*Dr. Trent Vermule*</u>
and
<u>*Dr. Nadette Vermule*</u>*.*

Please see the attached brochures and forms for further details on course selection, semester dates, orientation dates, housing programs, and other terms and agreements.

Best of luck with your studies!

Sincerely yours,

Quillian Abbott,
Head of Admissions, Ducreis University"

She felt her face go pale, and her hands start to shake, as she fumbled through the terms. She scanned over them and then plopped down on the couch behind her.

She put a hand over her mouth as Lily starting bursting, grinning hugely, "What? What is it?"

Ariettea handed her the letter in silence. She watched as Lily scanned over it and then started jumping up and down. The letter got passed to Alex and Elaina as Ariettea shook her head and looked at Lily.

"It's a full ride." She said in disbelief. "If I get into whichever program I apply to, that is."

Peter came over, now excited. "That's so awesome! So the school is paid for, and you'll get preferential treatment when you actually apply, but if your SAT scores were good too-"

"I got a 1340."

Peter's eyes widened, impressed. "Hats off!" He said, stepping away. "That makes my 1150 seem sad. But hey Ducreis took me in! It sounds like you're a shoo-in."

Lily plopped down to her on the couch. "Ari! You never told me you did that well on the SAT!"

Elaina rubbed her hand on Ariettea's shoulder. "This is so exciting! We have so much to celebrate tonight! Peter is here, your news, we're finally all healthy and home..." She fell back onto Alex's chest and closed her eyes, suddenly teary.

She shook her head and waved a hand. "I'm going to go get dressed for dinner," she said, backing away. "Be right out."

Ariettea jumped up. "Yeah, I need to change, too," she suddenly felt self-conscious of her bare face. "I should really call Trent and Nadette too." She started for the patio door.

"Well, hey, congrats again! Feel free to pick my brain over dinner! It's a great school." Peter said, following her slightly.

She smiled tightly, mouthed thanks, and stepped outside to make her calls.

She stared at her phone, thinking of anyone else to tell about her news. Her parents? She'd tell them eventually. Maybe if she decided on a program and actually going. She shook her head. What did she even want to go for? It was still such a murky question in her mind. She rubbed her temple with her free hand while she dialed Nadette.

The five of them trailed into The Shack only to be bombarded when all the waitresses saw that Peter was with them. He politely waved them all off and put his arm around Lily instead, his 5'11 frame nearly bent over.

Five is such an awkward number at a restaurant. Do you sit three on one side in a booth? Add an extra chair at the end of a table? Which is what they ended up doing. Peter diplomatically took the seat on the end, and Lily jumped to the other end, making Ariettea sit closest to him.

She could see two of the servers whispering and pointing at him, giggling. She looked back and forth between them and him, over her menu, her eyes the only thing moving. She could easily see the attraction; he was a cute guy. The humidity hitting his hair, bringing out the curl, his hoodie not hiding his tan skin, his attractive build.

Peter looked at her out of the corner of his eye, and she met his glance accidentally.

She raised an eyebrow, "You've got quite the fan club here." She murmured to him.

He smiled down at his menu, shrugged. "I think they like the hard to get game. I'm honestly just not interested, so I try to just brush it off."

She smiled at her own menu, thinking of all the guys she knew that would just love to bask in the glory of having multiple blonde 20 somethings fawn over them.

Lily looked down the table at him. "Oh, and just what ARE you interested in?" She asked with that twinkle in her eye.

He shook his head at her. "I'm not really looking right now. I've got the ministry and my job to worry about for now, and that's enough."

"That's the right attitude, Pete," Alex jumped in. "Always best to settle in before trying to do all that other adapting at the same time."

Ariettea looked back and forth between them as they continued on that subject. Peter talked about his preparation for the school year, his family, his new house he was renting. Ariettea kept waiting for sports or video games or his friends to pop up, but they never did. She stayed silent as he talked to Elaina about her flowers, the town, what books she was reading. He talked to Lily about her schoolwork, the beach, their favorite new tv show, as dinner progressed.

He finally looked at Ariettea, genuinely asked, "So what are you thinking of studying at Ducreis?"

She swirled a fry around in the salt on her plate. "I haven't decided yet." She said simply.

There was a pause as he waited for her to continue.

"There's a lot I'm interested in. I just want something short and practical. I want to live my life. I'm just trying to figure out what those two things are and mean."

He nodded gently. "Ducreis will suck you in if you're not careful. You definitely have to go in knowing what you want and sticking to it."

She smiled sadly. "That's what everyone back where I'm from thinks. It's all flash."

"Well, I guess that depends on what you think of as 'flash'. In my mind, it's different for everyone."

She smiled at him this time. "So, what did you think it meant?"

"For me, flash meant anything that went beyond what my goal was- to be a teacher so I can settle down someday soon."

"Ah-ha!" Lily piped up, pointing at him. "Do you DO want to find a lady!"

"I never said I didn't!"

"Whatever happened to the redhead?"

"My cousin?"

"Oh, you were serious about that?"

He rolled his eyes as he took in his last bite of burger. "You know why I'm hesitant." He said slowly, glancing at Ariettea, her knowing he was speaking of something she wasn't privy to.

Lily shook her head. "Well, the two of you should give it a go!" She said, pointing between him and Ariettea.

Ariettea jumped, "Lily!" She exclaimed as Peter and her parents did the same.

He held a hand out, "Not that that's offensive," he said to Ariettea.

She waved a hand at him. "Oh please. I think we both know Lily here and all her tricks to trying to help people find their happiness,"

Lily smirked, proud of herself. "Hey, the age difference is only six years."

Ariettea felt herself blush. How humiliating, the insinuation he could possibly be interested in her. She wasn't even half of what he would want.

"I think it's time to change the subject," Alex said sternly, giving Lily the evil eye.

"Hey, how's the congregation doing?" Peter asked him.

And just like that, the conversation went on. Ariettea watched as it ebbed and flowed between them all. She wished it were that easy for her.

As Alex was discussing with Lily what dessert to get, Peter turned back to Ariettea and lowered his voice, giving all his attention to her.

"To finish our earlier conversation- my best advice for college is to do something that supports the life you want."

Ariettea smiled at the ground. "The trick is figuring out what you want first."

Peter nodded, knowingly. "Sometimes, the answer to that is simpler than you think. I think we just all want to be happy. We have to actually test, and then see what and who makes us the happiest and build off of that."

She smiled coyly at him. "So, what does that look like for you, mister Peter?"

He laughed softly. "I just want to live a quiet life. Settle down, work, pray, that's why I chose teaching. Gives me summers off for what's important, and during the school year, I get to make my classroom and safe and happy space."

He looked over at Lily, who was now enamored in a story her dad was telling. "Lily taught me a lot about choosing what's important to me. Figuring out what that meant was just something that happened along the way."

Ariettea looked over at her, too. She smiled. She stared off at the sand lilies growing along the shore. Since meeting Lily, she saw lilies everywhere. They served as a constant reminder of a calm and happy place. All she knew was that she wanted to find that place within herself.

Karaoke music suddenly started to play, signaling the Friday night sing-off. They had always missed it, having wanted to avoid the massive crowds it always drew.

As all the fun songs started to play, Lily gasped and looked up at Ariettea. "Ari!" She said, grabbing her arm, "Let's do a song together!"

She looked hesitantly around, crowds pushing in around the raised circular stage in the middle of the deck. "I don't know Lily," She started, nervous.

"Ariettea," Lily grinned at her while shaking her head.

Ariettea relented and rolled her eyes dramatically. "Ok, I'll do it then." She sarcastically huffed before smiling back.

Lily's eyes lit up, shined even brighter than usual as she squealed and ran to pick out a song, dragging Ariettea by the hand.

All of a sudden, Lily had somehow gotten them put them at the top of the list, and they were on stage, and music started blaring.

Lily began to dance to the beat, not a care in the world what she looked like. Ariettea stood as stiff as a board as Lily looked out towards the crowd and got them to clap with the beat too as she continued whirling around in circles.

Lily wasn't about to stand still and sing a boring song. She was there to have fun, and she was going to make sure Ariettea did, too.

Ariettea felt the eyes of the crowd, feeling like she was being judged, her mind starting to spiral- but then she looked at Lily. Beaming, dancing, eyes shining, she felt her heart calm.

She could feel the bass drum beat in her bones as Lily yelled out the words to their favorite song. She returned Lily's smile as she sang out the next line herself. Lily ran over and grabbed her hand, twirled herself around before they started harmonizing and singing together, the way they had become so accustomed to doing. The restaurant crowd started cheering, and Ariettea didn't even care why. She and Lily faced each other as they pushed one another back and forth, trading off lyrics.

Suddenly, she forgot there were people there, and the world seemed to be going in slow motion. She felt such pure, unadulterated joy at that moment that it felt frozen in time. Dancing with Lily, singing karaoke, in South Carolina, happy.

Finally, happy.

Ariettea pulled back into reality and quickly spun, let her hair smack her in the face as she whirled around. She keeled over, laughing as Lily started dancing high kneed like a maniac. Ariettea stopped trying to sing the song; she was breathless from laughing and just joined Lily in her crazy, flailing dance.

In a crowded restaurant, on a stage, Lily was all she could see. No one else seemed to matter, but Lily.

Lily was everything.

She was everything Ariettea needed to realize.

Chapter 22

Ariettea sat that night, at the end of the deck before it dropped off onto the trail that led to the water. Her hands tucked under her thighs, she stared at the moon over the ocean. Her legs dangled off the edge, her flip flops were teasing the ends of her feet, about to fall off. She thought of herself a year ago, on the pier back in Michigan, watching her combat boots swing over murky lake water, wanting to plunge in. Now, she watched moonlight dance across soft ocean waves. She took in a deep breath of warm, salty, humid ocean air and sighed happily.

Peter and the Abonet's were all inside, chatting, exchanging goodbyes.

Her mind was stuck on that Ducreis letter. She thought about all the choices in front of her. All the things she really wanted. All the things she had dreamt of having. She smiled to herself, growing more and more confident in what she wanted to do.

Lily came up behind her noiselessly and sat down next to her. "I'll ask what's with the look because this time it's a happy look I'm not sure I've seen before."

Ariettea giggled softly. "I don't think I've ever seen it before either, to be honest."

Lily bumped into her shoulder with her own. "So...." she drew out her words. "Spill!"

Ariettea shook her head. "You know, I just keep thinking about what's made me so unhappy. Trying to identify it all but also forget it all. I've dealt with it all for so long without actually dealing with it. And being here, I still wonder if I haven't dealt with it all. But maybe dealing with it is just... Accepting. Accepting what happened, happened. What people are, they are. What I want, I want, even if I'm not always sure EXACTLY what that is."

She shook her head again. "I just think that sometimes deciding who you are, is deciding who you'll never be. And I at least know what that is."

She looked out towards the water, Lily knowing to just let her keep talking.

Lily always knew what she needed.

"I always get told I need to change my thinking. Change myself. I've even tried changing what people think of me. That was my parent's suggestion- show people the real you! But also, only show them what they want to see. I don't think it's about changing their thinking or even my own. It's not looking for the middle ground of people's approval, coupled with what I want. I think it's time for me to accept that there's more than one right way to do things."

She looked down at her feet, covered with sand. "But I just don't want to feel like I'm running away. Because then, all that stuff will follow me."

Lily shook her head fiercely. "I think you know the truth already. Happiness is not a place. Ari, you tried finding happiness there, and that environment doesn't allow you to find it in yourself. Some people and places are easier to find joy in or with. Leaving…"

She shook her head; her eyes scrunched in thought. "It's not taking an L. It's adapting and chasing happiness. Sometimes we have to find people and places that grow and adapt with us, instead of against us."

Ariettea looked over at her. "I feel different here, Lily. I want to go places, I want to go shopping, I want to have fun, get out of bed, I even want to eat. I want to do things. Become things. Being here… I just want to LIVE. You showed me what I wanted is real, it's something that YES, you CAN find. And I haven't felt that way in a long time. I can't lose that feeling again."

Lily scooched closer and laid her head on her shoulder, the ultimate sisterly pose they had mastered so well. "We BOTH need to learn to live, Ari. I'm glad we've been able to learn together."

Ariettea looked down at her head, the black curls that had grown out from a moppet into a bob.

"So, what about you?" She asked her. "Have you decided what living means for you now?"

Lily took in a deep breath and sighed happily. "I honestly don't know, and that's actually the best feeling. For so long, the goal was just to stay alive, to get back here. Now that I stayed alive, I just want to live. I want to go to school, spend time with my family outside of a hospital, maybe learn to play some video games, or watch football with my dad."

She giggled. "I'll never be a 'normal' kid. So, I just want to find my happiest version of normal. For the first time, I don't have a normal. I like that I don't have to know exactly what my future looks like."

"And that doesn't scare you?"

She shook her head. "Nah."

Lily popped up and started for the flower bed around the deck. She trailed through the throngs of lilies, her skin glowing in the moonlight, finally not translucent, but healthy, her long fingers skimming the tops of them all.

She turned back around to face Ariettea. She held her arms out wide above the flowers. "I'm just here for the lilies!"

Ariettea crossed her arms over her stomach and smiled at her. "Hey," she said. "Me too."

She scuffed her toes across the plastic beach trail. "I even think I might just stay where there's more of them to enjoy."

Soon enough, Nadette was picking Ariettea up to take her back to the airport. Trent came in the house with her, and they both beamed at Ariettea as she came around the kitchen corner. Nadette wrapped her up in a hug; her huge warm hugs were something that Ariettea hadn't realized she'd missed.

As she pulled away, Nadette took her hands into her own and admired her as she whispered, "The curves look good on you, gal."

Ariettea smiled back. "They feel good."

Trent came over and threw his arms around them both. "Ariettea is letting us hug her!" He yelled.

Her whole body started shaking with laughter.

She clapped her hands together as she pulled away. "So, since I've got the five of you all together, I have some news."

Lily jumped up and down in place, knowing what was coming.

"After getting the scholarship letter, I really started thinking- and in a different way than usual!" Ariettea laughed, holding up her hands.

"I've been able to pull away and think clearly for the first time in my life. So, the last few weeks I've been making calls and looking over brochures,"

She looked at Trent. "Brochures that I've kept with me since the day I toured Ducreis."

Her eyes sparkled as did his.

She took a deep breath, she herself shocked by what she was about to say. "I have officially been accepted into Ducreis University."

The room exploded with happy sounds and congratulations.

"What did you choose?" Elaina asked above it all, her usually quiet voice ringing out clear.

Ariettea took another breath, pushing air deep into her chest. "I chose nursing."

She let the breath out, smiled, and continued, "I'm going for a BSN, and along the way, I'm going to find specialized courses to be either psychiatric nurse," She looked at Trent, his soft eyes knowingly smiling back.

Then she looked at Lily, "Or a pediatric oncology nurse."

Lily was suddenly hugging her so tight that her arms were pinned down. "I'm so happy for you." Lily said softly.

Trent clapped his hands together. "I didn't want to be pushy, so I didn't mention it, BUT! Dr. Abbott told me about the scholarship, and I let him know that you were staying here so he could send the letter here. After he told me about it, I bought you a gift, just in case…"

He smirked. "I'll grab it for you; hold on-"

"Well, we can't let Ari leave without celebrating!" Alex jumper in. "Let's go to The Shack; we'll follow you out!"

They all filed out to Trent's car as he pulled something out of his trunk and handed it to Ariettea.

She held the item up, a maroon Ducreis pullover sweatshirt.

"I wanted to make sure that even if you stayed back North, you'd have a piece of us here."

She hugged it tightly to her chest, teary eyed, as she leaned into Trent for a side hug.

She examined it again, the Ducreis logo, shield and all, largely printed on the chest. She traced it with her fingers as Alex broke the silence.

"Our second daughter has found her way."

"And we get to call her our first daughter as she must be living with us for school, right?!" Nadette said excitedly.

Ariettea beamed, shook her head. "If you all will have me, after I pack up and come back down here, I'm never leaving you five again."

Chapter 23

Ariettea went home, expecting things to be incredibly awkward. With her family, with everyone she knew in that town.

And it was.

Every interaction was forced, painfully awkward, underlying opinions raging deep.

But for the first time, she didn't care.

"Have you told anyone I'm enrolling?" She had asked her mom.

"A few people, it's not like we broadcasted it."

Ariettea could feel the disapproval drip off her tongue.

"Matt asked, and we told him."

"Matt asked?" Ariettea asked incredulously. "That surprises me."

"Why?"

"He was just really distant when I left, like he didn't want anything to do with me anymore."

"Well, you didn't leave any room to get close to you before you left."

Ariettea set her jaw and looked over at her. "I've ALWAYS left room for people." She said evenly. "People just didn't want to fill that space."

"Because you push everyone away! You know you can't run from people. You can't be happy anywhere until you can get along with people."

"That's the thing, mom. No one here seems to understand that I'm not running from anything. I'm running TO something."

Things didn't get any easier the more people she saw. That next Sunday it was as if the entire congregation had questions. And with questions come opinions.

"So Ariettea," Cirise was saying, suddenly giving her the time of day. "We hear you've decided to enroll in... a... program? Down... South?"

Ariettea turned to her, smiling, trying not to make it smug. Through all the people telling her what she should, and what she would actually do, she was enjoying telling people that she was doing exactly what SHE said she would.

"Yeah I did," She said, matter of factly." My Aunt and Uncle are going to help me out, let me stay with them."

"How...nice!"

"But so far away, are you sure that's what you want, sweetie?" Matt's father asked from behind Cirise.

Ariettea nodded, trying not to be miffed. "I'm thrilled that I've finally made my perfect choice." She said kindly, almost condescendingly, but very firmly.

She thought of saying something like maybe she'd move back, maybe she'd change her mind along the way, but she knew those things weren't true.

She smoothed down her dress, the white one, that she had gotten with Lily and Elaina, her new favorite. Her stomach stuck out a little more than she was used to, and she liked it. She adjusted the tie at her waist and excused herself, backing away from the sad stares of her parents' friends, all thinking of how silly she was being, how much she must be hurting her parents.

She looked for Matt absentmindedly and found him with Mandy, who was sitting in her chair with a large church hat pulled over her eyes and her arms crossed tightly over her chest. Far from the flouncy attention seeker she left. She must have done something to bring the temporary ire of those around her. But as long as she sulked, she knew she'd get the attention she wanted. Matt poked her in the back, laughing, smiling at Mandy warmly.

Ariettea hated the feeling it invoked in her, seeing Matt flirt. She was over him! Wasn't she?

Mandy smacked his hand away and flashed him a dirty look. He said something that made his eyes sparkle, and she momentarily returned the smile, but then went back to sulking.

Ariettea waited to see if Matt would come up to her, but he never did. He hadn't even said hello to her since she had gotten back.

As she stood outside, basking in the sunlight, thinking of the coast, and subconsciously focused on the lilies in the planter in front of the building, she suddenly noticed Matt had been behind her, standing silently.

"Hey," She said, smiling confidently, turning to face him, on the step above her. "How's it going?" She exclaimed. "We haven't talked in ages."

She knew that her excitement was an irritant to him. He wanted her to be apologetic, remorseful.

He just looked at her, silently.

She continued, "Coming up on fall! College plans? Moving out? Anything?"

He looked at her with that look of irritation.

She just raised an eyebrow and waited, growing peeved at him.

"Always with the serious questions." He muttered, hands in his suit pants pockets.

Mandy came out of nowhere and suddenly pulled Cirise off to the side, tears in her eyes, ranting about something Ariettea couldn't hear. Typical.

"Nothing." He replied to her question, eyes on the ground.

Cirise overheard, threw a" sh" finger in Mandy's face and ran over, tried to answer for him, make him sound better like she always did, but he spoke over her before she could.

"Yeah, and what about you?" He said, purposely making it loud enough for everyone standing outside to hear.

Ariettea understood his tone, so she pushed him back. She knew he was playing dumb and she was not about to tolerate it. "Me? My mom said you knew since you'd asked…"

She trailed off just to watch him squirm. "But anyway, I got accepted into Ducreis."

"And will you stay there after school?" He asked, sharply.

"I haven't gotten that far ahead yet." She answered, her tone cutting. "I am going to enjoy the little time I have left of being young. Like YOU'VE always told me I need to."

He rolled his eyes to the side.

"So why not take that time and really ENJOY it?" Cirise suddenly said.

"Why won't I?"

"In school? Away from your family and friends?"

"Why do you all think that I don't have family and friends THERE?" She said simply.

Everyone outside grew quiet. Ariettea could tell that they felt like she'd just stabbed them all in the back.

But she didn't care.

She stole a look at Matt, and what she saw shocked her:

He looked the most hurt of all.

In a small town, once you have any sort of gossip or news, everyone needs to come confirm it with you, to see if you'll give them more information that they can pass on to their own friends, which would continue down the telephone game line.

Out buying boxes and packing tape, Ariettea had the luck to run into a couple of old 'friends'. She tried darting into the liquor aisle to hide before they could speak to her, but they followed her anyway. They bombarded her with questions- about her program, her housing, even asking how much the school was costing, was she going to get a job down there? Did she have one now? How was she even there paying for boxes and tape?!

She smiled sweetly and refused to answer their probes. She thought about bragging about her scholarship but knew it would backfire, people running around saying she was a pity student. She didn't owe them an explanation, anyway. So, she kept quiet, as their talk turned to other people's gossip.

"Ohmygosh, Ari!"

She cringed at the use of her nickname by someone she couldn't stand.

"Did you hear about what happened to Stacey? It was last summer all over again!"

Ariettea reached into her mind before realizing that, of course, she had no memory of it, she was an outsider. She didn't even know who Stacey was.

"I can't believe that was only a year ago! I forgot all about it!"

Ariettea had had it; she was over the small-town chattering. "Yeah, I know," She said, shaking her head. "A year is such a long time! It's good that we move past that kind of stuff, and we should try to keep it forgotten. Otherwise," She scoffed, "We'd have no lives of our own!"

She shrugged smugly as they stared at her, visibly angry.

"Well, I am still in the middle of a mess at home, so I need to get going." She announced, ending the interaction.

Fake, limp side hugs and pleasantries were exchanged, the 'let's do this again's' were said, and Ariettea pushed her shopping cart the other way.

She heard the whispers behind her as she walked away. Instead of trying to hear what they were saying, she pulled her cart off to the side in the cereal aisle and pulled out her phone.

"*Missing you!*" She typed out to Lily. "*Can't wait to get back there and have one last movie marathon before school starts.*"

Then she opened her thread with Nadette, sent a picture of the stack of boxes in her cart.

"*Ahhhh! Can't wait to help you unpack those!*" Nadette responded immediately. "*Trent is window shopping all the furniture stores here, determined to find you what he calls a 'study' desk.*"

Ariettea smiled down at her phone. "*I'm going to text him now; tell him I might need his help getting around campus for orientation.*"

She opened her thread with Trent. "*Nadette says you're shopping for a desk for me! Lol please don't do anything special to the room on my account. I'm already going to be asking you to help me around campus that first week.*"

"*Nadette ratted me out?! Figures.*" Then another bubble popped up, "*But on the subject of help... I can tell the summer has been good for you. But please let us in if the school year starts weighing on you. We're always here for you.*"

Then Lily's tone rang, "*YOU'VE GOTTA GET DOWN HERE ASAP! I MISS YOU TOO MUCH!*"

Ariettea grinned down at her phone. The love jumping out from the screen did much to warm her heart in the icy cold, judgmental air.

Part of the mindfulness and acceptance strategies she had worked so hard on meant accepting and letting go of all the things that had hurt her, while still learning from them.

But she still regretted not standing up for herself more.

At least now, she reasoned, she was finally doing that when she needed to. She had found that strength, that confidence, in herself.

She got to the part of her room that she had been putting off packing up: her closet wall, the one usually hidden by all her clothes, plastered with little pictures and notes, posters. All the things she knew she should have ripped down, thrown away, burned, long ago, but couldn't.

The train ticket from the day she spent in the city with Aspen.

The postcards that her once upon a time friend had sent from New York.

The tag off the shirt she had bought that day she had actually been invited by a group of girls to go shopping in the city.

The post-it notes she and Iris passed back and forth during class.

The concert ticket from the concert she went to with Luna and the other girls, the ones she spent so long trying to impress.

A packet of Taco Bell hot sauce that held a long-forgotten private joke.

The laces off the shoes that Brielle had drawn all over for her as a joke.

The movie tickets from all the rare times she had been invited to go with a group of people her own age.

She remembered everything, from every summer, every day she spent with her old friends. She realized that she didn't have to be consumed with any of it anymore. She could accept it and learn from it, but she felt free to move on.

She didn't know whether or not to throw away or keep the stuff. She decided just to pack it in a box for storage. It was still a memory of some kind, maybe even a good one, in a way.

She sat on her bed and picked up the glossy Ducreis pamphlet. She smiled, thinking about what was to come. Maybe, for once, thriving instead of just surviving. She laughed at herself, thinking of her face when Trent had said that to her.

She looked up at the last thing taped to her wall- a silly band that Matt had given her all those years ago when they were all the rage. She hated them, as she usually hated all fads, but he had pulled off the pink unicorn he wore as a joke, and handed it to her, knowing she'd take it as a joke, too.

Back in the days when they still had private jokes.

She'd never had the chance to formally say goodbye at the end a friendship. So she knew she couldn't leave things with him the way they were. She knew she'd regret it for the rest of her life.

It was time to say all the unsaid. She had to put it to rest before she left.

Because she was done keeping things hidden away in the back of her closet.

Chapter 24

She knew Matt would never agree to meet her one on one. But she didn't want to have that conversation with anyone else around, either. So, when her parents asked her to go to one last beach barbeque, she agreed, figuring it was her best shot at getting him alone.

It scared her, how nothing ever seemed to change in that small town. It was always the same group of people, with the same broken folding beach chairs, sitting in the same spot- the section of beach between the dune and the pier.

As the sun was going down the wind was picking up, the voices of everyone there getting lost in it.

She stood off and away from everyone, as she always did, but not as far as usual. She scanned the crowd waiting for him. She drug her bare foot through the sand, drawing circles and hearts in the soft, still-hot fluff.

As much as she had always searched for Matt in crowds, anymore, she looked for Lily, waiting for her little frame to pop up and run over to her. They had actually gone to a congregation picnic over the summer, and feeling safe with Lily, it was the first time she hadn't run away from a crowd.

Her mother was waving her over to the group, the ever-disappointed look on her face, the one she gave when Ariettea wasn't being social 'enough'.

She stood at the edge of the group with her hands in her back pockets, fingers trailing the outline of her cell phone, her lifeline to Lily. She was shocked that her mother wanted her in that particular group, the group of women- it was always the one she had never been old enough for. She was only half-listening to the conversation they were having, drifting from someone's Pampered Chef party to the new school year to… Mandy, suddenly.

"Ugh, that girl fried my last nerve over the summer," Someone was saying.

Ariettea flicked her eyes, but not her head, over to listen.

"You know Cirise took her to her court date, and she had the gall to ask her to take her shopping afterward."

"What court date was that for?"

"That was for the shoplifting charge."

"I can't believe she got into all this trouble!"

Ariettea felt a scoff escape, and then she watched words coming out of her mouth, seeing them in the air in front of her before she could stop them.

"All that surprises you why?" She asked, crossing her arms, deciding to commit to her question fully.

She received blank stares.

"Oh come on," She continued, shifting weight onto one leg, angling out the other. "Everyone gave her the attention she wanted- of course she'd keep asking for more."

Someone began to nod softly in agreement, "I guess maybe we should have seen it coming…"

Ariettea rolled her eyes and head backward. "Ah, so maybeeee people like Cirise and Aspen shouldn't have ignored me and doted on her less?"

Her mother elbowed her hard in the rib cage. "Ariettea!" She hissed, her eyes full of contempt, scanning the other women around them. "Stop!"

Ariettea shook her head. "No, I won't, mom. Not anymore."

She looked at the faces of the women around her, all in stunned silence. "I got dumped for being the good kid. By my so-called friends, and by everyone who I wouldn't lie the way Mandy did. I got stuck being either the goody two shoes or the disappointment."

She smirked in satisfaction. "At least now I'm choosing to own being the disappointment, while the person who everyone now realizes deserves that title tries to fight it."

Suddenly everyone was trying to refute her claim, tell her that they always knew she was a good kid, and that's why they just had to spend all their time helping Mandy.

She saw Matt walking down the dune towards the party out of the corner of her eye and cut off their blubbering.

"Speaking of disappointing people, I've got one more to disappoint now." She said, backing away.

She didn't care what they all thought she meant, because she was going through her head over and over what she wanted to say, but it changed each time.

She pulled her Ducreis hoodie, the one her parents had given her dirty looks for wearing to the party, down over her hands, and walked up to Matt before he could get caught up with his friends.

She smiled at him timidly. "Hey," She started.

He wouldn't even look her in the eyes. "Hey." He said, still trying to walk past her.

She sidestepped and stood in his path, holding her arm out. "Uhm, can I talk to you real quick?"

He shrugged and examined the ground.

She pressed her lips together so tight she couldn't even feel them. "Can we like…" she pointed towards the water. "Step away?"

He shrugged again but walked that way.

She matched his stride beside him, having forgotten how long it was, how he wasn't much taller than her when she stood close to him.

"Well, uhm," She drew out, wringing her hands together, "You know I'm going to be leaving soon, but before I left I just…"

She paused, chewed on her lip as they stopped at the edge of where the tide came in.

He rolled his eyes and sighed heavily but let her keep talking.

"We were so close, the two of us, for so long. And I miss it. I miss us." She said, motioning between the two of them, trying to get eye contact from him.

"I won't ask you what changed because I know you'll deny it… But I didn't want to leave before I had a chance to truly say goodbye. Goodbye in many different ways."

He shrugged again, and hands still in the pockets of his trunks, he mumbled something incoherent.

"What?" She asked, gently.

"I SAID," He snapped, looking up, his eyes finally locking onto hers. "Why would we have a problem?"

She felt angry heat fill her now shaking legs as she firmly planted herself in the sand.

"BECAUSE of things like THAT." She snapped as well, head jerking back.

"Look," She said, trying to calm down, running a shaking hand through her hair. "We haven't been right for a while now, you won't talk to me, you won't look at me, and I've asked you why. I just want to know the truth. And if you won't tell me, I just want to end things better than they've been left for the last year. I might never see you again."

A look of deep hurt slapped across his face.

Then he shook his head, regained the icy cold stare. "If someone else isn't talking to me, I'm not the one with the problem." He mumbled.

"What?!" She exclaimed, her voice rising.

She was glad they had walked far from the group and the wind was starting to howl, carrying their voices far away. Everyone was too consumed with pouring lighter fluid on the stack of bonfire wood to even notice the two of them.

"Me not talking to you? YOU haven't even LOOKED at me in ages., All I wanna know is how we can be cool again!"

"We ARE cool." He said, icily, his jaw set.

"We ARE NOT cool, Matt, and you know it."

He huffed and puffed for a second, moving side to side, and then glared at her.

"Why are you leaving anyway?" He snapped. "Are we not good enough for you here? Is that why you don't have any friends? No one is good enough for you?"

"Oh, Jesus, not this again! That's bull!"

"Oh is it? Then why are you so intent on leaving everyone again? What about your parents? I wouldn't leave my parents to go live with some distant relative or some little kid!"

"Oh, holy roller, excuse me!" Ariettea spat. "Excuse me for growing up and moving on with my life! Why does that intimidate you so much?"

"Oh yeah, ME intimidated by someone who can't get along with anyone, who has to leave because no one is good enough for them! From the minute I met you, you've complained about not having any friends, but how you want to get a job, move away, blah blah-"

"All I've ever wanted was to be HAPPY. Excuse me for thinking back then that I could confide in a frien-"

"Yeah, and what about all your friends you've had? Call Mandy up and be like 'Hey Mand, let's go shopping! But no, she's not good enough for y-"

"Get over yourself, Matt! You know I did! Many times! Mandy was just another person who made my life miserable!"

"OH! So she ISN'T good enough for you!"

"Sorry if I don't want to be around people I can't trust!"

"And you trust that little cancer kid?"

"YES, I DO trust that little CANCER kid!"

"Why? So you can come back here and whine when she's mean to you, too!"

"WHAT IS YOUR PROBLEM WITH ME? Why are you so mad that I don't like to have 10 million friends?"

"I have 10 million friends, and I wish you were one of them! I wish you could be with us!"

"I want MY friends to be more than empty-headed bodies, there just to fill space and increase numbers."

"Excuse me?"

"You heard me."

It was pouring out of her. All of it.

"So then that's what you think of me?"

"I never said that!"

"So, what DO you think of me?"

"I think you can be so nice and kind when you try. I know you can! You used to look at me, and I could see the care in your eyes, we used to talk for hours, about everything, about our futures, but now that you've spent all this time avoiding me and now that you're screaming at me I don't know WHAT to think of you!"

"Yeah, well, I think you're a stuck-up little snob, but if you'd try," His voice mocking, "You could be a LITTLE likable! I mean, you're nice and sweet and thoughtful and funny when you're not being snobby!"

"I'm snobby by trying to talk to you while also having my own life?"

They were both full-on yelling.

"Your own life away from where you should be!" He sniped.

"And why MUST I be here?!" She fired back.

"FOR ME!" He exploded.

Ariettea took a step back. "What?" She spat out, unsure of what emotion her exclamation carried.

He sighed, put his hands on his hips, then rubbed the stubble running down his chin.

"Ariettea," He started, waving a hand. "You're stuck up, you think you're smarter than everyone, and you drive me insane. But there is a reason you drive me insane. You're everything I'm not. You're kind-hearted when you actually want to be, you have this crazy sense of humor, you're fun to be around when you're not a tightwad. I look at you and see the universe in your eyes before you, and you have this look that says you can take it in your hands."

He shook his head. "And dear GOD, are you hot."

He clammed up and kicked the sand with his Nike as Ariettea felt her face blushing.

"So, when I left for the summer," She said, drawing her words out, trying to reason through it all.

"I was mad you did." He admitted.

"And even before that?"

"Before that, I saw in you that you wanted to leave. And it made me mad."

"But why?"

He looked into her eyes, and for the first time in a long time she saw that look. That caring look in those big brown eyes.

He wouldn't answer.

"I don't understand." She said.

He rolled his eyes. "Because I want you here!" He yelled at her.

"Why are you yelling again?" She yelled back.

"Because you're being stuck up again!"

"WHY?"

"Because it's you! It's always been you. I just.. AUGH! I LIKE YOU AND YOU DON'T GET IT!"

He stepped dangerously close to her and looked down into her eyes. She could smell his dark and musky cologne, and as her heart sped her brow furrowed, still trying to comprehend it all.

But then she got angry again.

"WELL if you like me, then why are you such a jerk to me?!"

"Because you can be so stupid!"

"Well if I'm so stupid, then why do you like me?!"

"Because I'm stupid!"

"DANG RIGHT!"

"WELL IF WE'RE BOTH SO STUPID, maybe we should go out!" He said, throwing his arms down.

"Maybe we should!" She fired back.

And then realizing what they had both just said, they both froze. She let out a breath that she didn't realize she'd been holding.

"Maybe we should." She repeated, mostly for herself to hear again, to make sure that's what she'd said.

He looked at her with that look again. He stepped even closer and put his hand on her back, confidently placed his other hand on hers, intertwining their fingers, sending chills down her arms and legs. He looked deep into her eyes, and that gravelly voice rang out clearly as he held her tight and asked, "Well, then why don't we?"

"Okay, okay, can you see me now?"

"I can!"

Ariettea stood bent over, trying to prop up her phone to show Lily her outfit over FaceTime.

"Yeah, okay, the picture is clear on my end too."

"Hiii!" Lily squealed, waving. She sat Indian style on the back deck, the ocean behind her.

Ariettea laughed into the camera. "Hey!"

"So this is crazy!" Lily said straight out.

"Just a little." Ariettea replied, trying not to blush, giggling like a schoolgirl.

"It IS crazy!" Lily exclaimed. "I'm helping you get ready for your first DATE!"

Ariettea looked down and smiled shyly.

"Okay, let's see!" Lily exclaimed. "Step back!"

Ariettea did, posing dramatically, letting Lily see her white dress, THE white dress, in its entirety.

"Cuuute!" Lily beamed. "Turn, turn!"

Ariettea spun.

"I love your hair!" Lily exclaimed. "It's so long again!"

Ariettea ran a hand through it, she had nervously curled it for hours, trying to get it just right. "Yeah it is..."

She thought of the day all that time ago, the day her hair had whipped Matthew in the face in the wind at the beach, the day she'd had that first lily handed to her.

"Are you excited?" Lily asked.

"Very."

"Nervous?"

"Extremely!"

"Well don't be. You're a catch, my friend." Lily beamed at her through the phone. "What did your parents finally say?"

Ariettea shrugged, picking up the phone and flopping down onto her bed. "I think they've finally learned that I'm going to do what I want no matter what. According to them I just go beyond reason anyway and never listen to anyone so they didn't really say much. I could see it in my mom's face that she was more shocked by it being HIM more than anything else."

Lily nodded slowly. "I mean... I was too. After all your history, for him to drop that bombshell..." She shook her head,

Ariettea could tell she was holding something back. "And?"

"And... I just hope that's truly how he feels."

"Why wouldn't it be?" Ariettea asked, defensively.

"You guys have been disconnected for so long; I want your coming back together to be...real."

"As opposed to?"

Lily waved a hand. "I'm not doubting YOU, Ari! I just want his motives to be pure, I want this boy to treat you the way you truly deserve, not just the way you think you deserve. Because you always deserve more than you think."

Ariettea smiled at her. "I just really think that this is what always should have been. We're finally where we're meant to be." She bit her lip and smiled at her lap. "I loved the way he looked at me, Lily. It was like he used to."

She shook her head, her curls bouncing around her face, cascading down her shoulders and back. "Those big brown eyes boring into mine…I saw something there that I haven't seen in a long time. The true him."

Lily smiled, consoling. "I hope so." She paused. "So, where are you going exactly?"

"We're going to eat at a steakhouse in town, and then he said we might go get a coffee or something after."

"So, he planned it all?"

"Sure did. He really took control."

"How sweet!"

"I know. That's how I know it's the old him."

"Ari," Lily said slowly, "which is it, though? The old him, or the true him?"

Ariettea shook her head, confused. "Why does there have to be a difference?"

Suddenly her phone beeped, a message popping up over Lily's face.

"Oh, that's him! He'll be here in 2 minutes, I've gotta go."

"Okay Ari, have a great time and tell me all about it!"

"I will, Lils. Bye."

"Bye!"

Ariettea tossed her phone into her purse and threw on her espadrille heels. She checked her makeup in the mirror one last time, the lighter makeup she had taken to wearing over the summer, the one with no black eyeliner rimmed around her eyes.

She heard a horn honk.

She ran out the front door just barely waving to her parents, not having the energy for another lecture on chastity or maturity.

She wondered why he didn't come to the door as she strolled down the driveway and opened the door of his white Subaru.

"Hi." She sighed, slipping in.

"Hey." He said, throwing his head back against the headrest, with the cutest smile she'd seen from him in a long time.

She felt like she had forgotten all the little things she loved about him, the way he drove with one arm draped over the steering wheel, the way his head moved without him knowing it whenever his favorite songs came on the radio.

"How was work today?" She asked him, searching for something light to talk about. He shrugged.

"A part-time job's a part-time job." He looked over at her and smiled. "So, basically nasty."

She smiled at him, knowing better than to suggest different ways he could get a better job. He'd only resent her for implying he wasn't good enough. But then again, how did he expect to even move out when all he wanted to do was work part-time and play video games? But was that even what he wanted anymore? She suddenly realized she didn't know anything about him from the past year.

"How was your day?" He asked her.

She snapped out of her thoughts. "It was fine; I finally got FaceTime working with Lily. It's been on the fritz for some reason lately."

He nodded. "Nice." He said flatly.

She wondered if he was still resenting her life away from there. She knew he was. But she didn't know what else to say. Shouldn't he carry on a conversation? Should she? They rode in silence for a few moments, both of them realizing how long it had been since they'd actually had a conversation.

"I guess this a bit new for both of us." She said sheepishly.

He shrugged, silently, her suddenly self-conscious if he had been dating while she was gone.

"Or, I mean, is it?" She stammered. "For you? I guess I don't really know what you've been up to, and I didn't mean to say-"

"No, I haven't been seeing anyone." He piped up, cutting her off. She bit her lip, unsure of how to tread.

"But have you… before?" She asked slowly.

His eyes flashed over to her, annoyance passing through the glance. "No, not officially."

She paused, and he rolled his eyes dramatically as his shoulders fell back.

"And no, not unofficially, either. Ariettea, can we just… talk to each other?"

She looked at her lap. "Like we used to?" She asked quietly. She could see him nodding.

"But… why did we stop?" She asked him gently. "Awhile back… Lennox had said something about… us. But there never was an 'us'. Or was there something I missed?"

"Ariettea, I think we both know there's been something brewing for a long time. But I just… I had to focus on finishing school."

"Was that your parent's choice or yours?"

"I make my own decisions, Ariettea." He said cuttingly.

He caught himself and tried to soften.

She wanted to ask more, ask if it was her, if she was a second choice, if she was the first choice but that his parents disapproved of, if his friends disapproved of. She'd spent all summer learning to not care about anyone else's approval, and there she was, obsessing over it again.

His voice lowered an octave as it took on that gravely tone she loved so much, at least when he was talking to her. "None of the past matters now. Now, we have all the time in the world."

Her face flushed, and her heart fluttered, a feeling she had forgotten about since they'd stopped talking. Still, in her head, she wanted to know what he'd been doing the past year that he wasn't saying. She also ignored the nagging feeling of wanting to point out that their time together was going to be limited, she was leaving.

"We haven't really TALKED in a long time." She said carefully.

Matt laughed good-naturedly. "Okay," He said with a smile. "Let's talk."

They tried talking about movies, what had come out the last year that they'd seen in common. Turned out, very few.

"Okay, so for the next date, we WON'T go see a movie."

"Agreed." She laughed.

She paused, realizing he was already thinking of a next date.

Then they tried talking about music. Another flop.

Then he tried asking her opinion on the new restaurants in town, that it turned out she didn't even know existed.

By the time they'd settled into the restaurant and ordered, they were still grasping for things to discuss.

"What did you do all summer?" She asked him.

"Just hung out, laid low, tried to keep up my GamerScore." He laughed.

She looked at him, confused. "Gamer score?"

He looked just as confused as she did, not understanding how she couldn't know what he was talking about.

"Yeah, on consoles you can see your friend's achievements in games and scores and it's fun to try and beat each other."

"Oh…" She looked around the restaurant, all the other couples all in rapt conversations. "I guess I had an outdoors summer compared to that," She said, trying to laugh, sound casual. "We spent a lot of time at the beach. I guess just laying low, too."

She waited to see if he'd ask more, what else they did, what it was like down south, but he didn't. He changed the subject, quickly.

They tried talking about classmates, mutual friends, but Ariettea didn't have many people she wished to discuss. She kept turning back to more serious conversations, as she was used to with Lily.

"So, are you still looking into getting a job at an architecture firm in the city?"

He shook his head. "Nah… it's too far, you know?"

She didn't.

"I want to stick closer to home, work for a while first before jumping into anything."

"Oh, okay, cool," she said slowly. "So, what have you been looking at?"

"I've been trying different things I can make a career of. But they want experience."

"Ah, yes, the experience." He shrugged.

"And you?" He already knew the answer.

"Well…" Ariettea paused. She was supposed to go to college in a few weeks. And here she was on a date with someone who refused to leave his zip code. "You know I'm going to school soon."

His smile fell. "Yeah." He mumbled, staring down at the table, fiddling with his napkin.

She decided to just put it out there.

"So, what does that mean?" She asked. "I mean, you said something about our next date in the car, what does that mean for our future?"

"Our future?" He scoffed. "There's not a 'us' yet."

"Yeah but it needs to be asked."

"I guess we just wait it out, Ariettea." He paused, trying to change his darkened tone. "You're always looking ahead, freaking out over details, can't we, just for now, maybe just the next few weeks, live in the now?"

Ariettea looked at him. Those eyes. Those big, brown, eyes were still boring into her own. It was like he could see right through her. But it was as if the sparkle that used to glitter through his eyes had died down.

But it was still Matt.

Finally, Matt.

The old Matt.

Her friend.

"Yes." She agreed.

"Okay."

"So, what are your friends up to?" She asked him, trying to seem interested in people she didn't like.

He told her about his friends, their summer, their jobs, their basketball games every Friday night, him and his boys were his life, there was no doubting that. "Nice." She smiled, trying to nod in all the right places.

"How was your summer?" Matt asked her.

Ariettea beamed. "It was great." She said feeling her heart warm. "I loved being by the beach all summer, I loved being with Lily, and I loved really getting to spend time focusing on me and what I want and God and just really deep stuff, you know?"

Matt smiled, tried and failed to suppress a laugh. "You sound like something straight out of a movie." He said.

His voice got high pitched, mocking. "God, Lily, beach, life!"

Ariettea tried to laugh it off, but his words stung. "Well, what's wrong with any of that?" She asked him, trying to sound casual.

He shrugged. "Nothing really, it's just kind of…"

"Kind of what?"

"Lame."

"Lame?"

"Yeah."

"Why?"

"I don't know; I guess it's just you're out of school, and you want to… I don't know; maybe we just don't have the same idea of summer fun."

"So, what's your idea of summer fun then?"

"Hanging out with friends, working, chilling, playing around."

"Yeah, and I did the same thing."

"Not really."

"What? You don't want to spend time on God?"

"I didn't say that."

"You think I shouldn't hang out with Lily?"

"Not exactly."

"Then what?"

She didn't want to argue, but she couldn't let it go.

"I don't know; I just think you get so serious when summer and life aren't."

"Life is serious, Matt. We're adults now, I mean, I don't think you can fault me for wanting to be serious. I have serious decisions to make. So do you."

He leaned back into the booth, sighed. "Okay. Okay. I understand."

She paused, taken aback he was agreeing with her. She smiled, seeing the old him once again.

"Thank you. I mean, if we're going to date…"

Her eyes trailed off, her gaze suddenly captivated by a vase of lilies at the front of the restaurant that she had somehow missed when they walked in. The thing about lilies was that there were so many different kinds; you could be surrounded by them and miss it.

She regained her speech, drug her eyes back to him sitting across from her.

"…I want to know you're serious."

He fumbled for words, then looked deep into her eyes again. "I am serious, Ariettea." He finally said. And in that voice…

She nodded. "Okay." She said softly, smiling at him and blushing.

She wanted to talk more, more about life, what he saw himself doing in a few years, but she promised to live in the moment with him, and she wanted to keep that promise. They chit-chatted more and more over dinner, trying to find things to talk about.

And they did.

The old inside jokes were still funny, the old bantering returned. She giggled like she used to when they would talk. It was like they were friends again. She had missed him as a friend.

"So, you wanna grab some Starbucks?" He asked her at the end of their meal.

She nodded, happy that he didn't want their date to end. Because neither did she. "I would love to."

Ten minutes later, they sat sipping decaf coffees. Ariettea curled her feet under her in an armchair, pulling a sweater tightly around her and her dress. Matt sat next to her, perched on the arm of the chair.

"This was really nice." She said, smiling, having to look up at him.

He had worn a button-down shirt, dark wash jeans. Every time they walked side by side, she could smell the men's soap coming off of him, the warm, attractive, strong smell that somehow smelled different than she was used to; older, mature. She liked it.

He nodded. "I think so too."

She let the quiet take her in. She found herself studying him, his sideburns, the stubble along his chin, the shape of his face…He caught her and laughed.

"What?" He asked.

She shook her head. "Nothing." She said, smiling.

He smiled back. "I know that look, Ari."

Her heart sped up. He knew her; he always did. She felt her cheeks warm. "Just admiring the view is all."

He chuckled, looked down sheepishly. "So," He began, staring at the floor. "Can I take you out again?"

She smiled, her cheeks still burning, for once in her life, not overthinking her answer. "Yes." She blurted, not thinking at all about what it meant.

He smiled back, stood up, and held a hand out to her.

She let his warm, strong grasp envelope her hand, seemingly tiny and pale, compared his large and dark hand. It closed around hers as he replied, "Good."

Chapter 25

It's been said that everyone dies famous in a small town. There's never been anything more truthful. Because everyone Ariettea knew, and a ton of people she didn't, knew about her and Matt within a week. Whispered conversations and not so subtly pointed fingers followed her wherever she went.

She was again being the weird one- officially dating someone. Everyone was used to fake dating, the kind where you lie to everyone and say that you're 'just friends' until you either get engaged or secretly break up. She couldn't help but believe that that's what had happened between Matt and Mandy, but she was too afraid to ask. She wasn't sure, though, if she was afraid of his reaction to the question, or of what the truth might be.

She was suddenly getting texts from people she hadn't spoken to in years; girls she had met in passing at parties and in school, and her old friends that had stopped talking to her, the ones she'd had falling outs with suddenly wanted to catch up. She ignored many texts, half of them she wasn't even sure who they were from, as she had deleted so many numbers from her phone over the summer as a catharsis.

She was stuck between wanting to confirm it to the world and wanting to hide it all away. She was avoiding everyone as best she could but wanting to talk with Matt one Sunday about their plans for the night, she hung around. Besides, she could tell from his looks that he'd shoot her as she ran out the door that he didn't like her bolting. Mandy made a beeline for her as soon as the amen was said, before Ariettea could make it across the room to Matt, to safety. She smiled, suddenly thinking of him as her safe place.

"Ariettea!" Mandy exclaimed in that loud, high pitched screech she made whenever she wanted to be overheard.

She tripped over a chair leg and practically fell into Ariettea's arms.

Always the drama queen.

"Congratulations!"

"On what?" Ariettea asked, sighing, hoisting her back up, fighting the urge to roll her eyes.

Mandy threw her head back and laughed, punched her lightly on the arm. "You and Matt! Silly!"

Ariettea gave her a fake smile. "Oh thanks." She said, absentmindedly, glancing over at Matt, who was enraptured in a conversation with his friends.

She wanted him to come help, she desperately tried to make eye contact with him from across the auditorium, willing him to look at her, but when he finally did, he looked away immediately.

"Sooo…" Mandy drew out, bouncing back and forth from the heel of her foot to her toes, dangerously close to falling down again, "Tell me the details!"

Ariettea felt physically grossed out at the thought of sharing anything with her. "There's not much to tell."

"Oh, you liar!" Mandy exclaimed dramatically, throwing her hand down at her side, the thwak of her hand against her leg purposely loud enough to get everyone to look over at her.

Ariettea shrugged, trying to get rid of her. "We went for dinner, that's all."

"That's all?!" She rolled her eyes at Ariettea and shook her head.

She sighed dramatically. "Okay, alright, if you don't want to share, I'll go ask Matt!"

She flounced away before Ariettea could stop her.

Ariettea felt the irritation well up in her as Mandy approached Matt; flaunting her short skirt and long legs. Why did Mandy need to act like there was some big juicy secret?

And... Why was she leaning in so close to Matt?

And why was he not backing away?

Ariettea felt confused, could she call Matt her boyfriend yet? Could she feel jealous? Was she allowed to feel jealous? She could just hear Lily in her head-

'No one is allowed to tell you what you can and can't feel. So feel it. Quit running from your feelings. Hiding from them means keeping the good ones out.'

Ariettea watched from afar as Mandy laughed and talked with Matt, leaning in and pulling back, her hand resting on his bicep, the one bulging through his dress shirt rolled up to his elbows. He just shrugged and laughed himself, leaning into her grasp. But she could tell that at least he wasn't giving her what she wanted, because she never got the smug look of gossip acquired on her face.

Ariettea smiled to herself, happy he wasn't blabbering on about them. But ...Wait, was she? Why wasn't he proud of her? Of them? She shook her head, yelling at herself, hadn't she just had the same internal conversation about herself? What was wrong with her?

"Ariettea," Her mom said, coming up to her. "Maybe you should stop staring at Matthew and talk to some of the other people here."

Ariettea looked around at all the people who had chosen to ignore and ridicule her for years, the people she had decided she didn't have anything to prove to anymore.

Her mom noticed her hesitation and rolled her eyes, leaned in close to her and whispered, "Ariettea, you're going to embarrass Matt by being rude to everyone."

Ariettea pulled away sharply, nearly snarling as she asked, "Why would I EMBARRASS him?"

"You really think he's going to want to date someone who doesn't like the people in his life? If you're going to be together for a long time, you're going to have to start caring what these people think of you."

"I will NEVER care about that, again. Besides, I'm leaving this place at the end of summer, with or without him."

Her mother sighed, looked around, made sure no one was watching as she grabbed her arm and whispered back, "Quit being so stubborn and fighting what people say just to make a point!"

"I've never been trying to make any sort of point! I've only ever been me! I'm not about to start playing a role."

She pulled her arm away, and walked over to Matt, placed her hand on his arm where Mandy's had been. But instead of stepping towards her like he did Mandy, he pulled away at her touch.

"Hey," He said lowly, looking around, grabbing her hand. "Let's talk later, yeah?" He squeezed her hand under the tops of the chairs, where no one could see. Then he smiled warmly at her as he walked away.

She held onto the feeling of his touch as long as she could after he had walked out. She stood there, alone, like she always did, feeling more confused than ever.

Everyone started saying they were spending too much time together. In just three short weeks, they discovered each other all over again. They remembered just how different they were, but they also remembered how well they worked together.

She had taken an interest in basketball, him patiently explaining games to her as they watched them together, her head resting on his shoulder on the couch. Her favorite thing was when he'd take her outside after dark, when the fireflies were out, and try to teach her how to shoot a basket. They'd end up just sitting on the blacktop of his parent's driveway, talking. Even though his parents constantly looked outside, thinking they were doing otherwise.

He took to her favorite books, diving into the first one she'd suggested to him, even though he'd avoided reading it all through high school. He learned all her favorite Starbucks drinks and randomly bring them over to her house.

He'd throw his arm around her shoulders the days they'd walk up and down the pier, to the lighthouse and back. Strolling down, holding his hand, to finally feel more than a handshake, but to feel his fingers intertwined with hers, him holding onto her tight and strong, sent electricity down through her arms to her toes.

She loved hanging off his arm as they walked into a restaurant.

She loved seeing him smile at her from across the room.

But as much as she loved every second they spent together, the thought of leaving was always nagging at her. Her departure date was drawing closer and closer, much faster than she had anticipated.

She was trying her best to keep up with Matt's all-day texts along with Lily's and Nadette's.

One week before she was set to leave town, they spent the evening walking along the shoreline after another coffee date. She tried to avoid the lapping waves from splashing her legs up her dress, a red flowing piece, made of satin. He walked where the sand was dry to avoid getting water on his dress pants.

They had come from a fancy Italian restaurant, him in trousers and blazer, looking more dapper than his usual skater boy style.

She wanted to freeze the moment in her mind, as she already had with so many photos of the two of them, their faces now taking up her lock screen in place of the photo of her and Trent.

The thing was, as much as Matt wanted her there with him in the present, she wanted her future down south more.

And he knew it.

They both knew her heart was somewhere else.

She still didn't do well with present only thinking. Her mind was always ten steps ahead of the current moment, although Lily had helped her reign that tendency in somewhat.

She smiled at the thought that maybe her summer down south had been to prepare her for their relationship.

Her hand intertwined with his, they silently strolled, both knowing the conversation that was about to come. They had been avoiding it all night.

She stopped walking and pulled his hand. "Matt," She said softly.

He paused, then turned around slowly to face her.

She looked deep into his eyes, and then down at her bare feet. "Matt," She began again, "This relationship is something that…" Her eyes wandered down the coast. "… I've wanted for so long, but never thought I would get."

She looked back up at him, his jaw clenched, those chiseled features popping.

"I was afraid that I had lost you forever when we stopped talking. I mean, all I wanted was to say goodbye to you before I left, and now here we are…"

She trailed off, turning to stare at the sunset behind them.

She paused to let him say something, anything, but he stayed silent.

"I've avoided talking about the future, just enjoyed the now, with you. That's something I've actually been working hard to learn all summer."

She smiled, but the smile left just as quickly as it came.

"But I AM leaving for Ducreis in a few days. So now we HAVE to talk about what happens next."

He nodded, slowly, deliberately.

She took a deep breath, "I've thought a lot about this, and Lily and I have been best friends long distance, we've grown closer and closer being so far apart, I think we can do the same!"

She was talking faster and faster, almost pleading. "We can spend weekends and holidays and summers and breaks together, talk every day like we do now, and-"

He squeezed her hand and then let go as he reached inside the pocket of the jacket he was wearing. He pulled out a single red rose that she had no idea he had been carrying.

She stopped talking as he handed it to her slowly.

"Ariettea," He said, looking down. "I've known that I like you for a long, LONG time." He paused, cleared his throat. "I know I don't want us to break up."

"I don't either-" She began.

She saw something on his face, something new…

Her mind was racing.

What if he wanted to come with her?

Would he really do that for her?

That's a big commitment so early on.

But they had both known each other for so long already…

Her heart was pounding as he cut her off.

"So, I don't want you to leave." He said firmly.

She zeroed in on his face, watched the corners of her vision turn black. "What?" She blurted loudly.

He took back her free hand. "Ariettea, I want to date you, I want to be with you, I want to talk to you every day, I want to see you Sundays and Thursdays, I want to see you when I get off work, I don't want you to be so far from me."

His own voice sounding pleading, he paused again to turn it to firm, commanding. "I don't want you to go."

Her head was spinning; she started to feel dizzy.

"But-but, I've enrolled," She stammered, "I've packed, I-"

"You can UN-enroll, you can UN-pack." He said to her plainly.

She looked into his eyes.

What about the scholarship?

What about Lily?

"Matt," She gasped out, eyes suddenly darting everywhere, "I... I can't stay here for... a summer fling."

She searched his face for some sign of what he was thinking. His gaze came up from the ground and settled squarely on her face.

"I love you, Ariettea." His words hung in the air as she desperately dug around in her head for the right words to say.

Her mind was going to everything she had planned, everything she expected, everything that she had wanted her entire life...

But.

But she knew that more than anything she just wanted meaning, a reason to exist, something in her life that would actually last.

She felt herself starting to shake. Then she felt Matt's hand tighten on hers. She squeezed back, held onto it, strong and... safe.

She wanted to stop; to analyze everything, weigh the pros and cons, think about what it all meant, not just to her but to everyone else that had planned with her.

But what had overanalyzing ever gotten her? She had known him for so long, and things were going so well, and college could always wait...

He had just told her he loved her.

He LOVED her.

She hadn't been sure she'd ever hear those words from anyone. And she didn't think she'd ever hear them from anyone else, either.

She suddenly was searching for Lily in the distance, as she had learned to do any time she was nervous. She looked at the lilies tucked into the sand dunes, blooming strong at the end of summer. Lilies followed her everywhere, every big choice she had made the past year. And she had to make a choice, right then.

"Okay."

She had to tell Lily first and as soon as possible. It wasn't news she could just sit on, not even for a night.

Despite the time, she got on FaceTime with Lily as soon as she got home.

Lily answered, under a pile of pink blankets in bed, her eyes squinting, and her hair smushed down on her forehead. "Ari? What's up?" She whispered.

Ariettea was suddenly at a loss for words.

Lily saw the look on her face and bolted straight up. "Hold on; I'm going to go outside; my parents are asleep."

Ariettea herself paced across the Berber carpet in her bedroom as she listened to Lily paddle down the hardwood floor and through the sliding door out to the deck. She couldn't bear to look at her reflection in the black screen as she waited for Lily to reappear. She was pale, her eyes popping out a little too much.

Lily bobbled the camera in front of herself as she pulled a knit blanket around her shoulders. "Okay... What's up?"

Ariettea paused, found herself chewing on a fingernail.

"Did something happen on your date tonight?"

Ariettea nodded.

"Okay, what did the jerk do? That no good, low life-"

"He told me he loves me." She cut in, softly.

Lily softened, but still looked confused. "He what?" Then she smiled. "Well, that's great! Isn't it?"

Ariettea nodded her head, her eyes started to burn. "He asked me to stay here, Lily." She paused. "And I said yes."

There was a silence. Ariettea could clearly hear the lapping of the waves behind Lily as she processed.

"Like... For good?"

"...I don't know, for now, at least. Probably."

"But I mean, is that what you...want?"

Ariettea sat on her bed, tucked a leg underneath herself. "I want him." She tried to gather her thoughts. "I want happiness. And I mean, isn't that what I've been trying so hard to learn? That happiness isn't a place? That you can find it anywhere-"

"Yeah, and some places are easier to find it in."

"Some people, too! I mean, wasn't I moving down there for all of you guys?"

Ariettea could see the hurt on Lily's face before the words had ever left her mouth.

Lily stopped herself from speaking. Looked around. The blue moonlight hit the high points of her cheekbones as she thought.

She looked back to Ariettea. "Ari, I think you need to chase what makes you happy. You're going to be the best judge of that. I just know how happy you were away from there. I would hate to see you stay for this one thing. One thing that was non-existent when you were at your happiest I've seen you and is also among ten other bad things you've hated and have wanted to get away from your whole life."

"But that's the thing; this relationship was never here for me before." Ariettea fought to keep annoyance out of her tone.

"Yeah but all the bad stuff was and is either way."

Ariettea played with the quilt on her own bed.

Lily sighed.

"Maybe everyone here is right. Maybe my finding happiness should happen anywhere. If I can't find it here, then I'd be leaving for…" She trailed off, not wanting to imply that Lily was nothing. That her whole new family was somehow inferior to Matt.

"I want to be by you guys so, so much. But I owe it to myself to see this thing with Matt through. It's been a long time coming. Maybe this is what's always meant to be. Maybe the summer prepared me for him. I've just got to wait and see."

Lily smiled and nodded. "Well, as long as you're happy, Ari, I'll always support you."

She beamed at her. "Thank you, Lily. That's the kind of support I need in my life." She had a twinge of realization that wasn't something she was going to get living there.

Lily coughed and Ariettea jumped. "Oh, man, I'm sure you're freezing. I'm sorry for waking you. Go back inside; we'll talk more tomorrow. Promise."

Lily grinned at her, wadded up her blanket and stood. "I'm counting on it."

Ariettea jumped suddenly, "Hey, wait, Lily?"

"Yeah?"

"Why was your first thought that he did something to hurt me?"

Lily shrugged, the blanket threatening to fall off her thin shoulders. "Just… His history with you. I think you're able to see the good things, but me, as your best friend, I have trouble seeing beyond the hurtful history, the one that's more recent."

Ariettea said goodnight again before she hung up and sighed.

She hadn't been sure who would be harder to talk to, Lily or Nadette. After all the trouble Trent and Nadette had gone to, the amazing offers they made, the support they were giving her, and she was going to hand it all back.

But it was for Matt.

Who loved her.

What she didn't think of was the people who had taught her to love herself.

Waking up, she had to tell her parents next, before Cirise could. She had to face them before she could even brush her teeth and call Nadette.

She tried explaining all the things she'd told Lily, but they didn't react as well as Lily had.

"So, all of a sudden, you're throwing away all your plans for this guy?" Her mother exploded. "I can't possibly understand your reasoning!"

Ariettea exclaimed, "You guys HATED me leaving here, and now you hate that I'm staying! Which one is it? Which one is the 'right' choice?" "

The balanced one!" Her father piped up. "We didn't want you running off chasing some unrealistic life. But we REALLY don't want you throwing away your life from some guy."

"But he's not 'some guy'! This is Matt we're talking about!"

"Yes, Matt, the guy who wouldn't talk to you for a year! How can he possibly tell you he loves you when you've only been together a month?"

"Because we've known each other since we were kids! We've got a jump start on knowing each other; we're years ahead of other couples."

"If that's true, then where do you see yourselves in a year? Two? Five? What's the long-term plan for you guys if you're giving up the long term plan for yourself?"

"College can wait. He can't."

"Why not?"

Ariettea stopped. She didn't have an answer for that.

"Everyone has ALWAYS jumped all over me for being too critical, too analytical, too cynical, and for once, I'm just trying to follow the feelings instead of calculating everything."

Her parents sighed. "I just don't agree with it. And after all Nadette and Trent were offering you…"

"Don't guilt-trip me for trying to do what's going to make me happiest. That's all I've ever wanted my whole life."

"And you've always said that means leaving here. All of a sudden, you're happy to stay?"

"You've always said I need to be happy anywhere. I'm doing all the things everyone has ever told me! Why is that an issue now? Because I'm not doing it the way everyone wanted? Because I didn't lie my way through high school only to go the other direction? I am going the other direction than what I said. But at least I never lied about who I am."

Her mother rolled her eyes and turned around to finish cooking breakfast. "You're 18, Ariettea. How do you even know who you are? You're not going to find yourself in a relationship."

"But I am going to find love. Acceptance."

"Has he ever accepted you for who you are, though? I thought he was always telling you to go out and make friends, go to parties, cut loose. So what, you're doing that now? Or he doesn't think that's right anymore?"

"I… don't know. That's why I have to stay here and figure it all out with him."

Then came Nadette.

Sure, Lily was her best friend, the person who she spent the summer with, the person that had taught her the most, but Nadette and Trent were the ones always willing to help her make the permanent choices.

She went through her spiel for the third time, and surprisingly it was the hardest time.

"Ariettea," Nadette said slowly over the phone. "We've gotten to know you so much over the past year. I know how important making your own decisions is to you."

Ariettea lay on her back, staring at the framed picture of her and Trent on their college tour, sitting on her nightstand.

"So I can't tell you what my opinion ion your choices. But can I ask you something?"

"Of course."

"You've only been together, what, a month?"

"Yeah."

Nadette's warm voice asked, "He says he loves you. You haven't told me what you love about him."

"What do you mean?"

"Tell me why this guy is so deserving of you."

Ariettea stopped, at a loss of how to answer. Leave it to Nadette to ask a question while making her out to be more deserving than she actually was.

"He makes me laugh." She said, finally. "When we're together, I feel special. I love the way I catch him staring at me from above his menu at a restaurant. We just… always have fun together."

Nadette was silent. "Can I give you a piece of advice?" She finally mused.

"Always." Ariettea chirped.

"One thing that I'll never forget learning when I was your age is that there is a big difference between loving someone, and loving the idea of them."

She called Matt, her brain feeling like mush and her heart so uncertain.

"What's up?" He answered, sounding far away.

"Just a tough day." She said, setting her head in her hand.

She hadn't showered or even changed out of her sweatpants. Her hair felt greasy as she flipped it to the other side of her head. She felt sick that she couldn't find a way to explain it. She didn't want him to feel like Lily and college were more important than him. But shouldn't a girlfriend be able to tell her boyfriend anything about her life? She looked over at the rose he had given her the night before sitting on her bedside table, next to the picture of her and Trent. Two clashing worlds.

"I'm just having a hard time canceling all the plans I've made." She admitted.

"Well, it's a good thing you and I have our own plans then."

"… I guess-Yeah. Of course… But do you want to go to dinner or something tonight?"

"Can't." He said quickly, nearly cutting her off. "I'm playing ball with the boys tonight."

Ariettea fumbled for words. "Well, can you, could you skip it just this once?"

"Ariettea, I go every Friday, you know that. It's guys night."

She felt uncharacteristically timid. "Well, I was just hoping that we could spend some time together, I mean, I just want to be with you. I NEED to be with you."

He sighed. She could hear him shaking his head. "What about Sunday night?"

"No, I'm going to dinner with my family, remember? It was something we planned as a going away thing. But hey, you could come!"

"You want ME to cancel, but YOU can't?"

She felt taken aback, not sure how to interpret his tone of voice. "Matt, this is my family, it's important to me. I'm sure you can understand."

"Well, we just saw each other last night, anyway."

"So then you don't want to come?"

She heard noise in the background.

"I gotta go. Work."

"Okay, b-." And then the call was over.

She stared at the phone incredulously. "He hung up on me." She muttered to herself.

She shook her head. 'I'm just used to people coming when I call.' She scolded herself. 'Lily always being there for you isn't realistic or even fair. Gosh, I'm such a drain on everyone. Look what I've put all these people through in just one day.'

She lay back on her bed and stared at the ceiling, her stomach starting to ache, feeling homesick for something while being in her own bedroom.

Chapter 26

Matt texted her Saturday morning, the first she'd heard from him at all since the morning before, as he would never answer any messages from her on 'guys night'. She had sat alone all night, trying to distract herself from feeling what she could only describe as jittery guilt.

"Do you want to go out tonight?" His text popped up.

She smiled at her phone, her heart calming at hearing from him. She was being selfish, of course, to ask him to stay in touch with her, even if she felt she needed him… right?

They set up a time for him to pick her up, and she went about her day. It was the day she was supposed to have left for Ducreis.

She sighed, then took in a deep breath. This was what was meant to be.

She was accepting it.

She just wasn't ready to eat her crow in front of the whole town.

Ever the planner, even dating Matt, she went out applying for jobs. Here there and everywhere, just something small to hold her over until… well, she wasn't sure until what. It was something she had said she'd never do; take whatever job came her way first without thinking of how it would contribute to her life.

She was finally learning that everyone was right when they told her that the money is enough contribution to happiness. At least, she was trying to learn it.

She thought about Trent coming home in his scrubs, kissing Nadette on the cheek, both of them happily babbling about their days. Surely work had nothing to do with it, right? Since they had each other?

And now she had Matt.

She turned in her application at the coffee shop and moved on to the next one. She saw a therapist's office that had advertised online for a receptionist, and applied there, thinking of Lily. Everyone in town always sneered at that office, making fun of and whispering about anyone who even thought of going there, the crazies. But Ariettea thought of Lily and all the therapy sessions she'd told her about and shared with her, Ariettea learning that feelings are meant to be felt, and through her own sadness, she'd seen Trent's support and what a difference it made. So even though she knew she was suppressing far too many emotions to be healthy, she smiled as she turned in that application, feeling somewhat closer to her family down South at that moment.

When Matt texted her that evening that he was in her driveway, she had just finished pulling on her Ducreis hoodie that had been a size or two too big, but now fit just right, paired with a pair of dark wash skinny jeans that hung on to the hips she had seemed to grow that summer.

He never came to the door for her, so she ran outside and whipped open his passenger side door, but only to find Lennox sitting there.

He snickered at her, tossed his head, saying, "Backseat." Before slamming the door in her face.

Her cheeks burned, and she wasn't sure if it was with hurt or embarrassment. She softly opened the backseat door and slipped in gently.

Matt looked at her out of the corner of his eye. "Hey," He said lowly, but not in the warm voice she was used to, but the cool guy act voice she hated hearing when he was around his friends.

She smiled tightly at him, waiting for an explanation of what was going on before she'd sit back and put her seatbelt on. She could see Lennox roll his eyes from the way his head moved as Matt finally turned all the way around.

He looked at her expectantly. "What's up?" He sighed.

She shook her head, her eyes wide. "You tell me…" She smiled, trying not to seem like THAT girl.

"We're going to get wings." He said flatly.

Her eyes darted back and forth from Lennox to Matt. "WE are?" She asked, putting as much of a casual tone on it as she could.

"Yeah, I mean, come on, you made such a big deal about not seeing me last night," He droned, "I thought the three of us could go out and have fun together."

She smiled at him, fluctuating between warm happiness that he wanted her to hang out with his friends, and confusion at his tone of voice.

She nodded as excitedly as she could and sat back as they drove off. She shook her head at herself as the boys talked, bantering back and forth, ignoring her. Of course, she was being THAT girl. He had asked her out, not on a date. They were different things, right? Of course. She was such an idiot. She wasn't even trying to talk with them! She scolded herself again as she leaned forward and tried to seem interested in what they were talking about.

"Did you see the achievement I unlocked, though?" Matt was saying.

"Oh, what for?" Ariettea asked, trying to sound supportive.

Lennox turned his head to look at her and scoffed.

Matt waved a hand. "It's a game thing."

"Oh, like at your game last night?"

Lennox chuckled to himself and looked over at Matt, shaking his head.

She saw Matt's grip tighten on the steering wheel. "No, Ariettea," He said, annoyed, hitting the syllables in her name sharply. "It's in VIDEO games."

"Oh..." she breathed, trying not to sound stupid.

"Geez Ariettea, you think you could at least TRY to be interested in what your guy here is?" Lennox sneered.

Her cheeks burned again.

It was just like Nadette said, he loved her, but she wasn't pulling her weight. 'I'm the worst girlfriend ever.' She thought to herself.

Girlfriend.

Why did Lennox call Matt her 'guy' and not boyfriend?

"Well, I'll just have to have my boyfriend show me." She said, putting all her effort into sounding excited.

It was one of many comments that went unacknowledged.

She let them talk as they drove, and when she got out of the car she went to grab onto Matt's arm like she always did- because he always offered it out to her, but he pulled away before she could touch him and walked side by side with Lennox, leaving her trailing behind.

It didn't end when the two of them sat together on one side of the booth of the local bar and grill, leaving her alone on the other. She bit her lip as she listened to the loudly playing pop hits music, the songs that were always overplayed in restaurants, feeling frustrated but desperately trying to be the girl he wanted her to be.

The girl she should be.

"What do you like to eat here, Matt?" She asked, putting as much cheer in her voice as she could.

He didn't acknowledge her.

"Matt?"

Nothing.

"MATT."

"What?" He asked suddenly, sharply, jarringly.

She pulled herself back and away from him, not realizing she was doing it. "Uhm, I was just asking what you like here." She smiled gently, but he said nothing.

"I just asked like, three times." She said with a laugh.

"Too loud to hear, sorry." He picked up a menu and flipped through it, ended up spinning it around on the table with one finger.

She waited for him to ask her if she wanted to split any appetizers like they usually did, but he said nothing.

He and Lennox started talking together about the food instead.

Ariettea kept trying to join in. "Yeah, my mom likes the nachos." She put in.

Nothing.

"Oh yeah, I've heard the desserts here are great!"

They ignored her or couldn't hear her; she couldn't tell. She didn't think the music was THAT loud. But maybe she was wrong. She usually was. She sighed and picked up her phone.

"Playing on your phone?" Lennox taunted, suddenly interested in her.

Ariettea bore her eyes into his face, the one she'd always described as slimy and freckled at the same time. "You're playing with my boyfriend." She shot.

"Ooh! Her boyfriend!" He laughed, shoving Matt on the arm.

She looked at Matt, confused. "What?" She asked.

"Nothing, nothing." Lennox said with a coy smile.

She tried not to roll her eyes, tried to keep herself from losing her temper.

She tried to take advantage of the pause in the boys' conversation, "I was just looking at an alert about that new movie we were talking about going to? It's getting good reviews."

"The one with that actress you like?"

"Yeah!"

"Oh, we already saw it."

She looked at him blankly.

"Len and I."

"...Oh." She said slowly, again trying to hide yet more hurt.

"You've gotta know Matthew has a life outside of you." Lennox sneered at her.

She couldn't even look at Matt or bear seeing his look of confirmation, so she just silently sat back into the booth wall and relented.

It seemed to make them happy.

They ignored her until there was a chance to poke fun. That had been one of the things Ariettea had loved about Matt, that they could joke around, but this, this was just too much. This was the side of him she hated.

She looked at her leftover fries, full. Her jeans were starting to cut into her stomach. She readjusted her hoodie and when she caught Matt staring at her, but not with the same smitten look he usually had.

She laughed and said, "I need to go on a diet Monday!"

Lennox leaned forward and grabbed her fries, shoving them in his mouth. His long pasty fingers dripping with grease waved to her as he asked, "Why not start now?" He smirked, that wide, snakelike smirk she'd hated seeing as long as she'd known him.

"What?" She asked, not sure if she was confused or hurt or angry.

"Start now!"

She looked to Matt for help, who just started laughing instead when she met his eyes.

"Gee, thanks, guys." She said, her insides stinging, burning, her stomach suddenly threatening to make her revisit what she'd just eaten.

"C'mon girl! Wearing a hoodie on a date? Hiding something?" Lennox mocked.

"Oh, so this IS a date?" She snapped, shooting Matt a look. "I hadn't noticed. Oh, unless you meant this is a date between the two of you." She pointed between them.

She rolled her eyes and took a deep breath. She looked down at her hoodie; the one Trent brought her the day they took her home, the day she told them she was going to Ducreis, the souvenir of them and Lily.

"This is my favorite hoodie." She said slowly, staying as calm as possible.

This was just how they joked. She needed to roll with it.

Until Lennox shot out, "Of that dumb school!"

Her eyes suddenly shot to his, hot, furious. She was feeling the same thing she'd felt all of high school, the need to defend herself, to have to try and get people to understand, the same feeling she'd worked all summer to forget.

To never feel again.

She was used to welding confidence, she'd come home with it, but now she was just back to fighting feeling embarrassed, desperately trying to explain to others what she wanted and why it wasn't wrong. A habit she had long given up, even before she left.

"And just what makes it dumb?" She threw at him hotly.

He just looked at her, smiling, enjoying goading her on.

But she wasn't about to back down.

"I'm waiting." She said evenly.

Matt laughed, "Tell her, Len."

"Where to begin!" He grinned devilishly.

Matt sat silent, staring into his coke, poking it with his straw.

She wanted him to help, to defend her, to tell him to lay off. But nothing. His face bounced back and forth between mocking and disgust.

"Maybe let's start with that dumb little girl it's by!" Lennox thundered.

Ariettea felt the disgust rise into her mouth.

She felt the fight or flight.

She wanted to either punch him in his wide toothy smirk or run.

She couldn't even look at Matt as she threw her hands in the air and got up.

"Oh, she's running away!" Lennox jeered over his shoulder, that statement loud enough to hear over the music.

She made a beeline for the bathroom. 'This is why I've always hated him.' She thought, throwing herself up against the wall, her head smacking against the white tile. 'And people in general.' She felt the cynicism well up and didn't even try to push it away.

She enjoyed the pain that came with her head hitting the wall, no pun intended, and threw her head back to hit it again. She sighed. There she was, a couple months back at home, already looking for ways to hurt herself again.

It just had to be her.

She scoffed. That attitude would have followed her to Georgia, and she'd have been just as miserable there, who was she kidding?

She had a bitter taste rising in her mouth as she pulled her phone out of her hoodie pocket and turned it over in her hand. She thought of reaching out to Nadette, to Trent, to Lily, but they were all people she'd abandoned, and who probably never actually cared to begin with. They'd just put up with her the past year and would have gotten just as fed up as people like Lennox who'd known her long had, had she stayed down there.

She shook her head, disgusted with herself. She was getting what she deserved.

She suddenly stepped forward, and dry heaved into the toilet bowl, fighting to keep her dinner down.

Lennox was right, starting now, she wasn't eating much of anything, anymore.

Another heave came, and she had to drop to a knee to avoid passing out entirely. The dirty bathroom stall was spinning around her so badly that she didn't care whatever dirt her knee was sitting in.

"Breathe." She could hear Trent saying.

She shook her head fiercely, squeezing her eyes shut, trying to push his voice out. Trying to make herself her Lennox's taunts, the truth, instead.

She went back to the table and slid back into her seat. Matt bored his eyes into her with fury flaming behind them.

"Oh-ho-ho, she's back!" Lennox's taunt came. She ignored him as Matthew continued his glare.

"That was rude." He chirped.

She looked at him, confused.

"You didn't ask if you could leave. You just left."

She felt all the words in the English language escape her mind as she struggled for words to respond.

"Did I need… permission?" She asked slowly.

Matt rolled his eyes as the checks arrived, three separate ones. He slid her receipt over to her silently.

She just looked at him for a second.

He always paid, always. She always offered to pay, but he never just expected her to.

Her eyes narrowed as she steamed. It had to have been Lennox's fault.

This wasn't Matt.

She needed to be nicer to his friends to make him happy. She needed to focus on him and what he needed and how to make everything work.

She softened her face as much as she could. "So, are we going to Starbucks then?" She asked with a smile.

"After wings?" Matt asked her incredulously. "Uh, no."

"But, we always do, even if it's just for iced tea or dessert."

"Well, obviously, not tonight." Lennox snipped.

She snapped her head over at him. "Would you just shut up?" She snapped. "This is our date, not your boys' night out."

"Woah, better tame your GIRLfriend, Matthew." He nudged him, laughing. "The last girl never claimed you as her boyfriend, guess you've got some labeling to get used to, boyfriend."

She looked at Matt, confused.

What last girl?

"We should go." Matt mumbled.

She gave him a dirty look and he threw his arms in the air.

"What is wrong with you tonight, Ariettea?" He snapped. "I'm trying to get you in with my friends. I guess it's true you've never liked them. I thought you were cooler than that. Why are you acting like a little brat?"

Ariettea bit her lip and set her jaw. "Because YOU are acting like a little boy, and you know what Matt, I don't WANT to date a little boy. I want to date a MAN. And you SURE aren't acting like one!"

"Oooh!"

People we're starting to stare.

Matt stomped off to the parking lot.

Ariettea sat with her arms crossed in the BACKseat of the car on the way home. Matt said nothing to her the whole drive until she went to get out of the car.

Her hand on the open door he whirled around, "HEY,"

She stopped, relieved he was going to apologize. "I didn't say goodbye." He said shooting daggers.

She realized he didn't mean it apologetically, but commandingly.

He leaned back into his seat, still facing her, his expression livid. "We'll talk later."

She steamed all night, pacing her bedroom back and forth, back and forth.

She didn't know what to do.

She felt so utterly alone, more alone than she'd felt, even before meeting Lily.

It was like the hope of meeting some new friend was gone, and she was truly alone.

Were she and Matt over?

Was this just yet another fight over friends that they'd get past? They'd never fought like they had the past year as long as she'd known him.

She thought it had just been his feelings for her. What if it wasn't?

She looked at the clock. She was supposed to have been in Trent and Nadette's guest room, her room, at the point. She was supposed to see Lily the next day, go to orientation the day after that. But she was… here. Instead.

It was supposed to be the better choice.

She had to make it the better choice.

Happiness is a choice… right?

Cirise came up to her that next Sunday morning after the final prayer. She expected some lecture on how she should be treating her son better.

Ariettea watched Matt and Lennox across the room, laughing with each other, Matt not even looking her way. Mandy sauntered up to them and smacked Len on the arm, the three of them diving into some sort of private joke and laughing.

"So did you guys have fun last night?" Cirise asked her.

She looked over at her, and saw she was genuinely asking. Did Matt not tell them anything?

"Oh, we, um,"

Ariettea stammered before Cirise jumped in,

"Matt never tells us anything!" She said laughing, waving a hand. "He comes home and recounts his basketball games in great detail but get him to describe a date, and then well, he has nothing to say!"

Ariettea stayed silent, not knowing how to feel about that.

"But, I did want to ask you how everything is going, you know, settling in here?" She smirked. "Look at you, after all those years of insisting you'd be leaving, proving the rest of us right!" She laughed.

Ariettea smiled, tightly. "Yeah, I've been trying to find my way of fitting in here, I guess. Looking for jobs."

"Oh yeah? Where at?"

"A few coffee shops, some stores at the mall, a vet's office, a therapist's office-"

"A therapist's office?" Her mom repeated, coming over. "You didn't tell us that!"

Ariettea shrugged. "I didn't think it was a big deal?"

"Which one?"

"It's on Franklin Street."

Her mom and Cirise looked at each other.

"Ooh, did you know that's where Emma went when she… had that… problem?" Cirise said in a hushed tone, eyes darting around the room.

Her mom nodded vigorously. "Her mother told me she had to see a psychiatrist too!"

Cirise shook her head.

Ariettea looked back and forth between them both. "Am I missing something?" She asked bluntly.

They both looked at her simultaneously.

"You'd really want to work around…" Her mom looked around, then whispered, "unstable people?"

Ariettea squinted at her.

"Well you know, people that say they hear voices or that they're 'depressed'" air quotes, "Or even cut themselves!"

Ariettea felt fire shoot through her arms and legs, and then her limbs and face went ice cold. She felt simultaneous shame and anger.

Before she could fully process, Cirise spoke up, "You know people like that just need to get up and pray more, get out more. Snap out of it."

Ariettea held a hand up. "Woah, woah. Seriously?" She was past annoyed, having nearly forgotten the ignorance of their small town. "I know people that have seen mental health professionals, and it's totally healthy, just like taking care of migraines or the flu, or just need maintenance."

Her mom and Cirise stared at her.

"I guess that time in the city really did get to you!" Cirise said, surprised, holding a hand to her chest. "We're not therapy people, Ariettea." She scolded, "We're friends and family people."

Her mom looked at her, almost scared. "Who do you know that needed mental help?" She asked, her tone suddenly hushed again.

Ariettea rolled her eyes. "Trent is an ER Doctor; he talks about mental health all the time, and very openly. And Lily and her parents are really open about getting therapy to emotionally deal with her illness."

"Oh well, that's a bit different, in Lily's case." Cirise piped up. "For your uncle, he must deal with those… strange people all the time."

She waved a hand, as if waving their germs away. "But Lily, I mean there's still prayer. But still, she's dying, right?"

Ariettea felt her face curl up in disgust. "No." She said curtly. "She's not."

She pulled her purse up on her shoulder. "I guess that 'big city' just taught me a more balanced look on things. At least more balanced than most people here."

She looked back and forth between the two women.

"Excuse me." She said, pushing her way past them and out the door.

Her mind danced back and forth between being glad she stood up for what's right and being terrified of the bridges she was burning with the people she was stuck with.

She found Matt in the parking lot, alone.

She suddenly felt afraid, thinking he was all she had left. She had to fix things. Apologize. But she was still ticked with him, and he clearly was with her, as she tell by the look on his face when she approached him.

"We need to talk." She said as gently as she could, the words still coming out clipped anyway.

He sighed. "Talk talk talk." He mumbled.

"Excuse me?"

"Nothing."

"It's not nothing, Matt! Be an adult and talk to me!"

"What do you want me to say?"

"Uh, 'I'm sorry' for one!"

"For what?"

"For acting like a jerk!"

"Oh was that when you were acting like a baby?"

"So you don't expect me to be upset when you bring your friend on our date and ignore me the whole time?"

He just looked at her blankly, almost as if she weren't even there.

"Well?"

He didn't say anything.

"And what about all the rude things Len said to me?"

"He was just kidding."

"Oh really? Does he always 'kid' about people's life goals? Friends?"

"What are you TALKING about?" He asked with disgust.

"What he said about Ducreis and Lily!"

"Well…"

"Well what?"

"Well he was kind of right!"

"WHAT?!"

"Oh c'mon Ariettea. You must know that all that crap is stupid. A little girl with cancer, a college to follow your DREAMS?"

"It's not STUPID, Matt! Why are you all of a sudden acting like you can't stand anything about me anymore? If that's how you feel about me, maybe this whole thing needs to come to an end. Maybe we ARE just too different."

He sighed, ducked his head down, threw a hand on the back of his neck, and pulled. "Okay, okay. I'll talk to Len. He just feels…left out since we've been going out."

"But Matt… We agreed we are both serious about this relationship. What will he do if we get MARRIED?"

Matt shook his head, annoyance washing over his face. "You know how I feel about young weddings, Ariettea."

"Matt you just told me you love me, that you want me to stay here for you, with you, give up a life I'd planned for you. How can you say all that and then act like we're just nothing more than a couple?"

He held up a hand, dismissively. "I'll take care of Len."

He suddenly started to walk away.

She tried to keep up with his long legs in her high heels. "Matt, wait,"

He stopped without turning to face her.

"What do you love about me?"

He turned around, scrunched his face up at her. "What?"

The two of them the only ones in the large concrete parking lot, she felt utterly alone, despite being with him.

She stepped forward and came close to him. "You told me you loved me." She said, Nadette's words ringing in her ears. "What do you love about me? Why do you love me?"

He shuffled his keys back and forth, from hand to hand. "Ariettea, that's… I don't know how to answer that."

She shook her head, took another step towards him. "Why not? How can we love each other without being able to answer that?"

"It's not like you ever said it back." He muttered.

She stopped.

Had she not?

Why not?

"So, tell me why I should." She said gently.

He shoved his hands in the pockets of his suit pants. He kicked the gravel with his shiny black dress shoe. "You and I can laugh together in a way I've never been able to with anyone else." He said, his eyes flashing up to meet hers.

"We can talk in a way I've never been able to with anyone else. You have this stubborn streak and wild heart that I somehow hate and love at the same time. You see everything so dang seriously that it makes me stop and look at myself, too. You make me want to be a better man when I'm with you."

She felt her cheeks warm as he stepped forward and pulled her hand into his.

But she couldn't look at him.

She couldn't look at him because of that one lingering question, "You keep saying we have something you haven't had with anyone else… I've been careful not to ask this… But was there someone else?"

He shook his head, stroked her hand. "Why would that matter?"

"Please, Matt. Just tell me the truth. I hate seeing other girls talk to you and not knowing what you may have had with them."

He dropped her hand quickly.

"But why would any of that matter?" He snapped.

"If it doesn't then why can't you tell me?"

"Because I don't want you getting jealous over stuff that wasn't even real!"

"Lennox has mentioned another girl more than once. How your parents shouldn't find out about me after the last one, how the last girl never called you her boyfriend-"

"Because I've never officially dated anyone before you."

"Okay but what about unofficially?"

He put his hands on his hips and shook his head at the ground. He stayed silent.

"Am I a second choice?" She asked, trying to keep her voice steady. She felt like a needy brat, asking for all this validation.

His eyes flashed up to meet hers. "What?"

She took a deep breath. "Am I just what was left over after Mandy?"

He looked angry. "Mandy?"

She rolled her eyes, flopped her neck back and looked at the sky. "Come ON, Matt. I'm not blind or stupid. I deserve to know what the two of you had, because I can't help but notice she's still always around you."

"Talking to girls doesn't mean dating them, Ariettea. It never has. It's not my fault my mom tried helping Mandy out and being there for her, when no one else was." He looked her up and down derisively.

She held in her offense as much as she could. "So then what did Len mean? What was the real reason you stopped talking to me for so long?"

Matt sighed again, looked around the parking lot. "Mandy has always been just a friend. I'm friends with a lot of girls, I always have been. I always will be."

Her stomach burned.

"Everyone has always known there was something going on between you and me. When my parents finally caught on that the way I felt about you wasn't just going to go away, they made it clear that my dating anyone in high school wasn't something that they were going to support. Mandy was just there to talk to in the meantime."

"And your parents were okay with THAT?"

He chewed on his lip.

"They think that little of me?" She all but whimpered.

He shook his head. "It's not like that."

"Then what IS it like, Matt?"

He shook his head again as he stepped forward and put his hand around her back, pulled her close, jarringly.

The wind picked up and blew her hair back away from her face; she could feel how long it was by the way it pulled her head back as it wrapped underneath his arm.

Her heart pounded as she wrapped her arm underneath his, put her hand on his shoulder.

She smelled the aftershave radiating off his sharp jawline.

Even with her heels on, he was still taller than her.

He looked down into her eyes.

"It's like it's always been you. Just know that at the end of the day, it's always been you."

As warmth spread throughout her body and down to her toes, she tried to push back the thought that she still couldn't tell him what she loved about him, though.

Chapter 27

Time went on, as it always does.

Weeks went by.

Ariettea slowly slipped back into the life she had lived her entire existence. Except now, instead of fighting against the grain, she was falling into it.

Or at least, trying to.

She tried her best to keep in touch with Lily, as she always had, but Matt got so funny whenever she brought Lily up.

"Matt, you've always told me to get more friends, why do you hate that I talk with Lily so much?"

He had shrugged, sitting next to her on the couch in his parent's living room, Xbox controller in hand, eyes fixed on the tv screen. "I just think it's a weird situation. And there's people here you should focus on instead. Why do you think I gave you a rose instead of a lily the night I asked you to stay? That wasn't an accident, I want your mind to be here, with me."

The next week, renting a movie, "Oh yeah Lily and I saw that movie-"

"Oh geez."

The next week, "That reminds me of what Lily and I were just talking about-"

"Yeah so did you hear about Kyle?"

She finally stopped herself any time she wanted to say anything about her. Which made her feel guilty for even texting her, like she was betraying Matt.

On the other hand, she felt guilty for NOT texting Lily, her best friend. But it wasn't like Lily was that talkative, either, starting her own school year, getting into life back home still.

"How is Matt treating my girl?" Her last text had asked.

"We're having a lot of fun together :)"

"Yeah, but that's not what I asked ;)"

Ariettea burned with annoyance. Lily had never been in a relationship, where did she get off giving advice? It was a message she just didn't answer.

But for some reason she still left the lilies hanging in her car instead of the rose, trying to hang on to the best of both worlds.

She started working part-time at a coffee shop downtown, serving up frozen coffees to people she'd gone to high school with, her parent's friends, all the people she had sworn she was never going to see again. She was trying to integrate herself into their world, for the first time.

Her new world.

With her working at a coffee shop and around food all day, her appetite started to dwindle. At least, that's what she told herself the reason was. She tied her apron a little tighter around her waist than she was used to one day before pulling out her phone to check on any messages from Matt. There weren't any.

He had begun a new job at an auto body shop in town, excitedly learning a trade. She tried to be supportive, excited too, but she hated seeing him stuck in a field he had always sworn he hated.

She tried to talk to him, "Are you sure this is the best fit for you?"

"Yeah, of course. Why wouldn't it be?"

"I just remember how much you hated auto class in high school. You only ever took it because your dad wanted you to."

"What are you saying? That I took this job to make my parents happy? So what if I did! I try to think of others in my life, and not just myself."

She had put her coffee shop's baseball cap on and gone to work, feeling like the pot who had called the kettle black, as she clocked into another shift at a job she kept trying to tell herself was meaningful, that she didn't hate.

She looked around at all her coworkers talking and laughing like it was so incredibly easy for them. It felt like high school all over again, her, standing alone, just trying to get through what she needed to do so she could go home.

She found herself zoning out, staring into a carton of heavy cream, thinking about the jobs she had wanted, what she had pictured. Everyone was right, it didn't matter the job, she was just going to be miserable no matter where she went.

She was starting to wonder why she was even trying, anymore. She wanted to reach out to Lily, but she felt like were just too far apart anymore, that maybe Matt was right, and she needed to focus on the here and now, not the there and them. Lily was just so different from her new life, anyway.

She ran her fingers under her eyes, picking up smudged black eyeliner onto her fingertips. She closed her eyes and tried to breath.

This was what she wanted.

She needed to be happy.

Happy is a choice.

She tried her hardest to focus on her and Matt, their present, having fun, but her overthinking mind wanted to wander to the future. She was torn, part of her knowing that she had learned to let emotions in on her decisions, but not sure where the line was of heart vs. head.

All she knew was that her head was set to explode if she didn't let some of it out.

She had been there before and was slowly inching towards self-destruction again.

She knew Matt wanted to just have fun together, so she tried to gently bring it up over dinner, "I know that we agreed to enjoy the now," She said to him slowly over pasta. "But that was before I was staying here, and not going to Duceris. It's been a couple of months I've been...home, now. So...I think we should talk about some future...stuff."

She waited for him to get angry, roll his eyes, but to her surprise, he nodded.

"Okay, what should we talk about?" He asked, setting down his fork, giving her his full attention.

"Well," she began, "I think we need to know where we are going with this. We both owe it to ourselves even more than we do to each other to know what we want." She said, realizing they should have talked about all that a long time ago.

Matt crossed his arms on the table, looked at her thoughtfully. "I mean, we both know we want to be together, right?"

She nodded, feeling trapped. "Of course, but what past that? I gave up a whole other life to be with you instead."

The words felt like knives coming out of her mouth, they hurt her so much.

"Are you saying you gave up something better? What, I'm YOUR second choice?" He snapped.

She shook her head vigorously, waved a hand. "No no, not at all. You know me well enough to know I don't do anything that isn't my first choice, or what I truly want. All I'm asking is that since this is my life, your life, our lives, here, not just a high school fling, we know where we each stand on long term issues."

He fiddled with the white tablecloth underneath his hand, pinching and pulling it, not looking directly at her. "What's more to know than that we want to stay together as long as possible?"

She stammered, looking for a response to that, baffled as to why he sounded like there was an end for them eventually. "I more so mean after that, I mean years from now, what we want, where we see ourselves."

"What do you mean?"

"Like houses and jobs and kids and-"

"WOAH!" He held up both his hands, asking for a full stop. "I'm 18! I don't want kids right now or anytime soon!"

"Of course not! But those are the things we always used to talk about together growing up."

"Yeah, before we were a couple. We were kids with silly dreams of careers and white picket fences."

'Silly dreams' rang through her head as she tried to keep taking over that voice.

"Right, so that's why we have to talk about it now, in this stage we're in."

He sighed again, threw himself back into the booth, and stared at the ceiling. "I just don't understand why we can't just enjoy our time together."

"Right now, I'm just muddling through a job I don't care about, living at home, I just want to know what my plans are going to be from here on out. I had it all planned and now… I have no plans."

He smiled slyly, pointed a finger at her. "Ah, ha! See, I always told you all that planning was nonsense."

Her face burned as she stared down at her plate, swirling her food around, not quite able to stomach it.

"In 10 years," He said slowly, "I see myself in a house with a family. Does that answer your question?"

She pushed more pasta around. "What about five years? What about next year? What about all the goals your parents told you to have?"

"Right now, I'm just working and saving money. I'll get to all that eventually. Come on, Ariettea, you're always ten steps ahead. Just live with me here, now. Please."

She sighed internally. If only he knew how much more so she was living in the moment than she ever thought she would be, or even wanted to be.

"I feel like I'm constantly eating crow," Ariettea was telling Lily over the phone, the first time they'd talked at all in over a week. "I spent my whole life dying to get out of here, and now I'm trying to force myself into what everyone always told me I should and eventually would."

Lily cleared her throat. "Changing your mind isn't something to be ashamed of. You could have come down here and changed your major or decided you hated the east coast and wanted the west coast. There's nothing wrong with chasing happiness. That's what we all SHOULD be doing."

Ariettea pulled at the hem of her baggy band tee, then pulled on her neck, her muscles always stiff, rigid. "Except now, I'm trying to find happiness here. Anywhere. Isn't that what you taught me? I mean, that's the same thing."

Lily paused. "But is it, though?"

"If you're not happy anywhere, you won't ever be truly happy."

Lily paused again, talking slowly. "To some extent. But finding ourselves also means realizing where and who we're meant to be."

"I thought I found myself. But I must have been wrong. So, it scares me."

"Why were you wrong?"

"I almost moved away from the relationship I've always wanted!"

"But again… just like you keep saying happiness isn't a place, it can't be a person, either."

"I found happiness with you!" She was suddenly annoyed with a kid trying to tell her where her happiness should lay.

"And besides, romantic love is even stronger than friendship." She spat.

Lily gently continued speaking, "Had you come and met me and hated it here, I hardly think you'd have moved here for me. You know that's true."

Ariettea closed her eyes. "So, what are you trying to tell me?"

She could hear Lily lay down, picturing her flopping onto the blue couch in their living room. "Happiness is different for everyone. It's not a place or a person, but those can be a big factor. It's whatever it means to you. Just make sure that you don't lose yourself in trying to make something fit. All this, good vibes only, choose happiness stuff isn't real. For some people, there's much more to it than that."

Ariettea sighed. "I guess I've just got more real-life things to focus on now." She crossed her arms over her chest in defiance, resting her chin against her phone and shoulder.

Lily cleared her throat again. "All I know, Ari, is that I used to hear way more happiness in your voice when you were running your own show."

"Well, maybe I was just fooling myself."

"Well then, you fooled me, too. And Nadette and Trent and my parents. But still, what others think doesn't matter. Only you know what's really going on."

By the time they ended the call, Ariettea had curled herself up in the corner of her bedroom, pulled her knees to her chest, laid her head on them.

She was fighting so hard to find the meaning in her life there, but she just wasn't finding it as easily as she had… somewhere else. She was being stupid. She had Matt. Matt was there and real and made sense. He wasn't some imaginary maybe. She already had him. She called him and asked him to come over for a movie night.

As he threw his arm around her on the couch and pulled her close, she felt her whole body tingle. She laid her head on his shoulder and sighed.

"So I was thinking of maybe looking into enrolling in some classes nearby, picking up the major I was going to at Ducreis." She told him.

He pulled his arm away from her, herself almost falling down as he pulled away. "What? Why?"

She pulled a leg up under her and looked at him, confused. "Why not? Matt, my whole life, I've told you how much I want a life that's meaningful to me."

"So, I'm not meaningful to you?" He snapped, looking hurt.

"No, that's not at all what I'm saying," She said, her face scrunching up in confusion, trying to calm him.

He went on, "If you want meaning outside of us, go in the ministry, work on your faith, go make some friends, your being alone all the time isn't good."

She felt steam rise off her head. "Matt, I'm tired of having this argument with you. We've been having it for years. I want a life FULL of meaning. And I will never be that social person. It's just not me. And that's ok."

"Yeah well, I AM a social person. That's why I can't bring you along with my friends!"

She felt her head jerk back and a look cross her face. "You never invite me." She said, stoic.

"Because I know how you are around people. You keep trying to find this great answer to something really simple. You have to work on yourself. Being happy isn't that hard."

Her stomach churned. "For some people, it is."

He shrugged, thinking she was just being difficult. "Well, then there's something wrong with them. Look, I'll bring you out with me and the guys and our friends next Wednesday when we go."

She stared at him. "Go where?" She asked, befuddled.

"Bowling." He stated. "We go every Wednesday."

Again, a blank stare. "You never told me that?"

He shrugged. "You don't own me."

That one stung.

"No and you don't own me, but I always keep you filled in on my life because I want you in it, every aspect of it." She fired back.

"Well, it's hard when you don't get along with my friends."

"And what about mine?" She snapped. "You always told me I was anti-social and weird, and I went out and got a very good friend, and all you've ever done is made fun of her. You've never even met Lily!"

"She's a kid who lives far away. You have to create adult relationships here, Ariettea. What people here think of you matters."

She sighed, heavily. It was something she'd heard her whole life. "You always hang out with kids, playing football and video games."

"Yeah, with people here, who aren't boring, who understand how life here works."

"Well what if we take a trip together down to see her? You could meet Trent and Nadette too, see the town, the school," She was getting more and more excited as she talked.

But she stopped suddenly when she saw the look on his face. "What?"

"I just think you need to get your head out of that place."

She shook her head. "I won't argue about this with you, Matt." She said, rubbing the bridge of her nose. "I'm tired of arguing about this." She breathed. "I just want to watch the movie."

He nodded, happy his point had been made, that he had won the argument.

Instead of leaning back into him, she leaned the opposite way into the arm cushion of the leather sectional, not wanting any physical contact with him, or anyone else for that matter.

For the first time in her life, everyone around her seemed to approve of what she was doing. They approved of her finally taking their advice.

A midweek day after work, she was sitting in a Mexican food to-go place with Matt and his mom, pushing some nachos around in their little paper tray.

"Ariettea, have you given any more thought to what else you're going to do here? Expand your ministry?" Cirise was asking her.

Ariettea looked at her, blankly. "I… I've just been trying to enjoy the moment lately." She answered, embarrassed, looking over at Matt.

He shrugged. "It's not a bad idea, Ariettea."

She felt ganged up on. She was constantly looking for something more to do with her life, but her idea was never the right one.

She pulled her long black sleeves down over her wrists, the sleeves that had grown baggy once more, and pushed her food away. "I mean, I've honestly been thinking about looking outside of town at some classes and jobs…" She trailed off, seeing the look of shock come across their faces.

She looked at Matt. "I mean, I've got to plan for my future, right?" She was suddenly unsure of herself.

"That doesn't have to mean away from here." Cirise said.

"No, not at all, I just-"

Cirise suddenly got up and took all their plates to the trash can.

Ariettea looked at Matt, concerned. She lowered her voice, "What did I say wrong? I'm just trying to be smart about things…"

He shrugged and looked at his lap. "It just always sounds like no one here is good enough for you."

She sighed, rolled her eyes, threw her hands on the table. "Matt, why is it I'm not good enough for YOU? Why is it that I can't seem to do anything right around here?"

He looked at her, blankly. "It's always been the same things with you, looking for ways out of here, talking down to everyone."

"I thought you said you loved the stubborn streak you saw in me."

He shook his head, standing up and taking his horchata with him. "There comes a point you have to realize just how uncomfortable you make people."

Her eyes burned as those words echoed through her head on the way home. Everyone's words seemed to echo in her head anymore. Even when she lived there growing up, she'd been able to ignore them, even if they still hurt. Now, she was giving them her full attention and they hurt even worse.

She was never good enough.

Not for that town, her family, her friends, and now not even Matt. The one whose love was supposed to be the strongest.

The horrible realization washed over her and punched her in the stomach- her mother was right. She WAS an embarrassment to Matthew.

She threw her keys down in the bowl by the front door when she got home.

She locked herself in her room and started to pace.

Not good enough.

No one likes you.

She started to chew on her thumb nail. She hated herself. Everything about her was wrong, no matter how hard she tried.

She started shaking, started wanting to find something sharp. She heard Trent's voice pop up in her head, from that phone call so long ago. "Please call me, Ariettea, whenever you want to self-harm. I'll help you through it, I promise."

She looked at her phone laying on her bed and started to bounce on her toes. She wanted to call. But after what she did to them... she couldn't. They had to hate her just like everyone else. Gosh she was such a disappointment.

She didn't want to talk through what she was feeling.

She didn't want to feel anything.

Anything except something sharp digging into the skin on her forearm. The pain that matched what she was feeling inside. The pain she deserved.

Chapter 28

"Matt, if I'm truly such a disappointment, then why are you with me?" She had asked him to meet her after work that next day.

It was January, so the long sleeves she needed to cover her wounds didn't seem out of place.

Sitting on a park bench of an empty playground, shivering in the cold, his brown eyes softened as they stared into hers.

He reached out and grabbed both of her hands in his. "Ari, I never said that you were," He said warmly.

"But?"

"We all just have to work on bettering ourselves, right?"

She nodded slowly.

"Isn't that what you came home saying you learned over the summer?"

Her eyes locked on the ground, glazed over then blurred as she thought of the summer. "More so accepting who we are…" She said quietly, almost to herself.

He squeezed her hands to make her look back to him. "You'd only ever embarrass me if you didn't work on yourself."

She stared at the empty flower boxes around the park, knowing they'd been full of lilies all summer.

He reached out and cupped her face with one hand.

She could see the difference in their skin tones down the side of her face, his warm dark skin, and her ever whitening pallor. She wanted to close her eyes and lean into his big warm hand, but she just didn't feel like being touched anymore.

"You are so funny and sweet-"

"But what about responsible, smart?" She jumped in, yet limply. "Those qualities always seem boring and disappointing to you."

He shook his head at her. "I just want to enjoy you." He smiled. "Why don't we focus on trying to have more fun? We'll loosen you up."

He let go of her hand and face and squeezed her knee instead. "That's why I asked you to stay here. We've got to choose happiness, you know?"

She tried to force a smile for him, tried to push Lily's disagreeing voice out of her head.

He suddenly laughed. "It's a good thing I'm with you; no one else would want to teach you how to act like a normal person."

She chewed her lip as she reached for her forearm, rubbed it so the wounds underneath her sleeve would burn. She really was the disappointment she had always known she was.

He was right, she was lucky he wanted her. She needed to work on being more of who he wanted her to be; who she was supposed to be.

When she was a young teenager, there were those rare instances when she'd get invited places. The older she got, the rarer they became. But every once in a while, the older women she knew would decide she was mature enough to let her come out to dinner with them. But then once she'd developed opinions of her own, ones in opposition to theirs, suddenly she wasn't old enough to go with them anymore.

So, she was shocked when an invitation came for her to go out with Cirise and her friends for a girl's night out.

Her first inclination was to talk to Lily about it, get her perspective, but she quickly scolded herself for thinking of asking a 14-year-old what to do about an adult problem that wasn't even a real problem.

She didn't want to go, but on the other hand, she did. She felt a sense of pride, satisfaction for getting invited somewhere because of being herself. She figured it would be like being out with Nadette.

So, she put on her sequin tank top and black blazer, high heeled boots, and met the women at a local pub.

Mandy was the first person she saw as she walked in the door.

Of course Mandy would be there. She had probably always been invited. She was always in their favor, no matter what she did.

Once she and Matt had started dating, Ariettea liked to pretend that Mandy didn't exist; that she didn't see her talking to him every Sunday, that Mandy's name didn't still come up in conversations about outings Ariettea had missed, never been invited to.

She begrudgingly slipped into the high-top chair beside her and across from Cirise.

She just didn't want to talk about Matt with Mandy. He was hers now, no matter what they did or didn't have in the past. But she hated the fact that Cirise still loved Mandy.

Ariettea took in a breath, ready to try and involve herself in her new life. She tuned into what everyone was talking about. Once the margaritas arrived, the words started to really flow.

"Thank GOD I have a night once a month to get away from my husband!" Someone down the table was lamenting.

The woman next to her threw her head back and agreed. "I just can't be around him this much! He comes home, and it's like dealing with my kids. I just need time away from him. I need to be around people who get me!"

Ariettea felt her face scrunch up, her brows knit together. Why would they marry men who they didn't like being around?

Cirise saw the look on her face and laughed. "Oh Ari…" She shook her head. "You'll understand soon enough! It's just a part of marriage to need time away from each other."

Ariettea looked at her thoughtfully, trying to choose the right words to respond with. "I guess I just don't understand why I'd want to be with someone that I need time away from." She said quietly.

Mandy scoffed next to her. "Don't you want to be around people who understand you?" She took Cirise's margarita and took a swig.

Arietta looked at her in shock and waited for a scolding that didn't come.

"I guess I've been a loner for so long I've never had that. I'm used to having a single person in my life that just gets me." She just didn't elaborate that she was talking about Lily, and even Nadette, but not Matt.

"Girl, please." Mandy shook her head. "Men are good for some things… "She winked. "But not others."

Ariettea felt her eyes widen in shock. Did she seriously…?

Her eyes flashed over to Cirise, still wide.

She laughed. "You're so innocent!" She dissolved into belly laughs as Mandy joined in.

Ariettea chewed her lip and she stabbed the lemon in her glass of water with her straw. She thought of Trent and Nadette, kissing after a long day of work, laughing over the table at private jokes that they still held from college. The way they looked at each other after almost 15 years of being together… And then there were these women, eager to get away from the men in their lives, disgusted with everything about them.

"I guess I am…" She finally responded to Cirise. "I just love the relationship my aunt and uncle have; I've always pictured having something like that someday…"

Someone from the other end of the table shook her head. "Well, those picture-perfect couples are either lying or are the exception to the rule! But even if they're the exception, they're lying!"

Everyone at the table laughed together, except for Ariettea.

She was so lost and confused, was she expecting a fairy tale with Matt? Was she doomed to the life that these women were describing?

"You'll see as you get older," Mandy nudged her with her shoulder, "Real relationships aren't nearly as pretty as you think they are at the beginning."

Ariettea glared at her before staring into her lap. Why did Mandy act like she was older than her? Because she had more experience with men? The thought sent a chill down her spine as she tried not to shiver at it.

Cirise reached across the table and patted Ariettea's hand. "I want all the happiness in the world for you and my son," She said with a sad smile. "But I also want you to know what reality is when it comes to marriage. Everything is fun and together now, but once you've been together a few years, all that sparkle fades away, and you're left with the cold reality that you ARE different people, and you need to each lead your own lives."

Ariettea squeezed her hand, trying to find some reassurance as she asked, "Then why be in a relationship at all?"

Cirise smiled. "Love is real. Sex is real. Having a partner in life is real. But you have to realize that those things aren't all they're cracked up to be."

Ariettea didn't understand; she didn't feel like her question was answered.

She looked at her purse, thought of pulling out her phone and asking Nadette for her perspective, her advice, but these women… They were the ones living real lives, there, in that town.

Maybe her journey wasn't about finding happiness, she thought, as much as it was about accepting it for what it is, not just what she thought it should be.

After that night, she quit answering Trent and Nadette's messages altogether. It just hurt too much and was too confusing.

And she realized she was finding less and less to talk about with Lily, she had stopped responding to her ever-lessening texts. For the first time since they'd met, they weren't texting daily.

She was lying on her bed, after yet another monotonous day at work, twirling her stupid barista ballcap around on one finger. She was miserable and utterly lonely. She knew she couldn't talk to Matt about how she was feeling, and Lily couldn't possibly understand her new place in life.

It had been so long since she'd felt so alone.

How could she feel so alone when there were now more people in her life than ever before? People who she was making happy by bettering herself for them?

But then she thought of Lily's face. The one that showed so much concern and just begged for you to be happy, begged for you to be yourself. She missed that feeling. That feeling Lily gives you when she teaches you things you never knew about yourself...

Before she could stop herself and tell herself she was being an idiot, she decided to call and hear Lily's voice, hear the ocean in the background.

She started slowly changing out of her work clothes as she held the phone between her shoulder and ear.

The phone rang… and rang…and rang until Elaina answered.

She sounded tired. "Hello?"

"Hey, Elaina, it's me."

"Hey, Ari." She said, sighing happily.

"You sound tired, is everything ok?"

"We're hanging in there, you know?"

Ariettea felt a knot in her stomach. "What do you mean? Is everything ok?"

Elaina paused, her end of the phone becoming dead silent. "Did Lily not tell you?"

"Tell me what?" Ariettea truly felt like throwing up now; she had to stop a gag in her throat.

"Oh, Ariettea, I'm sorry, I thought she told you. She said she would. Ari, Lily is in the hospital in Ducreis,"

'No, no no no no no.' She wasn't sure if she'd said it aloud or in her head, but suddenly, all the negative thoughts that Matt put in her head about Lily disappeared, until the only thing in her head was Lily.

"The cancer is back."

Ariettea felt a numb shock flood through her. Her stomach dropped.

This can't be happening.

She should have known.

She COULD have known.

"When?" Ariettea choked out, the word barely even formed as it left her mouth.

"They've been running tests and consulting with different doctors for a couple of weeks now," Elaina said. "And they admitted her a few days ago. Oh, Ariettea, I'm so sorry, honey, if we had known you didn't know…" She trailed off, again silent.

"I know, of course. Uhm," Ariettea's voice broke, wavered. She squeezed her eyes shut tight, trying to pull herself together, feeling her eyeliner grit together, a feeling she'd thought she had forgotten.

"Can I come?" She said, her eyes flying open. "There? To see her?"

"Always."

A quick and sharp goodbye flew from her mouth, and then she threw her phone down onto her bed as she yanked a duffel bag from the top shelf of her closet.

She stuffed her essentials in it as fast as she could. Jeans, but which jeans? They were all too big. Dresses? Shirts? Instead, she just grabbed leggings, hoodies, everything she'd lived in for so long in the past that she had been living in again.

Fifteen minutes later, she ran out to the living room to leave and saw her mom. She told her what was going on.

"I'm leaving." She looked around desperately for hey keys, shaking.

"For where?"

"For there, mom! For there!"

"Ari, you can't drive-"

"MOM I'M GOING!" Ariettea exploded.

She stopped, threw a hand on her forehead, closed her eyes, took a deep breath.

"This is Lily." She said just above a whisper. "This is no option for me."

Chapter 29

She knew she had to talk to Matt before she left. It wasn't something she could just drop over text. Mostly because she was afraid of how he would respond. She texted him that she needed to talk to him, asked him to meet her at the park because she didn't want to drive to his house across town.

She hopped out of her SUV, leaving the engine on and the heat running as she walked up to him.

The wind was gusting, the January air cold and harsh as it smacked her in the face. She looked up at the sky, grey and dark, as it stayed during the long Michigan winters.

"What's this about?" He asked, defensively.

She felt her head jerk back as she crossed her arms over her chest and approached him. "It's Lily." She said. She shook her head sadly. "The cancer is back. I'm on my way out of town now."

"Now?" "Now." Matt scoffed.

He paused, looked around him, put his hands on his hips, making what he thought was a power play, a move to control the conversation.

Then he looked back at her. "Just like that?"

"What do you mean just like that?"

"I mean, this kid calls, and you run to her?"

"Yes, Matt! This is my best friend! Of course!"

He scoffed again. "Are you telling me the truth?"

"What?!"

"We just talked about you having more fun, fitting in here, you go out with my mom's friends once, and now you run out of town?"

"MATTHEW!" She chirped, shocked, throwing her hands down. "Lily has CANCER, what do you not GET about that?!" She snapped.

Suddenly it was as if all the resentment she had towards him over his not wanting her to leave peaked.

"What don't I get? What I don't GET is why you act the way you do! This spoiled princess, running away to her poor little friend with cancer!" His voice shrilled in mockery.

"You need CONSTANT validation!"

She felt her stomach heave.

"It's sickening. She's the one you know you'll get it from, that's the real reason you're leaving!"

"You say I need constant validation; maybe I just need someone who actually cares about what I want! Who I am, how I feel!" Ariettea exclaimed.

"I don't even understand how you can say that when you don't give me any- all you do is tell me what you want me to be! WHERE you want me to be!"

"I want you here," He pointed to the ground, "What's wrong with that?"

"What's-" She stammered, crossing her arms again as the wind blew her hair back, the cold slapping her in the face.

With that sting, she finally lost it, let all, ALL the rage out of her.

"What's wrong with YOU?! I gave up college, I gave up my best friend, for YOU- not for us, for you. And now you're acting like I haven't done anything for us."

"For us?" He asked angrily. "What have you done for US? I take you to dinner, to Starbucks, I give up time with my boys for YOU, try to make you look better, keep you happy, CONSTANTLY VALIDATE YOU and stroke your ego, and what do you give me?"

"MY FUTURE!" She screamed. "That's all I've ever had, it's the only thing that kept me alive, and I gave it all up for you!"

"Future. Pht." He scoffed. "Go to college to 'help people' and 'be with family' whatever. You're so full of yourself."

He snarled, "And alive? You're such an attention seeker. Everyone knows your pathetic brooding act. Everyone knows about your pathetic threats."

Her stomach dropped at the realization that her mother had gone around talking to people about her depression, her suicidal ideations.

What good gossip sessions they all must have had at her expense.

She wanted to scream every vile thing at him she could, she knew she could tear him to the core with her words, but she held back. She wouldn't stoop to his level nor was he worth it.

But he kept going, "You wanna know the truth?" He asked stepped toward her, his face scrunching up in anger.

She wanted to take a step back, but that hard steel feeling came over her and she stood her ground and leaned even closer instead.

"I asked you to stay here because I didn't want you leaving and going down to spend time with some weird little kid at some stupid college." He spat in her eyes.

"No one else wants to even be friends with such a stuck-up snob, let alone date. I did you a FAVOR by being with you."

His head snapped as it bobbled towards her then back in finality.

She looked around, tongue in cheek, shaking her head in disgust. She felt like she had so much, yet nothing to say to him.

"So it was all a lie? That you loved me? Is this why you'd never talk about our future together? All while I gave mine up so we could have one together..."

She started backing away from him, almost scared of him, and the look of rage enveloping his face.

She backed towards her car, realizing she'd left the door open to in her haste to talk to him.

"You're the one who never loved me. Who loved that place more than me all along." He yelled, staying in place.

"Apparently because that's the only love in my life that was real! Well thankfully," She jerked her head around in a circle,

"I'm taking my future back, because we are DONE."

She hopped back up into her car and floored it, seeing him shake his head in disgust and wave a hand dismissively, like he cared nothing about whether they were together or not.

She glanced back in her rearview to see him already walking away.

She ripped the two lilies that were hanging from it and chucked them out the window, her hand stinging as the ice that had started raining from the sky hit it.

Driving way too fast, swerving in and out of lanes she put as much distance between her and that town as fast as she could.

No stopping for gas or pretzels or a Diet Coke, she just had to leave.

Part of her wanted to cry, wanted to scream in anger, in hurt, but the other part didn't want to feel anything.

She couldn't feel anything. That's how it had to be. She wasn't sure she had been feeling anything lately, anyway.

She gripped the steering wheel, getting on the highway, her face set in stone.

A drive Ariettea had never made before; the trip to Ducreis was a good 17 hours.

She somehow managed it in 14.

For the first four hours, she sat stoic, in complete silence, as the sky became less and less grey the further south she drove. The sun started to set as a dull ache set itself into her chest.

Every breath hurt to pull in, and every blink felt forced.

She felt cold.

She felt hard.

She couldn't have made the tears come if she wanted to.

She felt her eyes intermittently narrow, her brows furrow in disgust as her hands clenched and unclenched the wheel.

She was shutting down.

She caught a glimpse of herself in the mirror as she was changing lanes. Her eyeliner was smudged, her nose was red from the bitter cold, and the rest of her face was as white as a sheet. She looked lost and angry. Beaten down and throw away.

She looked at her hands, shaking on the wheel. They were icy and pale, enveloped by the sleeves of her hoodie. It hadn't taken long for her clothes to grow lose again, to take over her frame. For her cheeks to lose their rosiness, and go back to sunken, blue veins gleaming through. For her jeans to hang just ever so loosely around her waist.

As the sun started to go down many hours into her drive, her thoughts turned from everything bothering her to only Lily. She suddenly felt so selfish for boohooing about her breakup for so long, when she should be more concerned with her best friend, lying in a hospital bed, dy-

No.

She didn't know that yet.

All she knew was that she was sick.

She'd beat it before, and she'd beat it again. This was just another step in the journey.

She just had to get there.

She pushed her car way over the speed limit, flying through mountain ranges, knowing her parents would kill her if they knew she was driving like such a maniac. She just couldn't handle thinking about Lily until she got there, until she was with her.

As she pulled off in some little Tennessee town to get gas and a Diet Coke after the sun had gone down, she stared off at the thunderous mountains in front of her.

She took her hand off the gas pump and crossed her arms, leaned back into her car. The air had started to warm up just a bit, enough for her to notice but not the locals still running in and out of the gas station in down winter coats.

She chuckled to herself. Everyone's lives were different everywhere. And no one really knew what someone else was living… or sometimes even who they really were.

She stared off into the mountaintops that were kissing the stars, and she wanted to dive deep into them, never come out, never have to deal with anyone ever again.

She shook her head; how close she'd been to being able to dive into a new life. But her, the overthinking old soul had been suckered in by a hoodrat who just wanted to have fun. Her, the person who watched the waitress's expressions as she ordered her food to know what they thought of her order, missed giant red flags from him. Why hadn't she seen them? How did she ALLOW herself to get so stupid? Where did her brain go? She suddenly felt as if she deserved to be treated the way she had been, by being so incredibly ignorant. She hated herself for it.

The gas pump clinked and made her flinch, jump out of her thoughts. Her mind was working overtime to overthink what she hadn't even halfway thought of the past seven months.

In those racing and manic thoughts, she was suddenly panicking about where she'd stay once she got there, would Trent and Nadette be ok with her there? Would she have to rent a room somewhere? How much would that cost?

And work! Oh, work. She found greater satisfaction than she ever should have by texting her boss she wouldn't be in the next day and was quitting, before blocking her number. Another thing that now was over, but never even should have been.

She sent Nadette a text summarizing the situation and asking if she could spend just a night with them.

She didn't see her response until her next bathroom break, "***You never even have to ask! Please don't even think about staying only one night—You have a key; we will see you when we see you. Please keep us posted and let us know what you need, and we will get it, or do it. Hugs.***"

Ariettea finally parked her car in the Ducreis hospital garage at 3 am. Normally, she would have never felt safe walking through a dark parking garage at that time of night, but it was Ducreis. It felt like home.

It was home.

She made her way through the lot and outside, the sea breeze whisking her hair back, salty, mossy, and humid, even in January, to the only unlocked door at the main entrance.

She ran her hand through her hair as she walked into the lobby of the hospital. It felt stringy and greasy as she flipped her part to the other side of her head. Her hoodie had become unzipped and had sagged down on one shoulder, her combat boots, always slightly unlaced, were lapping at her ankles, the strings hitting the marble floor and echoing with every step.

She walked exhausted but determined toward the elevators, not expecting to see anyone. But that's when she saw the sky-blue scrubs standing by the front desk.

Trent.

"Ari!" He proclaimed. He enveloped her in a hug, and as much as she wanted to melt into his warm arms, her body went stiff. She couldn't handle being touched anymore.

She limply laid a hand around Trent's arm, and he let go.

"Nadette told you." She mumbled to the ground, pulling her messenger bag up onto her shoulder.

"Yeah, I'm working nights for a couple of weeks for a buddy on vacation. Perfect timing... I guess, not that anything about this is perfect," He put his hand at the base of his neck and pulled. "I just wanted to make sure someone was here for you when you got here."

'Here for you'...

Ariettea nodded distractedly, her eyes glazing over on the elevator buttons. "Thanks." She all but whispered. "Is Lily in the same room?"

The sadness in Trent's kind eyes only deepened as he looked down at her. "Yeah, same one. She uh, says her name should be on it by now." He smiled, trying to look casual, throwing his hands on his hips.

Ariettea scoffed. "Great place to claim for your childhood." She rolled her eyes.

She waited for him to flinch, to ask if she was ok, to say anything, but he didn't. He let her be.

He knew better.

She couldn't stand still any longer. Wordlessly she passed by Trent and forwent the elevator, hopping up the stairs to the left. The same stairs she knew led to side beach if she were to just go down a floor.

She came out of the door and only had to turn left before she could turn and slide open the door to Lily's room.

Her heart pounded as she approached. She was terrified of what she would see.

The room would have been pitch black had it not been illuminated only by the strong moonlight coming in the large windows. The blinds were slightly open, so she peered through the glass doors and saw Lily, asleep. Ariettea's eyes immediately shifted to the heart monitor. Still beating. Still breathing.

And she herself breathed out the breath she didn't realize she'd been holding.

She looked over at Alex and Elaina's usual spots on the window side of Lily's bed. Just Elaina tonight.

'Ok, if Alex isn't here, then Lily must be ok,' She reasoned.

She didn't want to wake Elaina, but she had just driven fourteen hours and wasn't about to just leave. She was suddenly unsure of what she had expected to find there in the middle of the night.

She slid open the sliding glass door as quietly as she could, shut it behind her. She looked over at the chair around the corner, hidden by the blinds, the one she had long claimed from all her visits, and jumped- Peter was in it. Asleep as well. He had a brown leather messenger bag overflowing with test papers at his feet, red pens spilling out, and a teacher's guide teetering on his lap. His blue button-down shirt was crumpled and wrinkled, like he had been up there for longer than he would have admitted, had he been awake.

She stepped over to the window, far from all of them, and teetered on the thick sill.

Even though her body blocked the moonlight coming in, she could still see Lily. She was pale. Paler than when they'd first met. Like the life was sucked out of her cheery face. 'She's asleep, you idiot.' She scolded herself. 'She can't be cheery when she was asleep.' But this was Lily. Yes, she could. But she didn't.

Her black curls were matted down wet around her ears. She saw Lily's bag under the bed and a black mound on top of it. Her wig. Of Ariettea's hair. She must have been worried that she'd soon need it again. The thought brought Ariettea's stomach into her throat. It hadn't been all that long ago that she had cut her hair off, met Lily, and seen a new world beyond her hometown. Beyond high school, beyond Michigan, and beyond Matt. Matt would scoff at the wig.

So, she purposefully walked over, bent down, and picked it up. She placed it on her hand and rotated her wrist. She thought about that day at the beach, the day of the lilies, after Matt batted her hair away from his eyes, laughed with her. Back when his eyes were so full of care and…life. His eyes looked dull anymore. There wasn't a gleam. At least not toward her.

She put the wig back down where she got it. Lily's real hair held happier memories, anyway. Running into the ocean fully clothed, seeing it glisten with the saltwater. Seeing her hair flying behind her as they rode bikes, bounce as they sang karaoke.

She turned away from Lily's bed to go back to her window perch. As she did, her boot squeaked on the standard hospital linoleum floor, the floor that replaced the shiny marble in the hallways and stirred Peter.

The book on his lap teetered as he tried to wake up and figure out who was in the room, dressed in black.

She rushed over and grabbed the book just before it hit the floor. His eyes met hers, and he finally registered who she was.

"Ariettea," He whispered. "What are you doing here?" His eyes searched for a clock, trying to figure out what time it was.

"I just got here." She whispered back. "Elaina told me…" She trailed off, embarrassed to admit that she hadn't known Lily was sick again. "that…Lily is sick."

She nodded her head towards the hall, motioning for him to follow her out there. They stepped out, and Ariettea handed his book back.

"Oh thanks," He said, blinking hard, still trying to get his bearings, "Did you say you just got here?"

She nodded. "I drove straight through. I had no idea she was this bad. Or even bad at all, for that matter. I had no idea anything was going on…"

Peter nodded, distracted, his eyes suddenly stuck on Lily, peering through the spaces between the vertical blinds. "Yeah, she had been getting fevers for a couple of months. The doctors kept saying it was just her immune system being low. And a week ago, maybe two? I don't know, anyway, it got really bad. Then they finally found the new tumors."

Ariettea closed her eyes. He couldn't say what 'it' was any more than he could.

"Elaina…Didn't say much. Didn't tell me much. Just that they're running tests and getting consults." She said with her eyes closed.

"What's their plan this time?" She asked, opening her eyes, trying to keep her voice from shaking.

Peter sadly shook his head. "I'm sorry Lily didn't tell you."

"Yeah, me too." She said sharply.

"No… I mean tell you… I'm sorry I have to be the one…" He put his hand on his forehead and sighed, his eyes closed.

"Tell me, WHAT?" Her heart pounded.

What?

Another long road?

Another extended hospital stay?

"They said they could start chemo again, but her body won't be able to handle it. It's been through too much. The illness spread so fast, and… very, very far, it would only prolong her life by 2-3 months as opposed to not starting it up again."

He stopped to swallow hard. His Adam's apple bobbed in his throat. "So," He cleared his throat, "there's nothing that they can do."

Ariettea felt her eyes start to burn.

Her stomach heaved.

No, no, no, no.

Her head started to spin, and she closed her eyes, put her hand on the glass to try to steady herself. She had drove down, thinking that it'd be a long road back to healthy. That she'd get there, and the chemo would start, and Lily would make it through.

Her eyes flew open and stared into Peter's. "How long?" She blurted.

"What?"

"How. Long?"

Silence.

"Does she have?"

Another hard blink. "At this point," He said sadly, choking up himself. "Maybe a month."

Ariettea felt chills rack her body, and a wave of nausea hit her like a ton of bricks.

Her whole life, she had been able to suppress any emotion, change her thinking, conceal- don't feel, but with Lily, all her emotions could never be stifled. Lily taught her that life brought feelings and that you had to roll with it because a lot of them were really great. So, anything concerning Lily was like a dam opening up the floodgates of emotion.

Her hand flew up to her forehead, eyes burning, stomach churning.

She turned, spun, and finally crouched down and hugged her knees, her back up against the glass.

Her world was collapsing around her, and so did she.

She wanted to scream.

She wanted to yell, but Lily was asleep, she couldn't wake up to this.

So Ariettea sat there, knees to chest, on a hospital floor, holding her breath and trying not to cry, trying to hold in dry heaves.

She didn't want Peter there to see, and when she looked up, he was gone.

As she gasped for air, she felt a hand on her shoulder. Peter was kneeling beside her, holding a box of hospital tissues, tears streaming down his face.

She gently took the box from him, feeling bad to admit she wasn't crying.

"I'm so sorry, Ariettea."

Her eyes welled up with tears again.

She took in a breath through her mouth, and shakily let it out. "I'm sorry too." She said.

Although she didn't know if she meant for herself, Lily, or him.

It took her a long time to collect herself, steady herself. Longer than anything usually did. All those times hiding in bathrooms, she could always pull it together and walk out, no matter how pale and shaky she actually was. But not now.

Peter silently stood above her the whole time, back to the glass, arms crossed, eyes at the ceiling. Normally, she would have resented his presence, but she could feel his pain just as strongly as her own.

She finally released the grip on her knees and went to stand up. Her feet had long ago fallen asleep, and as she grabbed the wall to steady herself, Peter quickly helped her up. His touch was gentle yet firm.

"Thanks." She mumbled.

"Not a problem."

For a moment, they both stared through the glass, just watching Lily sleep.

More questions started to flood Ariettea's head. "Where's Alex?"

"He went up to their place to get some of Lil's things. Things…she's not going to be able to go back for." Peter answered.

"I don't understand, why can't she just go home?"

"She said that she doesn't want to spoil their house by dying in it. That she wants to remember it as a happy place herself. And that…" He chuckled, "That she will finally be here for the annual Gala, and she's absolutely going this year."

Ariettea scoffed, shook her head. "Sounds like Lily…"

She took a deep breath. Lily couldn't possibly be this bad. How could she not have known?

"Is she in pain?"

"Yes." Ariettea glanced over at him, harshly.

He shrugged. "Lily has always said you cut right through the crap. From how highly she talks of you, I respect you enough to tell you the truth."

Ariettea nodded distractedly. A sane person, finally. "Can they manage it?"

"They're doing the best they can."

"How can she go from fine to…this… in a month?" She burst.

She turned away from the door. "She's my best friend, how could she not tell me?" She all but whispered.

Peter walked around to face her. Hands in his khakis, he said softly, "She's been in remission for a good stretch. But we all knew the chances it would come back. Extremely low, but... It did, and it did quickly. They just found out the outlook a couple of days ago. I'm not sure if they've even processed it themselves. She didn't want you driving all this way-"

"But I would hav-"

"And she KNEW that. She knows you love her enough to do anything and everything for her. She's so confident in your care for her, and she cares so much for you, THAT'S why she didn't tell you, not because you lost touch or anything else you're implying."

She looked up at him suddenly, wondering how he could possibly be reading her thoughts.

He paused. "Lily talks about you all the time." He said, pulling his hands out of his pockets.

He smiled. "Ariettea, I don't think you realize what you've done for her."

She looked at him, confused. "What do you mean?"

"Well, she's been sick for so much of her life, in and out of hospitals, never really a kid, alone. No one ever took a genuine interest in a friendship with her. It was always sweet, kind, nice people who saw her as a dying kid. And you saw more. Lily has always been a sweetheart, but you gave her true happiness, friendship, a confidant. She thinks of you as her best friend, the same as you do her. And that's great."

Ariettea scoffed, scuffed her boot across the shiny floor. "I've not been the best friend lately." She confessed.

She looked up at Peter; she'd forget how much taller he was than her, well over six feet. "I've been having…relationship woes as of late." She said carefully. "My…ex,"

She rolled her eyes, half out of annoyance, half out of disgust. Partly of hurt.

"Took a lot of my attention. In a bad way. He always said Lily and I had a very odd relationship. That's one of the reasons we broke up… He used to say she was just a weird, sick-"

"Sick kid." Peter said with her.

She stared at him.

He scoffed with a smile. "I've had the same conversation. Granted, Lily and I aren't as close as the two of you, now that WOULD be odd, but she's always been like my little sister. She was my first tutoring student, and now my longest. I've watched her grow up, as I have myself. Watched her highs and lows… The three of them, they're all my family. At first, I think she had a crush on me, but that passed with time.

"But, like you, I've gotten the same speeches. About the sick kid, the dying girl, that weird child I spend too much time with. I used to take a drive up there every weekend during the summer. Alex took me to my first real bar," He laughed.

"Elaina taught me that you DO have to call a girl back if you want her to like you. And Lily…she just changes you. As a person. She makes you appreciate things. Not in a clichéd way, not a cancer kid changes the world way, but in a-"

"'Hey, I wonder if the sky was purple' way?" Ariettea laughed.

"Exactly!" Peter laughed with her.

"But then she'll look at you so serious and ask why you are so scared to live life?" She said softly.

"So, I'm not the only one she asked!" Peter laughed. "She's always told me she only asks when she cares. But we all know she's too smart for her own good." He smiled.

"She's a special girl." Ariettea said, looking back at her.

Peter nodded and turned to look at her, as well.

They were both quiet for a moment before Peter jumped and said, "Hey, did you really say you drove straight here from Michigan just now?

You've been on the road and had a rough evening. Let me go grab you some coffee."

Ariettea smiled.

"If you drink coffee, that is, or I can get tea or pop," Peter fumbled.

"Coffee is great." Ariettea cut him off. "Thank you." She reached for her wallet.

"No, no, on me!" Peter said, already walking away.

"No-"

"Something else Lily taught me!" He said. "Always pay for a nice lady."

"Thank you!" Ariettea called as he rounded the corner.

She sighed and turned back towards Lily. It was then that reality hit her again. After the moment of laughter, she felt guilty.

Lily was dying.

Ariettea walked into the room and curled up in Peter's empty chair, took a deep breath. She looked at Lily's pulse ox machine and hoped it was normal. She supposed she would have known by now had she started at Ducreis when she was supposed to.

She just stared at Lily. Peter said she was in pain, Ariettea searched for it on her face. She looked tired, but not visibly in pain. At least that was a comfort.

She laid her head on her knees and closed her eyes. She couldn't accept it. Lily couldn't die. There had to be a way out. They had to find a way to fix it. They couldn't be trapped... She finally felt a tear slide down her cheek, sink into the knee of her jeans.

Things had finally felt right over the summer.

And now they had fallen entirely back apart.

Even worse than before.

She'd finally let someone in, taken a chance on a person after having walked alone for so long. But at least they had had each other, gotten each other through so much. Over so much. She was going to lose yet another person. But at least this relationship had produced nothing but happiness. Until then, at least. Until soon, she'd have another person leave her.

'But she let you experience happiness for the first time.' She thought to herself.

Maybe this time, though, the hurt of the loss was worth it.

Chapter 30

A pain in her neck woke Ariettea up hours later. The sun was coming up over the brick and mortar peaks of the college in the distance. She turned her neck to the side, and the movement made a coat that had been laid over her slip to the floor. She grabbed it and smelled cologne. She looked over at Elaina and saw no sign of Alex, so the coat had to be Peter's. But where was he? She looked and saw him sitting leaning against the wall on the floor next to her, asleep.

She stood up and laid his coat on his lap. She almost kicked over a foam cup sitting by the chair of her leg. Her coffee. From Peter. She picked it up and opened the lid to take a smell. It couldn't be that old she reasoned; she'd just find a place to warm it up.

She slipped out the door and searched for a waiting or breakroom. She approached a nurse, her obviously just starting her shift, and asked if there was a place to warm up her coffee.

She tied her hair into a bun and tried to wipe away any smeared makeup from under her eyes. She took a few deep breaths and tried to compose herself.

When she came out of the break room, a nurse almost plowed her over running down the hall- towards Lily's room.

Ariettea felt her heart drop.

No.

No no no no, what was going on? She raced to follow the nurse, and when she came around to Lily's room, she saw Lily sitting in bed, visibly upset, and Peter and Elaina were trying to calm her down. The nurse was looking at the monitor, at Lily's racing heart.

She could hear Lily from in the hallway; "I have to call her! I have to get a hold of Ari! I need Ariettea!"

"She's having a panic attack. It's to be expected." She heard a nurse say behind her, rushing into the room as well.

Ariettea followed her in and flashed her a nasty look before looking to Lily. "Lily," She said.

"Ariettea!" Lily nearly screamed, pushing away the arms of those around her. "Oh, Ari!" She started to cry.

Ariettea jumped onto the edge of her bed. "Lily," She said, letting her climb into her arms. "Honey, what's wrong?"

Lily choked back a sob. "I had… I had a dream. I died, and you- you-you weren't here. I never called you. I'm so sorry I didn't call you!"

Peter knowingly grabbing Ariettea's coffee from her hand, and she wrapped Lily up. "It's ok!" She said soothingly.

She hugged her close, trying to calm her down. She stroked her soft hair as Lily's head lay on her chest. She realized then how odd that was for her, to be hugging someone, especially after having become so cold again. But as always, it was Lily. It felt right.

She tried to make light of it. She laughed, "I mean, I'm not too pleased with you for not calling me missy," She said, trying to look down at her. "But best friends have a way of finding things out."

She felt Lily giggle in her arms and released her embrace. "Who told you?" She asked, her teal eyes still glistening with tears.

Ariettea pushed her hair from her wet face, tucked it behind her ear. "Your mom. I was trying to get a hold of you and couldn't."

"I'm sorry."

"I'm here now," She grabbed both her hands in her own. "That's all that matters." She smiled warmly, and Lily smiled back.

She realized just how much she had missed that smile.

A nurse knocked and came in. "We need to clean Lily up for the day if you guys could step out." She said, smiling.

Ariettea and Peter took their leave.

Ariettea glanced around at the nurses, all hustling into rooms, pushing carts, and she thought again about how easily that could have been her. Or at least, how easily she could have been learning it all. But because of Matt… Suddenly the thought dawned on her that with Matt gone, she was free to do what she wanted. But then she glanced back at Lily's room, the blinds drawn, and she knew she couldn't. She couldn't do whatever she wanted; she had Lily to think about.

She felt a twinge of pain. So, was that truly it? Was it really all over with Matt? All that time she put in, all those feelings, gone? What if…when…Lily was gone, would she feel the same way? All the memories, moments with him, where would they be? Tucked away with memories of everyone else that had left?

No. No, she wouldn't let that happen. Not all things end badly. With bad memories. If Lily was going to… go, then they'd have good memories. They were all good memories. And she was going to make sure things were good all the way… All the way until the end.

"Wanna grab a coffee?" Peter asked, jolting her out of her thoughts.

She felt awkward, getting coffee with a random guy. "You got me one, remember?" She motioned for him to give her her coffee cup back.

"So, no, thanks, I'm going to go see if I can find my Aunt and Uncle."

Peter smirked and laughed, "Ok, I'll see you then."

"See you."

Ariettea turned around to start heading towards OB. On the same floor as Lily's, but a different wing, it wasn't a far walk, and she knew Nadette liked to do early morning rounds.

As she passed the nurses station, she saw a woman standing there in business wear, looking for help. She caught Ariettea's eye, and even though she had tried to ignore her, she opened her mouth to ask a question.

Ariettea stifled the urge to roll her eyes. "Can I help you?" She asked irritated.

"I'm looking for a nurse, or someone to tell me where I can find a room. I know a lot of the patients here know each other; do you know what room Lily Abonet is in?"

Ariettea tilted her head to the side. "I'm sorry, who are you?" She asked, shaking her head, narrowing her eyes.

"I'm sorry, I'm new, this is my first appointment of the day," The lady apologized, digging in her leather handbag.

She pulled out a business card and handed it to Ariettea. "I'm Jorie Maybelle, with the hospital's hospice care."

"Hospice?" Ariettea repeated incredulously. "And-and you're looking for Lily? W-Why?"

"I can't really discuss that," Anna said. "But, hospice, as you know, is end of life care, it's for when-"

"For when there's nothing left to do." Ariettea finished for her bitterly.

Jorie didn't respond. She just looked at her sadly. "I'm sorry." She said softly.

Ariettea shook her head. "It's the corner room on the right." She mumbled as she brushed past her.

She threw her coffee into a trash bin so hard she splashed herself, and then tore the business card into as many pieces as she could as she walked off.

She was angry, she was scared, and she felt lost.

She found herself strolling the hospital grounds, having given up trying to find Nadette, but just trying to get her head together. Trying to grasp what was happening.

Literally overnight, she had broken up with the only person that had stayed in her life longer than a couple of years, and she found out her best friend was dying. That there was nothing to be done. And there wasn't long left.

There was no changing the facts. She remembered her high school psychology class. The five stages of grief. Denial, anger, bargaining, depression, and finally, acceptance. She knew she was in denial- This couldn't be happening. It couldn't be true. It had to all be some nightmare. She'd wake up in her bed at home, to a text from Matt, the kind Matt, and everything would be back to normal. Lily would be in remission, and she'd be… Where? Where would she be? Where had she been? Gallivanting off with a guy that ended up a total loser? Not even paying enough attention to her best friend to know that she was sick?

She shook her head in disgust. She really thought his love could be stronger than Lily's. All this time she thought Lily had changed her, she was a better person, more understanding, happier, forgiving of the people that had hurt her. But maybe she was just like the rest of them, using friends when they were needed and dumping them when things started looking up.

She flopped herself onto a bench just inside the college grounds, not realizing she'd wandered so far off. 'Well,' She thought to herself. 'At least I've reached the anger stage.'

She saw Peter walking up to her, hands in his pockets, as always.

As soon as he was close enough to make eye contact, "Hey, what's up?" She asked, not giving him a chance to speak.

He looked at her, his head slightly angled, as if he knew something more was wrong than the obvious. He straightened up, though, when he saw the look on her face harden.

"Hey," He said, trying to look casual, trying to pretend he didn't notice the look. "Lily is up and dressed. I thought you'd want to know."

He couldn't even finish his sentence before Ariettea was up and walking back up the path to the hospital.

"Awesome thanks." She said over her shoulder, not waiting for him to keep up pace with her, which he did anyway, hopping a few feet to catch up.

"That was my favorite bench here." He said out of nowhere.

Ariettea glanced over at him, confused. "What?"

"Where you were sitting, the bench, the trees, the stereotypical ivy-covered buildings, and brick pathways…" He smiled up at the sky. "I loved this school." He said.

"That bench was my favorite spot in the whole campus. To study, eat between classes, have a coffee… Well, besides this tiny spot on the beach no one really knows about."

"The one you can see from Lily's room."

Peter smiled. "Yeah, I think any of us who spent a lot of time in Lily's room know that spot." He mused.

"I never realized you were so…present." She said, feeling the sting of her own recent absence.

"Well, certainly not as much as you!" Peter laughed.

She just stared at the ground.

Peter fumbled with his words in response. "Well I mean since Lily has never really been able to go to school, she's always needed a tutor, and her longer stays here corresponded to my years in college, and I, of course, was broke, alone most nights,"

He started to stutter, "Not in like, a lonely weirdo bad way, but like, a, I'd rather study than drink or pick up girls way…I mean, I was just available to tutor and needed the cash…"

He shook his head. "I'm not presenting a good image of myself here, am I?" He said self-deprecatingly but still smiling.

Ariettea laughed. "Nah, I get you. I've always been the same. Not that I got to go to college here."

'Or anywhere.' She added silently.

She shook her head in disgust at the thought, then caught Peter looking at her.

"I mean, I could have!" She said, looking over at Peter for the first time. "You know that I got in here. To Ducreis."

He nodded.

"But I just...took another option."

"Another college?"

"No."

She could feel the awkwardness in the silence that followed as Peter tried to find an appropriate response to that.

She took pity on him and continued, "I chose to stay close to my boyfriend." She said slowly.

"My EX boyfriend." She corrected quickly.

She shook her head. "Honestly, I wish I had come here and stayed close to Lily instead."

Peter looked consolingly down at her. "Hey, don't beat yourself up about that. I got caught up in work a lot this past year." He said sadly. "You can't stay somewhere for anyone else. You also can't go around expecting the worst."

'Two of my specialties.' Ariettea said to herself silently.

Peter tried to push the conversation on. "Yeah, it's been a crazy year. They try to prepare you for a job but teaching elementary schoolers when you yourself are only 23 is a trip!"

She was still yelling at herself as they walked back into the hospital. It was her own fault she didn't know. It was her own fault she had let their friendship slide.

Peter mumbled on, "Not that I have to care about that much now... Asking for a leave of absence in your first year of work doesn't bode well."

Ariettea laughed, bitterly, as she pressed the elevator button. "Hey, I bypassed college and a dream job, then I quit my sad coffee house job over text on my way here, so I think I've got you beat."

She looked over at him. "Hey, how'd you know where to find me?" She asked, suddenly quizzical.

He smiled. "Like I said, it's the best bench here."

As they rounded the corner to come down the hallway to Lily's room, Ariettea's heart rate sped up. She felt suddenly nervous about what she would find. She tried to calm down, to prepare to hear Lily's excited voice call out her name as she walked in. But Lily could only get out the first syllable before a coughing fit hit her.

"I told you to keep the mask on, Lily." Elaina scolded, jumping up to readjust the oxygen mask on her face.

Lily held it to her face begrudgingly as Ariettea leaned in to hug her.

Lily smiled. "I KNOW I must be sick when I get an Ariettea hug without asking for it!" She said with a laugh.

Ariettea sat on the bed. She couldn't help but notice the blue veins popping up out of Lily's skin, a translucent white shade she had never seen before.

"You have some explaining to do, bestie." She said quietly.

Lily cocked her head and smiled softly. Then she looked around at her parents, Alex having arrived, and Peter. As if to send them the signal that it was-

"Coffee time!" Alex exclaimed. He clapped his hand on Peter's shoulder and put his free arm around Elaina's waist. "I'm buying! Let's give our girls the room." He said, winking at Lily.

Lily nodded as they quickly filed out.

'Our girls.'

They really had taken her in. How quickly she'd forgotten.

Ariettea glanced over her shoulder, she noticed Peter heading for the elevators, but Alex and Elaina took a left into the waiting room. She could see the tears already streaming down both their faces, hands intertwined. They were all putting on a brave front for Lily. Or so they thought. It was always Lily who ended up putting on a brave front for them.

As was demonstrated when she asked, "What's with the all-black, Ari?"

Ariettea looked at her, taken aback at first. Then, suddenly, she just felt at home. With Lily. But that wall she had worked so hard to take down had somehow made its way back up. And it made Ariettea hesitant to answer.

Lily noticed. "Ari? My eyes are up here, not on my blanket."

Ariettea looked into her eyes. Those once effervescent teal eyes, now missing their keen sparkle that everyone had grown so accustomed to seeing.

"I've always worn all black." She responded casually, thinking of Matt asking her why she wore black to weddings.

"Mmm, not all summer, when you had on flowy skirts, when you finally wore tank tops that showed your scars,"

Ariettea felt her own head cock to the side in shock.

"Oh yeah, I noticed." Lily nodded. "And what about the night you Facetimed me when you were going out with Matt, that night, you were wearing white"

"Sounds like you already know what's going on." Ariettea said looking down once more.

"I could tell there was more than just me running through your head." Lily said softly.

She reached out and grasped Ariettea's hand. Ariettea had to fight the urge to recoil. Not only at the feeling of human touch, but at the feeling of how ice-cold Lily's long frail fingers were.

"What happened?"

"Nothing."

"It's most certainly not nothing."

"We broke up." Ariettea had to fight to make the words come out without catching in her throat.

"Why?"

Ariettea scoffed, rolled her eyes, trying to roll back the tears that were trying to well up. "Because he's an idiot." She said, looking at Lily.

"Ari," Lily said, "Come on. Let's not have this conversation for the millionth time. Don't block it all out. I've watched you be miserable for so long, and then come out of it and grow into a happy person. I don't think I can watch you be this miserable again. You've got to let yourself feel."

Ariettea scoffed again, trying to stifle her disgust. "Feel? Feel what, Lily? Feel hurt? Feel betrayed? Just like I've always felt from every person in my life? How is feeling it going to make me any less miserable?"

She stood up and turned in a circle, arms out, palms up. "Why are you even worried about me?" She raged on. "You're the one who's sick, the one I raced down here in the middle of the night for, the one whose parents are sobbing in the waiting room. And you want to hear about my BREAKUP?"

She shook her head, let her arms fall and smack her legs.

Lily adjusted herself in her bed. She folded her hands in her lap as she said, "Well, now we're getting somewhere."

Ariettea just stared at her blankly.

"Well, anger is an emotion." Lily said. "When we first met, all I ever got from you was indifference."

Ariettea shook her head, bitterly. "He's just another person that left. Another person that broke me, broke the heart I never knew I had. But it doesn't matter, Lily. HE doesn't matter. All I care about is you right now."

Lily took a deep breath and began to stare at the ground before continuing, "That's the thing. I'm not so ignorant as to not know that I'm sort of proving your point here, I mean, I'm sure you're thinking, look, another person about to leave me…" Lily trailed off, shook her head, looked back up at Ariettea.

Her voice wavered. "But even if the loss of me breaks you, Ariettea, which I know it won't because you're the strongest person I've ever met, I need you to know…"

Ariettea now noticed Lily fighting back tears.

"Our friendship made ME." She sniffled. "You were, and are, the closest friend I've ever, and will ever, have. The most loyal. You always acted like I was some saint, yet you forget your own value. And I really hope you realize it someday and count it as highly as I do. And maybe it's selfish of me, to attach myself to someone I might have to leave one day, but that's a risk we all take any time we make a connection. And we have to decide if it was worth it. I never planned to hurt anyone. I always planned on outliving you all."

They both laughed through tears at the break of tension.

Lily bit her lip, "I'm telling you all this because I know you want to know why I didn't tell you sooner that I was sick again."

Lily's lip quivered, fighting a sob. "It was because I couldn't be the one to leave you again. I couldn't be one of those people to hurt the amazing girl that you are."

She gave in to the sobs, her lips quivering uncontrollably. "I wanted to deny it, I wanted to think I could fight it again, but Ari… I can't. I'm so sorry; I just can't beat it this time."

She sobbed more as Ariettea felt tears start to stream down her own face.

"It's not that I don't want to, but my body can't. And I'm so, so sorry."

Ariettea rushed over and wrapped Lily up in a hug. She wanted to tell her don't say that, it will be alright, we will get through this, but none of those words could mean anything. Not anymore.

Lily pulled away from Ariettea to look her in the eyes. "So, Ari, I know that you're hurting, and it kills me that Matt did this the same time my body decided to do this, but please, please…. Please don't shut down again. You're too amazing; you've got too much good in you to close yourself off. And there are too many good things still out there to open your heart to."

Ariettea's own lip quivered as she stifled her own sob. She bit her lip as she looked down into Lily's teary, red eyes.

"Matt already made me shut down. He shut me down months ago. There's no more good out there. There's not another you."

"So, what happens now?" Ariettea found herself asking, uncharacteristically outspoken.

She was standing in the empty waiting room with Alex, Elaina, Peter, and Lily's doctor. She wanted a solution, she wanted cold hard logic and a way to fix everything.

The doctor shook his head. "We make her comfortable."

Peter nodded, clapped a hand on Alex's shoulder, and jumped in, "We give her things to enjoy. We stay with her. We make sure he's not alone."

Ariettea felt her face stiffen, did he think she had left Lily alone on purpose? "Obviously." She snarled his direction, barely loud enough for anyone else to hear.

"What was that, Ari?" Elaina asked, sincerely.

Ariettea shook her head, crossed her arms. "Nothing."

But she knew Peter had heard from the look he gave her.

The doctor looked at Ariettea and Peter. "I've been told to treat you both as family members, so I'm going to tell you both what I've told Elaina and Alex; Lily doesn't have much time. The cancer has spread so rapidly, so viciously, that we can't expect her to last more than a month."

Tears silently rolled down Elaina's face once more as Alex took her in his arms.

"So yes," The doctor said, "Give her things to enjoy. Keep her happy, and we'll keep her as pain-free as possible."

The doctor, unwilling to say, 'until the end', excused himself and left, and Ariettea turned to Alex and Elaina.

"So, she really doesn't want to go home?" She asked, arms still hugging her chest.

Elaina silently cried in Alex's arms as he answered, "No. And we respect her enough as a human being to not force her. To be honest, it is easier here with pain management, meds, extra help…" He trailed off, eyes hazing over, showing how much he hated talking about it all. Elaina hugged him even tighter and buried her face in his chest.

"They aren't moving her to the hospice floor, though?" Peter asked.

Alex shook his head again. "It's her room." He said with a broken smile, his face starting to twitch as he fought back tears.

There was too much emotion… she had to get out of there.

"Hey, so I'll let you guys get some time with her. I really need to get in touch with Trent and Nadette."

She started to turn, to back away towards the door, but she paused. Lily's voice ever echoing through her mind, 'You can't go through life not feeling, Ari.' It was her hardest lesson to learn. Everything around her, every bad thing that had happened to her the last two days wouldn't have happened had she just kept her walls up. But then she wouldn't have Lily at all.

She hesitated, then stepped forward and put her hand on Elaina's arm. "We'll take care of her together. I promise."

Ariettea started to head out when Peter ran up behind her in the hallway, said to her back, "I wasn't trying to make a dig at you."

Ariettea stopped, hearing her boots scuff on the floor as rolled her eyes before turning around to face him.

"Noted." She said coolly, nodding towards him.

"Honest." He said, taking a step towards her, hand out.

She crossed her arms over her chest, daring him to step closer.

"Look," He began, stopping, still a few feet away, feeling her force field go up. "You and I have been passing ships. You've been with Lily in the summer, school breaks, all the times I've not been here. And vice versa, I've been here all the times you haven't. And that's not meant as an insult. You and I, one of us has always been by that girl's side, and I just want to keep it that way. And if one of us is gone, I'm sure Alex or Elaina will be there. That's all I meant."

Ariettea nodded.

"I know how it is to be adopted by this family," He laughed.

Ariettea smiled, as it was a feeling she was familiar with as well.

"And I know how well Lily was hiding this from you." He said in all seriousness. "Don't blame yourself. I begged her for the last month to tell you. But she didn't want to take you away from your relationship and happiness."

Ariettea involuntarily rolled her eyes.

Peter looked at her confused.

"I'm sorry," She apologized, rubbing the bridge of her nose, fighting a headache. "I guess I just hid a lot from Lily too it would seem."

Peter still looked confused but was too polite to ask for clarification.

"I told you my ex was less than supportive of our friendship, but that wasn't something I ever told Lily." She shook her head. "But maybe she knew. And that's why she didn't tell me this was going on." She pondered aloud.

"Just because Lily didn't say anything, doesn't mean she didn't know. Lily would definitely let you figure things out on your own if she thought you needed to." He said.

"I think that's why she gave you so much space. She talked about you all the time, but never your boyfriend. So, I could only assume she didn't care for him."

"Why wouldn't she tell me, though? I always listen to her." She mumbled, mostly to herself.

Peter shrugged. "Sometimes, we need to figure out things on our own for them to have the most effect."

She nodded silently. 'I just wish I knew what I actually want now.' She thought, before scolding herself that she only be thinking about Lily.

She cleared her throat, "Hey, well, I'm here now, so if you need to take care of anything, go hang out with your guys or whatever…"

She trailed off, waved a hand, trying not to sound snarky.

Peter put a hand on the back of his neck as he shook his head. "Eh… the whole 'bros' scene has never really been my thing."

He chuckled, threw his hands up. "I did the whole large group of friends thing through college and it just…."

He shook his head. "Wasn't me. The feeling was mutual on their end, too. I was usually the one bringing the group down, wanting to go get coffee instead of beers."

Ariettea began to smile.

"Yeah, yeah, I know I'm weird…" Peter shook his head.

Ariettea threw up a hand, "No! No, you're not. I mean, I always think I'M weird for having been that person all through high school, but maybe it WAS everyone else who was crazy!" She crossed her arms and shrugged, shook her head, still laughing.

Peter joined in. "I guess we can see why we both got adopted by these people." He looked down the hall at Alex and Elaina talking to Lily's nurse.

Ariettea continued to laugh, the tiredness hitting her, slapping her into slaphappy.

"It's like you're the version of me that I was supposed to be! Had I not turned into this epic disappointment, the failure of those amazing people behind you,"

She shook her head as Peter stepped forward, his face serious. "Hey, never say you're a disappointment,"

"Oh you don't even know me." She snapped, taking a step back, looking him up and down, mad that she felt like she was Jekyll and Hyde-ing him.

He shook his head again. "Hey, I'm another version of you, remember?"

He smirked as she rolled her eyes.

"Right, right, I'm only a disappointment if I don't better myself, right?" She asked bitterly, waving her arms out wide, hearing Matt's words ringing through her ears.

Peter squinted his eyes and shook his head even more. "No… Ariettea, no human ever has the right to tell you that you're a disappointment. And you- you're REALLY nowhere near a disappointment in any regard, from any angle. Look how much Lily loves you, how little she tries to change you, aside from telling you to be happy, and I know that's how she is because that's how she was with me."

He chuckled. "It seems to me that you're fine the way you are. Don't let anyone tell you otherwise."

She unlocked the front door to Trent and Nadette's townhouse and called out for them both. The house was empty.

She dropped her bag by the front door with a thud, but then noticed the framed picture sitting by the key tray on the side table. Her and Trent on their Ducreis tour. She smiled as she picked it up and stroked it with her thumb.

A voice rang out and made her jump, "You look at that picture the same way Trent does." Nadette called out from around the corner, her slim frame leaning up against the doorway. "Sorry to make you jump, I just pulled in the back."

"Hey," Ariettea gasped, putting the picture down.

Before her hand had even left it, Nadette had he wrapped up in a tight hug. She tried to reciprocate best she could as she still stared down at the picture.

"Yeah, I guess there's always that 'should have been'." She mused bitterly.

Nadette grabbed her shoulders and shook her head. "Hey, we're here now, we can't change the past. Just the future."

Ariettea felt her shoulder deflate, her face fall.

"The future isn't looking too good right now, Nade…" She stared down at the wood floor, tracing the grain as far as she could see.

"What's wrong?" Nadette pulled her arm, bringing Ariettea's eyes back to her.

She shook her head. "It's bad, Nadette. It's really bad."

She dropped to the floor, and crossed her legs over each other, looked up at her Aunt. "Lily is dying. Like, really dying."

Nadette slowly lowered herself to the floor, her grey pantsuit flaring out from her ankles as she removed her heels and sat facing Ariettea.

"They can't fix her this time." Her voice cracked, wobbled.

She played with her fingers as they sat in her lap.

Nadette reached out and touched her knee. "Why do I have the feeling that's not the only thing going wrong for you right now?"

Ariettea looked at her, her hazel eyes searching for some answer to Ariettea's pain.

"It doesn't matter." She leaned back onto her hands. "Nothing about me matters right now."

"Ari, you'll never be able to give Lily what you want to, what YOU want to, if you're falling apart yourself."

"Then, I just have to pull it together."

"This many broken pieces, dear, you need to take a few minutes and put it back together slowly."

"Why not just leave them where they are then!"

"Because life isn't black and white, Ari. There isn't perfection or absolute destruction, either."

She leaned forward and took Ariettea's hands into her own.

Ariettea looked down at them, remembering that Matt was the last person to have held her like that. She wanted to physically recoil at the thought, but she let Nadette hold on.

Ariettea held back tears. "I screwed up so bad, Nadette."

She chewed on her lip. "It's ironic. You know, I was the perfect kid. I never ever got in trouble. I read my Bible; I lived like a Christian; I was as kind to people as I could be. I got good grades, tried to make friends, tried to forge a path, but... But it was just never good enough. It was never good enough because I wasn't doing 'enough'. I wasn't friendly 'enough'. I wasn't Christian 'enough'. And all the kids that were enough? They fell so short of the ridiculous throne they tried to put themselves on, but people still praise them more than they've ever thought to even think of me because I never tried. As long as you put on the face that people want to see... You're fine. You're supposed to be fine."

She shook her head, stared at a cobweb on the ceiling. "I wasn't fine. I was never fine. I used to spend so much time reacting and responding to everyone else that my life had no direction. Other people's lives, problems, regrets, and wants set the course for my life. Once I realized it was ok for me to think about and identify what I want, need, remarkable things started to take place in my life. I finally had what I always wanted. But then… I tried to put that face back on…" She trailed off.

"I've always been told I think too much, that I lead too much with my head. So, after a summer of setting my own course, I really thought that putting on that face was what I wanted, but it wasn't.

"And the worst part is that it still wasn't enough. Even when I finally did all the things people told me I would end up doing, that still wasn't good enough for them. They wanted more and more and more from me. Leading with my head didn't work and leading with my heart didn't, either. So as much as everyone tells me there's no black and white, it's all I can see. And now, the one person who tried to teach me to use both head and heart is going to leave me.

"So, I see that picture of Trent and me, and I see everything I've lost."

As a tear trailed down her cheek, Nadette slid over to sit beside her and pull her close.

"Have you ever heard, 'stay close to people who feel like sunshine'?"

Ariettea laughed as she sniffled. What a 'Nadette' question.

"No. No, I have not."

"Choosing happiness… It's not really a thing. Choosing people and things that make us happy is really the key. We have to chase it. We have to find the sunshine."

Ariettea laughed again. "I guess everyone back there was right. You can't run from things. But what they didn't get right was that you can choose to let them go instead."

"You always say 'back there'. You never call Michigan 'home'. Nadette commented, laying her chin on top of Ariettea's head.

Ariettea leaned into her, grabbed her arm as she answered, "I had to learn that happiness isn't a place, and gosh, it's most certainly not a person. But if home is where I feel the sunshine, at least I know I can't feel it back there."

Chapter 31

Ariettea wanted so badly to be able to put a label on what they were doing; her, Lily, Alex, Elaina, and Peter, but there wasn't one.

It was as if they were waiting for time to pass without wanting it to.

Trent and Nadette were in and out, of course, and Ariettea met a plethora of Lily's extended family that came to… say goodbye. She couldn't be there for that. She couldn't watch Lily smile and put on a brave face saying she'd see them again, while still thinking how unfair it was that she had to leave at all.

So mostly, it was just the five of them.

Alex and Elaina used to jump up to go get coffee when Ariettea first met Lily, to give the girls time to get to know each other, but now they stayed in their seats.

Peter used to run out because his tutoring session was done, and he had to get to class, but now he was there without books and stayed as long as the rest of the family.

They were a mod-podged family unit.

Hospice came in and pulled them all off to the side and explained how to care for Lily, what she might need, what might happen. They explained the pain she was in, the pain that everyone tried to avoid talking about.

There were bad days, better days, but no more good days.

She was getting weaker and weaker, but she never stopped talking about the Gala. None of them were even sure how she'd get out of bed to get downstairs to it… but it was Lily.

Ariettea kept expecting to hear from… well, anyone. Matt, his mom, Mandy, any of the ten million people that had texted her when she and Matt first got together, but no messages ever came in. Part of her was relieved, but the other part of her felt the stinging burn of a slap to the face. It was as if they had finally, truly kicked her out, happily, even though she was the one to have walked away. But she knew she was happier being gone even more than they were having her gone.

She went to delete all the pictures of her and Matt online, but just deleted all her social media apps, instead. Anyone she wanted to hear from could gather in the room she spent her days in, and that's all she cared about.

But she still felt that emptiness, that lost feeling. She wasn't sure if she even had a life anymore. But she couldn't even think about it. She ignored Nadette's advice to rebuild, Lily's advice to feel. She had to think about Lily. Only Lily.

She was rubbing lotion onto her pale arms one afternoon, her skin growing thinner and thinner along with the arm itself. Ariettea smiled down at Lily but couldn't find any words to say. And, as always, Lily read in between the lines.

She tried to pull herself upright. "Ari, can you take me outside? Can we go to the beach?"

Ariettea looked panicked over at Elaina, curled up in an armchair by the window. She shrugged at Ariettea as if to say, give her whatever she wants. "We can see you guys from here, anyway."

Ariettea half expected Lily to jump up out of bed like she had the year before, grab her IV bags, and toss them to her, but it was a much slower process.

Peter and Ariettea shared a look that communicated so much, a look that said everything the other person was thinking, which always meant whatever Lily needed. It was a look they had mastered. He helped her gather everything as Alex helped Lily out of bed.

They took the elevator instead of the stairs. Once they arrived there, on that small strip of sand in the shadow of the hospital, Ariettea nearly had to carry Lily to the shore, bundled in a fuzzy pink sweatshirt and wrapped in a thin hospital blanket.

They sat together in a sunny spot and stared at the water, like they had so many times in Baringvale. They both had the unspoken knowledge that it could very well be the last time Lily was there.

"This spot has always made me think of home. But you know that." Lily said, her voice not projecting as far as it usually did when accompanied by the sound of waves.

They both found themselves staring at the sand lilies, wilted, but trying to grow back for a new season.

"Home makes me think of our summer, and how perfect it was. I've always loved that place, but you gave it more meaning. Thank you for giving me that, Ari."

Ariettea smiled down at her. "I should be thanking you for it. You were the one who brought me there, kept me there really," She laughed self-deprecatingly, then smiled. "It was the best summer of my life."

"Well, I'm sorry you've had such a crappy winter and fall."

Ariettea began to bafflegab for words.

"Well, me, here, now, sick." Lily explained, as if it were all simply a matter of fact. "And everything you had to go through with Matt…" She trailed off.

She looked at Ariettea's stoic face. "Do you think you feel up to sharing what happened?" She finally, after weeks, asked.

Ariettea took a deep breath. "As much as I try to ignore what happened, pretend it didn't happen, all I can do is analyze it all. And all I'm sure that is real was that all we did was try to change each other. I wanted him to be the sweet guy I pictured, that I once knew, and he wanted me to be the outgoing girl he wanted. And neither of us was that person or was going to get that."

She shook her head bitterly. "You tried to warn me, Lily. I chose not to listen when you questioned my choice to stay with him over coming here, to Ducreis. And then he took up so much of my time that I didn't even know or notice you were getting sick-"

"That's on me." Lily said quickly. "I didn't want to interfere with what you and Matt were trying to build together."

Ariettea shook her head, scoffed, unzipped her hoodie so she could pull it tighter around herself. "It wasn't real." She found herself saying out loud for the first time.

"It WAS real, Ari. It was real to you at that time."

"But it wasn't real in any other sense."

"But at that point in time, he was what you needed!"

"No," Ariettea snapped, squeezing her eyes shut. "I needed to do what was best for me! I needed to go to school, put my best friend on a higher place in my life, not choose to run around with some guy who did nothing but put everything I love down, hated you, put me down, sided with everyone saying I wasn't good enough, that I'd be an embarrassment if I didn't change for him, who constantly chose his friends over me, still flirted with other girls, and who only told me he loved me to keep me from doing what I actually should have been doing, what actually would have been best for me, and then told me he did me a favor by being with me, because no one else could possibly want me."

It all came pouring out of her in a rage.

Lily was silent for longer than Ariettea thought she would be. She didn't want to look at her, see some caring expression.

Lily finally burst, "This loser said WHAT?"

Ariettea snapped her head down to see Lily's face full of hatred, a look she had never before seen.

"He told you he LOVED you to keep you from moving here when he didn't even want you?! Are you being serious, or are you being yourself and reading between the lines? Because if that's verbatim what he said to you, then I just can't..." Lily trailed off, her face scrunched up in fury.

Ariettea nodded silently. "He admitted to it the day we broke up." She said evenly, just above a whisper.

Lily shook her head, disgusted. "Give me his number! I want to talk to him!"

"He'd never listen or care. He lives in a world where he can do no wrong. Everyone lives there with him, too..."

Lily shook her head some more, and Ariettea could tell had she had the strength, she would have hopped up and started pacing.

"He was the biggest mistake of my sad life." Ariettea felt her heart breaking as she said it aloud. Her chest aches. "Love... all love, all people, scare me. Because love isn't something concrete I can hold on to, make sure it never leaves or changes."

Lily was quiet. "Ok but think of it this way. Let's reframe."

Ariettea laughed and rolled her eyes, pulled a leg underneath herself. "Ever the therapist."

"Shush you! Ari, look, he was always going to be in the back of your mind. Wherever you went, whatever you did, he would have been there. Maybe this was for the best that you got it out of your system. I don't want you to ever say anything in your life was a mistake. And I mean, can't we say that now you know what you want at least?"

Lily looked hopeful, always the optimist.

Ariettea stared at her combat boot buried in the sand, dug it in further. She couldn't find the words to say a single thing.

Lily looked at her sadly. "I was afraid that was the answer."

Ariettea looked at her, confused.

"I know you, Ari. You are putting your life on hold for another person yet again," Lily said to her, her teal eyes bloodshot.

"You are refusing to look at your life as a whole right now because of ME."

Ariettea jumped in, "Because you're SICK, Lily! Because this is where I need to be right now!"

"And what about when I'm gone?" Lily said with such force that it stung more than either of them thought it could.

Lily shook her head, crossed her arms.

"Ari, I want you to be happy. That's all I've ever wanted. From the day I met you, this poor broken soul, I just wanted you to be happy. We had a great summer together, and I watched in your eyes as each day went by, the pall lifting. I got to see you living! And here you are now, doing the opposite of living! I'm going to DIE. Ok, do you get that?"

The wind came and slapped them both in the face, blasting sand at them, giving just enough time for those words to sink in.

"I'm not going to be here much longer. I appreciate you being here now, but I would not, cannot, and WILL not, fault you for thinking of what you're going to do when I am gone. In fact, it makes me mad that you can't picture yourself doing anything! Here I am, still a kid, never even got to drive a car, and my life is about to end. So PLEASE, Ari, please, if not for your sake, then mine, LIVE your life! Even if you feel you have to wait until I'm gone, PROMISE me you will LIVE it!"

Ariettea struggled to find words, but Lily just kept on going.

"You are allowed to, and I INSIST that you do, find what you want to do, and go after it with all your might. Because some of us never fully get that chance."

Ariettea had so many objections, that it wasn't right, it was selfish to think about her future when Lily wasn't going to get one, that she needed to be mentally present with Lily there in the end. The thought scared her, thinking at all of a life without Lily. She couldn't bear it.

But as she looked in those teal eyes that were brimming with tears, all she could do was take Lily in her arms and agree, just to, if anything, give Lily some peace.

But even through her doubts, she started to wonder if Lily was right.

"Well, hey, we have the Gala to look forward to in a couple of weeks, anyway." Lily choked out.

"Yes, of course! It will be…" Ariettea swallowed hard, shoved her tongue against the roof of her mouth, trying to stave off tears. "Just as EPIC as we always planned!" She tried to hide the crack in her voice that Lily chose to ignore.

"Thank you, Ari. And you have to promise to try and have a good time!" She laughed.

Ariettea smiled tightly, wordlessly.

"I'm serious, Ariettea." Lily said harshly. "You know how much this Gala has always meant to me. You have to promise to have fun. Promise me."

Ariettea nodded, fearful of what would happen the days following the Gala.

"I promise." She whispered.

Ariettea stayed curled up in bed with Lily even after she dozed off not too long after they had returned from the beach. They had set up the laptop on the bedside table and put on whatever Disney movie was still left on Netflix. Ariettea kept curled up beside her, glancing down at her every so often, just to make sure she was sleeping peacefully.

Once she started to doze off herself, she pulled herself out of bed to head back to Trent and Nadette's, try to eat something.

Had she eaten that day? She had no idea.

She waved goodbye to a half-asleep Elaina as she stepped out the door, and saw that Peter was about to walk in. He paused and waited for Ariettea to come out of the sliding door.

"Is she sleeping?" He asked.

She nodded. "Yeah, she dozed off a while ago."

"Oh good, I'm glad. You know how hard it is to get her to rest during the day."

She smiled at him. She had taken it for granted, having someone else in the room who knew Lily so well.

She paused, uneasy with him by herself, as if she were waiting for him to continue talking or his permission to leave. She didn't realize how often she'd done that with Matthew.

"I should-" She pointed a thumb down the hallway.

"Oh yeah," He began.

She took it as her cue to start walking briskly away from him.

"I should be leaving too,"

She heard him say from behind her. She kept walking, unwilling to wait for him to catch up, to keep their conversation going. But he did.

He hopped in the elevator as the door began to close. She waited for a huff of annoyance from him that she didn't hold the door, but it didn't come.

She bit her lip. "Sorry I didn't know if you were going to leave right away or…." She trailed off lamely, not having the energy to find an excuse that seemed plausible.

He shrugged. "Yeah, I really oughta get home, throw a load of laundry on…" He grimaced. "I must sound like the most boring person ever."

She shook her head. "Boring, no, I find it fascinating to meet a guy that knows how to do laundry."

He laughed good-naturedly. "Yeah, when I moved here for school, I didn't want to live in the dorms, and my parent's place isn't far, but I've just been on my own for a good clip I guess."

She smiled at him. "That's honestly how I pictured my life after high school going. A few years ago, at least. But everyone always told me I'd never make it on my own…"

She waited for him to jump in, agree, maybe explain that he had some massive trust fund, but he didn't.

Instead, he asked, "Why not?"

She found a laugh/scoff escaping her body. "Ha! That's what I always asked, too." She shook her head, rolled her eyes to look at the elevator ceiling.

"So tell me, what's the best part of living on your own? Having room to breathe and think for yourself?"

He paused, thoughtfully. "Yeah, I guess I always had that even with my parents, but it's nice."

"You DID?"

"You didn't?"

"Not in the slightest. They liked to think they were open and progressive and let me think what I wanted… but it was pretty much as long as I agreed with whatever they said, then they got to say that I was thinking for myself. If that makes sense."

"So, you didn't agree, then?"

She shook her head. "Not on much."

"I'm sorry."

Another silent shrug as she wondered why the elevator was moving so slowly. She wasn't ready for whatever lecture he was preparing.

"I guess my favorite part of being on my own is having a whole house to myself all the time. It's quiet and mine to do whatever I want with, without having to get permission."

"So, what do you want to do?" She asked, stepped off the elevator and onto the marble tile of the ground floor.

He smiled shyly. "Uh, again, I guess I'm pretty boring. A good night in with a good video game or some friends and the freedom to either stay up all night or go to bed at 8 o'clock."

She rolled her eyes as she walked towards the front door.

"What is it with guys and video games?" She asked, not even trying to keep the edge of bitterness out of her voice.

"You've never played any?"

She shrugged, "Mario this or that. I'm sure nothing you'd be interested in. Nothing that can help your… gamer tag name score or whatever it is…"

He laughed. "You mean a GamerScore? Man, I've not looked at mine since I was in junior high."

She smirked, mentally somewhere else.

"What if I bring in a couple of systems tomorrow, we can all play some games?" He asked, bringing her back to that moment.

She shook her head, "Oh man, trust me I'm NOT a person you want to play video games with. I'll probably just end up messing everyone else up."

He smiled down at her as he opened the front door and held it for her as she walked out. "Come on, I'll teach you!"

"You'll teach me?" She asked, shocked, whirling to face him, suddenly wondering if it was shock or mocking in her voice.

"Yeah, why not?" He asked confused.

"Isn't that like some cardinal sin among guys? My ex made it seem like some… sacred place."

Peter scrunched up his nose and shook his head. "Nah it's not that serious. What, he wouldn't let you play?"

"I mean, I never asked-"

"Yeah, but he didn't offer?" He didn't wait for the answer he knew was coming.

He waved a hand. "Nah doesn't matter- tomorrow! Tomorrow we're all going to have a video game tournament! Lily'll love it!" He announced, clapping his hands.

"I can even set you up with your own Gamertag to start your very own GamerScore."

She laughed at him.

When he stayed serious, she shrugged and sighed. "Alright, I'll bring the snacks."

She parked on the street outside the townhouse and drug herself up the concrete walkup. She collapsed on the big comfy green armchair and laid her head on the arm.

Trent appeared from around the kitchen corner, leaned up against the doorway, crossed his arms.

She felt like ignoring him, but instead looked up at him silently, knowing her face was giving more away than she wanted it to.

He walked over and sat on the ottoman in front of her.

Her head still buried in the arm of the chair, she moaned, "I don't think I've ever been this tired in my life."

He chuckled. "I said that all through medical school. But I think you have more stress on your plate than I did."

She smiled as she turned her head towards him. "And how did you get through that?"

He put his elbow on his knee, leaned forward. "I had to take a step back every once and a while to let my mind and body catch up to one another."

"I don't think I have enough free time."

He smiled sadly. "You've been putting yourself through a lot. You're going through a lot. Are you holding up ok?"

She knew what he meant.

She sighed. She was tired of lying and hiding the nightmares she was living through.

"No. I'm not." She squeezed her eyes shut and buried her face into the arm and held her breath before turning back to him.

"Even before I knew about Lily… Matt destroyed me. He made me question what happiness really means. He and everyone else there convinced me that what we had was just the reality of happiness, that it's not the fairytale we expect. And that quote-unquote "truth" destroyed me."

She paused.

"When you're made to believe that the horror you're living in is happiness, it makes giving up seem a whole lot more appealing."

She saw his eyes grow even more worried than they already were.

"But my mind is too full of Lily to think about or sort through anything else right now." She said quickly, answering the question he was asking with his face.

He pulled his lips inside his mouth tightly, nodded before asking, "But what about when the dust settles?"

She closed her eyes. "Lily asked me that today, too."

She sighed. "I thought I had found my direction over the summer. And part of me still wants that direction, that decision, I don't think I ever stopped. But after falling on my face, having to eat my crow, I don't know what I'll do when everything is…"

She trailed off, a sick feeling she'd so far been able to fight off, finally overtaking her stomach.

"Over. It feels like everything is different now. I feel like a totally different person, but also completely regressed to the way I was before. Before I met Lily, before you guys jumped into my life… I'm just… Really lost right now."

She shook her head. "While we were in the midst of breaking up, Matt screamed at me that I need constant validation, that I'm a cocky brat who no one would ever want in their life. That my wanting to die was just attention-seeking.

"The thing is I never talked to him about that. So whatever opinion he had came from other people talking. I can only imagine what my parents were saying about me. Especially since they never bothered to talk to me.

"But honestly, I don't want anyone to save me. Not even Lily. I just want to have people around me that help me save myself."

He patted her knee knowingly before standing up, shoving his hands into the pockets of his jeans. "It's been my experience, Ari, that the difficult things in life don't define us; it's what we take from them that makes us who we are. That makes us better. We're so proud of you; we always have been, no matter what choices you've made."

"You were proud even after I ditched your amazing offer to live here?" She asked sitting up.

"Yes." He answered quickly.

She looked at him quizzically.

"Because you were finally choosing paths for yourself." He explained, "We always knew you'd end up on the right one, whichever one that meant for you. And we still believe that. Just..." He paused.

"Just please don't let yourself spiral when we're here to help, ok? Asking for help is never attention-seeking. It only seems self-centered to people that actually are."

She herself paused, holding herself back from asking just what help he was offering.

She stopped him as he began to turn away, "Trent," She said timidly, "How do you know if you need... medication?"

He looked at her thoughtfully before she continued, "Last year... On our college tour you mentioned medication and I shut you down. But how do you know if that's something you need? What do you even mean by medication? What medications are there?"

He sat back down in front of her. "I'm not a psychiatrist or even a primary care doctor, so I can't act like I'm an expert on it. All I know is what I see come into the ER and I see a lot of people on psych meds. What would be surprising to most people is the amount of college students on them. I think it's mainly because we've finally reached a generation of people who are open about their mental health and are willing to accept treatment."

She scoffed. "Unless you're where I'm from. Then everyone just says that 'we're friends and family people', not therapy people."

He smiled at her sadly. "There's still a long way to go for some people to understand that what we know now about mental health is fact, not opinion."

He paused. "As far as for knowing when you need it… There are some general guidelines. If you don't have enjoyment from things anymore, if you sleep a lot or a little, you gain or lose weight, you're always tired, and… I think anytime you're thinking about dying is a big red flag. Self-harm is always a sign that something isn't right."

His words hung between them for a moment, hitting her just a little closer than she thought they would.

"I don't think about killing myself." She finally said, softly. "I just think about how much easier it would be if I weren't alive."

"That's a slippery slope, though, Ari. Some people with major depression can somewhat function, albeit miserably, but one false step sends you tumbling down. That's why I worry about you after Lily is gone."

"If that's what's wrong with me, then why was I so happy over the summer? It can't be a medical problem if a good attitude can chase it away."

"Good things can mask a lot. But like I said, one bad thing happens and… Here you are. I think that would do the opposite of telling you it's a circumstance thing."

"So what, medication magically changes you? Don't they say therapy is just as good? Maybe that's what happened to me with Lily; it was a summer of therapy!"

He shook his head. "Each person is different. And no, the gym isn't therapy, and therapy is not just like talking to a friend, no matter what Pinterest tells you."

She laughed with a scoff.

He looked down at the ground before taking a breath. "Ari, you know major depression is diagnosed when those symptoms last two weeks or more."

Her eyes grew wide. "So, when it's been years…" She trailed off quietly.

"So, to answer your question, neither therapy or meds is a magic fix, and they're not always equally as useful. Some people need therapy to talk through bouts of depression. But other people have clinical, medical depression that is just the same as diabetes. People need insulin just as much as some people need medications."

"So, what, antidepressants?" She asked bitterly.

"For some. A lot of people think it's a magical little pill, and it's all better. But there are SSRI's, SNRI's, antipsychotics, benzos; there are things used off label like anticonvulsants and blood pressure medicine…"

"You sure sound like an expert."

"Again, just know what I frequently see. A lot of people come in because they're having issues with their meds, and they get sent spiraling."

He paused again. "I think the biggest thing to know is that even when you find the right medication, which sometimes is the first med, and is sometimes the tenth, it takes 6-8 weeks for you to feel better. So, if you do decide to try something, it's not going to magically fix things. Starting something now isn't going to help you get through Lily's death."

She stayed silent for a moment before asking, "How do you know that it's not just an out? An excuse to not work on yourself? That it's not just some lack of spirituality or faith?"

"Faith and true mental illness have nothing to do with each other. Let me be clear about that." He said, holding his hands up.

"Medication won't work unless you need it. If a neurotypical person took psychiatric medication, it wouldn't do a single thing for them."

"So, it changes your personality?"

"No, it just makes your brain work like it's supposed to."

"But isn't that the same thing?"

"No…" He looked away as he chewed his lip thoughtfully. "My best friend in high school went on meds our senior year." He said suddenly, looking back at her.

"His personality didn't change at all. But for the first time since I'd known him, he was sleeping at night; he was laughing at my dumb jokes, he actually wanted to go out to a movie every once in a while. But he still didn't like crowds. He didn't become outgoing. And he didn't change his college major or friends or hobbies or tastes in music or clothes…. He was finally just happy."

"And what, after he got into his 20's he went off the meds and is all better?" She asked bitterly.

"Mental illness isn't a teenage rite of passage." Trent said gently. "A lot of mental illnesses present or get worse in your early 20's. My buddy's tried going off them many times, just to end up exhausted and miserable."

She mulled over that. "If that's… If medication is something I wanted to pursue, I'd have to see a psychiatrist?" She asked slowly, scared. Not wanting to even speak the word.

"Not necessarily. A lot of people get meds through their primary care doctor. It's just if you want or need someone who is more adept in managing medications."

"Would you… Be able to help me get on medication?"

He shook his head slowly. "It wouldn't really be appropriate for me to be your treating doctor when it comes to this, especially. I can help you find a doctor here, though, and be around for any follow up questions you're too stubborn to ask."

She smiled, then nodded. "I still don't think I'm ready to do that… I guess I'm just trying to make sense of my life, and I want to do it on my own."

"I understand. But being on meds doesn't mean you're not on your own. You'd be on your own with a better version of yourself. Even though going through life on your own isn't some sort of badge of honor to wear. Sometimes getting help is the strongest choice you can make."

Chapter 32

They all knew that Lily was living for the Gala. She had had Alex buy two tickets for herself and Ariettea, he and Elaina deciding to hold up in her room to help her if need be, not themselves up for an actual party.

But nevertheless, they all threw themselves into making sure it was the best night possible for Lily.

In doing that, Ariettea found herself in a dress shop on the Ducreis downtown strip. The conversation between her and Lily the night before happened just before she left for the night, near midnight, as usual,

"You need a dress!"

"I HAVE a dress!"

"You need a fancy dress!"

"What makes you think I don't have one?"

"A NEW one!"

So, she relented. Now there she was, with Nadette on a Friday night after her rounds at the hospital, in a bridal boutique.

Ariettea eyed the high school seniors in the other corner of the store, trying on tiaras and those god awful ugly clear plastic shoes that should have died in the early 2000's along with overplucked brows. She didn't go to her own prom. She hadn't even considered it. And of course, no one had asked.

"THIS one!" Nadette said excitedly, bringing Ariettea back down to earth.

Ariettea looked over, she was holding a soft pink lace form-fitting gown. She cocked her head to the side, trying to find the words to not hurt Nadette's feelings.

"You hate it." Nadette said, slumping dramatically.

Ariettea tried not to laugh. "I don't HATE it...per se..."

Nadette started laughing herself. "Ok, ok. I should know by now. No pink." She decidedly set the gown back on the rack.

"So white tie?" Ariettea whined again, as she had been all afternoon.

"Yes, Ari, white tie! Gowns and tuxedos and NO combat boots!"

Ariettea smiled and shook her head, a smile dancing on her lips.

Her fingers roamed through the dresses on the racks… Orange, purple, green. Taffeta, lace, organza, and bedazzled to death. She couldn't fathom which brides would choose any of those dresses for their bridesmaids, so deep in thought, she found herself stopping at the end of yet another rack, hand on it, as she stared out the store window.

Her view had shifted from the prom-goers to the college kids, roaming the streets with books in hand, going in and out of coffee shops and burger bars, studying. Messenger bags slung over their shoulders as they walked down cobblestone sidewalks, the tree-lined brick-paved road, Starbucks sitting at their feet as they typed away on their laptops, sitting on a bench dedicated to some college alumnus.

"Ari?" She heard Nadette say from behind her.

Nadette quickly caught where her gaze was focused and put her hand on her shoulder. "Let's take a break, hm? Go grab a coffee."

Ariettea nodded silently and followed her the cafe next door. As they sat at the wrought iron table outside, the same one from the summer before, Nadette started to speak first,

"I don't blame you; you know." She said.

Ariettea looked over at her startled. "For what?" She asked, confused.

Nadette suddenly looked unsure of herself. "For staying home?" She said, uncertainly. "I mean, had Trent asked me at your age to be with him, give up things, important things, for him, I-"

"You would have left him! Dumped his sorry behind." Ariettea cut in, harshly.

She shook her head and sipped her tea, having been unable to order coffee, after having made so many being stuck in her coffee shop job for the past 7 months.

Nadette stayed silent.

"Look." Ariettea said slowly, staring down at her shiny white plastic to-go lid on her cup. "I never fully apologized to you and Trent… You guys spent so much time… Helping me get into Ducreis, offering me a free place to stay… And I just turned it down for… Some GUY who…"

She sighed. Placed an elbow on the table, ran her hand through her hair. Every time she did, she couldn't help but think of Lily.

She closed her eyes and then reopened them to look into Nadette's. "I regret SO MUCH, Nadette." She said softly.

She shook her head and looked off into the distance, leaning her chin into her hand. "It's not just about college, or a guy, or my best friend…" She took a shaky breath. "This is my life here. And I'm trying so hard to navigate through it correctly and I feel like I'm just drowning. A month ago, I thought I had it all together. Now, every single thing has changed, and I have NO IDEA what to think anymore."

Nadette, to Ariettea's surprise, nodded knowingly. "I know, sweetie. I do." She shook her head. "And don't feel like you have to apologize to us. Like I said, I don't blame you for making the choice you did."

"But WHY did I?" Ariettea said, rolling her eyes. "Why did I do all that? I didn't have a plan! ME! Of all people! I dove into something without thinking it through! Trying to lead by emotion, for the first time ever, and then realizing why I never, ever did that in the first place. I could have been here! I could have caught Lily's cancer earlier, and-"

"Hey," Nadette cut in sharply, slamming her coffee down, rattling the wrought iron table. "You could NOT have 'caught' Lily's diagnosis any earlier. That's not something you could have seen. Her doctors, her own parents didn't see it. SHE didn't see it."

"Maybe I could have."

"Don't do this to yourself, Ariettea. Don't. You have got to learn that you can't blame yourself for things like this. We aren't God, don't get to play God, and don't expect to know everything God does."

Nadette paused. "And the same goes for everything else. You can't expect to know how a relationship will turn out. You can't expect to know how a career will turn out. We plan the best we can, and then we jump! We jump with a prayer and hope that the rope of plans we've woven through life will hold us."

Her green eyes turned into a fiery hazel as she raged on, "You jumped, and it didn't hold. So what? There's a net waiting for you. So, you've hit the net. So, your plans failed, your world is falling apart. Take that net and sew your world back together. Grab it then jump again."

Ariettea was taken aback. She had never seen nor heard Nadette get so passionate about anything that wasn't happy or sparkly.

Nadette softened. "I can't imagine the terrible sense of loss you're experiencing, Ariettea. I can't say that just because you're young, you'll be able to, or should be able to, just pick up the pieces and move on. But I can say that as far as that boy goes, you'll have better love. Real love. As far as college goes, you'll figure it out. We all do. Especially you, because you're smart and strong. And as far as life goes, sometimes it hurts like stepping on a million Legos. Some things knock us down and keep hitting. They hit until we are blue in the face and bleeding out our butts. But what matters most is getting back up. I promise you that you CAN get back up"

Ariettea felt her eyes sting, she had to take a minute to form her next words, and Nadette knowingly waited.

She barely managed to whisper out: "But you can't tell me that getting over Lily will be that easy."

Her voice broke. She rolled her eyes trying to hold back tears.

Nadette reached out and put her hand over hers. "I don't want you to ever GET OVER Lily." She said softly. "You may never 'get over' a pain like that. But I don't want to see you let life knock you down and roll you over. That's not what Lily would want, either. You take your time. You feel your pain. You grieve your losses. You punch out anyone who says you're not entitled to that. But then you get up. And as for where you go from there, sometimes just getting back up is accomplishment enough."

Ariettea nodded. Nadette was telling her all the same things that Lily had been. As if fate were real, she looked across the street to the florist, where a bunch of high school boys were frantically buying corsages. She saw lilies blooming loud and proud in the window. She looked down at her cup again. Lilies didn't usually bloom until the summer. She smiled. HER Lily bloomed year-round.

"I feel like… I feel like thinking of a world without Lily is a betrayal to her." She found herself saying. "Like, here I am, trying to figure out where to go from here when she doesn't have anywhere to go at all."

She shook her head. "I feel like if I just focus on Lily, don't think about anything else…" She trailed off.

Nadette shook her head sadly. "That's not going to save her." She said quietly. "And it certainly won't save you."

"That's what Lily said." Ariettea whispered. More to herself than to Nadette.

"Ariettea, you're making the mistake of seeing this as an all or nothing situation." Nadette began, "It's not focus everything on Lily and don't eat, drink, or think of anything else. But it's also not looking so far ahead that you ignore what's in front of you. I think we're all trying to tell you the same thing, Ari."

"And what is that?"

"To live."

Ariettea pulled her scarf from around her neck, took a deep breath of the cool Southern air. It smelled like home. She caught a whiff of the flowers from the shop across the street. Again, her eyes found the lilies. They always, always found the lilies. And the lilies gave her an idea.

She looked back at Nadette, ready to change the subject. "After we find my dress tonight, I need to go out; I'll be gone late, there's something I want to do for Lily. Don't wait up, ok?"

Without asking why, Nadette agreed.

"So, does that mean you're ready to keep on shopping?" She asked with a cautious smile, accepting that their conversation was over.

Ariettea nodded, picking up her cup as she stood.

Many hours later, in the wee hours of the midnight, her surprise errands for Lily done, and with a garment bag from a dress shop hanging in the backseat of her car, she began her long drive back to Ducreis. It gave her time to herself. For the first time in weeks, she was stuck all alone trapped in her head without someone to interrupt her. She was being forced to stop and think, and for the first time she started truly thinking about what would happen to her next.

Matt had taken up so much of her life, long before they even started dating. After the relationship was over, she had been pushing him so far to the back of her mind she wasn't sure if she was over him, just couldn't deal, or just didn't even care.

No.

She knew she was over him. She was over him the moment he opened his mouth to start screaming at her.

But all that aside, here she was now, single, unemployed, and about to be without a best friend again. The same way she had been when she met Lily. But she was also different. She knew she was stronger. She had experienced things; a relationship, friendship, illness, working, all things that changed her so that she was nowhere near the person she had been when she met Lily. "Why the all-black, Ari?" Lily had asked Ariettea's first night back in Ducreis. She thought about it, looking down at her worn combat boots, shrouded in the darkness before dawn.

WHY the all-black then? Why let Matt rob her of the happiness that she had worked so hard to attain? To maintain, at that. Why had she let him break her? She shook her head, realizing that he didn't have to. He was behind her. Her hometown was behind her.

The what ifs of that place and those people were finally answered. She was fully capable of taking her happiness back. Not that it was purely a choice to make, it never is. But she knew she could make choices to make it easier to chase.

She knew there was one choice, one decision in particular that she was ready to make.

Once she had gotten back to Trent and Nadette's, finished loading up the pieces for Lily's surprise, she showered, put on makeup, put on clothes that made her feel more human. Made her feel less...black. A blue mock neck blouse, long sleeves underneath, black jeans, and a pair of velvet heels.

She texted Alex, Elaina, and Peter, in their ever-open group chat, that she'd be up to the hospital in a couple of hours.

She drove down to campus, parked in the hospital garage, but didn't go in.

She walked down to the college campus and made her way to one of the stately brick buildings, up the long steep line of steps and into a marble-tiled, wood panel walled room.

She took a deep breath as she determinedly walked up to the largest wooden door there and knocked. It swung open and she smiled up at the large man who answered.

"Dr. Abbott, it's nice to see you again."

Ariettea enlisted Peter to help her with her surprise. Alex and Elaina had to get Lily out of her room, so he helped set everything up.

She was always fighting the tendency to be on the defensive with him, ready to dispute whatever left his mouth, but she never had to with him.

As she went outside to grab the last load of supplies, he ran up next to her to walk beside her. She was never able to get rid of him just by walking away.

"You know I think I should apologize to you," She said suddenly.

Peter looked over his armload and down at her, surprised. "What?"

"I owe you an apology," She began again. "I've not been the nicest person to you. You were loved by this family long before I came along, but I feel like I've been making you prove yourself to me, and you don't deserve that. I don't deserve that from you. So, I'm sorry."

It felt like pulling a tooth, pulling those words out of her mouth.

He nodded, pulling open the door to the hospital. "You don't have anything to apologize for, really. This isn't the easiest situation for any of us."

She stayed silent.

"You don't know me well enough to owe me anything." He said.

She smiled at the thought, a guy who didn't demand unconditional respect from her. "Well, you don't know me well enough to owe me anything, but you still are respectful."

"And you aren't?"

She paused. "I'm usually told I'm not." She said with a pained laugh.

He shook his head as he pushed the elevator button. "Well, you have been. So, you don't have to worry about it."

He jumped to a new topic quickly, "So I was thinking about bringing Lily some of that ice cream that she likes, but I can't find it. I don't know what her second favorite is, all I know is that she hates mi-"

"Mint chocolate chip!" Ariettea finished with him.

She laughed. "Did they ever take you to Delicia's? One time, Lily and I went and…"

All of a sudden, she couldn't finish, she stopped herself, waiting for the sigh or the eye roll or the utterance of 'not this again'.

She looked up at him, "Sorry." She said quickly. "I talk about her and I WAY too much." She would have tucked her hair behind her ear had her hands not been full.

He looked down at her, confused. "I don't see why that would be a problem; she's your friend…?"

Ariettea stared into the cardboard box she was holding. "I spent my whole life in my head, wanting to be somewhere else," She said slowly.

"Lily taught me to live in the moment. When I went back to Michigan, I took that mentality too far. I saw only the present, and the people around me demanded that I not think of or about anywhere else. I mean, they always did, but they finally succeeded in forcing me. It didn't help that everyone was jealous of her. I think maybe they always were. Jealous, I mean. But no matter what, the past eight months, I've avoided talking about Lily as much as possible so that I wouldn't get yelled at."

They stepped off the elevator in unison.

Peter waited to make sure she was done speaking. "Well, you'll never have to worry about that from me." He finally said with a smile. "And not just about Lily. I don't think it's fair to police what anyone wants."

She smiled up at him, then had to hustle to keep up with his long stride. She felt like a midget next to him.

As she noticed his height, she couldn't help but notice his build. She was always trying NOT to notice. For a teacher, he was surprisingly cut. When he showed up in a T-shirt one day, she realized his arms were bigger than her head.

She shook her head. She was being inappropriate.

Peter smiled down at her as he took her load from her after he set his down in Lily's room. "So, tell me what else I missed in Baringvale over the summer."

Chapter 33

They arranged everything just so, Ariettea and Peter, and texted Alex to bring Lily back.

She was suddenly apprehensive; she wasn't sure if Lily would be able to walk down the hallway like they had planned without needing to sit down.

She and Peter stood at the entrance of Lily's room. The door and curtains closed.

Lily soon rounded the corner from the elevator and appeared at the beginning of the hallway: Alex with his hands over her eyes, and Elaina standing behind with tears in hers, followed.

"Ok, Lils!" Ariettea called out and down the long hallway, trying to muster up as much excitement as she could.

She clapped her hands together. "We have a bit of a surprise for you!"

She watched the smile dance on Lily's lips. She knew she would have been jumping up and down had she felt any better.

"I wanted to do something special for you," She began, trying to keep her voice steady, "And since the day I met you, you've talked about two things: The hospital gala, and the lilies at your house. The thing about lilies is that since we met, they seem to follow me everywhere. So, wherever I am, whenever I see them, I think of you. And I always will."

She took another breathe, feeling corny, but she kept going, "You see, generally, lilies are a sign of summer or a sign of warmth and sunlight, brightness and cheer. They are annual flowers, they come back every year, usually stronger than the year before and bigger. Even if you can't see them, they never die."

Ariettea's voice cracked ever so slightly. Her eyes flashed over to Peter and then back to Lily as she swallowed and continued,

"No matter how much adversity is thrown in their way or on top of them, they always find a way to push through the soil and grow and bloom and shine."

She took a shaky breath before she could continue. Peter lightly laid a hand on her shoulder, just briefly enough that it gave her the courage to continue, "Just like you."

She nodded to Alex and he removed his hands from Lily's eyes.

She opened them to see the hallway transformed into a tunnel of lilies. Oriental lilies, calla lilies, stargazers, forever Susan's, Turk's caps, Easter lilies, every single lily that the local florist had, and every lily they could get their hands on from other local stores.

Lily's jaw dropped as she took a cautious step forward. Her eyes lit up for the first time in weeks as she took in the scene.

The nurses and CNA's had helped bring in chairs, tables, even IV poles so that the lilies were all staggered to different heights.

It was a true tunnel of lilies from floor to ceiling, where, lilies hung as well.

The colors were so bright and vibrant, the hues so strong that it was beyond overwhelming. The oranges, whites, purples, the stripes, and spots, it was hard to take in.

"The way these lilies look to you is the way you look to us. Lilies are strong, vibrant, gorgeous, resilient, and all together- unforgettable." Ariettea was trying as hard as she could to put boldness into her words.

Lily kept walking down the hall, pausing to smell or touch the different lilies, nodding to Ariettea as she spoke, as if to encourage her to keep talking.

She had to unclench her hands from fists before she spoke again, "Because even when they aren't there, you know the place in the ground that they belong. And you can't forget them."

Elaina sobbed silently in Alex's arms, trying to hide it from Lily. Ariettea looked at her worriedly, but she smiled through the tears and shook her head, waved for her to go on.

Ariettea inhaled, "For the rest of our lives, when we look at ANY lily, I guarantee we will think of you. But, there is one special type of lily that holds a bit more meaning." She saw Lily's eyes light up even more, if that was possible. "There's this special orange tiger lily…"

To avoid clenching her hands again, Ariettea shoved her hands in the pockets of her boyfriend cut skinny jeans, the ones that had fit her so snug over the summer, but now fell sagging in the back waistband. She could almost swear she still felt sand in the pockets. The sand from Lily's home. Where she had driven the night, morning, before to get the most important of the lilies. The ones she continued describing-

"These lilies hold special meaning for a few of us here," Ariettea said smiling at the crowd that had gathered. "You see, Lily is named after these very special flowers. Her parents' home, which was her grandparents' home, sits directly on the beach in South Carolina. And the yard is overflowing with these gorgeous flowers. Which is strange, seeing as how lilies would usually have trouble flourishing as well as they do in that sandy environment. But they did. The front yard, the sides, the back, every inch of the house is choked full of these amazing flowers. And so, our dear Lily, like her namesake, has flourished through an environment in which others easily wilt."

She could barely make it through that part of the speech, directing it at others instead of Lily herself.

But she knew she had to finish looking at Lily. "And she has stood as tall, strong, proud, and as vivacious as those flowers."

She nodded to Peter who threw open the sliding glass hospital room door and yanked open the curtains with one clean sweep to reveal Lily's hospital room- filled to the brim with the lilies from her home.

The fiery orange flowers covered the chairs, the tables, filled the windows, and had begun to spread to the bed. Some hung from the ceiling, some sat in planters, some in arranged bouquets.

Lily and her parents silently entered the room, Alex and Elaina's hands white and clasped together, Lily's covering her mouth.

Ariettea stood in the doorway with Peter over her shoulder. "Tiger lilies don't bloom in the winter, but somehow these still are. I wanted to bring them to you so it would be like being at home. But don't worry, I left a bunch blooming outside your window."

Everyone ignored the unspoken truth that Lily would never see them there.

Lily shook her head in disbelief. "Ari…" She trailed off, spinning in a circle, taking in all the flowers around her. "Thank you." She said, whirling around and staring into Ariettea's eyes. The way she always had, as if she were looking deep into your soul.

Her teal eyes filled with tears as she rushed into Ariettea, wrapping her arms around her waist. Ariettea blinked hard, and she hugged her frail, tiny body, smaller than it had ever been, back, trying to ignore something scary she had just seen in Lily's eyes. Lily always looked into you as if she read you, but this time, Ariettea felt as if she had read Lily.

She saw something. Something she had never seen before.

Something that looked like the end.

"So, have you told Lily about your meeting with Dr. Abbott?" Nadette asked excitedly, nearly dancing as Ariettea sat putting on her combat boots.

She shook her head. "I wanted to tell them all yesterday when we were all together, but it ended up being such an emotional time that it just didn't feel right to turn it back on me."

She traced the threads on the couch. "I'm going to tell them all right before the gala tonight."

She looked up at Nadette, her blonde hair already done for the gala, half-up, curled locks gliding down her back.

"Then the gala will be like our celebration, Lily and me."

Nadette grinned. "So, Alex and Elaina aren't going to the gala?"

"No, just Lily and I."

"And that cute tutor?" Nadette said, smirking so hard that her dimples showed, her eyes twinkling.

"Peter?" Ariettea asked. "He's not a tutor anymore; he's a teacher now."

"Oh well ok then, so is the cute teacher going?"

"Not to my knowledge..." Ariettea said casually.

"Shame. You two would make an adorable couple." Nadette teased.

Ariettea rolled her eyes dramatically, "Nadette, I am SO not biting this baited hook. He's too old for me! And I have zero, less than zero, interest in dating someone anytime soon."

"Oh come ON! He's cute; he's smart, you know he's caring and sweet because he cares about Lily as much as you do-"

"Nadette, I've learned the hard way that there's way more to a relationship than cute and sweet." Ariettea said, an edge creeping into her voice. "I don't even think 'sweet' is a thing for guys anymore. I don't think love is all it's cracked up to be."

Nadette sat beside her quietly and put an arm around her. "Do you really think that what you and Matt had was love?"

Ariettea scoffed, "Not at all."

"Then how can you say love isn't great?" Nadette asked softly.

Ariettea sighed. "All the married women I know have nothing good to say about their husbands. None of them seem happy." She paused. "Please don't try to tell me that it's just that newness wears off, but love takes on a different meaning. Because that still just means true, hard, deep love doesn't last. So, I can't believe that it truly exists at all."

"Do you think Trent and I have a true love?"

Ariettea paused. "I love the way you guys operate as a team. You take turns cooking dinner, you kiss each other hello after a long day, you still hold hands when you walk…" She trailed off.

"But?"

"But I've had women tell me that you're the exception, you two. Either you're the exception or you're lying, or your reality hasn't hit."

"After over ten years of marriage, I tend to think we've faced quite a bit of reality."

She let Ariettea go and turned to face her. "You're still letting people tell you what's real and true versus what's not. Way too many people are stuck in miserable marriages and for some reason they like to flock together to complain about the same things over and over.

"You get to choose what happens to you. You get to choose how you're treated. You get to choose the type of love you receive. And when you make your choice, your well thought out choice, that love is not going to leave. Of course I hate the way Trent loads the dishwasher and he hates the way I organize the closets.

"But those things have nothing to do with love. Love covers all things. Love never fails."

Ariettea stood up, wrapped her arms around herself and walked over to the window, overlooking the street, stoic. "I don't think anyone will ever want me, anyway." She whispered to herself, her stomach-churning.

Nadette got up and came to stand beside her, to pull her to face her once more. "Ari don't you dare let that boy succeed in making you feel like you're not lovable. There are way too many of us here that disagree with him."

"Yeah, but how many guys?"

"Plenty!"

She sighed.

"Sometimes these situations, while they may make us question everything, show us who we are. Maybe what you want is being shown to you now in a way you wouldn't have appreciated or even seen before."

Ariettea nodded slowly before walking to the door, ready to end the conversation, "You know the last time I was leaving for a party, my mother was forcing me to go and I ended up alone and hiding and running."

She smiled and fiddled with her hands. "I think this is the first party I've ever left for that I feel excited, and most of all, I feel safe because of everyone that will be there with me."

Nadette smiled as Ariettea picked her makeup case up from the floor.

"Thank you for being one of my safe places, Nadette."

Ariettea walked into Lily's hospital room, bags in tow, to find Lily in the middle of a coughing fit.

Lilies still everywhere, Ariettea threw her bags on the only empty chair and rushed over to her bed. Alex and Elaina were already standing there, patting her gently on the back.

Elaina looked over at Ariettea, "She's been like this all morning. They've bumped her oxygen up; she's having a harder time breathing."

Ariettea nodded sadly as she placed a hand gently on Lily's knee.

Lily looked up at her in between coughs, over the top of the oxygen mask Alex was holding in place. "Ar--" She coughed. "I'm so glad you're here!" She said with a wheeze.

Ariettea nodded, trying to force a smile. "Are you sure you are feeling up to tonight?" She asked.

"Of COURSE!" Lily said crackly with one last cough. She smiled up at Ariettea. "This is something we've been planning for a long time."

Ariettea smiled back, tightened the grip on her knee and nodded.

Alex and Elaina went to make their exit.

"Oh wait, before you guys go... I have some news to share with all of you." Ariettea said.

They both stopped, and Lily straightened up in her bed, as much as she could, at least.

"Well," Ariettea began, "I-"

Just then, Alex's phone started to ring. He went to silence it but noticed the caller ID. "Oh I'm sorry Ari, this is a call we've been waiting on from Lily's doctor, can we catch the news later?"

Ariettea waved a hand. "Of course!"

Alex and Elaina hurried off.

"Well you can tell me the news!" Lily said behind her.

Ariettea turned around. "Aw Lil, you know I tell you everything, but I really wanted to tell your parents at the same time as you, just because they played a big part in it."

Lily's eyes showed a twinge of a twinkle, much less than they used to shine and sparkle in the past, but those teal eyes still shone all on their own, even as they had begun to sink in the midst of her pale thinning skin. The skin that had begun showing more and more veins and divots than ever.

"I have a guess… I hope it's right." Lily said happily, sighing.

Ariettea smiled and shook her head as she pulled up her bags onto Lily's bed. "Ok, who's getting ready first?"

"You!" Lily chirped. "I can't wait to see your dress! Is it something over than black?"

Ariettea smirked. "Ah Lily, come on. You know me better than that."

Over the next few hours, they slowly got ready, Lily moving at her own pace. She helped where she could, and gave suggestions, more so instructions, where she couldn't. She curled Ariettea's hair for her and swept it up while Ariettea applied her makeup.

"This hair, Ari!" Lily said happily from her knees behind her. "It's grown back so fast!" She paused. "I hope you know how much it meant for you to meet me that first time. After that, my wig meant so much more to me. It meant a friendship, truer than I ever thought possible."

Ariettea whirled around, not caring that her foundation was only on half her face. "And I hope you know that's the exact way I've always felt. Even if I've been terrible at showing it."

Lily reached out and squeezed her hand before motioning for her to turn around so she could hairspray Ariettea's hair. For a girl who had been sleeping nearly all day every day, she was expending a great amount of energy.

"Don't tire yourself out on my account, Lil." Ariettea found herself saying more than once.

To which Lily would answer: "I've been saving my energy for this day."

After giving Ariettea's updo one last pat of approval, Lily commanded, "Ok, go change before you help me!"

Ariettea ducked into the bathroom to change into her gown. The bathroom had become home to a good many of the lilies from the hallway the day before. The smell was overwhelmingly wonderful.

She examined her hair in the mirror, raven-black curls that had been carefully constructed, gracefully swept up into a soft French twist, with loose tendrils gracing the back of her neck. The remnants of her short haircut from so long ago.

Her black eyeliner pencil had been replaced by a softer shade of brown that faded into a delicate smoky eye and highlighted the soft hues in her eyes that were so rarely seen behind the layers of black.

The updo was perfect for her dress, and when Lily saw the gown she let out a gasp and clasped her hands to her mouth.

Black, lace, and off the shoulder, the slight sweetheart neckline stopped below Ariettea's collarbone and faded into a form-fitting bodice. A bodice of lace and tiny hand-sewn crystals carefully placed all over it.

Ariettea turned to show off the lace-up corset-style back. She carefully adjusted the sheer lace sleeves that gently held onto her biceps and turned back around. The tight fit began to flare out below her hips, and fell into a mermaid-esq satin bottom supported by layers and layers of tulle.

She placed her hands on her tiny waist, and looked to Lily for approval. "Well?" She asked hopefully.

Lily's eyes filled with tears. She was fighting them back hard. "OhmyGOSH, I LOVE it, Ariettea." She burst.

Lily swallowed hard as Ariettea reached out to take her hand. Lily held it up, away from her, and took in Ariettea once more. "I just... It's just YOU, Ariettea. It's just YOU embodied in a dress. This is just going to be the best night."

Ariettea fought back tears herself after that. She fanned at her eyes. "Ok, ok," She said, laughing.

"Let's get you ready!" She clapped her hands together. "Where's your stuff?"

Lily laughed, "Ari did I make you CRY?" She asked sarcastically, incredulously.

Ariettea waved a hand at her. "Nah, nah, never!"

Lily giggled, but it turned into a cough.

Ariettea looked over at her. "You're the only one I'll ever tear up for, though." She said softly.

Lily mustered up as much of a smile as she could. "No more tears tonight, Ari, ok?" She said very carefully. Almost as if she had been planning those words for a while.

She started to cough again and Ariettea went over to lay a hand on her back. "I'm always telling you to feel your feelings, but this is a happy night. So, no more tears!" Lily repeated, looking deep into Ariettea's eyes.

Ariettea felt herself nodding, almost as if under a daze. "Ok." She whispered as she rubbed her back.

She looked away and around the room. "Ok, but really, where's your stuff?" She asked, suddenly realizing Lily had nothing there for herself for the gala.

"Are your parents bringing your stuff?" She asked, confused, still spinning around.

Lily looked at her, shook her head, smiled casually, "Oh Ari... I'm not going tonight."

Ariettea was confused by the smile, and suddenly a weird pall fell over the room.

"Wh...What do you mean?"

"This was always the plan..." Lily said, turning to look out the window.

Ariettea tried to catch her eye. "What?" She repeated.

Lily continued staring out the window, looking down towards the beach. She started shaking her head. She suddenly jerked her head back to face her and locked eyes with her. "I need you to do this for me, Ariettea. I'm too sick. Yesterday.... Yesterday was a perfect last day out of bed…" She trailed off softly and began looking at lilies around the room.

Ariettea shook her head confused. "No, no, this wasn't the plan, we… We were going to go, you and me, together. Did, did the thing yesterday tire you out? I mean, I didn't mean-" She sputtered, feeling the color drain from her face.

Lily shook her head and smiled as she looked to Ariettea. "This was MY plan," She said slowly. "From the beginning. I always knew I wouldn't be able to go, and I knew you wouldn't agree to go without me."

She paused, laughed at the sentiment, confusing Ariettea even more, and continued, "But I NEED you to go for me, please?"

Ariettea felt her eyes sting.

"Do this for me?" She whispered as tears welled in her eyes.

Ariettea took her in. The short pixie moppet of soft black curls. The sunken in cheekbones. The hollow eyes, their teal fading and paling. Her zip-up hoodie sitting askew and falling off her shoulder, her flannel pajama bottoms curled underneath her. Of course, she couldn't go. Ariettea felt angry with herself for expecting her to.

"Of course." Ariettea said, her voice barely above a whisper. "I'll do anything for you." She said.

Lily smiled. She suddenly looked at peace. "Then promise me to have a good time tonight."

Ariettea nodded. "I promise."

"No more tears."

"None."

They smiled at each other. "I'll tell you every single little detail." Ariettea said, fighting the stinging in her eyes.

Lily smiled softly. "I'm sure you will."

Ariettea paused. "So, I'll still be with Trent and Nadette, but if you never planned ongoing… why did you get two tickets?"

Lily smirked. "One for you," She nearly sang, "and one for him." She said, pointing to the door behind Ariettea.

She turned around to see Peter standing there in a tuxedo, holding a clear plastic box containing a lily wrist corsage. His brown wavy hair gelled, his face clean-shaven, and his expression confused.

"What about me?" He asked, assuming his signature stance, shoving a hand in his pants pocket.

"You," Lily announced, "Are taking Ariettea to the gala."

Ariettea and Peter exchanged a confused and awkward glance.

"One of your famous plans, Lily?" Peter mused, stepping into the room.

Lily nodded, clearly impressed with herself.

Ariettea looked at Peter expectantly. "You've experienced this before I take it?"

He laughed. "Oh, we all have. Whether we know it or not. I'm sure you were under this master's strings all that summer you stayed with them. I know I was. And still am, apparently."

He cleared his throat and shook his head. "So, it turns out this isn't for you?" He asked, shaking the corsage at Lily.

She giggled. "No, sir."

Ariettea smiled down towards the floor, then up at Lily. Lily clapped her hands, perking up. Something momentarily flashed across her face, but then left just as quickly, before Ariettea could quite read it.

"Stand together!" Lily commanded. "Let me get a picture of this in my mind."

Peter awkwardly moved to stand beside Ariettea. She noticed once more how much taller he was than she, even in heels. They shared an awkward smile, and then faced Lily.

"Perfect." She purred.

"This is perfect?" Ariettea asked, just as Peter piped up, "Really?" They shared another glance before looking back to Lily.

She smirked. "Yup. Perfect." She laughed.

She then looked to Peter. "You, stay here. I have to have some words with you. Ari, give us five if you don't mind."

Ariettea nodded and stepped out of the room, picking up the bottom half of her gown as she walked out and pulled the glass door shut. She couldn't help but turn and watch in between the vertical blinds as Lily's facial expressions went all over the board, from serious to lighthearted, to laughing, back to serious, and then to that expression again, the one Ariettea couldn't quite read before it left. Lily pulled Peter in for a tight hug, then Lily was waving Ariettea in.

Lily patted the bed. "Sit for a sec, if you can in that dress."

Ariettea smiled as she picked up the bottom of her dress and walked over. "It was a prerequisite for all the dresses I tried on." She said, smiling as she sat down on the edge of Lily's bed, as she had so many times before.

Lily held out her hand, Ariettea took it in hers but it was so cold, she wrapped her other hand around it.

That same strange expression was on her face. Ariettea furrowed her brow. "What is this look, Lily?" She queried.

Lily's expression remained unchanged. "Ari, I need you to do something else for me tonight, ok? I'm sending you off to have fun. Please, please, for my sake, I'm asking you not to suppress your feelings tonight, or ever, but especially not tonight. Don't shut down."

Ariettea shook her head, seeing Peter pacing outside the room. "Lily, if this is about Peter... I just... I can't-"

"Ari, I hope one thing you take from knowing me, is to stay away from people who make you feel like you're hard to love." She cut her off. "The people that love you- let them, like you let me. Fall in love with yourself like I did. Fall in love with your life."

Ariettea squeezed her hand even tighter inside her own.

"The happiest moments from deep down inside me came from the darkest moments in my life. I want you to know and feel that too for yourself. You're going to come out of all this like the powerful, resilient, gorgeous woman you are, even if you feel like a shell of a person you once were or never was. But trust me. You are capable of so much more than you think."

Ariettea lunged forward to hug her, hard, pulling her in tightly, wrapped her arms around her. "I love you so much, Lily." She whispered into her head.

"I love you too."

She pulled Lily's hands into her own. "When I get back here tonight, I can't wait to tell you all what is coming next for me. You're going to love it."

"I'm absolutely sure." Lily grinned at her, fighting tears. She pulled Ariettea in for another hug. "I can't wait to hear all about the gala. Take lots of pictures for me, ok?"

Ariettea held onto her arms as she pulled away and looked down at her. "Everywhere I go, there seem to be lilies around me. Even tonight with that silly corsage…" She looked out at Peter, pacing in the hallway. "I'll be carrying a piece of you with me to the gala, anyway."

Lily squeezed her hands around Ariettea's as they sat on her own arms. "I hope you'll always have me with you."

"I guarantee you; you've changed me, you've taught me so much, gave me a better relationship with Trent and Nadette who have been lifesavers too, you have made my life into something that I can live. That's something I'll always have."

"I love you, Ariettea."

"I love you too, Lily."

She stood up to leave. "I'll see you later tonight, ok?"

"Yes, I can't wait to see you later!"

"Promise?"

"I promise."

Ariettea smiled at her as she backed away, taking in her huge smile, those teal eyes, knowing that once the gala was over, over the next few days, she might not see that smile again.

Chapter 34

Ariettea and Peter stepped off the elevator to see the hospital lobby completely transformed.

The lobby, open-air to all floors, had an atrium glass top letting the moonlight in. The wide-open marble-floored lobby normally held only a circular reception desk smack in the middle, but now was completely full of round party tables.

Tables that sat eight in elegant garden-style chairs, each with a gold bow on the back to match the black tablecloths, gold runners, and tall sparkling black branch centerpieces. There was enough seating for hundreds.

A band was setting up on a tall stage in front of a dance floor in the middle of it all.

Waiters in tuxedos whisked around with tall flutes of champagne and tiny appetizers on golden platters. While caterers busied about, running back and forth to the cafeteria where they had set up in the kitchen.

A bar had been set up by the front door, where hospital administrators stood greeting people as they came in. People poured in and were all finding seats, a sea of faces so overwhelming she nearly wanted to run.

But then she saw Trent and Nadette making their way over to her and Peter. Trent, looking dashing in a navy colored tux with matching bowtie, and Nadette in a form-fitting matching navy colored sparkling sheath dress that hit her normally straight body in all the right places.

Ariettea took a step forward, but stepped on her dress, having forgotten to pick it up. Peter immediately stepped forward and grabbed her arm, supporting her.

Ariettea caught herself, regaining her balance, and looked up at him. "Thanks." She said softly, waiting for him to release her arm, trying to stop her mind from flashing to that day at the beach with Matt, when she tripped after picking up the lilies, wanting his touch to linger.

After Peter already had to awkwardly place the corsage on her wrist, she hated making him touch her more.

Trent and Nadette approached, and as Nadette eyed Peter's hand on Ariettea's arm, she smiled coyly at her.

Peter quickly let go. "Of course." He responded to her thanks.

"Hey guys!" Trent said excitedly. He reached out to shake Peter's hand, which Peter reciprocated with a strong handshake.

They exchanged pleasantries as Nadette pulled close to Ariettea. "So the cute teacher did come!" She whispered excitedly. "And as your DATE?"

Ariettea rolled her eyes. She spoke up so all three of her companions could hear. "Lily didn't feel well enough to come tonight. So, we came for her."

"Oh, I hope the tickets didn't go to waste!" Trent said.

"They only bought the two for us, apparently." Peter said, sharing a look with Ariettea.

Nadette again, looked at Ariettea coyly. "Ooh so they set you two UP!" She said bouncing slightly, clutching her wrap around her chest.

Ariettea and Peter shared another quick look. Peter shrugged. "Well then, if that's the case, I am honored to have your niece accompany me tonight."

"VERY good answer!" Nadette said as she took Trent's arm. "Our table is this way if you guys want to sit with us."

Ariettea and Peter shared yet another look and started to follow them. They had become experts at reading each other.

Ariettea awkwardly followed Peter as they wove between tables until they finally got to theirs, right beside the dance floor. Peter pulled out a chair and stood behind it, waiting for Ariettea to sit. She didn't realize what he was doing at first, so she pulled out her own chair, and then felt her face flush as she realized what he was doing. "Sorry," She muttered as she quickly sat in the chair he pulled out for her.

"Maybe I should apologize," He said quietly as he sat beside her on her left. "I was brought up to treat a lady as, well, a lady, but I know you can take care of your own chair. I shouldn't have overstepped."

Ariettea shook her head, glancing at Nadette out of the corner of her eye, happily finding her engrossed in conversation with another couple at the table.

"Pulling out a chair for someone isn't a crime. You didn't overstep at all. It's just...not what I'm... I WAS... used to." She tripped over her words.

Peter looked down at his lap as he placed his napkin there. "Well, for THAT, I do apologize. On behalf of men."

Ariettea raised an eyebrow.

Peter cocked his head, as if to ask why she was confused. "Because you deserve much better than that." He said softly, simply, as if it were the most obvious thing in the world to him.

Ariettea felt her face flush as she busied herself with her own napkin.

Peter accepted a flute of champagne from one of the waiters, taking Ariettea aback until she remembered how much older he was than her. He cleared his throat and extended his hand to the other couple at the table, easily striking up a conversation. Ariettea admiringly watched him expertly and easily navigate conversing with the strangers. She yearned for that skill, to be comfortable speaking with everyone. Lily had brought her out of her shell, but not quite as much as Peter lived out of his. She plastered on a smile as the introductions kept going.

"Dr. Pavalli, this is our niece, Ariettea." Trent said to the greying woman next to him, motioning across the table.

Ariettea feebly waved. "Hello." She said, feeling so out of place.

"Oh, the famous Ariettea!" The doctor's kind brown eyes smiled back at her. "Trent and Nadette love to talk about you! You're in your last semester of nursing school, yes?"

Ariettea sadly shook her head. "No, I ended up not."

The doctor smiled, years of long nights showing in the wrinkles around her eyes. "From what I hear, you're well suited for the job!"

Ariettea looked over at a beaming Nadette. "Heart of gold." She said, her voice up in an octave of singsong, winking at Ariettea.

Ariettea felt Peter's eyes on her, and she tried not to, but then looked to meet his gaze. "What?" She asked shaking her head.

Peter shook his. "Nothing, I just… agree. That's all."

"Agree with what?" Ariettea pushed, confused at his vagueness.

He took a sip of champagne and cleared his throat. He was unable to meet her eyes as he answered. "That you have a heart of gold."

Ariettea felt her face flush yet again. She had expected him to say that he agreed that she should go to school.

On her left, Nadette patted her hand, "Well, Ari, now that you've told Lily the news…"

Ariettea looked at her, panicked, trying to convey she hadn't had a chance to tell anyone yet.

Nadette looked back towards the others at the table and announced, "Ariettea is going to start nursing school in the fall!"

Before Ariettea could turn back to Peter and explain, the hospital director stood on stage and began to speak into the microphone. "Welcome, everyone!" She went on a spiel of how the night was to progress; dinner, dancing, merriment, and all that. She then began to speak on the meaning of the gala. "Many here are in the oncology field; many here have someone they love suffering from cancer; many here are loved ones who have sadly lost someone to cancer. Tonight, we raise money for research and to improve the quality of life of our oncology patients here in this very hospital. One unique thing we do within the next few months is our 'Hair That Cares' campaign,"

Ariettea's hand subconsciously touched the loose tendrils that graced the back of her neck.

"We already have quite a few signed up, and we are expecting many mailed donations as well." Ariettea felt her heart tug. The simple act that had brought her so far… "…So everyone have a great time tonight!" The applause of the crowd brought Ariettea back from her mind.

Suddenly servers were everywhere, bringing out fancy plated meals. Peter glanced over at Ariettea. The noise level had again risen, and as she felt everything inside her tense up, he leaned in close to ask, "Are you ok?"

She again nearly jumped at his close proximity, suddenly realizing that aside from hanging on Matt's arm, she wasn't used to being so physically near a guy. She had never dated before Matt. Even then, she had always been the one taking his arm, setting her head on his shoulder. He never made any move toward her, even to simply ask if she was doing ok, even though he used to, as Peter was doing now.

She nodded unsurely, trying to muster up a smile. What was going on here? She was so used to being so incredibly self-aware; it scared her to feel so confused.

Peter began to carry the conversation for her. "So, what specialization will you go into?" He asked her, beginning to cut into his food.

Ariettea thoughtfully cut into her own chicken as well. "Specialization?"

"Yeah, in nursing?"

"Oh, right, I guess what I had originally planned, either pediatric oncology or psych."

Trent leaned over Nadette to say, "Dr. Pavalli, here is head of psychiatry at Ducreis Hospital."

Ariettea felt herself go hot and then cold, suddenly very nervous. 'I'm going to make you an appointment with a psychiatrist,' Her mother's voice rang in her head. 'Everyone knows your pathetic threats.' Matt's voice echoed after. She looked over at Trent, wordlessly panicking again.

Dr. Pavalli spoke up, her warm voice ringing clear, "We need more young faces in the field! It's your generation that's going to help end the stigma around mental health."

"Stigma?" Ariettea found herself asking.

The doctor nodded as she picked up her own champagne, "So many people are still terrified of the brain; therapists, medications, psychiatrists.... I specialize in treating young adults, so I know what people coming in are dealing with and are afraid of. People don't want to get help and admit being 'crazy', but slowly young adults are the ones realizing and telling everyone else that needing help doesn't make you crazy. Through your generation, people are starting to see psychiatrists as something other than a punishment from their parents or a sentence to lose their minds. We aren't scary!"

She set her glass down. "Or at least I hope so." She laughed.

Ariettea smiled back at her. She liked her warm, calm demeanor. She had pictured psychiatrists as cold, calculating, staring at you through glass with a clipboard, but Dr. Pavalli was quick with a smile and could make a joke.

"You're not." Ariettea finally said. Her eyes flashed over to Trent before back to the Doctor. "I'll admit, I'm still somewhat subscribed to the theory that you're all scary and plotting and reading minds," She chuckled, "and that you have to be terribly, irreparably damaged and crazy to seek help but... I do want to change that."

She paused, wrung her hands under the table. "I guess I want to change my view on it so I can help not only others, but myself as well."

Dr. Pavalli smiled at her, "It can be a hard belief to break, especially depending on the way you were raised to believe, the way you were told to believe. And it can be a funny line to walk; promoting normality of help but also emphasizing the seriousness of mental illness. We don't want people to think that by talking about it openly, it means that everyone is ill because while it's true everyone has mental health, it's not true that everyone has a mental illness."

Suddenly, Peter was adding, "That's something I really took to heart in college; I teach," He paused to explain, "So I know that we HAVE to be here for this next generation of kids mentally, but it all starts with us. That's my favorite thing about my classroom, being able to make it a safe place for these kids."

Ariettea felt her heart warm as she smiled at him. He was so kind. He was so... understanding of things she hadn't thought anyone else on the planet understood.

But she was seeing others who understood as well, as the Doctor spoke up once more, "There's still a lot of parents out there who make their kids feel either attention-seeking or, like you said, Ariettea, damaged. That's one of my favorite things about my practice, too, dispelling that. Making people feel understood, feel better, and then feel like themselves again. Maybe even find the person they've buried in their own mind."

Trent smiled warmly as he nodded, "Education is definitely the key here. So people know when they need help, and they feel safe enough to ask for it, safe enough to openly receive it."

Ariettea looked over to Trent. He raised an eyebrow, asking a silent question. She looked back at Dr. Pavalli, then back to Trent, and nodded softly. They both knew what she was agreeing to, and Trent looked at her in a way she was used to, with pride, but it somehow seemed stronger.

She stared back at her napkin in her lap, trying not to see the look he and the Doctor exchanged next.

Peter picked up the conversation for her, before she could nosedive into overthinking. "Any ideas on where you'll work?"

She took a breath and met his gaze. "Well, here would be my first choice! I mean, I feel like it's already home anyway." She said with a laugh.

Peter nodded in agreement. "Yeah, after going to school here, teaching Lily here, and even spending summers with them when I was in college, I just couldn't leave the South."

"Where do you live?" Ariettea queried, "I don't think I've ever asked." She said, feeling bad.

"Don't feel bad!" He said, waving a hand. "I live here. In Ducreis. Teach at the local school."

He suddenly fell silent. "I guess… I guess that's why I've absolutely had to be here so much." He said sadly. "I was right here the whole time, not so far from their house, but I was so caught up in my first year of working that I wasn't with her as much as I should have been."

Ariettea shook her head. "I'm sure she understood."

Peter shook his head. "I really got selfish the past couple of years, I guess." He murmured.

Ariettea looked at him kindly. "Come on now," She said, cocking her head to catch his gaze. "Weren't you the one who told me not to feel guilty that I hadn't been here? I mean, I didn't even have a good reason to be as distant as I was. A new career is a much better reason than a crappy boyfriend."

"Well, we're both here now, right?" Peter said over the ever-loudening music. Ariettea couldn't help but notice the genuineness in his eyes.

"Right." She whispered as she busied herself with her food again.

"And both staying!" He said happily.

"Yep." Ariettea smiled up at him and held his gaze for longer than she had meant to.

"So, you're not from here then?" She asked, trying to get the conversation back on track.

They kept the conversation going all through dinner. It was the first chance they had had to actually converse with one another, without Lily or her parents or on a short trip to get coffee and back. She hadn't realized what a good conversationalist he was until then. Actually, she hadn't realized how much she liked talking to him until then. By dessert, they had exhausted most of the normal topics; school, work, families, home.

"So, before all this, what do you like to do when you're not working? Do you have a lot of friends here now that you've been here a while?" She asked cautiously, fearing the door it would open.

Peter sipped his champagne. "I have a few close friends." He said simply. "After work, I'm content to either make dinner at home and grade papers, or I'll go out and have some drinks with friends." He said with a shrug. "Being here with Lily and her parents, it's kinda my speed. I'm terribly boring. What about you? Will you miss your friends at home when you move here?"

Ariettea shook her head. "No," She quickly and happily.

It took Peter aback.

She tried to explain, "Lily's my best friend, so it'll work out good." But the smile fell from her face once she realized that Lily wasn't going to be around much longer.

Peter saw the pain suddenly wash over her face and understood. Ariettea traced the curve of the tablecloth in her lap and tried to swallow the feeling. But she could hear Lily in her head telling her to feel it. She tried her best to acknowledge it, feel it, and let it go for the moment.

Suddenly the band that had been setting up started to play, and Peter got a funny look on his face.

He looked down as he said, "So, Lily made me promise something before we came down here. A few things, actually,"

Ariettea nodded, "Me too." She said softly.

"But one thing was that… That I have to dance with you tonight." Peter said, almost wincing. "Don't be insulted," He said quickly, "I'm just not in the habit of asking girls to dance at parties…" He trailed off.

Ariettea laughed. "Me either!"

Peter beamed at her as he got the joke and chuckled. "Then, as bad as it sounds, I'm glad I'm not the only one who feels awkward here."

"Oh, I'm awkward, am I?" Ariettea joked.

Peter looked at her fearfully as she burst out laughing again. "I'm kidding! I'm very awkward!" She said laughing more.

Peter joined in laughing. "No, no, you're not." He said sincerely.

"Ah, but you haven't danced with me yet!"

"Surely you're as amazing a dancer as you are a dining companion."

"Yeah so I suck." Ariettea giggled.

Peter shook his head. "No way."

He stood up and extended his hand just as the band began an upbeat song. "May I have this dance?"

Ariettea stood up. "For Lily's sake, yes." She said as she took his hand. She tried not to meet Nadette's beaming gaze as he led her onto the quickly filling dance floor and put one hand on her waist and took the other in his.

She tried not to stiffen, but it didn't work well. "I'm sorry…" She murmured, trying to match Peter's footsteps. "I've never danced… with a guy."

Peter looked at her surprised.

"My ex wouldn't have been caught dead dancing with me." Ariettea scoffed.

Peter shook his head. "The more I hear of this guy, the less and less I like him."

"That makes two of us."

"But I can't say much. I love to dance, but my ex would never dance with me either." Peter admitted.

Ariettea shook her head as she looked up at him. "You ever wonder how we both ended up dating people totally wrong for us, and in all the same ways?"

Peter laughed. "Maybe we're the odd ones out of all this. Befriending Lily and chasing dreams and all that."

Ariettea chuckled and scoffed at the same time. "That's so LAME!" She said mockingly. "God, Lily, beach, life!" She said, mocking Matt's deep voice.

Peter chuckled under his breath. "Yep. Heard it all before." He said with a twinge of sadness creeping in.

"You don't talk much about her, your ex… exes?" Ariettea said slowly.

Peter shook his head and looked off into the distance. "Not much worth repeating." He said evenly.

Then he sighed and looked down at her. "I took our relationship much more seriously than she did. She wasn't in it for ME; she was in it for a boyfriend. She hated everything about me it turned out. I broke it off once I finally realized that. That was two years ago, and I haven't dated anyone since."

Ariettea nodded. "My ex was...the EXACT same." She scoffed again, unable to meet Peter's gaze. "He wanted to date me to keep me trapped with him. In the life he thought I should live. The life everyone wanted to force me into. Not even to live! But just force me into it."

She rolled her eyes. "I wasn't even looking for a relationship then. I thought he was my best friend. My partner. Someone to walk alongside me. But he just wanted someone to domineer. And that won't ever be me." She would have shrugged had she not been in Peter's arms. Trying to keep up a matter of fact facade when you can't gesture was more difficult than she thought.

Peter nodded understandingly. "I spent a lot of time looking for the right girl. Then there came a point I gave up looking and just focused on myself. I figured the right girl would make me notice her."

Ariettea nodded. "That's how I look at it too." She kept Peter's gaze just a second longer than she meant to.

Then she caught Nadette staring all the way across the room. Nadette shook her head at her, smirking playfully. Ariettea quickly tried to tone down the mood,

"I'm sorry for my aunt, by the way." She said, nodding her head towards their table.

Peter shook his head and laughed. "I should apologize for Lily as well then."

Ariettea shook her head this time. "I don't think any of us can ever dare apologize for Lily." She said with a laugh. "She's always got everything planned out just so…" Ariettea said trailing off, wondering exactly what wheels Lily was trying to set in motion.

Clearly, she knew, but still, there seemed to be some piece missing.

The band started playing a slower number, and many of the more casual couples left the dance floor. Ariettea smiled up at Peter, to free him of his obligation, and let go of his shoulder.

But as she tried to walk away, he gripped onto her other hand still in his, just a little tighter.

She stopped and turned back to him, seeing the pensive look on his face. "Another Lily promise?" She asked knowingly, smirking.

He smiled shyly to the ground. "In a way." He said, mysteriously. "If you're not comfortable-"

Ariettea shook her head and waved. "For Lily." She said, putting her hand back on his shoulder.

Peter smiled nervously as he replaced his hand on her tiny waist. They slowly swayed to the music, an awkward space settling in between them, the space that all the other couples had closed with their bodies.

They were avoiding eye contact with each other when Peter suddenly said, "Maybe not just for Lily."

Ariettea looked into his eyes, still struggling to meet hers. "What do you mean?" She asked slowly.

Peter took a breath, "Ariettea," He said, his firm yet gentle voice making her full name not sound like nails on a chalkboard for the first time in a long time. "You said that you weren't looking for a relationship back then, and I know it's still a fresh breakup, but… I really want to ask… What about now-"

Peter's words were cut short by a flash of blue light and an eerily calm voice announcing,

CODE BLUE, THIRD FLOOR PEDIATRIC ONCOLOGY. CODE BLUE, THIRD FLOOR PEDIATRIC ONCOLOGY.

At that moment, the world stopped moving, turning on its axis, and it felt as if oxygen and time stood still. Ariettea knew exactly who that call was about.

She felt a million miles of synapses and thoughts fly through her brain all at once, but they all led back to one word-

Lily.

They don't call code blues on hospice patients. But she knew in her heart of hearts it was Lily. For whatever reason, the code had been called. Was she reversing her DNR? Was it a mistaken call? Was it divine intervention?

Even though her mind was racing, she felt like she couldn't get her body to move fast enough.

She dropped Peter's hand from hers and simultaneously, seamlessly jumped out of her heels, leaving them silently sitting on the dancefloor.

Before she knew it, she had layers of tulle and lace balled up in her hands, and she was running barefoot with all her might across the lobby towards the elevators.

She slapped the button but, at the same time, realized she couldn't wait and started bounding up the stairs to her left.

Peter wasn't far behind, and Trent and Nadette were futilely trying to make their way to her as well. She expected one of them to call out to her, tell her to slow down, that it wasn't what she thought, but they all knew it was, too.

She pounded each step, taking two at a time where she could, chills wracking her body as adrenaline surged. She heard Peter clamoring behind her, trying not to slip in his dress shoes.

She flew up the last few stairs, having come up the north stairs she turned down the hallway and rounded the corner.

She was trying to see Lily's room, craning her neck for a glimpse, when she lost her footing and fell.

Her hands full of dress; there was nothing to cushion the fall. The tile met her knees with such force; she thought for a split second that they had shattered.

Her ears rung in pain, as she still strained to hear something, anything.

Her eyes darkened around the edges in agony as she stared down the hall towards Lily's room.

She felt stuck on the floor, feeling like she was frozen in cement, like she just couldn't move fast enough.

It was a straight shot to Lily's room, and there was no denying that the code had been called from there.

Way too many people she recognized; nurses, aides, respiratory therapists, and doctors ran into the room from the other adjoining hallway; crash carts lined up outside the sliding glass doors. There were too many people in the way to see through to Lily's bed.

"Ariettea!" She heard Peter call out behind her, worriedly. She ignored him, not wanting his help, and forced herself up off the ground and into a sprint again.

She ran all the way up to the sliding glass door where a male nurse held out his hand.

"We need you to wait out here." He said firmly.

"NO! I HAVE to get in there!" Ariettea said, trying to push past him, still straining to see through the crowds.

She could hear the wailing siren of a flat line, begging someone to do something so that it could register a heartbeat again. The pulse ox machine that had beeped slower and slower the past weeks was screaming out too, almost as if it felt the pain in the room.

She could hear Elaina screaming, yelling voices filling the room as Ariettea tried to push through.

"Please!" She implored.

She felt hands wrap around her waist and pull her back. She looked angrily at the nurse and then realized it wasn't him; he was in front of her.

She looked down at the hands that belonged to arms in a tuxedo.

"Peter!" Ariettea exclaimed, slapping at his hands, large and easily encircling her whole waist. "Let me go!" She screeched vehemently.

"I can't, Ariettea." He said sadly. "For Alex and Elaina."

The crowd in the room cleared and Ariettea saw Alex and Elaina, standing on the far side of Lily's bed, Elaina sobbing uncontrollably, and Alex holding her shoulders, tears streaming down his face as well. It wasn't some pretty cry you see in a movie; Elaina was on the verge of hysteria and Alex was trying not to let his own broken pieces fall as he futilely tried to hold together his wife.

All Ariettea could see past that was Elaina holding on dearly to one frail little white hand.

Medical staffers were filing out of the room, all still blocking Ariettea's way in.

Them and Peter.

Tears streamed down almost every one of the nurses' faces, and a pall hung over them.

Ariettea placed her hand on the glass and peered into the emptying room, where she saw Lily's outline lying motionless. The monitors went from screaming, to silent, as they were turned off one by one.

Ariettea felt her hands go cold. She shook her head. "No, no, they have to do something!" She exclaimed to anyone that could hear her.

"DNR," Peter said, coolly, painful gravel creeping into his voice.

He slowly let go of Ariettea, and as he did, she realized she could barely hold herself up. She leaned against the window for support.

She listened as Lily's doctor profusely apologized that the code was called, it's standard for the unit since it's not a hospice unit, etc, etc, etc. His voice faded out with the rest.

By then, Alex had joined in sobbing with Elaina, and Ariettea heard Peter sniffling behind her.

When you expect a death, it's supposed to be calm, loving, that's what the hospice nurses had preached so hard.

But this wasn't that.

This was pure, unadulterated pain.

Everyone's voices started sounding like they were fading further and further away.

Ariettea tried to look at Lily, to see her face, but either she couldn't see it, or couldn't register it. She just kept shaking her head.

"No. No, no, no, no." She kept repeating out loud.

Peter slowly walked into the room, and Ariettea just stood and watched. He put one hand on Alex's shoulder and one hand on the bed as he dissolved into sobs himself.

"You can go in now, dear." An older nurse said as she walked out. "To say goodbye."

Ariettea stared at the three of them surrounding a lifeless bed.

'No more tears. Especially tonight.' She heard Lily say in her head.
Tears burned the corners of her eyes as she watched everyone, EVERYONE, around her cry.

'No tears tonight.'

The realization hit her like ten semi-trucks-- Lily knew.

She had sent her away to the gala because she knew. She knew that it was the night.

She had known weeks before.

When she told her to feel her feelings, she didn't mean Peter… she meant after she died.

Once again, everything around her slowed to a standstill.

She felt like an alien in her own body. She held her hands up to look at them, trying to figure out if they were even her own, the corsage on her wrist mocking her, that lily still alive.

Her hands shook uncontrollably, ice-cold, as she held one to her face and one to her chest.

The floor underneath her seemed to suddenly tilt, like a dream, a nightmare. She tried to steady herself but found herself staggering.

She took a breath in, trying to regain her balance, but took in too much air instead, causing her to gasp. She was starting to hyperventilate.

She looked over again at Lily's bed, a small lumpy outline in the sheets, completely and lifelessly still. She looked back to the crying trio, registered Trent and Nadette coming down the hall, but then again heard Lily.

'Promise me.'

Ariettea looked at the clock on the wall. It was just after 9. She had three hours until it wasn't 'tonight' anymore. Three hours to keep her promise.
Her last promise to Lily.

She was trying not to be angry at her, how was she supposed to feel her feelings but also not cry? When she didn't want to do either.

She kept shoving her pain down her throat for it only to come back up in dry heaves.

When Peter looked up to see where Ariettea had gone, why she wasn't in the room with them, she was already gone.

Chapter 35

She ran like lightning down the back stairs to the beach. The same ones she and Lily had gone up and down so many times.

She ran, still barefoot, from the backdoor, across the concrete walkway, and to the small strip of sand.

The sand was cold and wet, compacted down under the deep darkness of the hospital's shadow.

The wind blew hard and fierce, pockets of cold spring air biting through the warm humidity that normally permeated the Georgia coast, even at night, hitting her bare chest like needles.

It was just like Lily described, how dark that stretch was in the middle of the night. She thought of all those nights they spent in Baringvale at The Shack, watching the sunset, and even after it was dark, it was still warm and comfortable. Not like the cold she was experiencing then.

She ran across the beach, yanking her dress up from underneath her feet, the layers on netting caked with sand, getting caught up in her toes.

She was trying to run from everything. From all the pain, the hospital, from everyone that would be looking for her, from Lily's lifeless body. She wanted to be as far away from it all as possible.

She stopped running when she reached the water's edge.

The waves were churning up in response to the harsh spring winds, the high tide of late night. They crashed into the shore, into the rocks, creating white foam that crawled up to her feet.

She thought about diving in, swimming out, possibly even letting herself sink down into the unrelenting black water.

But she knew better. For Lily at least.

The wind was deafening but the night was still somehow silent. The silence and solidarity she had always craved were mocking her. She finally understood why people fear silence. It felt like the world was crashing down around her, like she was in a room with the walls closing in, even more so than usual.

She felt her eyes burning from the wind, the grit of the sand and salt air stinging, but she couldn't let herself cry. She wasn't even sure she felt like crying. She wasn't sure if she felt sad or angry.

She was numb and somehow still in pain.

All she knew was that it hurt.

It hurt like someone was punching her in the stomach and then the chest, bashing her over the back, over and over and over again. Something was beating her from the pit of her stomach to the back of her throat.

And that's where the screaming came from.

From deep inside herself, she started screaming.

With balled fists at her sides she screamed at the top of her lungs, her voice being carried out to sea in the howl of the wind.

She finally let her legs go out from underneath her without trying to stop them, and dropping to her knees, she let the water soak her dress, let the tulle between her toes rip and tear more than it already had.

She thought about Lily, talking about swimming in a ballgown. That made her scream more.

The water, carrying up through the bottom layers and up into the lace bodice, soaked her. The waves crashed against her knees as she screamed.

She crossed both her arms over her stomach, hugging her shaking body, and screamed.

She screamed and screamed kneeling on the ground until her throat was raw and numb.

After some great time had passed, she somehow found herself pushing back away from the water's edge and sitting down in the sand.

She drew her knees into her chest, not caring that the corset back was ripping open, and hugged them tight with her sandy, pruny hands as she shook cold, wet, and alone, but hoping no one would find her.

She watched the waves pound in for hours and hours, but it still felt like time had stopped. Sometimes she thought about nothing at all, but mostly she thought about Lily. And how she was gone. Really, truly gone.

How funny a thing, she thought, that someone could be there one minute, and gone the next. Gone from this life. You can't talk to them or even send them a letter. It's not a long-distance relationship, it's not a fight where you aren't speaking, it's not even a missing person, but the person is really and truly gone. Nonexistent.

She started to shake harder, unsure if it was from the cold, exhaustion, or pure emotional distress.

She sat motionless, just staring out at the pitch-black ocean. Everything was so dark that you couldn't see where the water stopped and the sky started. She stared so long, that it took her by surprise when the warm glow of the sun started to creep up over the oceanic horizon.

It was the dawn of the first day in a world without Lily.

And that thought nearly broke her open.

She could feel her heart in her chest, it felt like it was tearing itself apart.

Out of what seemed to be nowhere, she felt warmth envelope her shoulders. She looked up to see Peter putting his tuxedo jacket around her shoulders.

Even through the darkness, she could see his eyes were red and bloodshot. He sniffled as he silently plopped in the sand beside her. He stayed silent.

"I should have known I'd find you here." He finally said after a while. "Aside from home, this was Lily's favorite spot."

Ariettea nodded mutely. She tugged at the tuxedo jacket and pulled it closer to her.

"There was one more thing Lily asked me to do before we left for the gala." Peter said, his voice rough and uneven, like a boy starting puberty, as he stared out to the sea.

"She asked me to take care of you tonight. I thought I knew what she meant..." He trailed off. "But I guess I didn't. Now I do."

She looked over at him for the first time since he had sat down. "She told me to feel my feelings tonight. And I guess I took it to mean what you thought she meant, too."

Ariettea looked back out towards the water. She shook her head, trying to listen to what Lily would be telling her to do- Speak.

"Sometimes there are these big moments in our lives, where there's this event that marks your life so significantly, that there's only the time before that, and the time after.

"I can't decide if that moment is meeting Lily, or losing her. Everything I do, I'm doing for the first time in a world without Lily." She said, trying to keep her voice from breaking.

"I'm watching the sunrise in a world without her. I'm talking to you for the first time in a world without her. Every minute that goes by is a new minute without her. I don't know how I'm going to get through every minute of every hour of every day of every week that goes by as a new moment that I'm experiencing without her on this planet."

Peter nodded. "I think what Lily would say is... Don't do it alone. I mean, you're out here for hours, soaking wet, trying to handle this all completely on your own. Let someone help you."

"Alex and Elaina just lost their daughter; I'm not about to make them comfort me." She snapped.

She recoiled at her own words, realizing he was only trying to help. Only trying to say what Lily would.

"I need to keep myself together for them. I couldn't do that inside. Not in that room." She said softly.

"Well, you're out here all alone, who are you keeping it together for now?"

Ariettea looked at him thoughtfully.

"Seems to me," He said gently, "You're only putting on a front for yourself."

Ariettea shrugged, trying to push the emotions down with her shoulders. "Always my own worst enemy," She scoffed.

"Lily made me promise I wouldn't cry tonight." She tried to explain, voice breaking, her eyes filling with tears.

"It's 5 am, Ariettea." Peter said gently. "The night is over."

And with that, she broke.

She choked out a sob, her hand flying to cover her mouth.

Peter slowly and gently, but very firmly, put his closest arm around her and pulled her in. She wanted to fight back, to push him away, but she let him hold her as she sobbed. She leaned her head into his chest and cried until the sun came fully up.

All the things that she had pent up, Matt, school, and now Lily's death all came bubbling to surface and she couldn't stop it. She was taking in all the pain, all the feelings, and letting them hit her.

She sobbed and sobbed and sobbed, pain pouring out of her, all her makeup running and burning her eyes.

Peter wordlessly held her, but not silently, as he had begun to cry too.

She looked up at him, chest aching, eyes stinging, and said, "You know what hurts me most?" She took in a shaky breath, trying to keep her body from letting another sob escape.

"I told you but not her, that I got back into Ducreis. I got another full scholarship. I'm finally going to follow a path that means something to me. It's all because of Lily, and she had to die without knowing."

Another tear escaped, trailing down her nose. "I did something so that I could live the life she always told me I deserved. But she'll never know. She died without knowing that she changed my life."

Peter wiped away a tear of his own. "She knew." He said with a slight sniffle. "She knew full well that she changed all our lives."

"But I didn't get to tell her." Ariettea shook her head. "I should have just come the first time. I should have shown her then. But I didn't. I chose some stupid boy. And now she'll never know that I finally made the right choice." She said, dissolving into sobbing again.

"Lily had faith in all of us, Ariettea. She believed in everyone even when you had no faith in yourself. There were so many times I wanted to drop out of college, when even my faith in God started to shake, but she could always take one look at me and know what I was thinking, and tell me not to give up because I would be doing something I loved one day. She had such faith for the future of everyone.

"So believe me when I say that even if you made a choice that she didn't agree with, she still believed in you and knew you'd do the right thing. I personally want to keep her alive by keeping that faith. In myself, in you, in everyone.

"I've listened to Lily talk about you for two years, Ariettea. She worshipped the ground you walk on. She thought the world of you. She never said a bad thing about you and even when she told me you weren't going to be moving here for school, she told me with a smile that you were on the right path for you. So don't you ever think that you disappointed her. She believed in you. So you believe in yourself FOR her." Peter commanded.

Ariettea sniffled. She stared at her feet as she stretched them out in front of her. "She talked about me a lot?" She asked, bottom lip quivering, her voice barely above a whisper.

Peter nodded, very serious. "ALL the time." He shook his head, his arm still pulling her close.

"Lily believed you could do great things if you'd only let yourself try. She was always saying that happiness was out there for you, but you had to find it in yourself first."

Ariettea nodded, stifling a giggle. "Yeah she was always telling me that too." She said, thinking of all their conversations, their texts, phone calls.

"So how did you find it?" Peter asked softly.

"Who says I did?" Ariettea fired back, meeting his gaze, her voice still soft.

"Lily." He said gently. "She told me tonight before we left for the gala. She said that she had seen you find that happiness before. And she made me promise to help you find it again."

"Well she gave you quite the list of tasks tonight, didn't she? Following me around must be loads of fun for you." She said bitterly.

Peter ignored it. "Well what did she say to you?"

Ariettea stared out at the water. She took a deep breath and wiped the wetness off her chin. "She told me to fall in love with my life." She paused. "I may not know how I'm going to live in this world without her, and I may not know what I'm going to do tomorrow or the next day, but I do know that I'm going to do what's best for me, and not just for Lily's sake or her memory, but for me. Because what else do we have in life but faith and happiness?"

A tear fell down her cheek, and then another. She felt Peter's fingers trace her shoulder reassuringly. She reached up to wipe the tears from her face, smearing wet sand onto her raw skin. She looked at the lily on her wrist, wet and smushed. She took a deep breath and inhaled the warm cologne radiating off of Peter.

Then she jerked away, "I need to go see Alex and Elaina." She said determinedly, pushing herself up suddenly, Peter's jacket falling from her shoulders.

He stood up as well as she brushed the sand off her hands.

She then looked down at her dress, wet and sandy, and could suddenly feel the grit of dried run makeup on her face. "I should probably go home and clean up first." She said sheepishly.

"Can I drive you?" Peter asked, gesturing towards the parking garage.

She waved a hand. "No, my car is here. I've got to get it eventually. But thanks."

She started gathering up her dress in her hands, and Peter came behind her and helped, handing her a wad of wet lace, swinging his jacket back around her arms.

She met his eyes when he did, feeling his hands brush down her arms, noticing for the first time the flecks of gold in the deep green of his eyes.

"Thanks." She whispered as she began to hurry off, trying to leave him behind as he tried to follow her. Because her heart had skipped a beat. Because it scared her. She wanted to leave him behind, walk away like she always did, shut him out.

But she mentally paused.

She let the feeling sink in. She felt it.

She stopped suddenly, "Your car is parked there too, right?" She asked abruptly, turning around to him.

Peter nodded, taken aback ever so slightly as he finished catching up to her, as he always did.

She tilted her head towards the garage. "Walk with me?" She asked with a smile.

Peter smiled back softly as she let him take up pace beside her.

Chapter 36

The funeral took place, of course, back in Baringvale.

Alex and Elaina's house was bustling with friends and family at a luncheon after the memorial service. Trent and Nadette were there, of course, Alex and Elaina's family, and some close friends from the congregation. Not a lot of people but enough to make the tiny beach house feel even smaller than usual. No one wanted to sit outside, away from everyone else.

Ariettea watched everyone mill around her in a blur. She stood in the kitchen, the kitchen she knew so well, backed into a corner, clutching her bottle of Aquafina with a death grip, wishing she could just vanish.

The day had already been hard enough, singing the songs, saying the prayers, seeing all the pictures.

She still expected to see Lily's head pop around the corner somewhere, her bright smile and shining teal eyes beckoning Ariettea to follow her out of that miserable place.

She felt her throat tighten at the thought, her eyes wandering to Lily's bedroom door, wondering if Elaina had packed anything away, or if she even would.

She thought of the lilies that she had left blooming outside of Lily's window. Lilies from their lily day at the hospital surrounded her, as they had at the memorial, now in the kitchen, dining, living, and bathroom. All rooms full of the somehow still blooming flowers.

She took a deep breath and looked around, trying to calm herself, but she couldn't.

She had to get out.

She slammed her water bottle down on the kitchen counter and slipped as quickly as she could out the sliding glass door.

Still, lilies surrounded her as her bare feet ran down the deck. She ran, loving the feeling of the decking underneath her as she made her way down the long and winding walkway to where it dropped off to the beach path.

She stood at the end and crossed her arms over her chest, letting the warm wind whip through her hair, pushing her dress between her legs. She had worn the white dress Lily loved. She looked down the beach both ways, still looking for Lily.

The weather that day was anything but what you'd expect for a funeral; warm, sunny, windy, and kind. Spring had come early. She wanted the sky around her to be grey, raining, the sea before her angry, like the night Lily died. She wanted the earth to reject this day, to rebel against anything sunny or happy, but how fitting that like Lily, the sun always shines even when you want it to rain.

The wind whipped through her hair again, and she thought immediately of Matt, all that time ago, walking on the beach, batting at her hair, asking why she wore black to a wedding. And here she was, wearing white to a funeral. Whatever would he say about that?

"Do you always wear white to funerals?" A voice called out from behind her.

She smirked as she replied without turning, "Yeah," She called out, "And black to weddings."

She dropped her arms and whirled around to see Peter walking down the boardwalk towards her.

"You always look gorgeous." He beamed at her and stood beside her, shoving his hands in the pockets of his three-piece khaki suit, sans jacket, coral-colored shirt sleeves rolled up to his elbows.

"Sorry, was that creepy?" He asked sheepishly.

Ariettea shook her head. "Actually… no." She said smiling.

He looked back to the ocean and took in the sea before them just like Ariettea had. He took a deep breath in. "I never get tired of this place."

Ariettea looked up at him, having to squint slightly in the sun, and smiled softly. "My best memories are here." She said gently.

He met her gaze and smiled back.

She held it for a second before looking down at her feet.

"I was actually trying to find you," Peter said shyly. "I wanted to check and see how you were doing… If you're ok?"

She drew in a deep breath and nodded, forcing a smile. "I'll just be happy when this is all over." She said letting out the breath.

Peter nodded in agreement. "Yeah, it's been… hard." He said with a sigh, staring down at his own feet, sans shoes.

She shook her head staring out towards the water. "I still expect her to pop up and run past me, out into the water."

"Fully clothed, I'm sure."

"Hey, it's her favorite way to swim, you know."

"I do!"

They both let themselves fall into laughter.

A long pause ensued.

"I keep asking myself what happens now." Ariettea began. "I mean, the funeral's over, the dinner's been had, everyone else is just going to carry on with their lives, and I'm trying to figure out what step I take next."

Peter looked at her confused.

"I mean," She explained, nodding, "I start school, but not until the fall, so what am I going to do until then?"

"Well," Peter began, stepping forward, moving closer to her. "You could always move down to Ducreis early, get the lay of the land, learn the cool hangouts, meet people. Or just… Stay in and watch movies with the people you already like."

He reached out to gently graze his fingertips against hers.

He smiled coyly at his feet. "I mean… That suggestion is admittedly self-serving on my part but…"

She felt her cheeks flush as she smirked.

She could already hear the naysayers in her head, 'You two will never last! Your relationship was born out of tragedy!' She smirked even more as she thought, 'So were Lily and I.'

She looked over at him and met his gaze, reached out and grabbed hold of the hand still grazing her own, "Well maybe you can show me your favorite places."

"I'd like that."

She squeezed his hand before she let it go.

She looked at the orange lilies surrounding them, around the house, and then at the ones sprouting up through the sand.

"You know I feel like wherever I go, I always see lilies." She said, breaking his gaze, thinking of the corsage now hanging from her rearview mirror.

"Or maybe it's just that I notice them more than I used to. But, either way, it'll always be a reminder to be happy.

"To chase that happiness.

"I'll always have her with me.

"In lilies."

Lilies

Lilies: My story

I started writing 'Lilies' when I was 15 years old and in the depths of my first depressive episode. I wouldn't be diagnosed with major depressive disorder until I was 22, but it was something I knew I was dealing with on and off for many years, and it was something deeply impacting my life as a teenager. Like Ariettea, I wanted to die because I didn't believe the future I wanted was attainable because everyone told me it wasn't.

As a preteen and into my teens, I lived completely in a world of fantasy. All-day, every day I was picturing myself somewhere else, usually living in a tv show that was actually real life. Whatever shows I watched, I dreamt of living with those characters. Each of those characters I interacted with I needed at that time. I also dreamt of my writings being turned into TV series and movies, where I not only wrote, but starred in and co-directed. As silly as it is, I still picture turning this story into a movie; thinking of where we'd film, who would star, direct; I can vividly see the gala and all the celebs we could invite to the filming.

I tell you this to explain that 'Lilies' started out as a fantasy of my own, where I went off to visit some long lost relatives and met this kid who taught me that happiness is a choice and brought me out of my depression. It wasn't until later in life that I realized what an erroneous statement that was, that happiness is just some simple choice. So once I moved away from my hometown the moral of the story changed from choosing happiness anywhere, to chasing happiness wherever you need to. That's why it took ten years to finish. Ariettea was me and I learned the same lessons she did. I grew with this book, and it grew with me.

So this story is deeply meaningful to me, especially since I chose to go in a mental health heavy direction, which is something I didn't originally plan to do. I hemmed and hawed and agonized over which direction to take the story, and I had to go with what meant the most to me, what I found the most meaningful. I am a huge advocate of breaking the stigma and teaching our teens to take care of their mental health, teaching PARENTS to take care of their kid's mental health.

As a nearly 25-year-old woman who has finally accepted the state of my mind, the mental illnesses I have, that I will always have, I've finally found my voice and I'm so excited for you to hear it.

Belle Meramec

Thank you for reading 'Lilies'!

I'd love for you to leave me a review on Amazon, or wherever you bought this book!

Let me know if you think I should write a sequel in your review!

Please also share it with your local library if you enjoyed it!

-Belle

Belle Meramec

Belle Meramec has been writing novels since she was a preteen. She is a Midwest native who now lives in the South Chicago Suburbs with her husband. 'Lilies' is her first published work. Check out her Instagram, @BelleMeramec for info on upcoming novels and content, along with behind the scenes details on the creation of 'Lilies'.